HOME
WRECKER

BOOKS BY J M DALGLIESH

HOME WRECKER

J M DALGLIESH

Bookouture

Published by Bookouture in 2024

An imprint of Storyfire Ltd.
Carmelite House
50 Victoria Embankment
London EC4Y 0DZ

www.bookouture.com

ISBN: 978-1-83525-801-9
eBook ISBN: 978-1-83525-799-9

PROLOGUE

My family home is a murder scene. How on earth did I screw up so badly that I've ended up here?

Using the wall as a brace, I make my way through the ground floor. I'm less worried about slipping on the blood-smeared marble, more so about cutting myself on the broken glass.

All I can hear is the ticking of the grandmother clock coming from the hallway. It's so surreal to be in the house when it's this quiet. When I'm up and around at three in the morning everyone else is always sound asleep, but the house never feels this subdued. Can what happens within a home permeate its walls?

I look around the hall. The smashed mirror is in pieces, shards as long as my forearm interspersed with the smaller fragments, each one as sharp as a butcher's blade. The cuts on my hands hurt like hell. Blood is streaked down the walls of the stairwell and along the hallway, pooling in places where the skirting boards meet the floor. I still have its bitter taste in my mouth. My right eye is still swelling and will soon close completely. That side of my face is numb, and my lower lip has split just off centre. It hurts to talk now.

Not that I have anyone left to talk to.

I gently and painfully probe my face with my fingertips. My left side feels like it's on fire, but the bleeding has eased a little. I have to move slowly or the wound will open again. I know I should go to the hospital, but they'll ask too many questions.

The stairs to the basement are shrouded in darkness. But I know what lies in the shadows and I don't want to see it, not again. Leaning against the wall to catch my breath, I take out the folded envelope I've been carrying around in my back pocket these last few weeks, staring at the handwritten address. I recognise the writing, but I haven't dared open it.

I should. If ever there was a right time to face my past, then it's now. Slipping my thumb along the seal, I let the envelope fall to the floor and unfold the single sheet.

It opens with *My darling daughter*.

My eyes water and I try swallowing, but I can't. Covering my mouth with my hand, I read the first lines.

I am here for you whenever you need me. Whatever has passed between us is now history, but our futures, we write those for ourselves.

I clutch the letter to my chest and tears fall. I can't control it anymore.

If I'm honest I don't even know who I'm crying for. I never allow myself to cry, not now. I'm not supposed to, but I guess that doesn't really matter now. Swallowing hard, I look around at the carnage of what was once a happy home.

They said they would come back. Come back and fix the mess we made. But some things can never be fixed.

I know this is what had to be done. But in my wildest

dreams, I never could have imagined what had gone before or that it would go this far.

ONE

SOPHIE

Two weeks earlier - Friday

Roused from a moment of calm by the announcer's voice, the doors open. Stepping onto the platform, my gaze sweeps over an oversized poster promoting a new feature at the nearby Sherlock Holmes Museum. Passing through the maze of passageways, I emerge into Park Square. Bright morning sunshine. The sound of passing vehicles.

From here it's only a three-minute walk to our home on Chester Terrace overlooking the 400-acre Crown land of Regent's Park. It's a haven of natural beauty, albeit carefully manicured, within inner London. The Beckhams, Kate Moss and one of the brothers from Oasis live in – or at least own – houses around here. Not that I've ever seen them myself, but we rarely see our neighbours at the best of times.

A couple of passers-by shoot me sideways glances, maybe recognising me, as I stride past them, but I don't pay them or the park's manicured gardens, with its trees burgeoning into leaf as spring passes into early summer, much attention. The nights are still chilly, and the daytime temperatures swing between unusually cold for spring and the warmth of summer. All of my thoughts, however, are on my home, and what is waiting for me there. How am I going to play this today? There's no manual for dealing with motherhood. I wish there was, I really do.

It seems to me that the sound of traffic is muted as I mount the steps to our Georgian terraced home, on a gated private road bordering the park. It's not closed off to the public but unless you live here, you've no business passing by which provides us with ample privacy. Sliding the key into the lock, I take a moment to steady myself before entering.

Now my heels click on the polished marble of our entrance hall and I'm taking off my coat as the door closes. I see a figure in my peripheral vision appear at the far end of the hall, pausing and leaning against the door frame beside the entrance to the kitchen.

Hanging up my coat, I steady myself and check out my reflection in the giant ornate mirror on the wall. The hair and make-up team do a wonderful job of masking the fact I'm not sleeping well, hiding the shadows as well as the lines at the corner of my eyes, but it does lead to a somewhat unnatural appearance, stiff and highly polished. My hair is up, I think it looks more professional that way, although others disagree. Still, I'm not complaining. I hear people say they wish they looked as good as me. Without the team at the studio, I wouldn't look much like Sophie Beckett off the telly, either. It may only be a little after midday, but I feel like I've completed a day's work already.

Usually, I leave the studio before ten o'clock, but I had a meeting with the production team and didn't pick up my messages – and the numerous missed calls – until much later.

I'm weary, and I really don't need what I know is about to happen. Not today, after my nightmarish time at work. Straightening my blouse, I put my shoulders back, exhale softly and turn around.

'Where is your sister?'

'In the kitchen,' Chas, my towering teenage son, says, gesturing to his right with a nod. He's the responsible one of the two, but he does put a lot of effort into presenting himself as a Californian surf dude. Thankfully, he doesn't dabble in the recreational drug culture, or any actual surfing either seeing as the required surf is hard to come by in London. 'Brace yourself,' he says, with the hint of a bemused smile. Chas is utterly unfazed by anything that comes his way. But, of course, this isn't his problem, it's mine.

Sitting on the window seat of the front-facing sash window of our Georgian terrace, her back propped up on several cushions, brown eyes fixed on the tablet in her hands, is my daughter, Katie. She is highly focused on whatever she is doing. Either that or she's ignoring me, head down, trying to hide behind her shoulder-length hair. I lean towards the latter.

Katie is twelve years old and going on eighteen. Although that is doing a disservice to Chas, who is that age already and shows none of this spiky behaviour. She seems to have bypassed the transition from sweet child to temperamental teen and just gone with *full-on awful* as her attitude of choice.

She ignores my arrival, the volume on her device deliberately set to unbearably irritating. I set my bag down on the nearby breakfast table – four chairs and a bench seat set back against the wall – with a thump and stand in the middle of the kitchen, waiting for her to acknowledge me.

'Well?' I ask curtly. Her eyes flick towards me and away again. 'Katie?' She lifts her right hand in a slow, exaggerated movement and pauses her video.

'Well, what?' she asks, turning to face me, arching her eyebrows and peering through her hair to meet my gaze. Her features are so finely sculpted, high cheekbones and a complexion most women would kill for. She could be a child model if that was her thing, but she would have to get out of the yoga pants and hoodies first.

'What do you have to say for yourself?'

Her brow creases, puzzled. 'Good morning?'

'You know full well what I'm talking about, Katherine!'

'Whoa,' Chas says behind me. 'Proper naming her.' Ignoring my chastening glance, he looks at his sister with a smirk. 'You thought you were in trouble with the school, but now you're really going to get it.'

'Not helpful, Charles,' I say.

'Hey, don't bring me into it!' Chas beats a hasty retreat. 'Good luck, little sis.'

'Get to your lecture,' I shout after him, but my focus is already back on my daughter. 'What were you thinking?'

'I guess I wasn't thinking,' she says.

'Well, I guess that is something.'

'What?'

'I'm glad you didn't plan it, at least.' She looks away, averting her eyes. 'You planned it?' She shrugs. 'Katie! You've been back in school for three days! How can you possibly—'

'She deserved it,' Katie says, with a Gallic shrug. I close my eyes, lips pursed, desperate not to lose it. That won't help, but as usual, she's not making it easy.

'You were suspended for three weeks and you've only been back for three days—'

'Two and a bit,' she says, wrinkling her nose.

'What?'

'I don't think today counts as a third day. I was home by ten o'clock.'

'Don't try and be cute with me, young lady.'

'I'm just saying.'

'And since when do you have the school call your brother and not me, or your father, for that matter?'

'I did have them call you, but you were busy and wouldn't come to the phone.'

'I was on live television, Katie. How do you expect me to take phone calls—'

'Which is why I had them call Chas. It's called *using my initiative*. At least I know my brother will be there for me.'

That's true, Chas is unlikely to be at university where he's supposed to be.

'That's not fair, Katie, and you know it. I have to work—'

'Yeah, yeah, yeah... I know.'

'As soon as I was off air I picked up the messages and called the school.'

'Well, there was no need because I was already home. And I suspect I'll be here for a while.' She sits back with a smug smile and crosses her arms defiantly.

'What on earth were you thinking?'

'You've already said that.'

'You set fire to your friend's locker—'

Katie sits bolt upright, the smile gone, and glares at me, raising a pointed finger. I note she has taken the time to apply nail varnish. 'Firstly, she is not my friend, *at all*.'

'I think that's clear, yes.'

'And secondly, I didn't set fire to her locker—'

'That's not what the headmaster says—'

'I set fire to the *photograph* of her boyfriend, which happened to be in her locker at the time.'

'You could have burned the entire building down!'

'Don't be so melodramatic,' she says, rolling her eyes. 'No one is focusing on the real issue here.'

'Which is?'

'How Olivia, who, let's face it, is the biggest bully in our year group, thinks she can get away with lording it over the rest of us, is beyond me. Then she takes up with Freddie—'

'You set fire to her locker over a boy? Are you serious?' I ask through clenched teeth.

'No, I did it because someone dared me to.'

'Who?'

'That doesn't matter.'

I'm at a loss, a total loss. Katie attends one of the best independent schools in the city. She has so much to be grateful for, everything to give her the best start in life, and yet she does something like this. 'Just wait until your father gets home from the office and hears about what you've done.'

'Yep, pass the parenting buck, same as always. Why take responsibility yourself when you can get Dad to deal with it?'

'I beg your pardon?'

'Nothing, forget it.'

'You're a fine one to talk about taking personal responsibility, Katie.'

Katie hauls herself to her feet, gathers her tablet and goes to walk past me. 'Whatever. I'm going to my room.' She reaches me and I grab her upper arm. She's grown a lot this past year and she's barely a head shorter than me now.

'You don't get to walk away from me, young lady. Don't you dare.'

She sighs, shooting me a withering look. 'What else is there to say?'

'Three days!'

'Two,' she says, holding up her index and forefinger. 'And a bit.'

'You could face criminal charges—'

She giggles mockingly, tossing her hair, and I can feel the seed of indignant fury expanding in my chest. 'As if!'

'You are going to be in big trouble!'

'The school won't dare risk the negative publicity criminal charges would bring. They'll never do it,' she says confidently.

'You could be expelled!'

She cocks her head, sweeping her hair away from her face and raising her chin. 'You say that like it's a negative.'

'Katie Morton, I...' I don't know what to say. 'You're...'

'I'm grounded?'

'Go to your room!'

'Thank you. It's about time.' I release her and she stalks away from me.

'And you can leave your tablet on the breakfast bar, you'll not be seeing it for a while.' It's not much of a win, but I'll take anything that comes my way just now.

Katie, two handed, slams the tablet down on the surface as she passes, and I'm glad I bought the shockproof travel case otherwise the screen would be done for. Then she leaves without another word.

The flash of anger subsides, leaving me with just a throbbing headache. Rubbing my palms against my face, I push the heels of my hands into my eyes. It really feels like I'm losing her. Like I've failed.

The next morning, I steel myself for another battle as the elevator pings as the doors close and Katie walks into the kitchen, looking around and stifling a yawn. She's in her ever-present hoodie, a style statement if ever I saw one. Katie will use the elevator, an addition Scott worked into the plans during the renovation prior to our moving in. The house is terraced, narrow and there's a lot of stairs, but I won't use the lift, not since I got stuck in it for eight hours that time.

'I thought I heard Dad's voice.'

'He's just left for his run, he'll be back soon. Are you hungry?'

She nods and climbs onto a stool at the breakfast bar. I suppose this is pre-teen communication that translates into *Mum, please can you make me breakfast.* This is a classic interaction where neither of us wants to discuss the elephant in the room: my daughter's behaviour.

One of the reasons we came back to the UK from France was to give our children the benefit of growing up with the best opportunities available to them. Well, that and a much-needed fresh start for all of us. Now, Katie's trajectory threatens to wreck all our best-laid plans, and her own future.

The tension in the house is palpable. Passions are high. My husband, Scott, and I are struggling to understand how we got to this place, let alone what to do to fix things. We both have demanding careers in media that demand our attention while our daughter seems hell-bent on self-destruction.

She's still grounded from her last little escapade at the school, and at this rate she will remain so until she turns eighteen. Initially, Scott used his exemplary negotiating skills to have the school offer Katie a stay of execution when they threatened expulsion, commuting her punishment to an enforced absence. They decided not to go to the authorities on that occasion, thank God. I can imagine the newspaper headlines if they did, although I may face those headlines anyway at some point. But, I suspect, that will be because of other reasons and not related to my daughter.

Somehow, I doubt she'll be let off the hook this time.

So, we'll need to find another solution for Katie while we try to find a school willing to take her. Schools talk to one another, especially when it comes to a pupil expelled for arson. Okay, arson might be a bit of an extreme description, but it is the school's stance. And I can't really blame them.

Only two years ago, Katie was the kindest, most loving little girl you could hope to meet. But things have changed. I know I shouldn't be pandering to her, but I don't know what to do, how to act. I'm afraid of making things worse.

I'm so far out of my depth here that I may as well be treading water in the middle of the Pacific.

'What would you like?'

'I'm easy. Could I have some toast and cereal?'

'Yes, of course.'

I duck into the pantry and return with two slices of whole-meal batch bread to toast. Crossing to the fridge I take a carton of orange juice and set that before her on the counter with a clean glass just as the doorbell chimes.

Approaching the door, I realise I haven't showered or got properly dressed yet. I threw on whatever was convenient when I got out of bed as I didn't want to wake Scott, oversized jogging bottoms and a scabby jumper, seeing as it's still chilly first thing. At the weekends we share a bedroom, but when I'm due into the studio in the early hours I tend to sleep in the guest suite at the top of the house.

Who on earth is calling at this time on the weekend? We don't tend to get unannounced visitors.

I'm hoping I haven't forgotten something important, but it wouldn't be completely unlike me. I had a tennis tournament back in June which I'd completely forgotten about. Tennis isn't really my thing, but we joined the club for the sake of improving Scott's networking connections. Scott is a media executive, commissioning and developing television programmes for studios. With so much competition, knowing the right people and being able to speak to them at almost any time has become essential.

Take exercise, they say. *It's good for your mental health.* I'm sure that's true, but every time I set foot in the club, following the event we never talk about, I saw people whispering about me behind their hands. Scott insists that no one knows, and my psychiatrist would never speak openly to anyone about what is said during our sessions, not even to his wife, but I see the way they look at me. They're all wondering how a basket case like me could end up married to a man like Scott.

My husband is handsome, charming and charismatic. Men

who are charming have this ability to set others at ease, and this enables them to get you to do what they want. Charismatic men, on the other hand, don't need to do that because you will be drawn to them, and then you will do what they want. Occasionally – rarely – you meet someone who is capable of both. And that's Scott. Men, women, everyone, fall at his feet. It really is something to behold when you witness him in action. He manages it with such ease.

It's a cliquey social group, those at the tennis club and in Scott's circle in general. If you're on the periphery then it's a lonely place. They smile, welcome you warmly, invite you along to certain events. Not all of them obviously, not the more intimate events, but the bigger occasions, definitely. They want to draw you in close enough to assess your value, but not so close as to make you one of them. Not yet. They want you to feel comfortable in their presence. After all, they need to be able to get behind you before they can stick a knife in your back.

I'm sure no one missed me panting and lurching around the court like a drunken geriatric.

Pushing my thoughts about the tennis circle behind me, I reach the door and peer through the spyhole. Whoever it is, she has her back to me. I can see people in the park opposite, exercising their dogs, I think. Taking a breath, I open the door.

A young woman, five foot five or six tall, turns and smiles as she sweeps a length of hair away from her face, blown across it by a gust of wind. A gust that rustles through the leaves of the manicured potted plants screening the drop to the courtyard entrance of the basement below. She's a brunette, twenty-something I'd guess. She could be in her early thirties, but she has none of the telltale beginnings of wrinkles that might give it away.

'Good morning! Mrs Morton?' she asks, beaming, her hands clasped together in front of her holding a folder. She has a small black bag over one shoulder. Her teeth are brilliant white, but they're not perfect. She's had them whitened but she hasn't flown to Turkey or anything. She's sporting a navy business suit over a white blouse, tie-detailed and frill-trimmed, and sensible heels.

'Beckett,' I say politely, feeling incredibly under-dressed suddenly, and using the door to shield me from view. She must be here to meet with Scott. 'I'm afraid my husband isn't here,' I tell her, opening the door and gesturing for her to come in. She enters and I hurriedly close the door before the great and the good of Chester Terrace see me in my grunge-wear. 'He'll be back soon though.'

'Thank you, Mrs Morton.'

'Beckett.'

'Oh yes, Beckett. I'm so sorry. You're on the television, aren't you?'

I nod. I still go by my maiden name, much to Scott's chagrin. It's a battle he's never been able to let go of but one of the few I've persisted in fighting.

'That's right,' I say, adjusting my clothing although I know it makes no difference to my overall look.

'They did tell me, but I'm afraid I don't get to watch much television these days. Plus I've not been in the country for a while.'

'Oh, really?' I ask, vaguely curious. 'Where have you come back from?'

She's looking around at the entrance hall now, studying the decor, the mix of marble and wood panelling along with the accent furnishings. I'm used to that when people first enter our home. It must seem like they are stepping into a boutique hotel. Scott's taste is such that the appearance is lavish and yet also understated. How he – or his interior designer – managed to pull that off is akin to alchemy in my book.

'I've been working abroad,' she says, turning her focus back onto me. She seems a little embarrassed that I've caught her staring at our home, and she flushes slightly. 'Most recently in France and Switzerland, South America before that.'

'Wow. You certainly get around—' The second the comment leaves my mouth I'm backpedalling. 'I didn't mean that the way it came out—'

'It's okay, Mrs Mort— Beckett.' She reaches out and gently places a hand on my forearm. Her fingernails are immaculately manicured and painted with a deep-red colour to match her lipstick, and her suit fits her so incredibly well.

Her presentation is stunning but then that would be expected from someone who has lived and worked in both France and Switzerland. The ladies on the continent are very meticulous about their appearance. Joggers and a sweatshirt just wouldn't cut it in either country, not for receiving visitors in polite society.

'Hello.' We turn to see Katie's head peering around the corner from the kitchen, eyeing the two of us suspiciously.

'Hello,' our visitor says to my daughter, smiling broadly. I realise I haven't asked our guest her name, which feels very rude now. 'Katie, this is...' I look to her, hoping she'll pick up the direction of travel for herself.

'Deanna,' the woman says without skipping a beat. She walks forward and extends her right hand toward Katie, who steps out from the sanctuary of the kitchen, wiping the palm of her hand on her thigh before accepting the handshake.

'Katie,' Katie says as they shake hands.

'I'm very pleased to meet you, Katie. Is that chocolate spread on your lips?' Katie immediately licks it away, nodding. 'That's one of my favourite things to eat for breakfast, too. The hazelnut chocolate spread is my personal fave, as long as it doesn't contain palm oil—'

'Using palm oil is so bad for the habitat of the orangutans,' Katie states, her eyes narrowing.

'That's right, and of course we should do what we can to

reduce the felling of trees to make the oil,' Deanna says confidently.

'Consumer power in action,' Katie says, nodding furiously. 'It's the only way to enact change on a corporate level.'

I didn't know she cared all that much about, well, anything really. I do wonder if this is one of her teachers filling her head with lines like these. Either that or she's following some activist on social media.

'Although,' Deanna continues without missing a beat, 'the manufacturers are getting wise and now they're renaming palm oil with other names on the list of ingredients to fool us.'

'Well, they won't fool me!' Katie says triumphantly, and she's probably correct. Katie is nobody's fool. 'Are you here to see my dad?'

'Yes,' Deanna says. 'I am.'

'Would you like some orange juice while you wait?'

Deanna glances at me. I gesture to her to be my guest, and she smiles. 'Yes, I would like that very much.' Katie grasps her hand and leads her forcefully back into the kitchen. Deanna glances awkwardly back at me and almost stumbles but seems cheerful enough as she is led away.

I've never seen Katie take to someone like that before.

She's certainly not that friendly with me. She hasn't been for a long time.

TWO

Katie has Deanna perched beside her at the breakfast bar. The crusts of her toast are on the plate pushed to the edge of the counter. I wouldn't normally approve of chocolate spread on toast at breakfast, I mean, we're not Dutch, but I need to choose my battles carefully lately. Otherwise, we'd be at war every day.

I'm clearing away while the two of them are poring over a map Katie has unfurled from an atlas that I didn't know she had. Seeing my daughter so enthusiastically pointing to regions, mountains and rivers is really quite something. She must have gathered a fair bit of knowledge from her time at the school. I don't know where she found the time when shuffling between detention and punishment duties.

For her part, Deanna seems incredibly comfortable, leaning in and showing what seems to be genuine interest. She is even making encouraging sounds at all the right moments which is a skill I wish I had. I've learned it – learned to blag it, to be honest – because it has been necessary in my role. We have at least one, if not two or more, guests to interview daily and that's not including the politicians who do the morning studio rounds with the given narrative of the day. I can fake it in many ways but Deanna, I recognise, is something of a natural.

I'm loading the dishwasher with the breakfast clutter when Chas comes into the kitchen.

'Whoa, nice addition.' I look at him reproachfully, ignoring the fact he reminds me of a creature of the undead, thin, bordering on gaunt and pasty. Clearly he's had far too much partying and a severe lack of sleep, but bearing in mind what time he got to bed I'm impressed he's up, seeing as it's not even midday. His floppy hair sits across his face, and he moves it aside, momentarily licking his dry lips as he looks across the room. He tilts his head towards his sister and Deanna, lowering his voice to me. 'Who's the... the... er... brunette?'

'Is that how you were raised to speak about women?'

'Er, no, but...' He lifts his hand and gestures towards her surreptitiously, as if to point out the obvious, just as Deanna lifts her head, glances in our direction and smiles. Chas flushes instantly and grins back, turning his hand gesture into a mini wave.

Chas is right, Deanna is attractive. She's spent time styling her dark hair which hangs in waves beyond her shoulder. She's layered it, both with the cut and styling. It would take me an hour to achieve that look, and I'm not confident I'd ever look as good as she does.

Her make-up is also applied perfectly. I'm certain most men in my present life, and my previous one, would say she has a natural beauty, and doesn't need make-up. However, women know differently. There's a real skill to applying make-up so it doesn't show to the untrained eye and offers the appearance of a bit of lipstick and nothing more. Not that Deanna has applied a full mask, far from it, but she has pulled off that most coveted look: understated beauty.

'Close your mouth, Chas, you're drooling.'

'Huh?'

I elbow him gently in the side and he flinches, caught off guard. Deanna is pretending not to notice, a smile playing on her lips, but Stevie Wonder would have seen his reaction to her.

'You also might want to consider getting dressed.'

Chas looks down at himself, horrified. 'Damn!' he says under his breath. 'You could have warned me we had company.'

Looking to make sure we're not overheard, I pull Chas closer to me. Scott would be devastated if his appointment started with having to apologise for his son's behaviour. 'You should find a girl your own age.'

'There's something to be said for an older woman,' he whispers with a smile. I elbow him again, only harder this time. 'Ow!' Both Deanna and Katie look up then and I smile sweetly while Chas rubs his ribcage. 'I'm going to take a shower.'

'Make it a cold one!' I tell him. Deanna looks at me curiously. 'I said, would you like a drink? A hot or a cold one?'

'No, thank you, Mrs Beckett. I'm okay.'

'Scott will be back soon.' She nods with a smile, before Katie points out something else to her. As she leans in, she draws a smile from my twelve-year-old, and I can't help the pang of jealousy that nags at my chest.

I hear the front door open, and I step out into the hall. Scott has one hand resting on his side at waist level and is sipping from a bottle of water, sweating from the exertion but, other than that, he's the picture of tranquillity. His T-shirt is clinging to his chest, emphasising his impressive upper body physique, and despite the outward appearance of calm he is breathing heavily. Scott works out at the gym two to three times a week, but I'm pleased he aims for an athletic build rather than going for out and out muscle which seems to be the trend these days. 'How did you do?'

'As I expected. I shaved thirty seconds off my best.'

'That's great.' I look towards the kitchen. 'There's someone here—'

'I need to take a shower before my video call.' Scott is what anyone would class as a workaholic, but he's passionate about what he does. He demands the best from himself and of those around him, including his family. I know he won't work all day, but if needed, he'll always make time. He hurries past me, placing a hand on my waist and kissing my cheek before moving off and taking the stairs two at a time.

'But there's—'

I'm a little confused but I wander back into the kitchen. Deanna smiles at me, slipping off the stool and crossing over. 'I'm sorry, but I didn't expect things to be so informal. I thought we would be interviewing today.'

'Interviewing?'

'Yes, the agency said the lead time was short and, well, I am here and available, so—'

'The agency?'

'For a tutor, for your daughter?' Deanna says. 'Tamsin arranged an interview for this morning. She said you would both be here, you and your husband.'

'Tamsin? Oh, Tamsin sent you?' Deanna breaks into a nervous smile, nodding. My confusion must be written across my face.

'Yes, that's right.' Her eyes narrow. 'You did know I was coming? Tamsin said she'd spoken to—'

'Oh yes, of course,' I lie. 'It's absolutely fine.' I look down at myself now, feeling self-conscious. 'I would have got dressed, well, I am dressed obviously, but—'

'It's okay, Mrs Beckett—'

'Sophie. Sophie will be fine, thank you.'

'I can stay with Katie,' she says, glancing at my daughter, who nods glumly in her direction. 'If you want to go and get changed or something. It would give us some time together to see if we get along.'

'Yes, thank you.' I look between them, wondering why Scott hadn't mentioned any of this to me. 'I'll only be a minute.'

I leave the kitchen and head up two flights of stairs. The sound of running water greets me from our bedroom suite; Scott is showering. Opening my wardrobe, I fish out something half decent to wear, a burgundy skirt along with a cream blouse. There are numerous questions spinning through my mind. Is this what Katie needs; will home-tutoring be better for her than school? What are Deanna's qualifications? Why didn't Scott discuss this with me yesterday? He must have organised it so quickly, amid the flurry of panic after Katie's expulsion and all his efforts to prevent the school from escalating matters with the police.

I suppose the most important question has been answered already, bearing in mind how she's found an instant bond with Katie. Half the battle with my daughter is getting her to engage. For six months now, at least, it's been the domestic equivalent of the Western Front, only less likely to move.

She seems young though, Deanna. Or is that my vanity getting in the way?

Scott appears in the walk-in wardrobe, fresh from the bathroom, a towel wrapped around his waist. He's momentarily startled by my presence but his easy smile flashes across his face soon enough. 'I didn't hear you come in.'

'We have a tutor downstairs. Tamsin sent her over,' I say.

'That's great!'

'When...' I want to phrase this diplomatically, 'were you going to tell me about it?'

'What?'

'Hiring a tutor?'

Scott laughs momentarily and then his brow creases. 'We talked about it.'

'We did?'

He laughs again, a little incredulously now. 'Yesterday,

remember? When I came home early to discuss what we were going to do?'

'Oh, right,' I say, frowning. I remember options coming up but not actual decisions being made. 'I guess I forgot.'

'You forgot?' Scott arches his eyebrows and sets about choosing what he's going to wear.

'Never mind. Anyway, she's downstairs.'

'Good.' He hesitates before slipping his arms through a white shirt and begins buttoning it up. It's a slim fit, hugging his athletic frame. 'Listen, Tamsin knows what's what. Her agency comes highly recommended, and we have to do something quickly, irrespective of what the outcome is with the school governors. Katie's already missed a lot of school this year, and we can't have her falling behind.'

'Yes, okay. You're right.'

Scott finishes buttoning up his shirt, leaving the top two undone. Coming to me, he gently places his hands on my hips, pulling me into him, and meets my eye.

'I know it seems rushed, but honestly, we got very lucky. Tamsin said there is such demand for high quality educators that the full-time options are thin on the ground. Many of the tutors on the books are also teaching, so just wait until Katie's reputation gets around. No one will touch her unless we pay triple the fees!' He tightens his grip around my waist. 'It's all going to work out just fine, you'll see. Okay?'

He raises his eyebrows, inclining his head. I meet his eye and he's humouring me with that impish little smile of his and I tilt my head, and nod. 'Okay.'

'Right. So, do you like her?' He pauses, his eyebrows knitting.

'Deanna? Yes. She seems nice.'

'Okay, great. Well, I have my call and then I'll be down.' He scans the rack of neatly pressed clothing on his side of the wardrobe and selects a pair of grey-check tweed trousers with a matching waistcoat. He looks so good in this combination. To be honest, he makes any combination work.

I lay out my clothes on the bed and go into the bathroom. Scott is fixing his dark hair which, irritatingly, takes him all but the briefest of moments to run some wax through, followed by two passes of a comb, and he's done. I admire his reflection in the mirror, and as I tie my hair up, I notice that my roots are showing, before heading into the shower cubicle.

Turning the water on, it's still warm from Scott's shower and I spend as little time as possible washing, trying my best not to get my hair wet. I wouldn't normally care about drying it if I wasn't heading out to work or to socialise, but today, with Deanna downstairs waiting, I have less time and more motivation not to be outshone in my own home. Lame, vain and a reflection of my current levels of self-esteem, yes, but it's the way I feel.

Showered and dry, I slip into my clothes which feel tighter than I remember. Studying myself in the full-length dress mirror in the corner of the dressing room, I see my efforts to avoid the natural frizziness in my hair were in vain. The humidity has made it look like I've just come back from a day at the beach. It will have to do. I salvage things as best I can, put on a bit of lippy, nothing too dramatic, and I'm ready to face the world.

Voices carry up the stairwell, energetic and good humoured. I hear Katie cackling at something, and it strikes me that I haven't heard that sound – her laughter – in so long that I can't remember when it last happened. It's joyful to my ear, only I'm not present. Reaching the foot of the stairs, I catch a glimpse of myself in the mirror hanging in the entrance hall. I don't look too bad at all.

When I walk into the kitchen, Katie is no longer at the breakfast bar but sitting at the occasional dining table at the far end of the kitchen. The sash windows are open and the gentle hum of traffic can be heard drifting in from outside, but that is punctuated by chatter and laughter. Deanna is next to Katie with Chas at one end of the table. Scott is at the other, to Deanna's right. They all seem very relaxed and comfortable with one another, laughing at something Scott has said. Deanna flicks out her hand, touching Scott's forearm, drawing his attention to her and he smiles warmly.

I realise I've been holding my breath, and I exhale heavily as I step forward, managing to stub my toe on the leg of one of the breakfast bar stools. I wince, trying hard to suppress a yelp. Scott looks at me, followed soon after by everyone else.

'Are you okay, darling?' he asks. I don't know how long I've been standing there watching them.

'Y-Yes, of course.'

Scott stands up and comes towards me whilst Katie jabs a finger at something in her book, chuckling gleefully again. Deanna gives her a playful nudge and even Chas is grinning. What has someone put in the water this morning?

'Are you sure you're okay? You look a little pale.'

I meet Scott's gaze. He's sporting an odd expression as he approaches and puts a hand on my shoulder while I nurse my toe, balancing on one foot. My eyes shift between him and our children and he leans in and kisses my cheek as I right myself, gingerly putting my foot down.

Over his shoulder I see Deanna looking at us. Her eyes meet mine and I can't read her expression, but she holds my gaze for longer than I find comfortable, before she looks away, turning her attention back to my daughter.

THREE

'Sophie?' Scott says, grabbing my attention with a gentle squeeze of my shoulder.

'I'm fine, honestly.'

'Come and sit down,' he says, leading me out of the kitchen and back into the hall where he guides me to the bench seat beneath the stairs. 'You do look pale,' he says again, touching my forehead. 'Are you coming down with something?'

'I don't think so. I'm fine.' At least, I was fine until about an hour ago. 'I didn't sleep well.' This is true, although I haven't slept well for weeks. 'I'll be okay in a minute.'

'Have you taken your—'

I raise my hand. 'You know I don't like to—'

'I know, but you know what Doctor Sheldon said.'

'I'm fine, just give me a minute.'

Scott nods glumly, and I can see he's not impressed but if I took everything Dr Sheldon prescribed me then I'd rattle as I walk up and down the stairs. 'Fine. It's your body.' I look at him, but he won't meet my eye. Clearly, it's not fine at all.

'I was hurrying, that's all. I haven't had any breakfast yet either.'

'Sophie, I know you're busy and I understand that you want to lose weight, but you need to stop skipping meals.'

'I'm not, it's just I got sidetracked with Katie, and then Deanna arrived.' I'm keen to shift the focus of conversation away from me. 'How are you getting on with her anyway?' I can hear the thinly disguised envy in my tone, and I hope Scott doesn't detect it. He doesn't seem to notice, and a thought strikes me. 'I thought you had a meeting.'

'Yes. Postponed because his flight was brought forward. Frustrating, but we'll squeeze it in later today, although it'll probably be this evening now.'

'Ah, right.'

'As for Dee—' He glances towards the kitchen.

'Dee?'

Scott's expression cracks and he arches an eyebrow. 'Oh, Deanna. She likes to be called Dee. Her given name is actually Deianira, but Deanna is the anglicised version, so she's gone with that to make it easier for people.'

They've certainly been getting to know one another quickly. 'Right, and *Dee* is for those who can't handle names of more than one syllable?'

Scott takes a deep breath and tilts his head in that way – the way he does whenever Katie comes home with another letter from her teacher – and I feel much as our daughter must have, like a disappointment. 'It's important that she feels comfortable.'

'Well, I'm not one for shortening of names, so I'll stick with Deanna if it's all the same with you?'

Scott narrows his eyes, looking amused. 'What? No shortening of names, huh? Like Katie and Chas, for example?'

'They're children's names, and our children at that. It's different.'

'Yes, you're right,' he says, grinning. 'Completely different.'

'It is!'

'Absolutely.' He nods. 'Totally different.'

'You like her, then?' I ask, changing the subject.

'Her credentials are impeccable,' he says, glancing toward the kitchen as we hear the three of them laugh at some joke or another, 'and I've scanned through her CV and it's excellent. She's already improving Katie's French accent.'

'Quick worker. She's only been here for a couple of minutes.' I think I managed to keep the edge of bitterness away from my tone. Scott stares hard at me and mock winces. Perhaps I didn't.

'Come and see what you make of her. If you don't agree—'

'So, you've decided already, you want to take her on?'

Scott shrugs in that way he does when he wants to look as if he hasn't decided but, in reality, he has and is simply waiting for me to catch up. 'She seems like a breath of fresh air, honestly.'

'But we have to follow up on the references surely.'

'Of course,' he says calmly, 'but if she measures up to half of what's documented on her CV, then I think we've found the answer to our problems.'

'They say seventy per cent of someone's CV is a lie.'

'Do they indeed?' He stands up and holds out his hand, and hauls me up onto my feet. I do feel quite unsteady; I really should eat something. Scott notices. 'Are you sure you're okay? I could give the doctor a call, get some advice?'

'That's not necessary, honestly. I'm just a bit tired, it'll pass.'

'If you're still feeling like this tomorrow—'

'Then you can call Doctor Mengele, and I'll happily pay him a visit.'

Scott sighs. He's never shared my sense of humour when it comes to our family practitioner. The man's first name just happens to be Joseph, and the thought has kind of stuck in my head, never to be dislodged. The truth is, I'm not keen on doctors telling me what to think or do. They always give this impression that they know better than anyone else – professional arrogance maybe – and better than me in particular. And I dislike it.

'Come on,' Scott says, slipping his arm around my waist – hopefully in an affectionate way rather than in fear of me collapsing – and together we walk back into the kitchen.

We almost bump into Deanna as we round the corner. 'Oh, I'm sorry. I was just coming to see if everything was okay,' she says, smiling at me with concern in her eyes.

'We're fine,' I say, returning the smile. 'We just needed a moment.' I'm aware that the *we* in this is something of a *royal we* but I've known this woman for barely five minutes. She looks younger now for some reason. Perhaps it's the light in this part of the house. Maybe my instinct was right that she's a twenty-something, but I'd thought – or hoped – she was at the higher end of her third decade.

'Oh, good. You had me worried there for a moment.' I study her. Has she got a medical degree as well? 'I love your house.' She looks past Scott, her eyes catching mine, and they linger briefly before she scans the kitchen and then looks through into the entrance hall. She's already said all of this, to me, earlier when she first arrived. Does it really warrant a second outing of flattery?

'Thank you,' Scott says. 'It was something of a personal project to renovate and bring it forward whilst maintaining the period features.' I have to give it to her, Deanna knows what buttons to press to enrapture my husband. 'It's also listed, so we had to get it right.'

'You've done a remarkable job, it's stunning. I can't wait to see the rest of the house—' She stops and holds up a hand. 'I'm sorry, I'm not normally so presumptuous. I've only just walked through the door, and I've barely spoken to Mrs Beckett, but I feel a real sense of connection with you and your family.'

Is that so, I think. *Or do you see a connection with my husband?*

'Sophie will be fine, I'm sure,' Scott says, glancing sideways at me, looking for a corroborative gesture. I'm reticent. By her own recognition, she's only just walked in.

'We'll have to check out your references—'

'Sophie,' Scott says – there's the tilting of the head again – but I'm going to stand my ground. Somewhat irritatingly, Deanna agrees with me.

'Of course! I wouldn't let a total stranger have complete access to the most precious person in my family without checking them out properly either! You are far too intelligent for that, Mr Morton.'

Yes, she's irritatingly nice.

'Purely an academic procedure, I'm sure,' Scott says, fixing his eyes on me. I smile, much like I do when the red light comes on, on top of the camera in the studio, and nod firmly.

'Purely academic,' I repeat and Deanna's smile falters for a fraction of a second before broadening. Katie appears beside us, and she's almost eye to eye with Deanna. I forget how quickly she is growing up sometimes.

'You're not leaving, are you?' Katie asks her.

Deanna meets her eye and then glances between me and Scott. 'I don't know if your parents have any more questions for me, especially your mum?' I look at her suspiciously. 'We've not really had a chance to get to know one another, have we?'

'I don't,' Scott says and then looks at me pointedly. 'I've seen enough. How about you?'

'No, I don't, not really.' I look at Deanna. 'If my husband has covered all the bases... but as I say, we'll look at your CV and follow up on the references—'

'Which look terrific, by the way,' Scott says. Deanna blushes.

'Thank you, Mr Morton.'

'Scott,' he says, extending his hand and she takes it. He encloses her hand with his left as well, smiling. 'I think you know we have a somewhat tricky situation here,' he says, glancing at Katie, 'and we need someone like you. We have a good fit here, I believe, so don't worry.'

Okay, you can let her hand go now, and you can pull away, too, Deanna. Any time you like.

'Does that mean I can show Dee my bedroom and the rest of the house?' Katie asks, looking at her father and then me, more as an afterthought, I'm sure. Scott releases his hold on her hand, finally. Deanna is being offered access to Katie's bedroom, already? Katie scowls at me if I even dare to enter uninvited. Perhaps that's the issue, I'm not invited.

'I don't see why not,' Scott says and I smile, conscious of the crow's feet cracking in my face. Deanna, led away by a delighted Katie, glances back at us both apologetically. Scott looks at me. 'You have doubts?'

'I've only just met the girl.'

'Woman.'

'I beg your pardon?'

'She's a woman, not a girl. We shouldn't belittle her just because she's a bit younger than...'

'Who, me?' I ask but Scott is saved by the approaching Chas.

'Well, she's got my vote,' he says, grinning. I can smell something different on our eighteen-year-old. I think it's a mixture of spray-on deodorant and something else more familiar, Scott's cologne.

'Well, I can see the positive influence she's already had on you, Charles.' He looks at me with incomprehension. 'Maybe she could get your grades up as well.'

Chas angles his head. 'Fine by me. But I'm acing my course right now, and you know it.'

'Get away with you,' I say, gently swiping at him with the back of my hand. He deftly avoids it and trots out of the kitchen backwards, scooping up an apple from the fruit bowl as he passes, offering it into the air in a salutatory wave with an accompanying grin.

'That's three votes in favour,' Scott says. I roll my eyes and he shoots me an apologetic look. 'I'm only saying.'

'*Only saying*,' I repeat, shaking my head. Reluctantly, I must admit, Deanna seems perfect. I guess she wouldn't be here if she wasn't qualified, and if she has Katie onside then she'll likely last more than a fortnight. It is highly unlikely we'll be able to get Katie back into anything other than a state school, and even they might baulk at the prospect. No, I think we'll need Deanna, or someone similar, at any rate.

I can't seem to shake this sense of unease though. Something feels off in my family. That might not be because of Deanna; it's a feeling I've had for some time now. That's not to say life is or has been unpleasant, but our home life has certainly been on a downward trend, like we're going through the motions. I'm sure this is probably pretty common in a marriage. In the beginning everything is exciting, to be together, to feel one another's touch is nothing short of exhilarating. It was for us anyway. No, that won't last and when you bring children and careers into the mix it will become more mundane. But even so, there should still be a spark between us, or something that separates us from simply being housemates, sharing physical space but with lessening emotional connection. When did that happen?

It's almost like there's been a clock counting down these last few years, and every now and again something in our relationship disappears. I don't know what will happen when we reach zero.

I notice Scott's gaze lingers on Deanna and Katie as they round the half landing and go upstairs out of sight.

She certainly has his attention.

FOUR

Monday

Monday is cited as the most unpopular day of the week in most surveys. It stands to reason, for anyone who isn't working on a rotating shift pattern or working in the retail or hospitality sectors. For those people Monday might offer them a welcome day off. Although, what you would do with a Monday when everyone you know is likely at work themselves so that's your social engagement gone, and good luck taking yourself off to the cinema and being viewed as someone a tad odd by the staff.

My alarm sounds at three in the morning. Even if you love your work – and I do – it is an ungodly hour to surface. I'll forgive it if it means travelling to an airport for a long weekend in Dubai but to cross London in the early hours... no, thank you. I throw back the duvet and brace myself against the chill of the night. It's not particularly cold but I tend to sleep with the window open when I sleep alone otherwise the stuffiness of the air gives me a headache. I'm also tired, having struggled to find the sanctity of sleep again after retiring shortly after seven o'clock last night, and I always feel the cold more when I'm tired.

I've been sleeping in the guest bedroom five nights a week for months now. Occasionally I still sleep with Scott in our bedroom, but it's rarer now than ever before. With my new job, our hours are just completely different. My alarm goes off at three in the morning, and Scott doesn't have to get up until closer to six. I'm in bed for seven, which is when he gets home and he wants to shower, fair enough. Obviously, that wakes me up, and when my alarm goes off in the middle of the night, it does bother him. Also fair enough.

The guest room is more of a suite than simply a bedroom. There is a full bathroom along with an adjoining dressing room, and the king-size bed swallows me whole. It is at the front of the house on the third floor, and it has access to the garden roof terrace at the rear.

I've separated out my clothing and transferred what I would wear for the studio into this room. Many people think we arrive at the studio and are handed whatever we are going to wear during the broadcast upon arrival but that really isn't the case. Perhaps it was at one time, but not these days.

Stepping out of the shower, I walk back into the bedroom and look down at the three outfits I've shortlisted for the day. Usually, I've already chosen before I attempt to sleep the night before, but today is different. Embracing my dithering, I've set out clothing representing three different categories and which one I go with will set the tone for the future.

The first is in the style I've adopted over the last few years. It's stylish, professional and businesslike. The second is, let's face it, a complete and utter capitulation in the face of what Sam, my producer, said to me before I left on Friday. It is still professional and stylish, although the cut is lower than I am comfortable with these days, unless I'm out with my husband, and, to be honest, even he prefers me not to dress like this. I'm also not dating the almost two million people watching from their own homes. The length of the dress reaches to mid-thigh which, under most circumstances, wouldn't be an issue but the sofa I sit on is low and the table before me is even lower. The chance of a mishap is, therefore, highly likely.

The final choice is a compromise. A compromise in that it matches neither option but offers a bit of both. As with most compromises in life, it will leave no one happy and will serve only to kick the can down the road for a bit longer. Somehow, I don't think the production team or Scott will be impressed.

My mobile beeps and I scoop it up. There's a text message from my agent, Magda. What on earth is she doing up at this hour?

The text brings a smile to my face despite it offering no help with my current predicament. Magda must have picked up more than I'd thought during our brief telephone call on Friday. I read it again, shaking my head.

High collar and below the knee say professional, but certainly won't command attention.

The message from my agent, who has my best interests at heart obviously and not her commission, is to go with my own instinct. However, said instincts will likely garner a lesser value contract or no contract at all, if I'm unlucky. Oh, how pleasant it would be to have no need of scruples or a personal moral code.

That thought stops my deliberations in their tracks. *A moral code.* How easily these can be shaped and adjusted by a specific need. Anyone can rationalise their actions. Personal morality can be shifted.

I choose the middle ground option. There are enough cans bouncing around in my life as it is. One more loose one lying around won't make all that much difference.

I'd better get a move on. The driver will be here to collect me in fifteen minutes, and he is never late.

I pull on the skirt which reaches to just above my knees. The blouse is cream, has a ruffled neckline and heavily embroidered front panel, long sleeves and the cuffs match the front. Topping off the outfit with a suede burnt-orange multi-style blazer, I stand back and admire myself in the mirror, angling to one side so I can see how the line of the skirt's cut hugs my hips. Admiring my reflection, I cut a pose like I see the girls do all over social media these days.

'They'll notice me in this.'

Leaving my bedroom, I'm startled by movement from the shadows. Katie comes into the light emanating from the bedroom behind me. I hesitate as she approaches, those big round doe-like eyes of hers staring at me. Is she frightened or angry? Haunted, maybe. I can't tell in this light.

'Katie, are you okay?' I ask, reaching out to her. She stops just beyond my reach, and I decide not to push my affection onto her. 'Can't you sleep, darling?' She is just standing here in the darkness, in her pyjamas, staring at me with a strange expression. 'Katie?'

'Why are you here?'

That's a puzzling question. 'I'm going to work.'

'But *why* are you here?'

My eyes are adjusting to the dim light offered through the sash window overlooking the rear on the half landing between floors. The window is cracked open, and I can see the drapes shifting slightly in the passing breeze. That's odd. There's no reason for that window to be open. I can see Katie more clearly now my eyes are adjusting. Her expression is vacant, eyes staring straight at me, or possibly through me, I'm not sure.

'Do you think it's time you went back to bed, darling?'

She stares at me with blank emotionless eyes for a few moments longer. Blinking once, she turns and walks down two flights of stairs and into her own bedroom. I follow her. Katie climbs back into bed, pulls the duvet across her and lays her head down. She's motionless, eyes closed, arms wrapped tightly around a soft toy. It's her tiger, I think, although in the darkness it is hard to tell. She's getting a little too old for soft toys now, but she still clings to that tiger most nights.

As I lean over her, she doesn't flinch or acknowledge my presence. I make sure the duvet has covered her properly and she is breathing soundly.

I don't think she was awake. My sister, who I haven't spoken to in years, was prone to sleepwalking. I'd have entire conversations with her on detailed subjects and she'd remember nothing of them the following day. I've never known Katie to do the same, though, but maybe I've just never caught her before.

I can hear a car approaching and I cross to the window, shifting the curtains fractionally to look down onto the road just as my car draws up in front of the house. Returning to Katie's side, I lean over and gently kiss her forehead, sweeping a loose strand of hair away from her eyes before heading back onto the landing.

Then I scream.

FIVE

'Everything all right?'

My heart is racing and I'm breathing heavily as I look up at Scott standing on the stairs. He smiles sheepishly. 'You scared the hell out of me!' I say, keeping my voice down.

'Sorry. I got up to use the bathroom and... never mind.' He looks past me into Katie's bedroom. 'I thought I heard voices.'

'It was only Katie. I think she was sleepwalking. Between the two of you, you've managed to shave years off my life tonight.' Scott descends to join me on the landing and peers into our daughter's bedroom. How she didn't wake when I screamed, I'll never know. Katie's breathing is shallow now, almost imperceptible.

Scott turns and looks at me with a puzzled expression. Is he doubting me? He returns to me, wrapping his hands around my waist and pulling me into him. 'I'm running late, Scott. The car is already here.'

'Saif can wait a minute longer. I am going to miss my wife,' he says. He says it lightly, but there's something deeper within his tone. Regret or disappointment, I'm not sure which.

'I'll see you later. Will you be late home tonight?'

He draws a breath, looking up and away. 'No, I think I want to be back earlier today. Spend a bit of time with my hot wife.' Such flattery is very transparent, but it is also very effective. I smile and he returns it. Kissing me on the cheek, he releases his not so firm grip on my waist, and I set off down the stairs.

'Go back to bed,' I whisper over my shoulder. 'You need your beauty sleep.'

'I'm way ahead of you,' he says as he makes his way back up to our bedroom.

Descending the stairs, I know I'm flustered. Usually, I'm on autopilot to get out of the house and into the waiting car, but tonight – this morning – my autopilot isn't calibrated and is malfunctioning, my thoughts flitting between work, home, my husband and Katie. Lately any deviation from the norm seems to throw me out of kilter, exaggerating every hiccough into something greater. I'll sort myself out in the backseat and by the time we pull up in front of Media House, I'll have my game face on.

Coming to the front door, I go through my last-minute checklist which is pretty much my coat and bag. I have both, the coat under my right arm and my bag over my left shoulder. With one hand on the door handle, I take a deep breath before pulling it open and stepping out to face another day.

The night air feels cool against my skin as I descend the steps in front of the house to the waiting car. Saif is already beside the rear passenger door, waiting to open it for me. I feel like a movie star being collected for an awards ceremony, only in a hired Prius, driven by an African migrant practising his broken English. Despite me telling him a hundred times that I am quite capable of opening my own door, he insists and I've stopped arguing. I aim a frown in his direction, and he shoots me one of his toothy grins.

'Not on my shift, Miss Sophie,' he says.

I've just put on my seat belt and Saif puts the car into drive, making ready to get underway as a thought enters my head. Grabbing my bag from the seat beside me, I unzip it and scan the contents. It's not here. I start rooting around just in case it's sunk to the bottom, but it's not there.

'Damn.'

Saif glances back at me as the car moves off. I look toward the upper floors of my house and see a figure at an upstairs window. One of the windows in the guest suite. My suite. I turn my head as we pick up speed, craning my neck to see out of the back window but we are on the move and the house is dropping away from me.

'Everything all right, Miss Sophie?' My head snaps around to see Saif's eyes observing me via the rear-view mirror.

'Yes, everything's fine.'

'You have forget something? I can stop and go back. We have time.'

I glance at the orange digital clock set into the dashboard. We don't have time. We'll be cutting it fine as it is.

'No, no, it's okay. Honestly, keep going.'

He accepts my decision, but still furtively glances into the mirror several times as we leave the pale facade of Chester Terrace and beautiful Regent's Park behind us. Who was in my room, and why?

Or is this my overactive imagination seeing shapes in the darkness, again?

SIX

The broadcast today is not running to plan. At least, not for me. My usual runner, Megan, isn't on shift. Thomas is taking her place today, and he doesn't offer me anywhere near as much support as I have come to expect, no, to rely on, from Megan, who is an absolute godsend. It doesn't help that he seems to have the ear of my co-host, Michael, either. The two of them are thick as thieves in between segments. I say that, but it's more Thomas laughing almost hysterically at every quip Michael offers. It is clear who has the power on this show and everyone – Megan excluded – is looking for a leg-up.

Sam, the show's ever-present producer, beckons me aside as the broadcast cuts to the regional studios. I slowly get up from the sofa, my feet feeling like lead weights. If he's going to launch into me, then I'd much rather he waited until the end of the programme. That way, I can hold it together until I'm riding the Tube when I can allow myself a pity cry and no one will comment, acknowledge or even care.

'Sophie.' He has a pained expression. It's probably his gout playing him up again. I'd feel sorry for him if he wasn't so... no, that's harsh. I do feel sorry for him. He has his masters, just like the rest of us, and he's doing his best. 'I just wanted to have a word about our conversation on Friday.'

'I know. I've been thinking about it too, and—'

'No, please,' he says, holding up his hand to get me to stop talking. 'I think I chose my words poorly.' Ah, so that's it. He's fearing an email to HR. As if I'd do that. It'd be the death knell for my career if I went down that path.

Sam pauses, taking a deep breath as he thinks through his next line – never a good sign – and then removes his little round glasses; they are frameless, and without them his eyes look all beady, a bit like a mole. That description ties in with his silky dark hair, smooth complexion and slightly rotund appearance, and being only five-five, it does leave him open to nicknames. Not that I would ever partake. I have enough going on as it is without falling foul of mocking the bosses.

I must admit to feeling a sense of smug satisfaction at not having given in and worn outfit number two. Although, I'll never let on to anyone about how close I came to doing just that this morning. 'And I would like to apologise if I said anything untoward,' Sam continues. 'I can see how upset you were by what I said, and it was in poor taste.'

'Sam, don't worry. We're all looking to achieve the same thing here. We all want the programme to be a success.'

His expression brightens, a weight seemingly lifted from his shoulders. 'Thank you, Sophie. That's very kind.' He glances down, taking in my appearance, which feels a little creepy bearing in mind he's apologised barely twenty seconds ago for objectifying me last Friday and insinuating I wasn't attractive enough. That is the polite way of saying it and, incidentally, is not even close to his appalling comments about my wardrobe. 'I see my comments didn't affect your style choice.'

'I took on board what you said though, Sam.' He looks at me curiously. Something tells me the apology has emerged out of an innate desire for self-preservation rather than the dawning of a less misogynistic attitude from the production team. This conversation will be revisited later, I'm confident of that. 'I think there is a compromise to be had.' He nods and smiles. Why on earth did I say that? I know why, it's because I have this insatiable need to be liked and to please people. Even at the expense of my own sanity. I wish I knew where that came from.

Thomas comes alongside us, winking at me, and pointing toward the sofa.

'Two minutes,' he says, smiling artificially before slinking away to attend to his golden ticket: Michael. If he wants to get the other side of the cameras, then he'll need to improve his deliverance of fake authenticity.

'Thank you, Sophie,' Sam says awkwardly, before hurrying from the studio set and making his way back to production. I retake my position on the sofa, Michael pointing to the strips of white tape stuck to the carpet off camera, where my feet need to be placed, as he always does.

'I saw Samuel having a quiet word with you there.' He's either fishing or he knows full well what we were discussing. 'I presume he was trying to extricate himself from some hot water.' He knows. He definitely knows.

'It's all fine,' I say. If there's one person I won't confide in with the details of a serious conversation, then that person is Michael, one of the most indiscreet individuals I have ever had the displeasure to work with.

'He drew the short straw, the poor chap.'

I look sideways at Michael as Thomas silently counts down the final ten seconds before we go live. 'What straw?' Michael glances at me, arching one eyebrow in that sanctimonious manner he has.

'To speak to you about dressing like an old maid. I told the powers that be how you need to be far sexier to keep your seat next to me on this sofa.'

The red light on top of the camera is illuminated and my

jaw is hanging like a sleeping drunk. Michael is sporting his best *Good Morning* smile to the nation and the Autocue is stationary.

'Er, g-good morn—'

'Good morning!' Michael steps in, taking the opening that was scheduled for me. 'Welcome back, and have we got some great items for you to look forward to. Coming up this morning, we have...'

One day that toupee he wears will slip and I might point it out to him or I might not, depending on how much I detest him on that given day.

The remainder of the broadcast passes without event and I'm leaving the studio before half past nine, slipping past Sam, who looked like he was gearing up for another awkward conversation.

I thought Friday's conversation was Sam trying to improve the ratings of one of his shows. I didn't realise that there had been group discussions about me, about my appearance, and that they'd reached the conclusion that an intervention was required. My first thought should have been outrage. I mean, how dare they? But it wasn't. It is now, obviously. Who the hell do they think they are, telling me what I should wear or how I should present myself, like I'm an object rather than a person?

It's not that I wasn't angry on Friday, but I won't lie, in the main I was embarrassed. *It was utterly humiliating.* All of my achievements, my interview techniques, the highest ratings this programme has ever had, all disregarded with the focus switching to how short my skirts are.

I look for Michael, but he's long gone. Apparently, the tweaks *they* have in mind to improve the viewing numbers don't affect him. To be fair, why should they? Michael has been presenting this show for years now. He also works on the weekend lifestyle show: visiting farms, outlying donkey sanctu- aries, or similar, and highlighting charitable activities in communities across the country and not just the capital. Nice work, if you can get it. Seemingly, he has had no involvement in the downward trajectory of viewing numbers prior to the departure of my predecessor, just like I haven't in the rising numbers since I came across.

I can't hang around the studio today. Every look, every glance could be shared with someone who thinks I'm past it, not good enough, or that I shouldn't be there. It's stifling, claustrophobic. Also, I'm keen to get home. Deanna is starting with us officially this morning, and Scott is working from home to greet her because I can't be there.

There's no reason why it won't go well, given how quickly Katie took to her on Saturday, but we will see. However well the two of them hit it off, Katie can burn through anyone's goodwill in a matter of weeks, if not days.

Despite the apparent healthy beginnings, I'm irritated by Deanna. She seems perfect, but I know perfection is an illusion.

I can't wait to get home.

SEVEN

There are delays on the Bakerloo line. Some poor soul wound up on the tracks and the knock-on effect has turned a Monday morning commute into a bit of a nightmare. Luckily, Scott invested a great deal of time and energy into teaching me the tricks of the trade when it comes to navigating London in these scenarios.

It would be far easier if I had my mobile. How I managed to leave the house this morning without it is beyond me. These days, to leave your phone behind is like stepping out of the house with only one foot attached. You would hope to notice that you're hopping along rather than walking, but if your mind is elsewhere, and mine certainly is, then I suppose it is easily done.

Usually, I would have a carriage almost to myself. By the time I'm heading home the morning commute is over and everyone who needs to be at their desk for nine o'clock has made it. The mass movement of people is over until closer to four in the afternoon when things go haywire again, descending into some obscure form of managed anarchy as millions migrate across the city like a flock of starlings. That is aside from heavy tourist periods, special events or security situations. Some of this you can plan for, but much of it is beyond anyone's control. Today is one of those days. It is carnage on the network.

Add to this scenario a drubbing from a new weather front that batters the capital, and it all adds up to a rather bedraggled – somewhat frazzled – Sophie who arrives back at Chester Terrace. Finally, I slip my key into the lock and enter. Sounds of laughter carry from the kitchen. My coat proved to be more style over substance and is far from waterproof. I pretty much have to peel it off and the suede burnt-orange blazer I thought was such a good idea at three o'clock this morning now has watermarks running through it. It's done for. My hair has gone in all directions. Frankly, examining my reflection in the hallway mirror, I look an absolute state.

I hang my coat up and I'm not concerned about the floor. The underfloor heating will take care of the runoff. My shoes, also suede, are a write-off too. The jacket... I hold it aloft, studying it. Maybe it can be salvaged but I'll need to run an internet search for that one. I can imagine the look of pity I'll get taking it into the dry-cleaner's. Maybe Martha, our house-keeper, will have a solution. She's pretty good with these domestic crises. I badgered Scott into getting us some help for the house, and Martha is so much more than a part-time house-keeper; she is my rock.

I head toward the sound, stopping at the threshold of the kitchen. At the far end there's Katie hunched over her books with an energetic-looking Deanna sitting alongside explaining something to her with theatrical use of arms and hand gestures. I had energy like that once, I'm sure.

What I didn't expect was to find Scott passing our new tutor an espresso, then leaning back against the counter of the break-fast bar with a cup of his own.

I can't recall the last time he hung out with me over a cup of coffee when he was supposed to be working. Should I be annoyed that no one has even noticed I'm home, an hour later than expected as well? Katie is engrossed in her studies which is a good thing, I guess. Scott's looking on with a contented expression. He used to look at me like that once, too.

I think Katie and Deanna are working on pronunciation of Latin phrases. I didn't study it myself, but that's what it sounds like to me.

I enter the kitchen and set my bag down on the counter. The sound alerts everyone to my presence, and I swear I didn't throw it down but something inside clatters against the surface. Scott seems irritated; he doesn't care for loud noises. His gaze settles on me, his eyes narrowing, before that quick smile of his returns. To be fair, I'm a mess.

Deanna glances my way and smiles, but doesn't break off from whatever it is she is talking through with Katie. Scott comes over, reaches out for a hug and hesitates as he casts an eye down me.

'You look like you've had one heck of a day already.'

'Yes, I do, don't I?' I reply somewhat snappily. In my defence, it's been an awful day and it's only just got going for most people. 'You picked the right day to work from home.' His frown deepens.

'You say it like I had a choice,' Scott says. 'It's Deanna's first—'

'Yes, I know. Sorry.' I didn't mean to make him feel like I was attacking him.

'That bad out there, is it? You should have called. I'd have sent a car for you.'

Now he tells me. 'I couldn't, I didn't have my phone.'

'But you always take your phone,' he says, surprised.

'Trust me, I too can also see the heavy dose of sod's law in all of this.' He leans closer and kisses me on the cheek. I smile gratefully and then look past him. 'How is everything going this morning?'

Scott steps to the side so I can observe Deanna and Katie's interactions. 'See for yourself. It's going incredibly well. We were just about to take a break with our coffee. Would you like one?'

'Yes, please.' An image of Scott sitting alongside Deanna, chatting over a cup of coffee, comes to mind and something instinctive, something dark and unpleasant, flickers inside me. He moves toward the machine, but I grip his forearm. 'Actually, no. I think I'd rather take a shower first and get changed.' Deanna is immaculately presented. More like she's at her first day at a financial services institution rather than taking a twelve-year-old under her wing.

She must have felt me looking at her because she glances up, making eye contact for slightly longer than is normal, and then returns her focus to Katie. My daughter slides her exercise book over and Deanna scans the page before raising her hand for a high-five. To my surprise, Katie accepts and their palms slap together with accompanying smiles.

Then Katie pushes her chair back, jumps up and runs around the table with her book clutched against her chest, triumphantly waving the book in the air. She lands before us with an enthusiastic bounce, grinning. 'I can do it!' she says.

'That's great, love!' Scott says. 'I'm so proud of you.'

'Me too, darling,' I say, touching her cheek, but it's her father's approval she seeks more than mine and her eyes flicker to me with a pointed glare – unseen by Scott. She flinches away from my touch and looks back to her father. Smiling at him, Katie puts the exercise book down on the counter and strides out of the kitchen to make the most of her break. That probably means YouTube or something similar.

'She's a smart girl,' Deanna says, joining us with her coffee cup in her hand. 'She could do very well if she concentrates.'

'Yes, she is smart,' I say, watching Katie disappear up the stairs. 'Very.'

'She's getting on just fine. I don't think you have anything to worry about with her studies.'

'That's lovely to hear,' Scott says. He looks at me. 'Are you sure you don't want that coffee before you take a shower?'

The image returns to mind, Scott and Deanna alone together, only more powerful than before now that Deanna is standing in front of me with her perfect hair and make-up, and a natural, gorgeous smile. 'Sure. I'll have one before I go up, yes, thank you.'

Deanna's observing me, sipping her drink, eyeing me over the rim. She is wearing glasses today and is more obvious with her make-up which I find pleasing. Maybe she does have natural blemishes she needs to cover after all. My mascara has run. Hers, though, is perfect. She must have arrived before the weather turned, although it's been raining steadily since six a.m. I listen to some of the weather reports during the programme if Sam isn't fussing around me.

'Did you get caught in the rain?' she asks while Scott prepares my drink with that contraption that he adores. It's all stainless steel and chrome, manual pumps and gauges. Apparently, it extracts just the right amount of coffee in the allotted twenty-five seconds to ensure the espresso isn't too bitter. It's an art form completely lost on me. For me, a tin of freeze-dried Nescafé was the height of caffeine decadence growing up. Okay, decadence is pushing it, but sometimes I miss the simplicity.

'I did, yes. Is it that obvious?' I ask, with the trace of a self-deprecating smile. Deanna smiles but doesn't respond to my comment.

'This is lovely coffee, Scott,' she says, turning his way. 'Is it a South American blend?'

My husband inclines his head with a smile. He's impressed, I can tell. 'Yes, it is. Guatemalan.'

Deanna sniffs delicately and sips again. 'I can really taste the chocolate, and a hint of cherry in there too, I think.'

Scott finishes wiping down the machine with a lint-free cloth and returns with a fresh cup for me, passing it across the counter and nodding. 'You are very good. There's apricot in that one, and a touch of cinnamon too.'

'I missed that though,' she says, smiling. 'You clearly know your coffee.'

'It is a vice that I have, that's true.'

Scott has very few vices that I am aware of. He seldom drinks alcohol and is very particular about what he eats. He's not a calorie counter or anything like that, and he isn't a vegan or an extremist when it comes to nutrition, but he does insist on minimal consumption of processed foods. That applies to everyone within the family. A treat for Katie is certainly not a trip to a fast-food burger chain.

'You didn't have any trouble getting here this morning, Deanna?' I ask her. There is a moment where she is still beaming at Scott before she breaks off her gaze in an almost seamless, silky movement of the eyes, turning to me.

'No, no trouble at all. I'm staying nearby, on the other side of Holland Park.'

'You live near Holland Park?' Scott asks, surprised.

'No, not exactly. I'm just staying in a dorm. I haven't had time to sort anything longer term since I got back.' Deanna's expression darkens and she looks suddenly dejected. 'I've been out of the country for some time and the capital was always expensive but now... it's ridiculous.'

'Are you staying at the hostel?' I ask her. It's the only place I know locally that won't set you back over a hundred pounds a night. She nods.

'It's only temporary.'

Katie hustles into the kitchen. I hadn't heard her come

down the stairs. It is very unusual for her not to be forced back to her studies; Deanna must be a positive influence indeed.

'I have to admit though, if I can't sort something out soon, I think my stay in London will be a brief one.'

'Well, I for one hope that isn't the case,' Scott says glumly. He checks his watch. 'I have a call. Please excuse me.' He finishes his coffee, puts the empty cup into the dishwasher, as always, and leaves the kitchen. Katie appears at my side, handing me a bundle of letters and my mobile phone.

'Where did you find this, sweetie?' I ask, examining my mobile. It's switched off.

'In the downstairs cloakroom.'

That's odd. I don't remember going in there this morning. Maybe it was last night before I went up to bed and I just forgot about it, I was so tired.

Deanna finishes her coffee and follows Scott's example by putting the empty cup straight into the dishwasher.

'That's perfect, Dee,' Scott says jovially as he steps back into the kitchen, scanning the room for something. Spotting his pocket diary beside the coffee machine, he gathers it up, holding it aloft as he turns to leave. 'You'll fit in around here, I can tell.' Deanna smiles and I half-heartedly note the exchange because I'm focused on the letter in my hand.

I recognise the handwriting, and I can't quite believe it.

Why now? It's been years, and I thought I'd left all of that behind, long ago, but I guess I was wrong.

EIGHT

'Sophie?'

I turn to face Deanna, quickly folding the letter in the palm of my hand, as if she'll recognise the handwriting of the address. That's crazy, I know, but it's instinct. 'What?'

'Is everything all right?' she asks me.

'Yes,' I say innocently. 'Why... why wouldn't it be?'

'I don't know,' she says, studying me. 'You seem distracted. Is everything okay?'

'I need to get cleaned up.' This is true. I'm self-conscious as it is, but I also want to get out of these clothes and into something dry. I can see mascara clumped in my eyelashes and my skin has absorbed the smell of the underground. 'Can you manage down here?' I ask, glancing around. She nods confidently. Of course she can manage. She's perfect.

Backing out of the room, the envelope held tightly in my hand, I mount the stairs and I don't look back. I can feel her eyes upon me, and I almost miss a step but manage to style it out. I can hear Scott on the phone as I pass his study but I don't look in on him. I don't stop until I'm into the guest suite upstairs, closing the bedroom door.

Unfolding the envelope, I'm considering opening it but I'm nervous. Not now. There are too many people in the house. So I put it under my pillow and glance at the door. They'll not come looking through my things, will they?

I lay out my clothes before going into the bathroom. I don't want to be wearing a skirt for the rest of the day, so I've kept it casual, a pair of jeans and a large, hooded sweatshirt. It's not because I want to unwind and be comfortable, but because I want to hide. Being judged at work on my personal presentation is making me want to avoid being looked at, being seen, by anyone. But as I look at them now, I'm not so certain these clothes will make me feel any better. Deanna makes so much of herself, in an understated way, and I don't want to look like some middle-aged frump alongside her in my own home.

Heading into the bathroom, I set the water flowing and turn up the heat. Steam is forming on the mirror by the time I've undressed, casting my clothes to the floor in an untidy heap and stepping in. All I can feel now is the water upon my bare skin, and the sound of it cascading to the tiles below. I'm in my safe space, away from the world. Running my hands through my hair, brushing it backwards, away from my face, I feel clean again.

The handle squeaks as I shut off the water, stepping out of the enclosure and pulling a towel from the heated rail and wrapping it around myself. Running my hand across the mirror, I peer at my reflection as it fades away behind the steam. Spending time in the shower is a vice of my own. I get to be alone while I'm here, unless I choose not to be, obviously. Not that that is a scenario that's come to pass recently. I can't remember the last time I was intimate with my husband in the bedroom, let alone the shower, and I'm pretty sure that I'm to blame. It certainly isn't Scott's fault that I go to bed before either of my children do, and usually in a separate bedroom.

When I am showering, I have the time to allow my mind to

wander, to play events out in my head without interruption. To dream about things the way I'd like them to be, along with how I could make that happen.

Today, though, my thoughts are jumbled and incoherent. The situation at work, with the pressure to dress in a way I don't feel comfortable with has thrown me. Am I naive? Am I the crazy one for believing in a meritocracy, that if I perform well, I will be rewarded? Or do I have to dress like someone half my age, who's gone for a night out clubbing with her mates, in order to get ahead? I don't see Michael being asked to show a bit more skin. On the other hand, I could be reading too much into this. Scott often tells me I overthink things, but it's hard not to over-think it when they're talking about my body.

My father used to drill into all of us, myself, my brother and sister, that the world is full of people bleating about their own victimhood. If, he would say, they put half as much effort in trying to achieve their goals as they did into whining about the unfairness of life and how mistreated they've been, then they'd be on easy street. The world doesn't owe anyone a living and it is up to us to make something of ourselves. It was the foundation of his work ethic which was second to none.

I've certainly tried to follow that teaching. Am I living on easy street? To be fair, life is good. I have the house of my dreams, well, Scott's dreams, to be honest. My dream would be some land in the countryside, surrounded by rolling fields, peace and quiet, disturbing the wild deer as they ruin the flowers in my garden. Perhaps that is for another time, once our careers are done and the children have flown the nest.

Everyone talks about adjusting your work-life balance, making time for your family by putting boundaries in place. That's great, but I do wonder if it's even possible. My job is demanding, and a role in broadcasting doesn't lend itself to being present for my children. I'm trying to juggle these two conflicting worlds, and a daily planner, an app on my mobile phone, or calendar reminders just doesn't cut it. Perhaps I'm just making excuses. I see others managing it well enough.

It seems like only yesterday that I landed an internship at the studios. I never really considered that I'd wind up before a green screen in the weather corner, let alone get to work as a broadcaster, a national one at that.

My career is proving to be far more of an issue than I ever anticipated, demanding excessive amounts of my time and draining my limited mental energy, but it is something just for me. It is the one thing in my life that is still mine. And I don't want to give it up.

The day I was introduced to Scott changed my life. As much as I would like to think what followed with my career would have come to pass eventually, I know it's probably not true. I got lucky. It was by chance that I wound up working for Scott, and then hanging out in the office led to an impromptu audition to be a weather girl. That's what they referred to the role as, not a presenter, but a weather girl. That in itself probably should have been the indicator for things to come.

It still amazes me even now. I know what some people say, that Scott pulled strings to get me my start. Nothing could be further from the truth though; if anything, I'm pretty sure he'd rather I hadn't got my start at all.

With only the sound of the extractor fan reverberating overhead, I look at my reflection again. Wiping the moisture clear, I can see something of the youthful face that once spoke to herself in the mirror, practising what it would be like to be on television. To be a celebrity. *A celebrity.* What an awful word that is, and being one isn't what most people would expect either. 'You are a naive fool, Sophie Beckett,' I tell my reflection. 'There is always a price to pay in exchange for success, and you're just finding out what that is.'

When I was younger, I'd have been delighted to know where I have ended up. But now, with the strain my career places on my relationship with Scott and my ability to be the mother Chas and Katie deserve, I sometimes wonder if it is worth it. I love my job, despite its challenges, but I love my family more. And the mental toll the pressure is having on me is becoming increasingly severe. It's not just my high anxiety, it's these awful stress headaches, which feel like they're getting worse every week.

Moving into the bedroom, the thick carpet soft and forgiving beneath my feet, I go to the door and listen carefully just to make sure I'm not going to be disturbed. No one comes up here very often in any event. Scott put so much effort into harmonising the decor of the house, matching floor coverings in bedrooms and communal spaces, pale colours on the walls to link everything together. This room, every room in the house, is a reflection of my husband, smooth, stylish and inoffensive. Not that that should be confused with plain or boring, because it is anything but. Our home could grace the covers of a magazine and be the envy of anyone but perhaps a passing sheik.

Crossing the room to the bed, I glance over my shoulder before retrieving the letter from beneath the pillow.

I recognise the return address. Of course I do. I grew up there.

The knowledge that my father hasn't moved gives me a warm feeling, a familiarity with somewhere I belong.

But I can't go back. I wouldn't be welcome.

If that's true, Sophie, then why would he write to you after all this time?

Has someone died? Louise or Carl? No, my brother and sister are too young to have been ill, surely?

Biting my lip, I slip my thumb into the corner. Then I pause.

Closing my eyes, I try hard to quell the knot of anxiety I feel building in my chest. I can't handle this, not right now. I should destroy it, pretend I never received it.

But it's a link to my past. A link to who I am, even if I can't be a part of it anymore.

Instead of putting it back under the pillow, I fold it and put it into my pocket. The best way to keep something from other people is to keep it on your person.

I've spent too long in the shower, and I need to crack on. I can't hide up here for the rest of the day. I'm hoping Martha has returned from the shops with the groceries from the list I pinned to the fridge. I would like to make Katie her lunch today. Usually, Martha would normally take care of it, which is another of the many things that we don't pay her to do and that she does anyway, but I want to show my daughter that I can look after her too. Work has been so busy lately and seeing her interacting with Deanna has sparked something in me.

My critical side tells me I'm jealous and it's true, I am. I want some of that too. I want Katie to laugh and joke with me. Is that so bad?

Descending to the lower landing, I can't hear anything from Scott's study now. I knock gently and open the door. He has his back to me, his chair facing the window, gazing at the sheets of rain lashing against it. This used to be two rooms, but Scott had them knock out the wall in between to fashion a personal space larger than the entire ground floor of the house I grew up in. The wood panelling to the walls is original and painted in a satin white finish with the walls contrasting in the colour of squid ink.

On one side of the room is a seating area made up of an oxblood Chesterfield sofa and club chairs laid out in a U shape before a cast iron period fireplace with marble surround. Scott's desk is at the other end of the room, carved from mahogany, two metres wide with green leather covering it.

'Scott?' I ask hesitantly. He hasn't reacted, and I wonder if he's deep in thought or listening hard on a call. 'Scott?' I ask only a bit louder, not wishing to interrupt him. His chair slowly turns to face me, and he smiles.

'Sorry, love. I was miles away.'

'Thinking?'

He laughs. 'I'm always thinking.'

'Anything important?'

He sighs. 'It's always important, just different levels of importance. Nothing to worry about. Everything all right?'

'Um, yes.'

He fixes me with one of those looks that my husband is so good at, giving me an opportunity to say what's on my mind and at the same time conveying that he likely already knows what it is. 'You're sure?'

'Yes.'

'Only,' – he flexes his shoulders and brings his hands together in front, elbows resting on his desk, pitching a tent with his fingers before his face – 'I saw you received a letter.'

Did he see that? I didn't think he was there, but I suppose I was so preoccupied I wouldn't have noticed.

'A letter?'

'Yes, you didn't open it and put it into your pocket.'

'Oh, that letter.' I can feel my face reddening. 'That was nothing, just a circular. I threw it away.' His gaze lingers on me and either he doesn't believe me or he's considering. His look is intense, lips slightly parted. Is he waiting for me to say something else? I'm not going to. I'm feeling uncomfortable, like he knows I'm lying. His eyebrows flick upwards briefly and his eyes shine as he smiles, softening his expression.

'Did you? I thought you looked a bit pale, and I wondered what could have done that, that's all.'

'Just having a moment. I didn't sleep well, you know?'

'Again? We really need to work out what's going on with you, don't we?'

'I'll be all right.' I can tell he doesn't share my faith. 'I will, honestly.'

He stands, drawing a sharp breath through his nose. 'There is something else we need to talk about,' he says quietly.

'Oh?'

He nods. 'Yes. I spoke to the school first thing this morning, and there's no way back for Katie.'

'I really thought they might come around, after all your calls on Friday—'

'Well, they do have a reputation for discipline, so we shouldn't be surprised, I suppose.'

'You did such a good job getting around them after the last time, that I hoped you'd be able—'

'As did I, but even I have my limitations. The final decision will need to be ratified by the board of governors, but I don't think they will take a pause to think about it. Let's face it, it's done,' Scott says, scratching at the back of his head. 'It looks like we'll have to stick with the arrangement we have with Deanna.'

'Really? I mean, there are other schools we can try.'

'That's true, but they all speak to one another and, despite money often playing the role of kingmaker when it comes to school places, no one wants a problem child on their books.'

'Katie' – I look over my shoulder just in case she has crept in unseen or unheard behind me – 'is going through a difficult phase, but she's hardly a problem child.'

Scott tilts his head to one side. 'Well, her track record of late says otherwise, does it not?'

I'm utterly deflated. I was banking on this being resolved positively. 'Where did we go wrong?'

Scott arches his eyebrows and shakes his head. 'Things have been out of kilter for ages. Maybe we just need to reset again.'

'Again?'

He meets my eye slowly. 'You know, like when we moved to

the UK. We've been through difficult times before, and we came back from them.'

'That's true. We'll find a way, won't we?'

He reaches out and draws me into him, gently rubbing the small of my back. Tilting his head, he winks at me. 'It'll all be fine, you'll see. Don't worry.' His affectionate embrace lightens my mood.

'Are you hungry? I was thinking we could have some poached eggs, maybe on sourdough with avocado. I know it's yours and Katie's favourite.' As soon as I say the words something nags at my memory, but it slips away.

'Used to be.'

'What?'

'Avocado used to be her favourite.'

'Ah, yes, that's it. She did say. I forgot.'

Scott fixes me with a curious look. 'It was a while ago, but you've not been around much recently.'

'Because I'm working—'

'I know, it wasn't a dig.'

'Never mind.' I shake my head. 'I can always do something else. I'm hoping Martha's back from—'

'Martha?'

'Yes, I figured she'd gone to the shops and—' I pause, noticing his puzzled expression. 'What?'

'Martha's mother is ill.'

'She is?'

Scott nods. 'She's just come out of hospital, Martha had to go down to Kent to care for her.'

'Oh, I... when did this happen?'

Scott almost laughs but suppresses it. 'This has been coming for a while, we just didn't know when her mother would be coming out of hospital.'

'I—' This is so odd. How could I forget something like this? 'Are you sure?'

Scott smiles but I can still see the concern in his eyes. 'Yes. I know you've been busy, but Sophie, are you feeling—'

'I'm fine! Now you've reminded me, of course I remember, it'd just slipped my mind, that's all.' Scott's studying me now, and I can't read his expression anymore. 'Honestly, I don't know what I was thinking. I'd better get to the shops then, otherwise we'll have nothing to eat.'

'Would you like some help?' Scott says, frowning and looking at his desk. 'If you're struggling, I could shift some things around, free up—'

'No, no. I can manage, don't worry.' I reach for his hands and smile, giving them a gentle squeeze. He responds with a half-smile, clearly finding it difficult to mask his uncertainty. 'You carry on and I'll get lunch sorted.'

'If you're sure?'

'Yes, don't worry. I'm fine.'

Downstairs, as I'm zipping up the coat I bought on our holiday in the Peak District a couple of years ago, I can't help but wonder what is going on with my mind. I have to get a grip. I can't have it all falling apart. Not again.

NINE

Thursday

Martha hasn't even been gone for two whole days, and the house is already descending into chaos. I should have tackled this last night, but I didn't know where to start, and now... it looks like we're living in student digs.

The kitchen counters have scummy residue in patches, some of it dried solid like glue and in other parts, slimy and unidentifiable. When Martha is around the surfaces are clear, but I've got packets, cartons and tins all over the place; some are open and others untouched. I've no idea why I've taken them from the pantry, let alone why I've left them out. The bins are full, too, and they're starting to smell. Why is there clothing thrown across the island? Is it clean or dirty? I've not got a clue, about anything.

Deanna is sitting at the table by the front sash window, resting her finely chiselled chin on a closed fist as if she's posing for some neo-classical sculptor, staring out across the park. Damn, she looks so poised and graceful. It's really annoying, bearing in mind I want to curl up into a ball behind the island

and stay there until the sun goes down. The study materials are laid out on the table, waiting to begin the day's lessons, but of my daughter there is no sign. I raise my eyebrows at Deanna and she smiles awkwardly. Clearly she doesn't know where Katie is either.

We had such high hopes taking Deanna on. Or, I should say, Scott did. As for me, I had my doubts which I'll admit have little to do with her capability as an educator and much more to do with other concerns, none of which I can articulate without coming off as a jealous old hag. Initially, Scott was proved right. Deanna and Katie hit it off and I had to feast on enough humble pie to, quite frankly, have me reaching for the indigestion tablets more than the recommended daily dosage.

However, as with anything Katie-related these days, inconsistency reigns supreme and after the early relief she has managed to reassert herself. And when I say *reassert herself*, I mean turn this situation into a farce. She's still getting on with Deanna, I've no doubt about that. It's me that my daughter has an issue with. It's almost as if a successful tutor makes me the winner and therefore, by default, she's the loser. My daughter hates to lose. She once walked out on a family game of Monopoly because she had to pay rent to her brother.

My mobile ringing stops me from walking into the hall and bellowing at her up the stairs. It's Magda, my agent and part-time agony aunt. Katie has until the end of this phone call to make an appearance or she's going to get a rocket up her backside.

'Magda! What can I do for you?' I answer as I head into the lounge to take the call away from Deanna's prying ears.

Magda has been with me for a couple of years now, pretty much from when I first started. I found her, much to Scott's disapproval because he wanted to use his contacts to seek out the best in the business for me, but I insisted, in a rare moment of clarity, that I needed this to be something I did on my own.

He relented, and I suspect figured I'd fall on my backside and beg him to help. However, Magda and I got on like a house on fire even when I was arguably the least significant client she had on her books. How things have changed. I think her percentage of this current contract paid for her new Mercedes, or the boob job. Perhaps both.

'Hello, Sophie. Kisses, darling! Long time no speak.' It hasn't been long at all but this is Magda, and for someone who deals in contracts most of the time, she does seem to adore a touch of drama.

'Here we go. Have they been onto you already?'

'About what?'

'Oh, nothing to worry about,' I say confidently. What Magda doesn't know, she can't nag me about. 'Listen, this isn't a very good time for me—'

'There never is a very good time, darling, but we need to talk. There have been some fascinating opportunities earmarked for the coming year. You're going to love them. I think we can significantly boost your profile, and that will give us leverage when talking to your current employers about how much they pay you to sit on that sofa.'

I'm listening to Magda relaying the planned trajectory for my career this year, while I look over to see what Deanna will teach my daughter this morning. If Katie deigns to show her face, that is. It looks like maths. There might be the root cause of her disappearing act, but I have a nagging feeling that it wouldn't matter what the subject is. She's waited until I get home to make it very clear that she's not doing what I expect of her.

I'll have to go and find her soon, but I must admit, the thought of going another round with my daughter fills me with dread.

'Magda, I sense you're building up to something. What, specifically, have you got for me?' I ask as I retreat from the kitchen, almost catching my foot on a bag for life that I managed to miss when unpacking yesterday.

'How are your legs?'

'Oh, don't you start! Sam's been on the phone to you, hasn't he?'

'Samuel from the studio?' Magda asks. 'Little man, pot belly, funny looking? No. Why?'

'Forget it, my legs are fine. Why do you ask?'

'Dancing, darling. Dancing. I know you can dance—'

'No, I really can't. Maybe a bit of a can-can at the work Christmas party once I've had a cheeky G & T, but aside from that...'

'Oh, well, you'll pick it up.'

'Dancing where?'

'*Children in Need* is coming up, and they are putting on a week-long special dancing competition.'

'You mean like *Strictly*, celebrity dancing?'

'Exactly, darling. You'll be ace! Think of it as an audition for the main show. The studios love to have popular presenters, household names, and you tick each and every box, Sophie darling. It'll be massive for you! When you make the final three—'

'I admire your confidence.'

'What?'

'If I make the final three.'

'Of course you will.'

'Except *I can't* dance.'

'It's a popularity competition above everything else, and what makes people popular with the viewers?'

'Er, talent?'

There's a soft chuckling coming from the other end of the line. Slightly irritating, if I'm honest, but Magda always means well. I think.

'No, darling. *Familiarity*, and who is more familiar to the nation's viewers than the person with the biggest smile who everyone wakes up to of a morning?'

'You make me sound like a slapper.'

'Smile, dance, be your lovely, infectious self, and you'll have it made. What do you think?'

'I know I've already said this, but it's very important and so I think it is worth repeating. I can't dance.'

'You'll have time to practise. Weeks and weeks in the build-up. You're finished in the studio by nine—'

'By nine thirty, but whatever.'

'Exactly, which gives you all day and the evening to find your way around the dance floor.'

'Except I am in bed by seven o'clock, and I have a husband and two children to manage as well as my career.'

'Speaking of your gorgeous husband, how is Scott?' Her tone always changes when she mentions my husband. I see it a lot. It's not only Magda, but almost everyone who encounters him. He has that level of charisma that draws people in. Women in particular, but he has this appeal to men too. I shouldn't be surprised. After all, it worked on me.

'He's well.' The truth is, I've barely seen my husband in the past couple of months. We haven't exactly been ships that pass in the night, rather we're not even sailing in the same sea. Granted, he's been around the last few days, but I wonder if he's just making sure Deanna is in place, Katie's not going to burn the house down and I... well, I'm not going to relapse, and then I think he'll be back in his office twenty-four seven.

Having the time together over the weekend to discuss Katie, and what we might do to resolve this situation has been a welcome change, despite the stressful topic.

I wonder, thinking of Magda's plan for me, what he would make of me taking on something extra on top of everything else we have going on? Scratch that. I know what he'll think. Not that he'll say, being more likely to brood on it for days if not weeks. When he finally voices his opinion, I'll be committed, and it will be too late by then.

'Shall I put your name forward, Sophie darling? It makes sense, trust me.'

She said the same when they approached me about moving from the regional breakfast slot of occasional presenter and primary weather presenter to the national studios. To be fair, she'd been right. 'Okay, sure, if you think it's for the best.'

'Lovely!'

'So, what was it you were saying?'

'About what?'

'Your chat with the money men.'

'Oh, slow going, I'm afraid. They had an initial offer of a twelve-month extension, but I pushed back, looking for three years.'

Three years? I never thought about doing this job beyond six months, let alone for another three years. Would my marriage stand it? There's no valid reason why it shouldn't, I suppose. Scott might be a little perturbed about the hours I have to keep, but we're still in the bedding-in phase of these changes. It'll work out. It always does.

'How did they take that?'

'Um, quietly.'

'That doesn't sound good, Magda. Are you sure about this strategy?'

'Don't worry, Sophie darling. I know these people. They'll try anything – and routinely do – to get what they want. I have their cards marked, never doubt it.'

'You sound very gleeful. I must say, I'm pleased you're not calling to ask me to fly out to Australia to eat assorted bugs—'

'Ooo, that's a point. How are you with insects? I forgot to ask—'

'Goodbye, Magda!'

I hang up, smiling, and feeling the pleasure offered by the

warm glow you get when someone speaks so positively about you. For a moment I actually believe her and set aside my self doubt. It really is the fleetest of moments though. My mobile beeps. This time it is Scott. I open the text message.

How is everything at home? Is she behaving herself? Update me when you can. And I think we should talk when I get home.

Is she behaving herself, indeed. Sometimes I wonder if Scott knows what's going on in his own home.

TEN

There is so much I can unpick in that short message. Is 'when you can' a thinly veiled dig at the fact I'm so busy with work and not around very much these days? Scott has a high-powered executive role in the media and has done ever since we first got together, but I don't think he is adjusting well to my own career soaring and taking me away from our family.

Ever since I've known him, Scott has been in great demand. He is so talented; he understands people in a way that most of us don't. As a commissioning editor for television, he's managed to bring multiple hit shows to the small screen across different continents, let alone countries. He's also charted a successful career path by never saying no to anyone, a course that's taken him from national television to global commercial studios and back again.

I swear if he'd just stay in one place for a while, he'd have nailed down one of the most senior positions in any of the big players. He could be the go-to man, but Scott struggles with a desire, a need even, for perfection. The people around him never quite manage to live up to what he wants to achieve, and so he moves around looking for the right team who can fulfil his vision.

Being so sought after, and so successful, leads to something of a trade-off. I hardly ever get to see him, but we have this wonderful life. A life that anyone would be mad to turn down. However, this is a life where I am primarily concerned with the children and the running of the home. Or at least, that's how it used to be, that was our arrangement. It was never necessary for me to have a career of my own. But that didn't stop me craving one. Now I have my dream career, but it has put so much strain on our family.

It's not like I am still expected to do as much as I used to do at home and with the kids, on top of my work. I know I shouldn't complain; I love what I do, and Martha goes far and away above her mandate with the shopping, cleaning and some-times even the cooking, taking so much of the strain away from me. She also makes it appear so effortless.

Looking around, the hallway has shoes scattered by the door. It's like they've just fallen off feet as soon as they passed through the door and been left there. I can't even see many matching pairs. Does Martha usually pick them up, and what about the muddy footprints all over the floor and... *are they leaves?* The park is forty feet away from the house. How on earth did someone manage that?

I am quite sure that if Martha isn't going to be around for even a brief period, I am really going to struggle. I'll do my best, but this is a big house, and I just don't have the time to keep on top of everything. We have a garden too – well, a roof terrace along with a basement courtyard – and there is a man who pops in to take care of those on a regular basis. I never see him, but he does a cracking job. At least that's one area of the home I'll not have to be concerned about, as long as we pay him on time. Scott takes care of that, along with all of the household finances. I know that sounds a bit old-fashioned, but it's simpler if only one person deals with it and Scott has more experience and confidence handling money than I do. Anyway, I've never minded having one less thing to worry about.

The children are my biggest concern, as always, and I worry about the impact a chaotic home environment could have on them.

Prior to all her recent dramas, Katie used to be manageable and as for Chas, well, his comfortable existence manifests in the modern affliction decimating the middle to upper classes these days, that of affluenza, resulting in a lack of get-up-and-go. He's also *a bit sketchy*, as the kids of today like to say, but his heart is in the right place. Sometimes I wonder if he has enough about him to pass his studies and make a career for himself in medicine. The visual evidence makes me doubt it, but then he comes home with his grades and he's top of his peer group every time, so what do I know?

Everything had been going in the right direction until Scott was headhunted for the job he holds now and at the same time my predecessor on the morning show managed to fall by the wayside... well, less the wayside and more onto a train line. The jury is still out on whether she meant it or not. Somehow, I managed to navigate the path of benefiting from tragedy without looking too upbeat about it. On-screen empathy, Magda calls it. So, my little part-time job transformed into a burgeoning career.

And it's true, what Magda said. I was just myself, then and now, which is both a benefit and a curse. I would never wish to garner advantage from someone else's pain, but they could hardly leave the chair empty, could they? Like that one time the production team left a tub of lard in a seat on a topical news panel show when one guest failed to show up for the recording. That was funny. This was not.

I suppose the politician thought they'd be in for a hard time and so ducked out on that occasion. When it comes to delivering bad news, people like that think they'll avoid proper scrutiny by sitting opposite people like me on the morning show sofa. Little did they know that particular morning, though. Holding the Home Secretary to account live on television has to be the high point of my broadcasting career to date. Seeing the expressions of terror on the faces around me, my co-host, Michael, my producer, Sam, and, of course, Sir David himself, still brings a smile to my face when I think about it. I never thought I'd be able to make him tie himself up in knots on live television, let alone that that'd lead to his resignation within twenty-four hours and threaten to bring the government to its knees.

Okay, that's an exaggeration, but it was the gist of the news headlines for the remainder of the day and it put my name into every household as a serious journalist, and competent interviewer. No one was more surprised than me. Scott was bowled over. What followed was something of a whirlwind around me, with a massive contract thrown my way where I could live the dream, a career in broadcast television. And I can still feel the trailing winds of that storm even now.

I've steered well clear of having social media pages, because I don't have the time or want to be so visible, but when I stumbled across the *Sophie Beckett Take-Downs* fan page, I did smile. When it hit almost one hundred thousand followers and was subsequently featured in the next news cycle as a story of its own, about me, I must admit to finding it gratifying. I speak to people daily that not so long ago I only ever saw and read about in magazines or watched on the big or small screens. Most of them are not what they want you to see, which is both eye opening and disappointing. Like the film star, perhaps not as big as he once was but still a name, who thought I'd leap at the chance to have lunch with him. I don't care how great he thought the room service of his hotel was, it wasn't going to happen.

Reputations are fabricated in the main. I want to see the real person behind the mask. That's hard to do in a five-minute segment on the breakfast show, but not impossible.

However, since I got my chance there has been something nagging away at the back of my mind. In my experience, when things go well, there will always be something that will come along and mess it all up. Only, on this occasion, I know already what that will be.

I've been expecting this hammer to drop ever since I got my first gig in front of the green screen. There is always the fear of dismissing the threat of a hurricane only for it to land within hours, and that's certainly happened before, but in this case, I already know *what will be the end of me*. It's not a matter of if, but when, particularly now that I have become something of a household name, not only in the homes on my street but across the country.

Someone will start digging at some point and then all manner of things will come out. Which will be first? I guess that depends on where they start looking. There is a pattern that follows people through the British media, and I'm in the early stages of that cycle. The twenty-four-hour cycle of social media and celebrity culture is such that the new face gets all the positive coverage but at some point, they run out of positive things to say. They get bored, or simply chase cheaper clicks. When that day comes, I won't be lauded anymore, I'll be lambasted.

I think I can count on my immediate family, irrespective of how estranged they are, not to dish the dirt but there will be others who'll no doubt crawl out of the woodwork. Past boyfriends, colleagues, former friends. I've made my fair share of bad choices, but I was doing the best I could at the time. I was young, naive and made brash moves that I'd never countenance now.

There is one aspect of my history that I fear the most as it doesn't translate well in the public eye. Scott has protected me from it so far, but I know how these things work and if it comes out then the vultures will destroy me. Once you've had a breakdown, the media love to see every aspect of your personality through that lens. And not only the media.

That's a concern for another day. Today, my concern is Katie, or should I say, my failings as a mother. It doesn't really matter how softly Scott begins the conversation, it is the course the conversation will take, I have no doubt. Our lives were settled, and everyone was doing just fine until I took this job. Ever since then, to outward appearances, things have been going great guns but, behind closed doors, it is becoming a comedy farce.

Sooner or later, somehow, this house is going to burn down. My public image aside, I'm certain my downfall will be a result of something happening within these four walls, and that thought terrifies me more than anything else. There are any number of people outside who will love to put me down for daring to step out of my lane, but the reality is, I'm quite capable of destroying my own life without anyone's external input.

As I head up to Katie's room a movement passes across the threshold of Scott's study and I stop for a double take. Is one of the children in there? Scott won't care for that; he's very particular about people being in his space. I walk to the door and poke my head in.

'Deanna?'

She starts, looking round at me and clutching her chest with her right hand. 'You startled me!' she says sheepishly. In her other hand, she's holding a framed photograph of Scott and me on our wedding day. He surprised me, first with his proposal and then again when he whisked me away to the Seychelles for the ceremony.

'Um, can I help you? What are you doing in here?'

She carefully sets the picture frame back onto the mantelpiece above the fireplace, adjusting it to ensure it goes back exactly as she found it. 'Sorry, I was looking for Katie.'

'She's still not with you?'

Deanna shakes her head. 'No, I'm all prepared for her but she's not come down.'

'Right, well, I'll find her,' I say, glancing around. 'You should probably wait for her downstairs.' She picks up on my hidden, and not particularly subtle, meaning, flushing red and shooting me an awkward smile.

'I'm sorry, I didn't mean to overstep—'

'No, it's okay,' I say, attempting to lighten my tone. It's not okay, she has broken with the norms of social convention, in my mind anyway, but I don't want to go over the top about it. 'It's just, this is Scott's study, and he—'

'Likes his privacy?' she says. I nod. 'I completely understand. So, this is where Scott hides himself when he's working from home?' she asks, looking around the room and then toward the photograph on the mantelpiece again. 'You both looked so happy. Was that taken on your wedding day?'

'Yes, it was.' We didn't go for a traditional wedding, choosing to keep it low-key. Scott wore a white linen shirt and pale blue trousers, while I wore a loose-fitting dress that hung off the shoulder.

'Wonderful,' Deanna says, her gaze lingering on it for a moment longer before turning to me. She smiles. 'You look lovely, both of you. So happy.'

'We were.'

I step aside very deliberately to give her space to pass by me and as she sets foot on the landing, I pull the door to the study closed.

'Right,' Deanna says breezily. 'I'll wait for Katie downstairs then.'

'Yes, I'll send her down.'

Deanna shoots me an artificial smile, to my mind at least,

and then heads off down the stairs, glancing up at me once more before she disappears. I can't help but think I'm going to find her going through my underwear drawer next. Or maybe Scott's. Maybe I'm over-reacting. It's not that odd, is it, to snoop around someone's home? We've all done it; it's almost irresistible at times. But something about Deanna is putting me on edge. This is my family, and I'm protective of it.

I'll talk to the agency, just to see if anyone else is available. In the meantime, my daughter needs an education, and if it has to be Deanna for now, then I'll just have to handle that.

ELEVEN

My ever-increasing to-do list is now bordering on a new level of classification: that of overwhelm. *What is the name of the lady at the tutoring agency Scott mentioned?*

I know Scott likes her, but if Deanna can't even ensure Katie takes her seat by ten thirty in the morning, then what chance is she going to have of making up the shortfall of missing the regimented timetable of regular schooling? No chance at all.

I'm searching for the agency's number on my phone, just as Chas descends toward me on the stairs. He's looking like he's dressed in clean clothes and he's even showered, a little knapsack tucked over one shoulder.

'I'm off to class,' he says.

'Lectures,' I say as he shoots me an impish grin. 'And you're late. It's already almost half past ten.'

'I'm not officially late for another three minutes,' he says over his shoulder, taking the stairs two at a time which is brave considering how slippery they are underfoot. They were supposed to be non-slip tiles but the interior designer suggested it would ruin the look. It's all right for her, she doesn't have to risk breaking her neck every time she walks up or down while suffering from periods of distraction, like me.

'Yes?'

I'm snapped out of my moment by the tone of a petulant pre-teen. How long have I been standing in the doorway to the cinema room? A while, I figure, but searching through my email inbox for the agency contact Scott sent to me is proving difficult.

Lifting my gaze, I see Katie, sprawled across the sofa, feet up on the footstool, wearing her tiger-print onesie and staring straight ahead at the screen. She may not be looking at me, but she did pause the film she's watching which is more respect than she's shown me at almost any point in the last three weeks. I should probably be grateful.

'Deanna is waiting for you, Katie. This doesn't look like Latin to me.'

Katie shrugs. 'Well, you went to a rubbish school.'

Not the response I was expecting. It's true though, my secondary school wasn't the best. Latin wasn't even on the curriculum. The teachers did their best, though, and the pupils didn't make it easy on them, me included. That final salary pension probably wasn't worth the grief in the end, but at least they got a fair number of weeks off in the summer, albeit in Bolton. It rains a lot in Bolton. It rains most days in the north-west of England to be fair.

I pick up the remote under the watchful scowl of my beloved daughter and switch off the projector. 'School first, revenge of the mutant zombie icemen, or whatever rubbish you're watching, later, okay?'

'What's the point?'

'The point, young lady, is that Deanna is waiting for you downstairs and if you choose to get yourself removed from school, that's on you, but you will be educated whether you like it or not!'

'Oh, why won't you just give me a break?'

'A break? Well, let's examine what you've achieved so far this term, shall we, and then see if you deserve a break?' Katie rolls her eyes. 'You've managed to hospitalise several of your classmates—'

'Um... exaggeration,' she says. 'Only three of them.' As if, somehow, three out of a possible twenty-two is a mitigating factor. 'And they deserved it.'

'Attempted to burn the school down—'

'Again! Exaggeration. I set fire to the photograph of Olivia T's boyfriend which she had in her locker.'

'And in doing so set the rest of the locker's contents alight and the locker itself.'

'Olivia shouldn't store combustibles in there. It is *clearly* stated in the terms and conditions they make us sign when allocating them at the beginning of the year. I mean, who keeps hair products in their locker at school anyway? But no, it's all *my fault!*'

I'm at a loss for words... almost. 'And, you've managed to exhaust even a well-qualified tutor from an agency of the best private educators available to us in the Borough of Camden. That's quite some feat, I can assure you.'

Katie's smile broadens and she does a little dance in her chair. 'Mini wave in appreciation of me then!'

'This is not funny, Katie.'

'Oh, it is, I can assure you.'

I purse my lips, feeling anger and bitterness doing battle with my inner critic, which sits on my shoulder and whispers into my ear, reminding me of my inadequacy as a parent. If I was better at this, then my daughter would never have been expelled in the first place. I point my mobile at her.

'You dislike Deanna anyway, so I doubt she'll be around for much longer,' says Katie snidely.

I pause. 'That's not true, Katie. I... I hardly know her.' Damn, what a time to hesitate. It's like swallowing hard and stammering when someone asks you if you've done something that you know full well you were doing but try to claim you weren't. Damning.

'So, I'm right, you don't like her?'

'She's fine.'

'Thought not.' My daughter is very perceptive. I must try harder to mask my micro expressions. Although, I'm not sure how micro they are when it comes to Deanna.

'Deanna is perfectly capable.'

'So what's the problem?' Her eyes narrow as she studies my face.

'Deanna is fine, for now. We need to assess her experience and see how you get on with her, that's all.'

'Oh, I get it now.'

'You do?'

'Yes, she's younger than you and you feel threatened.'

I scoff, but I can feel my face warming and I avert my eyes. 'We need to make sure she's qualified and that you're making progress.' Katie nods knowingly, a hint of a smile crossing her lips. 'And I want to see you heading downstairs right now, and whatever tasks Deanna sets you today, I want to see a clear and impressive effort from you by teatime. If not...'

'Then I'm banned from chatting with my friends online on a school night?'

'You're already banned from chatting online with friends on a school night.'

'Oh, yes, I forgot.'

'Have you been chatting with your friends online—'

'On a school night?' Katie asks, wincing. 'Erm, no,' she says, looking up at me hopefully.

'I'll have your mobile from you after tea as well then, please.'

She sighs, looking to the ceiling. I fix her with my sternest, no quarter given, look and jab a pointed finger at her. 'Teatime. And I want to see it without asking. Clear?' Of course, confiscating her mobile phone leaves me with pretty much no effective punishment if she doesn't toe the line. I'll have to cross that bridge and fight that battle when I get to it. And I will get to it.

'Crystal clear, Mother.'

I draw breath. 'And don't call me Mother. I'm not old enough to be called Mother. Mum, yes, or Mummy' – at a push, although it sounds odd coming from a twelve-year-old – 'will do just fine.'

'Oooo... kay.'

I know I've extended myself in this conversation, left myself vulnerable and open to attack – from a pre-teen. I've no idea where Katie gets her innate, natural Machiavellian ability to win through attrition. It's certainly a skill, one that will benefit her in life and if she ever goes into media. Although, she'd have to avoid being fired first, which I suspect would be a challenge.

As I look at her, I wonder again where I went wrong. She was such a sweet and loving little girl only a few short years ago. When she first found her love for drawing, she'd often present me with a picture she'd drawn just to give me something – no reason, no special occasion, just because she thought I might like it. I've still got them somewhere in my room. I could never bring myself to throw them away and even when she came across them much later and insisted they were lame, I still refused to throw them away. I can remember her smile, my pride reflected in her expression. She loved that I kept them, not that she'd ever admit it. To think that wasn't too long ago.

I know that somehow, this is my fault. There's no issue between her and her father and the sibling rivalry and angst that was a staple of my own childhood just doesn't seem to manifest between Chas and his little sister. Although, there is a significant age gap between them. Why am I the one who is struggling to connect?

It would be easy for me to blame her, but she's twelve. How much responsibility can I lay at her feet? Her actions have been getting more and more extreme, a level of violence and anger I could never have anticipated just a few years ago. Is she above or below the criminal age of accountability? I don't know; I've lost track since that uproar surrounding those young boys who murdered a toddler.

I wish I had a reference point for mother and daughter relationships. I can't even remember the sound of my mum's voice, I was so young when we lost her. Maybe this is how it always works. I can play around with fault and blame, and often do, but I know it's always going to be my fault. All of it.

'Teatime,' I repeat as I pause at the door. 'And get downstairs to Deanna, now. She's waiting for you and right now she's being paid to sit in our kitchen staring into space.'

'Got it!'

Katie's scowl deepens – who'd have thought that was even possible – as she hauls herself off the sofa and lurches from the room with an exaggerated walk, shoulders sagging. I dread to think what she's calling me in her head. At least it is in her head, for now. I follow her and watch as she stalks past Scott's study, making sure she does go downstairs.

When we first discussed this enforced educational venture, I figured we'd be able to make use of Scott's study rather than having lessons in the open kitchen. This isn't an arrangement my husband approved of though. It is his sanctuary within the family home. I thought as long as we tidied everything away before he got home, it would work. But Scott was having none of it, so lessons in the kitchen it is. My husband has a gift for getting his way, I'm always impressed by it. I was hoping he'd be able to get around the school headmaster and the board of governors but that's not going to happen this time. Katie has seen to that.

The first suspension was tricky enough. Scott worked something of a miracle in getting her readmitted after she slipped laxative into her classmates' lunch. As if that hadn't been bad enough, the medication wasn't supposed to be taken orally and led to three children requiring an overnight stay in hospital, along with a great deal of pain and suffering. A three-week suspension, a great deal of grovelling, and a commitment that such events would never happen again did the trick. Well, that and, I suspect, Scott's incredibly generous donation and the promise of fundraising efforts for the new science wing.

During Katie's previous suspension, Scott took time off work to be with her and he managed to get her to do some work, apparently. And initially, it seemed like Deanna was doing pretty well too, but things are clearly slipping and I have my doubts about her abilities to handle my daughter. I don't care what her references say, something tells me she is more used to dedicated, and, more importantly, motivated children who don't require their tutors to wear stab vests. Okay, I'm exaggerating. No one was ever seriously endangered by Katie, but she has become something of a terror to people in authority.

How long will it be before Katie properly mutinies and Deanna jumps ship? What would we do then? Scott can't take any more time off work, and neither can I. For now, Deanna seems happy to continue working with us, so perhaps I should hold my tongue. Katie might be acting up, but it's resistance to homework, not Deanna. She seems happy with her. So is Scott. Chas... let's not go there for now. No, it's only me who has a problem.

I follow Katie downstairs, still scrolling through my emails. At every turn of the staircase, she glares back at me. Moments later, she slumps down into her seat in the kitchen, thrusting her hands into the pockets of her onesie having pulled the hood up to hide much of her face. Deanna shoots her a broad welcoming smile.

A-ha! Here it is. I tap the screen, highlight the telephone number and a judicious use of copy and paste has the phone ringing as I leave Deanna to it. My work here is done, for now.

TWELVE

'Good morning, Steller & Co, how may I direct your call?'

I lean to my right and peer back into the kitchen. Deanna has Katie's attention. Katie looks up at me, it must be her sixth sense, and makes eye contact. I incline my head and make it very clear what my expectations are and Katie rolls her eyes, then sits forward and takes up a pen. I've won the battle. Not the war, obviously, but celebrate the wins whenever they come is my motto.

'Hello there,' I say with my best easy-going manner and telephone voice, as I step into the hallway, ensuring I'm well out of earshot, 'this is Sophie Beckett from Chester Terrace, I'd like to speak to Tamsin...'

'Oh,' the voice almost yelps excitedly; she sounds remarkably young, 'off the telly?'

'Er, yes, that's me.' I can see her grinning inanely down the telephone. This is not something I've become used to. In many ways, I hope I never do.

'Oh, right. Wait one moment.' I hear her adjusting the receiver and her pitch changes back to the formulaic, artificial tone she answered the call with.

Two pips sound in my ear as I'm placed on hold. I glance back at Katie, who is poring over her textbook, absently rotating the pen in her hand. Is she working or merely making a show of working? I can't see any words going down.

'Mrs Beckett! How are you?'

'Sophie, please,' I correct her. 'Lovely to speak to you, Tamsin. Thank you for taking my call.'

'What can I do for you today?'

'I'm just wondering, we might be back in the market for another tutor, if any availability has come up...'

'Oh, things haven't worked out with Deanna?'

'Hmm, no, it's not that.'

'Oh. Then, is there another problem?'

'Deanna's great!' I say, and I can hear the artificial upbeat nature of my tone and it grates on me, but I'm hoping Tamsin doesn't recognise it for what it is. 'I'm just wondering. Deanna is quite young, and I don't want to say immature, but maybe you have someone who is a little... um...'

'More mature?'

'Yes, that was what I was thinking. Do you, by any chance? I'm just not sure Deanna is a good fit for us.'

'That is a shame, it really is.' I can hear the resignation in Tamsin's voice. I can picture her scrolling through the people on their lists who are qualified to not only deliver a first-class one-on-one education, but are also trained in self-defence and survival skills.

'Do you have anyone available?' I ask this because she hasn't said anything for almost an entire minute and in a telephone conversation, that's an awfully long time.

'Well, as I explained to your husband, we have other options that we can call upon but they're not as qualified as Deanna.' That's odd, I thought Scott said there were no other options. 'Can I get back to you, Sophie? We are a little inundated with requests at the moment.' She pauses and I can almost picture her mind turning a question over, and wondering whether she should ask it.

'May I ask you to be clear, is there an issue with Deanna? Has she done something wrong?'

Damn. That's not a question I want to answer. I can't in good faith fault Deanna, aside from her wandering into my husband's study and touching a photograph. It's hardly a serious offence, even if it makes me feel a bit uncomfortable. 'Erm, no, she's been fine.'

'Fine?'

'Better than fine. She's great.' Damn. I hate my people-pleasing nature. Why can't I be selfish like everyone else and demand what I want for no better reason than because I want it? I want an unattractive, old, annoying tutor who will educate my feral daughter and not attract the attention of my husband. My husband, who has done nothing wrong or exhibited any signs of being drawn to Deanna.

I glance at a photograph of Katie and me on the wall among the many other family shots we exhibit in the stairwell. It was taken on a family holiday in Corsica. She'd hurt her feet walking on the hot sand of the beach and I carried her to the car. She clung onto me, and I swear her feet were just fine but she wanted that closeness with me. She was much younger then, carefree and very loving. She still is in many ways, just not with me.

This tutor shortage has me wondering if there are many other children living around Marylebone and Fitzrovia who have been expelled from their prep schools and require private tutoring on a full-time basis. Perhaps we are not too dissimilar from our neighbours after all.

'So, Deanna can stay with you until we find a suitable replacement?'

'Yes, that's it exactly!' I say, light-heartedly. 'Until we find a suitable replacement.'

'And the replacement should be old?'

'Older,' I say, as if that makes a difference. It sounds better in my head, but perhaps I'm trying to absolve myself of any guilt.

'Okay, please leave it with me, and I'll get back to you.'

'Yes, thank you, Tamsin.' I have my best telephone voice on now, calm and extremely polite. After all, I need this woman to help me. 'I'll await your call.'

'Speak to you soon.'

I'm not at all convinced the last thing she said will come to pass. I hang up and stare at Katie's image, beaming out at me. It's the same sweet smile she used to give me almost whenever I came home and entered her room, keen for her to know I cared. Those days are long gone now, simply memories that I treasure alongside those of my own childhood.

Perhaps we're not meant to find contentment throughout our entire life, and such feelings are purely moments in time, snapshots of treasured memories. But I want to believe that nothing is irreversible, and the pendulum can swing back toward me. I want that relationship with my daughter back.

THIRTEEN

A repetitive rumble rouses me. My body feels incredibly heavy. Looking across the room to the open shutters of the window, I can see it's getting dark outside. Where on earth did the day go? I roll onto my side and shooting pains stab me behind the eyes when I look at the digital display on the clock beside my bed.

I don't remember going to bed. I was coming up for a shower and a change of clothes after having lunch. My phone is vibrating, dancing its way to the edge of the bedside table and is about to drop off. I gather it up, peering at the screen.

'Tamsin,' I say, trying to sound like I haven't been asleep for much of the day, drawing a hand across my face and stifling a yawn.

'Hello, Sophie. I have some good news and some not so good news...'

'That is usually delivered as good news and *bad* news, Tamsin.'

'Well, we do have someone who might be available, which is the good news.'

'And the bad?'

'She is coming from abroad and it is unlikely she'll be in the country before next month.'

'Next month? That certainly is a problem.'

'I can appreciate your frustration, but as I said to your husband there are limited numbers of tutors available and—'

'We've no other immediate option,' I say, with resignation. My hands are tied here. I can't take a leave of absence from the studio, especially while Magda is negotiating a new contract for me. We need Deanna. I sit down on the end of our bed, sinking into the thick duvet that threatens to enclose around me like a giant, snuggly hot-dog roll.

'What do you think?' Tamsin asks and I have absolutely no idea what she's talking about. At what point did I stop listening?

'Sorry, about what?'

'About sticking with Deanna? She has a wonderful CV, and maybe you just need a bit more time for your daughter to build a rapport with her. Perhaps, in light of recent events, you might consider keeping the status quo?'

'Okay, yes. We will stick with Deanna for now, and I'll speak with my husband and come back to you.' I'm trying to sound breezy. This isn't a disaster. I know something is off, I'm not comfortable, but I can handle this. If I take a stubborn approach and dismiss Deanna, then I am screwed. That's if Scott would even let me do it. After all, it's not like I have a good reason, is it? Maybe it's just me who has the problem.

I'll find a way forward. There's always a way.

'Okay, well, do come back to me once you've spoken with Scott. How is he by the way?' There's that tone again. Oh, how I hate to hear it.

'He's great, Tamsin.'

'Wonderful. Do pass on my best to him and I hope to see him again soon.'

Again? What did she mean by again, and by soon? Maybe Scott knows the owner of the agency, that'll be it. Scott knows everyone. It's one of his things, his contact list. It makes Hoover's files look like a novella.

I hang up; the craving for that shower is growing stronger. That cubicle, although the name cubicle doesn't do it justice, feels as special now as it did on the day we moved in post renovation. It has two rain shower heads and could easily fit four grown adults comfortably inside it, not that that's my thing.

A voice pipes up. 'So, are we sticking with Deanna?'

My eyes snap open and I realise I'm lying on the bed now, staring at the ceiling. I don't remember lying back. I struggle to sit upright, my body losing itself in the heavy tog of the duvet and a sprung mattress that does you no favours when you try to get up from it.

My eyes drift over to the door where Katie is standing. How long has she been there? Her exercise book is in one hand by her side, a pen in the other. She might not have been eavesdropping.

'What's that?'

'Deanna. Is she staying or not?'

'Staying. For now.'

'But you might get rid of her?'

I nod slowly. 'Something like that, yes, but I wouldn't phrase it that way. I need to speak to your father about it.'

'Why? I like her. What's wrong with her?'

'It's complicated, darling.'

'Why?'

'It just is. As I say, I'll speak to your father.'

'How come he can be Father, but you can't be Mother?'

'Scott thinks Father is an endearing term, whereas I think Mother...'

'Makes you sound like a witch?'

Was that a statement or an observation?

'Something like that, yes.'

'You're repeating yourself.'

'I am, but it is the same response to different questions,

which is allowed.' My eyes narrow as she studies me. 'Do you want something?'

'Yes,' Katie says, walking into the room. 'How are you with the second declension?'

I exhale slowly. 'About as strong as I am with the *first declension*.' Katie sits down beside me on the bed, her book in her lap. She looks dejected. 'Can't Deanna help you with this? It is what we're paying her for, after all.'

'She's part-time, remember?'

'Oh yes. She couldn't help before she finished?'

Katie shakes her head. 'She had to go somewhere.'

'Had to go where?'

Katie shrugs. 'To see someone.'

'Who?'

'I'm not her PA. How should I know? You said I needed to have this done by teatime.'

'I did, yes.'

'So, can you help me or not?'

I sigh. 'I can try.'

'I'm sorry,' Katie says in a rare, for these days anyway, sign of humility. I look at her and she's sincere, but I'm unsure of what she's apologising for.

'You're sorry about what?'

'About causing trouble. I don't mean to, but it's hard sometimes.'

'What's hard?'

'Being me.' Katie shrugs. 'Sometimes, I don't think you understand just how hard my life is.'

'Is that right?' I say as I put my arm around her shoulder, and she leans into me, just like she used to back when she actually seemed to like her mum. 'I'm sorry things are hard, really I am. And I'm trying to understand. That's the thing about growing up. The challenges get harder, and,' I tell her, doing my best not to dismiss or invalidate her feelings, 'as much as we'd like it, there isn't a manual to tell you what to do.'

'I wish there was one.'

I hug her tightly, kissing the top of her head. 'I tell you what, one day we'll write one together. Then we'll both know what we should do. What do you think?'

'Until then?' she asks.

'Until then, we'll just have to figure it out as we go along, darling. But we'll get there, I promise.'

'I wish things could be like they were,' she says quietly. In that moment, I hear a nod back to the Katie I remember, and I can't help but wonder what's sparked it.

'Is there anything you want to talk to me about? Because you can, you know that, right? Whenever you like.'

She pulls away from me and shrugs. 'I guess. I know I'm being a pain, and I'm going to try and be a better person.'

This is a turn-up. The fleeting thought that she must be unwell comes to mind, but I won't say it. 'You're a good person, a wonderful person. It's just that you've been having a tough time of it of late. Believe me, I know what that feels like, to feel alone and as if no one understands what you're going through. We all make mistakes. I've made plenty, but there's never *no way back*. There's always a way to turn things around,' I say reassuringly, reaching out and taking her hand in mine, and giving it a supportive squeeze. 'We'll work a way through it. Okay?'

'I still need help with the second declension.' I scoop up my mobile. 'I don't think a search engine is going to help,' Katie says. I pat the side of the bed, encouraging her to lie down with me. She snuggles in beside me.

'Well,' I say, 'it's all I have, so it's going to have to do. And if I can't solve it, we'll just have to put a film on or something and the Latin can wait.'

As it turns out, my knowledge of the second declension is

woefully inadequate. I think my ability to competently assist with her homework peaked at key stage two, and Katie is past that age range and into key stage three, she's also bright enough to be further along in her studies than expected at this age. What I learned at school has become a distant memory. Therefore, when Scott pokes his head round the door an hour later, he finds us cuddled up watching an inane romcom.

'What's going on here then?' he asks lightly.

'Come and join us, Dad,' Katie says. Scott smiles and comes around to her side of the bed, while Katie adjusts her position to give him a fair share of pillow as a head rest and he gently puts an arm across her, his hand settling on my waist.

Maybe, just maybe, I can do this after all. I can get my family back, back the way it was. They mean everything to me. And I'll do anything to stop us falling apart.

FOURTEEN

Friday

The following morning, I wake feeling more positive than I have done in a while. I still haven't slept well, and I have another headache to contend with, but after last night I really feel like we might have turned a corner.

I don't have to go into work today, as the Prime Minister is receiving some bigwig delegation ahead of the Chinese Premier's visit. There will be a morning of interviews and panel pundits are in the news studio to offer commentary, and so our show was taken off the air to make way for the *serious* broadcasters. I should be annoyed, our programme being bumped from its slot when we could have done something ourselves, but I'm not. I get to spend a bit of unscheduled time with my family. I think we need it, what with everything that's been going on, and it's a relief to have no need for Deanna, today.

At lunchtime I halve and slice an avocado, and place it on a plate alongside a rolled piece of breaded ham, add some butter to several pieces of freshly baked French baguette – I found a pack of sealed part-bake in the pantry, bless Martha – and set it out on the breakfast table beside the floor-to-ceiling doors that open up the Juliet balcony. The sun is shining, and it feels warm. The sound of birds in the nearby park carries on the breeze but is soon drowned out by the general hum of traffic noise that signifies a typical London afternoon.

'Is that for me?' Katie asks, entering the kitchen and making for the table.

'Yes, I was about to call you.' I'm just finishing making her some blackcurrant cordial, and as she pulls out a chair, I set the glass down on a coaster beside her plate. I gave up just offering her water a long time ago because, simply, she didn't drink it. Katie looks at the glass, then the plate and her eyes drift up to me. She often has this near blank expression these days and, more often than not, she saves it for me. So much so, that I wonder if I'm imagining it much of the time. She turns her focus back to her plate.

'I don't really eat avocado anymore.'

'Since when?'

'Ages. I told you.' She hasn't got the derogatory tone in her voice though. This is the Katie who shares pertinent informa-tion rather than the one who sets out to cause me pain.

'Do you think you could manage it today? I mean, it's not like you haven't eaten it before.'

'I guess,' she says with a dramatic sigh. 'And this is white bread.' She jabs at the nearest piece with a pointed finger.

'Ah, right, you did say you don't eat white bread anymore. I did forget that. Do you think you could—'

'Yes, of course. I'll manage.'

Katie starts eating and I am grateful for the lack of another confrontation. A ring of pain circles my head from my eyes and forehead all the way around and back again. These headaches are getting really quite unbearable. Hypertension was my first thought and so I googled it. Turns out to be stress related, which does nothing to make me feel better. It's the sort of pain that

isn't relieved through maxing out the daily dosage of parac-
etamol and ibuprofen I took earlier. It did ease the tension in my
shoulders a little, but the throbbing came roaring back before
long.

I run the coffee machine and sit down opposite my daughter
nursing an espresso. It will not help my headache in the least
but a caffeine withdrawal headache on top would be too brutal
to imagine.

She really is a pretty girl, Katie. She wasn't what anyone in
their right mind would consider a beautiful baby, over-sized due
to bottle feeding and with a strangely square head shape that
always struck me as odd. Very quick with a smile though and
once the toddler years kicked in she grew into the most angelic,
gorgeous little girl. This is something that hasn't changed as
she's grown. I have no doubt she'll be breaking hearts all over
the place in a year or two, perhaps sooner.

I say nothing changed, aside for the angelic part obviously.
What was it the headmaster of her prep school described her as:
a consistent barrage of chaos who leaves carnage in her wake. I
should have that framed and hand it to her on her eighteenth
birthday. If it wasn't such a devastating situation that we
currently face, I'd likely find it amusing, but it's really not a good
thing to be so disconnected from her peers. To grow up a well-
rounded individual, you need the influence of others around
you, good and bad. That's how we learn, how we grow as individuals. If we can't get her back into school then I fear for her
wellbeing both in the short and the longer term.

Nothing is spoken between us for the remainder of lunch
and Katie eyes my cup of coffee as she finishes up.

'Are you not eating?'

'I had something earlier,' I lie, but I'm unsure why. Not
wanting to set a bad example, I suppose.

'Right.' Katie slips out of her chair and heads off.

'Erm, have you forgotten something, young lady?' She stops

and even though I'm looking at the back of her head, I can see her rolling her eyes before glancing back.

'Thank you for lunch.'

'You are very welcome, Katie, but I meant your plate.' I use my eyes to signal she should clear the table. Katie drifts back to the table and purposefully picks up her plate and transfers it to the counter beside the sink. It's not into the dishwasher, but baby steps. That one simple task is delivered with such unspoken, thinly veiled fury that it almost makes me smile. Only, I don't want this relationship with my daughter. It's painful and I don't know how to fix it.

The remainder of the afternoon is given over to random pottering around the house, while Katie gets on with some work that Deanna left her. I've always been uncomfortable policing my daughter, even more so now that she is in what Scott defines as her *difficult* phase. The light touch parenting model I prefer is a direct mirroring of my own father's style. He was less of a helicopter parent – he couldn't be because he was always working – and was predisposed to allowing us freedom to manage our own lives. It taught us all to be responsible, to look out for one another in the family, and it definitely helped maintain a harmonious environment.

I'd love to be able to pick his brains about all of this. I'm sure he could tell me where I'm going wrong with Katie.

I miss him so much. What would he make of our current situation? Even if he did think it was my fault, he'd never say so. He'd just find a way of communicating his view without making me feel guilt or shame. I'd love him to be here with me now, but that's another thing I can't change, no matter how much I might want to.

I find things to do to occupy my thoughts, anything to save me from worrying. As the grandmother clock in the entrance hall chimes to signify it is six o'clock, I have successfully managed to pick up a number of given items and move them from one place to another without actually achieving anything in the process. It does nothing to alleviate my stress headache and even less to relieve my sense of overwhelm.

The front door opens and instead of the waif-like entrance of Chas wafting in, the space is filled with the ever-upbeat voice of Scott.

'Daddy's home!' he calls, and an audible response carries from the floor above, reciprocating his enthusiasm. By the time I reach the hall, Katie bounds past me on the stairs and runs to her father, launching herself into his arms. This is how she used to greet him when he came home from work, albeit six or seven years ago. I never get a greeting like this, when I return.

Scott loves it when she acts like this, and I can't help but see this as a cultivated gesture on my daughter's part designed to wrap her father around her little finger. Frankly, she's not the same open-hearted bundle of energy anymore. She's fierce, calculating and very aware of the trouble she's in and what she can do to mitigate the backlash that's coming her way. Where did she learn these manipulation skills?

'Hello, munchkin,' he says, exhaling heavily as he recipro-cates, putting his arms around her in a tight bear hug and lifts her fractionally off the floor. She exhales as if he's squeezing her too tight. They have such a wonderful relationship. They say most fathers and daughters do, and that is also my personal experience. At least, it used to be.

'How was your day?' Katie asks him as he sets her down, relief in his expression. She's a lot bigger now than she used to be when she was half her age, and these greetings were a daily occurrence.

'Busy. Frighteningly busy! And how have you been getting on with your studies today?' Scott asks Katie.

She shakes her head. 'Not the best.'

'Well, all you can do is keep trying as hard as you can. And tomorrow is another day, isn't it?' She nods again. There is no dissent; she is quite comfortable with this suggestion. Had I made it, then there would be fireworks. Scott glances at me and I force a smile, although it's the last thing I want to be doing. 'Let me have a minute with your mother.'

Mother. So that's where she's getting it from. Katie smiles at him, spins on her heel and glides past me and back up the stairs without even meeting my eye. Scott watches her go and then turns his focus towards me, offering me an apologetic smile. At least, I think it's an apologetic smile.

He slips an arm around my waist and draws me to him. I can smell his scent, high quality aftershave that smells as good now as when he applied it after showering this morning. I can feel the strength in his arms, the athleticism of his upper body muscle definition, all in that one grip. He is a devastatingly handsome man.

'Hello, my beautiful wife.'

'Hello yourself,' I say, feeling awkward under such lavish praise. I don't feel beautiful. Being asked to wear more revealing clothes to work by your boss – your semi-boss – to be seen and, likely, judged by millions, isn't quite the self-esteem boost one might think it would be.

'I sense you have had a rough day,' he says in that gravelly voice that makes women melt when he applies it in their direction. It certainly works on me, past and present.

'I've had better.' Maintaining the embrace, he leans his upper body away from me and studies my expression with one eyebrow arched. How does he do that?

'Come on, tell me about it.'

'Oh, it's just... don't worry about it.'

Craning his neck to look down at me, Scott smiles. 'Well, I will worry, especially if you can't talk to me about it. Take a breath, arrange your thoughts and whatever it is, we can sort it out. We always do.'

FIFTEEN

Alone together in the kitchen, I take a deep breath and Scott fixes me with a knowing look. 'You're not having a good time of it right now, are you?'

I scoff, shaking my head. 'No, that's an understatement.'

'What's going on?'

'It's just all starting to feel like too much. We've got this whole thing with Katie, and then the studio—'

'What about the studio?'

That's right, I haven't discussed this with Scott. I tend not to be forthcoming with matters around my work. It's my thing, for want of a better description, and I know Scott will try to solve it. That's his thing, or maybe it's a male thing: when presented with a problem they want to provide a solution, when it's not always necessary. Just being available to listen would often be more appreciated.

'It's nothing really.'

He reaches over to take my hand. 'If you're upset by it, Sophie, then it is something.'

'Oh, it's just the execs being what they are.'

'That's why I prefer to work for the independent producers rather than the big broadcasters,' he says with a knowing grin.

'I know you do.'

'So, what are they up to? Is it the contract situation?'

'You know about that?'

'I know yours will be up later this year. Magda should be turning the screw—'

'She is, she is,' I say, nodding.

'Presuming you want to continue?'

I look at him. 'Why wouldn't I?'

He shrugs. 'No reason, I just thought with everything we have going on, you might take a break.'

'Why don't you take a break?'

'Me?' He scoffs.

'Well, why should I if you're not prepared to?'

Scott's eyebrows knit together then and he splays his hands wide. 'Easy, it was an off-the-cuff comment. Calm down.'

He's right, I shouldn't have snapped. 'No, sorry. I didn't mean that. It's just that I love my job.'

He tilts his head. 'I know, and you've worked hard to get to where you are. So, what's the issue?'

I really don't want to go into it. 'Honestly, it doesn't matter, but a bit of stability at home would help.'

'Okay, well, I'll try to do more,' he says.

'Oh, I didn't mean—'

'I know. But I can still try to be present more for you, and the kids. Katie, in particular.'

'That'd help.'

Scott stands up, comes to me and holds his arms out and I lean in for a hug. 'Things will get better.'

'I know.'

'Right.' He releases me, checking his watch. 'I don't have long.'

'But you've only just got home.' The doorbell sounds and he looks over to the window.

'Right on time.'

Scott goes to get the door and I cross the kitchen to the window overlooking the front of the house. I catch a glimpse of Deanna just as Scott lets her in. She comes into the kitchen with Scott a half step behind, his suede jacket in hand. Deanna looks less businesslike and far more casual than usual, like she's going out for drinks in a small dress that's not revealing but hugs her figure.

'Hi, Sophie,' she says, beaming. Her make-up is freshly applied and her brunette hair, giving off a lovely shine, has curls in it. She's clearly made an effort.

'Hello, Deanna.' I look past her to Scott. 'I wasn't expecting company.' He looks at me quizzically. 'What?' I ask.

'You forgot?'

'Clearly!' I say, not tempering my surprise. Scott glances sideways at Deanna, who smiles uncertainly, and then looks back at me.

'We are going out for a drink—'

'You are?'

Scott exhales sharply. 'To formulate an educational plan for Katie.'

'Without me?' I can't keep the hurt of being left out from my voice. Scott frowns deeply and heaves a sigh.

'Sophie—'

'Why?' I ask, wrinkling my nose. 'Why do you have to go out?'

Scott and Deanna exchange a look and she seems suddenly awkward. Scott's expression softens. 'Sophie, this was your idea.'

'Mine?'

He nods, lowering his voice. 'You thought it best if we did it away from the house, so that we could discuss it without inter-ruptions.'

'I... did?' I ask, confused. I snort, laughing it off as ridiculous, which it is. My husband is going to sit in a bar someplace, discussing our daughter over drinks with a woman half his age. Why on earth would I agree to this?

Scott is frowning at my clearly bemused expression, and Deanna looks concerned. 'We talked about this, and it was your suggestion that I go, Sophie?'

'I don't remember saying that.'

'Well, it was your idea, not mine.'

'Oh, I... forgot, I suppose.'

'Honestly, Sophie,' he says, pulling on his jacket and nodding to Deanna. 'Come on, we'd better get a move on.'

'When will you be back?'

'Later,' he says over his shoulder. 'But we'll grab a bite to eat while we're out, so don't worry about making me anything.'

It's a good job he's already turned his back on me because I'm absolutely furious. Deanna sees my face though and she seems uncomfortable. At least someone sees me. She smiles sheepishly, and then moves to follow him. 'Bye, Sophie.'

'Yes, have a...' I don't know what to describe it as. She doesn't say anything but nods and sets off after Scott. I move back to the window then, standing to one side of the sash windows and watch them leave. I swear Deanna glances up at the window and our eyes meet, but she doesn't show any reac-tion, so perhaps I only imagine that she sees me.

My husband doesn't look back. He's already deep in conver-sation with Deanna as they reach the car and Scott opens the passenger door for her, stepping aside as she sits down, lifting her legs gracefully into the car. 'You'd better keep those legs together,' I say under my breath.

'What's that?'

I jump, startled by Katie entering the kitchen behind me. She comes to join me at the window. 'What are you looking at?'

'Nothing,' I say, steering her back the way she'd come.

'I'm hungry. What's for dinner?'

'I've no idea.'

'Well, what are we going to have?'

'Something.'

'When will it be ready—'

'Just as soon as it is!'

Katie sighs, turns on her heel and walks out. 'I hate living here!'

'Yes, join the club,' I snap, hopefully too quietly for her to hear.

My mind sees Scott and Deanna sitting down for dinner. Scott isn't a pizza or burger man. He doesn't eat just anywhere. They'll be eating far better than we will be tonight.

Was it really my idea to send Scott out with Deanna? Why would I do that? Have I always been so forgetful? I do often lose track of what is going on once the routine of the week gets into full flow and anything extra is likely to fall by the wayside. I blame stress and lack of sleep, but I'm annoyed.

It's in the evening, usually in the kitchen, that Scott and I spend most of our time interacting these days. When we do get a chance to see each other anyway. I feel deprived of what little time we have together, as instead, he's out with her. That's just great.

Scott's a decent man though, so I can't doubt his sincerity. He'll genuinely want to ensure Deanna has the tools to do her job well. He is the type to lend a helping hand to those in need, if he can. He's done a lot for various charities over the years, linking up his contacts with organisations who need a boost. He's the kind of person who stops for a homeless person, gives them change or buys them a coffee. It is very much like Scott to put himself out for someone else.

As a teenager he was quite the gifted ballerino and, but for a ruptured anterior cruciate ligament aged fourteen, he would have maintained his place at the Royal Ballet School and likely gone on to be a professional performer. He's that type, my husband, driven to succeed and with enough self-discipline to ensure he excels at whatever he turns his hand to. You'd always want a Scott by your side if you were in trouble. He's remarkably focused.

I didn't know Scott back then, and it is one of those moments where fate intervenes and charts you a completely new course, because if he had stayed fit, then this life would never have existed. Where would I be now without having met him?

Why should I have any fear about him helping Deanna? This is Scott; it's what he does.

I don't trust her though.

Is it her or just other women in general? I'm not sure. I'm doubting myself: my career, my mothering skills and my ability to be attractive to Scott. I used to be so confident, but now when I look at myself in the mirror, all I see is a failure. The brutal reality is, I know Scott deserves better than me.

SIXTEEN

It feels good to be back in my own bed, with Scott. Friday and Saturday nights are the times Scott and I can be together most weeks, because the breakfast show is different on the weekends and I'm a Monday to Friday host, in the main. Unless he's out of town on business, of course, which does sometimes happen. It is an odd sensation to hear my husband's shallow breathing – and occasional snort as he breathes in.

I enjoy being near him, but it feels strange as I am so used to sleeping alone. I know this can't be a good thing in the long term for my marriage. Sharing intimate space is important, but then I do like the freedom to thrash around as much as I like, get up, read a book, not worry about waking him. Scott thinks I should take the tablets our doctor prescribed for me. The ones to aid sleeping, not the other ones. I don't like those; they make me feel drowsy and I'm worried about acting like some kind of zombie, sleepwalking through life.

I watch him sleeping. He's so peaceful, his chest rising and falling evenly, no fitful sleeping patterns for my husband. Unlike me, Scott doesn't seem troubled by stress at all, either from home or from the office. He's always busy and has a lot of pressure and responsibility but it doesn't faze him. Some people are cut out for modern life, all organised with plans in place for almost every eventuality. Some say people marry what is familiar to them, be that what they grew up with – mirror images of their parents – or important figures who have left an imprint on their lives, forming strong neural pathways as my therapist said. I prefer the old adage, that opposites attract.

Scott and I are certainly opposites. The calm and assured nature he brings to the family is immense, and a huge contrast to my more frenetic, anxious energy. Things bother him. I know they do. I see it in the micro expressions that flicker briefly in his facial features before he rationalises the situation and moves past it. Me, I ruminate on a given situation for days. Sometimes I'm still ruminating on things I saw, or said, years previously, wondering what I could have done differently. That's not normal.

Neither is it normal to be lying awake at three thirty on a Saturday morning whilst the rest of my family sleep soundly, expecting a lie-in for the weekend. Especially Chas, who crept in just over an hour ago thinking he was being stealthy and that no one would notice. I did. I was already awake, as I often am in the early hours before my alarm sounds.

Scott came home around ten o'clock after his evening with Deanna and I was already in bed, sleeping. Well, I wasn't asleep. There's no chance I could close my eyes with the thoughts I had running through my head. I pretended to be asleep when he came into the bedroom though. I'd have fired multiple questions at him, and he would have seen right through me. Then it would have kicked off for sure. He doesn't like it when I say anything that might bring into question his loyalty or suggests I have a lack of faith in him. I've told him it's not him, but other women I worry about. That doesn't wash with Scott, because if I doubt him, then it's a trust issue. I couldn't face the argument. Not this night.

Now Scott is snoring. I could give him a nudge and make him roll over but there's no way I'm going back to sleep anyway. My brain is already fully engaged, and the sun hasn't even come up. Slipping out from beneath the duvet, I do my best not to cause a wave of movement that might wake him. He deserves to sleep in or at least to sleep until a decent hour on the weekend. I probably don't need to be so careful, mind you. This bed is massive, handmade by craftsmen and imported from Italy, so I was told. I'm confident it wouldn't ripple if a giant of a woman got in or out of it, and the movement of such a slight figure – okay, slight is pushing it – such as me certainly won't wake Scott.

Pulling the bedroom door closed behind me, I head downstairs, and I'm surprised to see a shaft of light visible under the door to Scott's study. He probably left the light on before coming to bed. Scott will often keep odd hours, working late when anyone else would desire sleep. He's quite a machine when it comes down to it, so I wouldn't be surprised if he got another hour or two at his desk after getting home.

For a moment I thought I heard something beyond the door so, tentatively, I grasp the handle and ease it open, startled to find Katie sitting at Scott's desk, head tilted to one side and her face a picture of concentration. So much so, that she doesn't notice me at the door. Still in her pyjamas, she looks up at me as I walk in.

'What are you doing up at this hour?'

'I couldn't sleep,' she says glumly. 'You?'

'Same.' I enter the study and cross to where she is sitting, doodling a sketch on a sheet of paper she must have taken from the printer tray of the nearby machine. There's only one colour in use, black. 'What's this?' I ask as I perch myself on the edge of the desk next to her. Katie is back drawing again and she doesn't look up.

'It's me, Chas,' – she glances up at me as I look down at her handiwork – 'you and Dad.' The picture is of a large house, ours on Chester Terrace I presume. The Corinthian inspired columns and Georgian windows are a giveaway. There's the four of us, and in the background is another figure walking a dog, although it is hard to tell. She's talented, our daughter. Her grades in the core academic subjects are exceptional, despite her behavioural issues, but she also has this creative side that I don't see exhibited in her brother or her father. I know I'm biased, but this sketch wouldn't look out of place framed on the wall.

'Who's that?' I point at the figure.

'That's Sharon, our dog walker.'

I can feel myself frowning but I soften my expression. I don't want to put her off. This is the most creative thing I've seen Katie do off her own bat in months. I can't remember the last time she was drawing anything. 'She's pretty.'

'Yes, she is. I based her on Deanna.'

'I see. One thing though, we don't have a dog.'

Katie nods slowly. 'I know, but if we did, we would have a dog walker, and her name would be Sharon.'

'And the dog's name?'

'Dave.'

'*Dave?*'

Katie smiles and nods. 'Yes, Dave. It's a good name for a dog.'

'What if it's a female?'

'Dave,' she repeats. 'She's a dog. She won't care what her name is.'

I can't fault the logic. 'Dave it is.' She glances up at me.

'Could we get a dog, do you think?'

I sigh. 'Speak to your father.'

'He'll say no.'

'You're sure?'

She shrugs, continuing with her picture. I reach out to stroke her hair but hesitate and then withdraw my hand. She's not a little girl anymore, not really. Such a simple sign of affection that she once loved would probably be seen as infantilising her and wouldn't go down well at all. 'Do you want to come downstairs with me? I can make you something to eat and we could snuggle on the sofa like we used to when you were small.'

'When I had bad dreams?'

'Yes, exactly.'

'No, it's okay. I'm going back to bed.'

And with that, Katie slides from Scott's chair, leaving her sketch behind on his desk, and leaves the room without a backward glance.

Picking up the picture, I take a deep breath, trying not to feel hurt or disappointed. I should be glad she's going back to bed; she needs her sleep. Her drawing is a nice scene depicting the family all together which doesn't happen often.

There's something about the image though. Something dark and foreboding and not just because she's only used shades of black and grey.

Chas towers above everyone else, which is accurate, and there is a noticeable space between me and Scott. Also accurate. Scott is presented with his seemingly endless smile and I am the polar opposite.

On the face of it everything is fine, the family, the house, husband and wife, united. Scratch the surface and the reality is very different. She's managed to capture the atmosphere, rendering our entire marriage in one image of simplicity.

Scott says all the right things. He offers me verbal and even physical support with a touch or a hug, but it doesn't feel real to me anymore. It's like it's all for show, but who is the intended audience? Or maybe it's just me and my perception that's got it all wrong. Maybe I'm wrong.

SEVENTEEN

Saturday

Scott walks into the kitchen around seven, dressed in his shorts and an old T-shirt with his running shoes on. I've been up for a couple of hours already, and I'm nursing my second cup of coffee. Glancing at my notepad, I'm supposed to be making some notes on how I'll approach an interview we've got planned for the show next week, but all I've managed to write so far is *don't be too passive*. I check out my husband. He always looks immaculately turned out, even if he's just prepping to go for his morning run through the park as he is today. I swear he rolls out of bed like it. How he can have an eighteen-year-old son, a demanding executive job and appear so fresh each morning when I can feel my eyes hanging off my face by midday, every day, is beyond me.

He pours himself a glass of fresh orange juice and sips at it as he approaches me. I lean into him as he kisses my forehead. 'Morning, gorgeous.' It is lovely to hear, but I don't feel it.

'Heading out?' He nods. 'How far today?'

'Ten k... no more than that. I'm going for a personal best.

Want to come?' he asks with a smile. *As if.* I fell in love with running whilst training for my marathon attempt but knowing what my limit would be now, having struggled to maintain any form of fitness regimen this past year or two, it would only depress me when I pull up or watch Scott disappearing into the distance ahead of me.

'Another time,' I say lightly.

'Great.' He finishes his drink and puts the dirty glass in the dishwasher, and I can almost hear him tutting internally as he puts the other bits and pieces left on the counter into the machine, before rearranging a few things. He looks at me, smiling. 'I'll hold you to that.' I return the smile, wondering if I'll ever run again. Just as he's about to leave, he hesitates at the door. 'Has someone been into the study?'

'Today?' He nods. 'Katie was in there when I got up earlier. She was sitting at your desk and sketching a picture.'

'A picture?'

'Yes, of us, all of us.'

'Any particular reason she had to do it in there?'

He's bothered by this but is trying not to show it. 'She wasn't doing any harm.'

He looks at me impassively. 'I didn't say she was—'

'I know you're a bit precious about your private space—'

'Precious?' Scott asks. 'It's where I work. I have things in there that...'

'That what?' I ask, frowning. 'You're not a spy. What are you hiding?'

'I'm not *hiding* anything,' he says, sneering. 'It's just that I don't think she should be in there.'

'I don't see the problem.'

Scott's upper lip twitches, his eyes darkening. 'I don't want people in my study, all right?'

'Now it's people?'

'Yes. Keep her out away from my things.'

I scoff. 'Scott, what's the issue?'

He ignores my question. 'What did you say she was doing, drawing?'

'Yes, a family picture. Like she used to, when she was small.'

'That's a good thing,' he says. 'I've not seen her drawing for a while. I thought she'd dropped it completely.'

'Me too.' I get up and find the paper, holding it up as I walk towards him. He examines it, his brow furrowing.

'It's a bit bleak, isn't it?'

'In that case, you should leave some coloured pencils on your desk.'

Scott smiles. 'Yes, perhaps I should, but I'd rather no one used my study for doodling.'

'It's hardly doodling. She's very talented. It's creative expression.'

Scott holds a hand up, placating me. 'I know. I get it. But it's my study; I don't want anyone in there, at all.' For a moment, I had forgotten how much he treasures his inner sanctum. 'I'd better get a move on,' he continues. 'I have a meeting this morning and I'll need to shower beforehand. I don't want to be rushing.'

'Another weekend meeting?' Scott arches his eyebrows as if to say he has no control over when he's needed and working at the weekend is hardly a new thing, which is true. 'Will it take long?'

'We'll see.' He winks at me. 'Please speak to Katie and keep her out of my study.'

'Okay.'

'The park awaits. Back soon.'

'Yeah, have a good run.'

EIGHTEEN

Monday

On Monday when I get home mid-morning, I'm pleased to find Katie sitting at the kitchen table, seemingly in good spirits and paying attention to Deanna.

'So, I thought we'd do a little more on languages now and I could assess how you've been getting along with the French we've been working on. How does that sound?' Deanna asks. Katie shrugs but she doesn't complain.

'Okay. My French teacher says my vocabulary is passable but my accent sucks.'

'Did she now?'

'Sort of.'

'Well, I'll make my own mind up about that.'

I sit down on a stool at the breakfast bar, pushing all of the other mail aside. Other than the one I've been carrying around in my pocket, unable to open, for the last week, there is only one letter I'm interested in reading. This one is from Katie's school. Sliding my nail between the flap and the back of the envelope, I realise I'm holding my breath which is ridiculous.

It's not just about the education, it's also about the doors that are opened by attending this school. It has forged strong links with another, the senior school, where Katie would likely go next year having turned thirteen. Half of the places are saved for pupils attending her prep school, provided they pass the entrance exam. The arrangement with the prep school is such that the exams are taken a year ahead of any external applicant. Katie has already passed and her place will be confirmed.

However, this is all very much dependent on her completing Year 8 at the prep school. As things stand, they will never entertain her attending such a prestigious institution with an expulsion on her record.

Things were never this complicated for me. I went to my local primary. It was a dump. Then I progressed to the local secondary school which, you'll have guessed was, and still is as far as I know, also a dump.

Unfolding the letter, a very official-looking letter which is written in very official language, I exhale slowly before placing it down on the counter. I want to scream.

I need to speak to Scott, but first, I need to eat. Folding the letter up, I keep it in one hand and cross to the fridge. The shopping list I wrote out over the course of the weekend, for Martha, is still stuck to the door with a magnet. She's supposed to be back today.

'Katie?' I ask and both she and Deanna glance toward me. 'Sorry to interrupt, Deanna. Katie, where's Martha?'

'I don't know,' Katie says, returning to her studies. Deanna smiles at me and then joins Katie in shifting her focus back to the French lesson. I open the fridge and see the near empty shelves. Hopefully, Martha is at the shops.

I switch my phone on as I make my way upstairs. The door to Scott's study is closed and I can hear a muffled voice – Scott's – talking. I'll speak to him after I've showered. He'll know what to do. He always does.

My phone beeps and it's a message from Magda.

Call me.

I do just that.

'Sophie, darling,' Magda says, as upbeat and enthusiastic as ever. I often wonder if that is her natural default or whether she carries as much acting ability as many of her clients. 'Thank you for getting back to me. How was the programme today?'

I think on it momentarily. 'It went okay, I would say.'

'Very good. I'll cut to it. Contracts, darling.'

'Good news?' I ask hesitantly, pausing at the top of the stairs.

'That depends.'

'*That depends* is not often very good news, Magda.'

'Well, I think you're going to have to give a little in exchange.'

'Give a little what?'

'Play the game a bit more, if you know what I mean?'

I really have no idea what she's on about. 'Magda, what do I have to do?'

'The wardrobe needs an update, darling. You just *know* how much I love your style—'

'I had a conversation with Sam and he—'

'Apologised! Quite right too. However, there needs to be a little bit of give and take. A sacrifice, so to speak.'

'On my part, presumably.'

'I always said you were my smartest client, Sophie. If everyone was like you, I could retire early, a happy woman.'

'And I need to show a bit more...'

'Yes, not too much though.'

'What if...' I'm reluctant to ask this, but I'll kick myself every day for the rest of time if I let it pass, 'I don't?'

Silence, punctuated only by Magda's breathing. 'Well, it's not like they're expecting you to sleep with anyone...'

'No, just sell my soul—'

'It's hardly that, Sophie darling. It's...'

'I can be a professional broadcaster or' – and this catches in my throat, and I lower my voice – 'a sex object.'

'Oh, Sophie. Do the two *have* to be mutually exclusive?'

'Someone else said exactly that to me when I made this observation to them as well,' I say, recalling Sam, my producer, reacting the same way.

'Oh?'

There's something in her tone. I know Magda; I know her very well. She made a good fist of trying to make it herself as an actress, but she didn't get the traction she wanted and so she crossed the line into talent representation. She made the right call, because she's a terrible actress.

'Magda, have you been speaking to Sam?'

'I speak to everyone, Sophie darling. You know that. It's my job.'

'Well, I hope you gave him what for! He's a creep.'

'That's entertainment, Sophie. You just have to grease the wheels sometimes.'

I snort with derision. 'And what do you mean by that?'

'Just play the game a little, Sophie, that's all.'

'And by *play the game*, you mean what exactly?' There's a brief pause.

'I'm not suggesting you do anything you're uncomfortable with, Sophie.'

'And what is it you think I should be comfortable with?'

'Sophie—'

'*Magda*,' I say, mimicking her.

'You do need to be less precious about some things if you want to succeed in this business.'

'Is that so?'

My agent heaves a deep sigh. 'Honestly, Sophie, I do work very hard for you but sometimes...'

'Sometimes, what?'

'You make my job more difficult.'

'How?'

'It's a tough world out there, Sophie,' Magda explains, as if I'm some kind of novice.

'I thought you, at least, would be in my corner.'

'I *am* in your corner, Sophie, I'm just asking you to consider – just consider – being a little bit more accommodating.'

'I see.'

'So, you will?' Magda asks, her tone lightening.

'I'll *consider* thinking about it,' I tell her.

'You're a real gem, Sophie,' Magda says.

'Thanks, Magda,' I say, and she hangs up.

Is there anyone left I can count on?

NINETEEN

A few hours after my call with Magda, I'm trudging back through the arch at the end of Chester Terrace, arms laden with bags of shopping. There's been no let-up with the rain and I'm aware I must stick out like a sore thumb to anyone looking out of their windows. Most people either have home deliveries or their staff to do their grocery shop, and most certainly have someone at the house to receive it.

To be fair, that's been the case for me too, recently, with Martha. It feels a bit uncomfortable for me; I didn't grow up like this, with a silver spoon in my mouth. But let's face it, I need the help. It's been hard enough organising a family as it is what with Katie's extra-curricular activity programme, school play rehearsals, sporting fixtures and then supervising Chas and everything he is *supposed* to be doing. Throw in demanding careers for the two adults of the household and things can get out of shape very quickly.

Out of the corner of my eye I can see someone is watching me from the house next door to ours. I don't know who the owner is, but I see the housekeeper from time to time. She always has this look on her face when we see each other, one of disdain. Maybe she's not a fan of breakfast television. Everyone's a critic.

Labouring up the steps to our front door, I set the four bags down. Arguably, I should have left some of this until later but going to the shops twice in a day is going to test my logistical expertise. To think, before children, I'd happily make my way around three or maybe four different shops to get the products I wanted. Once I had a baby in tow, that quickly became a one-stop shop for everything.

The sound of laughter and a general murmur of conversation emanates from the kitchen as I struggle to shift the bags inside without knocking one or two over and spilling their contents. Closing the door with my heel, I miscalculate and manage to do what I thought I'd avoided. One bag topples to the left and I see fruit, vegetables and a box containing a dozen eggs fall out onto the tiled floor. I curse loudly whilst mentally whispering a quick prayer to avoid breakages and leaking. I can still hear laughter, and no one's come to investigate let alone offer to help.

I'm on my knees gathering the cherry tomatoes together which have escaped their packaging as Chas appears at the end of the hall. He comes over and helps me pick up the last few and then turns the carton of eggs upright.

'Did you get lucky?' he asks with eyes on the box.

'Only one way to find out.'

Chas tentatively opens the lid and peers inside. 'You should buy some lottery numbers.' He grins, tilting the box in my direction. 'A couple are cracked but other than that, you got away with it.'

'Great. It's my lucky day.' It feels anything but; however, I'll take what I can get right now. 'Can you give me a hand getting all this into the kitchen?'

'Yes, of course.' Chas picks up two bags, the lightest ones obviously. There's helpful, and then there's a teenager's idea of being helpful.

Chas is still single, as far as I know, and I can see why. He's a nice enough lad, a bit odd sometimes, but girls often quite like that. However, he's not overly attentive.

'Why aren't you in a lecture?'

'A double study period.'

'Which you're making good use of, are you?' I say, struggling with the weight of two bags despite having managed to walk home with four. Maybe I've hit the wall, and my energy is flagging, approaching the red line.

'What's the point in studying so close by if I can't make use of my home? I may as well have gone to stay in halls.'

That's a subject I've never broached with Chas. His A Level grades, although stellar, weren't quite good enough to get him into Oxbridge, or it was his poor interview technique that scuppered his application, but any of the Russell Group institutions would have taken him. Basically, Chas could have gone almost anywhere. I know I couldn't wait to get away from home when the prospect of higher education was dangled before me. I could go away to someplace new and be myself or, at least, have the space to try and find out who I wanted to be.

This is a teenager's rite of passage, as long as you can afford the fees or are willing to accept the debt. Perhaps both. I was more than willing to accept living in a bit of a dive, cheaply, with friends. There was damp in the bathroom and the pans and utensils in the kitchen always had a weird smell to them no matter how often or aggressively we cleaned them. Still, that was all part of it. Freedom. Above all else, it was fun.

None of this seems to appeal to Chas. He accepted a place at his first-choice medical school which was local. He could live at home and wouldn't entertain the notion that he was missing out on some of the best experiences that university had to offer by not moving into halls. Mind you, I'm not sure how many of his peers live in the manner in which Chas has become accustomed. Why would he change it?

Thinking back on it, I had a reason – many reasons – to leave home and never look back. None of which were related to my family, but more to do with the town I grew up in.

Scott is in the kitchen, leaning with one hand against the counter alongside his precious coffee machine. However, it's Deanna who is arranging the cups and working the levers, giggling as she presses and pulls the assorted buttons and chrome handles.

'No, no,' Scott says, reaching out and placing his hand on hers to stop her from adjusting a setting on the steamer. 'You have to wait until the boiler pressure hits ninety-three per cent otherwise the micro-bubbles won't be sufficiently pressurised and you'll end up with too much air in the milk.'

'And too much air in the milk means your foam won't be silky.'

'That's it, you've got it!' Scott says. Deanna grins triumphantly as she reads the gauge and releases the steam into the stainless-steel milk jug. Why am I irritated by this scene? Could it be because Deanna is making a process – one managed by tens of thousands of minimum wage employees the world over on a daily basis – seem like alchemy? Or is it her closeness to my husband that I don't like? I would hope it's the former but even I can't delude myself that much.

'You're picking it up much faster than I ever have,' I say, forcing a light tone to my voice, carting the bags into the kitchen. Scott is startled by my appearance and hurries over to help me lift the heaviest bag up onto the counter.

'I didn't hear you come in.'

That's apparent. 'I was stealthy.' He looks at me questioningly, but I avoid meeting his eye for fear he'll read my mind. They say the eyes are the windows to the soul, and right now, my soul is decidedly jealous.

'I've done it!' Deanna exclaims. Katie bounces across the kitchen to inspect the latte she's just made. 'The foam isn't quite right, though.'

Scott moves to assess it himself. 'Great for a cappuccino.'

'Then let's say I was making a cappuccino,' Deanna says.

'You're a fast learner.' Scott looks at me. 'Do you want our new trainee barista to make you a cappuccino?'

I'm so wired that a caffeine hit is the last thing I need. 'No, but a green tea would be nice. I'm going to make lunch.'

'Green would suit your eyes,' Scott says, coming alongside me and lowering his voice. My eye colour is brown, and he obviously knows that, but he's always preferred to call it green-ish brown. Wishful thinking, on his behalf. 'I'll have to give lunch a miss. There's an impromptu call. Sorry.'

I frown at him. 'You should eat—'

'I did. Deanna made me a quick sandwich.'

'Of course she did,' I mutter.

'What's that?' he asks.

'I said, that's great.'

He smiles. 'With help from her sous chef, Katie, of course.'

'Of course.'

Scott kisses me on the cheek, glancing down at the floor. I'm dripping rainwater from my coat onto the wooden floor. It's pooling at my feet. That's one of my husband's pet hates. He thinks we should take exterior clothing off at the door. He's right, but I don't care, not today. He smiles and kisses me again. 'Don't worry. It'll mop up.'

'Has Katie had lunch too?' I ask as he makes to leave. Our daughter is already back at her makeshift desk at the kitchen table, Deanna alongside her, getting back into work. Chas has set down the bags he carried through and disappeared, clearly not keen to help put things away.

'No, not yet. She's waiting on the avocado.' Scott winks at me. Sarcastic sod that he is at times.

'I'll sort something for her.'

But Scott has already left the kitchen, returning to his study.

TWENTY

'It must be quite a challenge for you,' Deanna says. I almost didn't register she was speaking to me. I'm rinsing the salad leaves in the sink next to our pantry. Was it a question or a statement? I poke my head around the door.

'Sorry, what did you say? I had the tap running.'

'Managing your home, looking after your kids, alongside having such a successful career. It must be challenging.'

I shake the water from my hands and bring the colander holding the leaves back into the kitchen. 'Yes, it has its moments.'

Deanna is leaning against the breakfast bar. Katie has gone to the bathroom.

'I can imagine. I've no idea how you do it. I only have to look after myself and that's difficult enough.'

'Well, you figure it out I suppose.'

'Do you have family to help?'

I glance in her direction and shake my head. 'My mother passed away when I was very young, barely Katie's age now come to think of it.'

'Oh, that's such a shame.' Deanna looks at me with

mournful eyes. 'Do you remember much about her?' She meets my eye and then looks down. 'I'm so sorry, that's none of my business. I shouldn't have asked—'

'No, it's fine, really,' I say, forcing a smile and resuming my task. I've set out two plates, Chas having declined a proper meal in exchange for picking something up on his way back to lectures. Deanna has also, politely, chosen not to join us, saying she wants to take a walk across to the park with her lunch. If the rain ever lets up anyway. 'I don't remember much about her. I can't even remember what her voice sounded like.'

'Do you recall spending time with her though?'

'I do, but she was very sick for a long time before she passed. Much of my childhood was spent fetching things for her, that type of thing. It wasn't what you might call *quality time* that we shared.'

'I'm so sorry.'

'That's okay. It was all such a long time ago now. I still have fond memories of her.' Images of my mum lying in her bed come to my mind. I haven't thought about her in a long time. It's not a period of my life I find easy to think about, let alone discuss. Not only is it painful for me but there are things in my past that should remain there.

'And your father. Is he still around?'

'No, not so much. He lives a long way away. We don't see much of him.'

'Ah, Katie said something like that.'

'She did?' I ask, setting the colander aside on the drainer, allowing the leaves to dry while I cut some slices of bread from the artisan loaf I bought.

'Yes, we were translating relations as part of her French work. It just sort of came up.'

'Right. Of course.'

'It's a shame that he doesn't see much of his grandchildren.'

I shake my head. 'He lives up north, so it can't be helped

that we don't see a lot of him.' That's a lie, but one I'm comfortable telling.

'He wouldn't consider moving down this way then, to be closer?'

I smile politely and shake my head. 'No, I don't think that'll ever happen. Besides...'

'Besides?'

I wish I hadn't added that. The last thing I want is to be discussing my family relationships, especially with someone I have barely just met. I busy myself putting salad leaves onto the plates, adding some cherry tomatoes as well. I bought a caramelised red onion houmous at the shops, too. That, along with a selection of cheeses. Katie likes French cheese, the deli ham and the tandoori infused ready-cooked chicken and that's lunch pretty much ready. 'Oh, just that I envy those people with large extended families living nearby. It must be nice to have people around, offering support if nothing else. Particularly when it comes to the children.'

'I'll bet you and Scott don't get much time alone together, either.'

I don't wish to confirm that, despite it being true, but I'm not going to lie and deny it either. 'As I say, it's a challenge. We're both busy people.'

'What about Scott's parents? Don't they help?'

I never got to meet Scott's mother. She passed away a few years before we met, so I've only ever seen her in photographs and there aren't many of those.

Scott's parents were divorced when he was young, and he went to live with his father, who was a media executive much like his son is now. They moved around a lot, living in various parts of Europe and North America depending on his father's career. How much Scott saw of his mother, I don't know, but he doesn't speak about her much which indicates that she wasn't a constant in his life, I suppose.

'His father lives abroad.'

'Oh, exciting! Anywhere nice?'

'California, I think.'

'You think?'

'Well, the US anyway.' I thought it was California, but now I'm not so sure. 'Yes, probably California.'

'That sounds fantastic. I've always wanted to go there, live up in the Hollywood Hills, walk along the Sunset Strip and all of that.'

'Sounds good.'

'Have you ever been? To Hollywood?'

'No, why would I have been?' I ask, transferring the plates to the table. Deanna helpfully moves some of the study materials aside.

'Oh.' Deanna is leaning forward now, as if we were two old friends nattering away, as I set the table for lunch. She is easy company to be fair. 'I just thought, what with Scott's job, and you being in television too, that you might have the chance. Your lives must be so exciting.'

I suppose our life must look compelling from the outside, but it's nowhere near as glamorous as one might think. 'I tell you, if they offered me an outside broadcast opportunity over there, I'd jump at it.'

'Would you?'

I think on it for a moment. I've no idea how we would make that work in our current set-up – and it is never going to happen anyway – but hypothetically, a trip to the place where the sun always shines is not something I'd pass up. 'Heck, yes!'

Deanna giggles. She giggles a lot, it would seem.

'How about you?'

'What about me?' she asks, recovering her composure.

'Your family. I mean, you're staying in a hostel right now, aren't you?' Deanna nods. 'Have you not got any family nearby who could put you up until you find your feet?'

Her expression turns sombre. 'No, I'm afraid not. Like yours, both my parents have passed away.' I'm surprised by that. Deanna can't be older than thirty and she looks much younger than that. It's a very young age to have lost both parents already. She catches me looking at her.

'Sorry, I don't mean to stare, but you seem awfully...'

'What?' she asks, cocking her head.

'Young, to have lost both parents, I mean.'

She smiles. 'I hear that a lot, don't worry. It's true. My parents separated when I was young. I don't really know my mother and my father died in a car crash.'

'I'm sorry.'

'As you said,' – she tilts her head to one side, matter of fact – 'it was a long time ago.'

'What about friends? Couldn't you stay with someone? I know we pay fairly well, but after agency deductions, tax... Staying in the hostel is going to bleed you dry.'

Deanna cocks her head and then slowly nods. 'I know. I'm already thinking that working in the capital wasn't my best decision.'

'So, friends are not an option?'

'No. I've been living abroad for so long, pretty much all of my working life.' She smiles. 'All seven years of it.' This makes me smile as well. 'I'm really enjoying working for you, but if I can't find a solution, I'm afraid I'll have to think again.'

Katie returns then from her not too brief sojourn to the toilet and Deanna retakes her seat while I finish making lunch. Chas leaves for his afternoon lectures and time will tell if he is actually attending or simply making it look like he's attending. If it is the latter, then he'll be thrown out before the year end. He doesn't seem to be taking his studies very seriously and in medicine that's just not going to work.

Katie and Deanna close their books and Deanna excuses

herself, making ready to head out into Regent's Park for her lunch break.

Admiring the simple, but delicious, lunch I've prepared, I have to admit to being pleased. It all came together well but despite this, I'm still nervous as Katie picks up her knife and fork.

'Is it okay?' She nods. 'Really?'

'Yes, it's okay.'

'You are special to me, Katie. You know that, don't you?'

She doesn't respond, focusing instead on eating. 'Can you call me KD from now on?'

'Excuse me?'

'I want to be addressed by my initials, K and D.' She shrugs. 'KD.'

'Why? Are you planning a career as a hip-hop artist or something?'

She shrugs again. 'It's cool. KD is a lot like Katie, if you were an American.'

'But we are not American, and this is London.'

Katie fixes me with a pointed look. 'What difference does it make to you what I'm called?'

'Well, right back at you,' I say, setting my knife and fork down. 'What difference *does it make* what you are called?' She narrows her eyes and slams her cutlery down, before slipping her legs out from under the table and stalking out of the kitchen. I sigh, biting my bottom lip painfully, struggling to understand what just happened.

'I think that might be my fault,' Deanna says, wrinkling her nose from where she is at the doorway. I thought she'd left for her walk, but apparently not.

'In what way?' I ask quietly, glancing over at her.

'My friends call me Dee. I find Deanna sounds a bit pretentious. I think it may have inspired Katie.'

I pinch the bridge of my nose between thumb and forefinger, eyes closed. 'It's okay. Things have been a bit difficult recently. She'll get over it.'

'It wouldn't hurt to humour her though, would it?'

Is Deanna really offering me unsolicited parental advice? 'I'm sorry, what did you say?'

Deanna shifts her weight between her feet, the first sign that she acknowledges she may be overstepping. 'I just meant—'

'I know what you meant, but I'll parent my own daughter, if it's all the same to you?'

'Yes, of course. Sorry. I didn't mean to make things worse, is all.'

I wave away her apology. 'No, I'm sorry for snapping.' I shake my head. I can see the genuine guilt in Deanna's face, and I know she meant well. I overreacted, as always. 'Your presence with us, with Katie, has made her smile, and I haven't seen her this interested in her studies since... well, in quite some time. And, seeing as it doesn't look likely that Katie will be readmitted to school anytime soon, I hope you'll stick around for a bit.'

Deanna comes over to me, her lips pursed. 'Really? Do you mean that?'

I meet her eye. 'Yes, yes, I do. You have been good for her, I think.'

She smiles warmly, appreciating the comment. 'Thank you. Only...'

'Only what?'

'Forgive me, I shouldn't say.'

'No, please, go on.'

'Well,' – she rocks her head from side to side – 'I kind of get the sense that you're not happy with me being here.'

'No, it's... um...'

'You don't like me?'

'That's not true.' And it isn't that I don't like her, it's that I don't like her being in my house, having such a strong connection with my child, and being around my husband... definitely being around my husband. 'It's fine, don't worry. There's no issue.'

'If you're sure?' Deanna asks. 'I don't want to cause a problem.'

'No,' I say, holding up my hand. 'It's fine.'

She smiles, apparently relieved. 'Mind you, it might not be an issue soon anyway.'

'How do you mean?'

'Like I said before, I don't know if I can sustain what I'm doing for very long, living like this. I'm sorry to add to your burden, but I don't think I'll be able to keep this job for much longer. London is just too expensive for me.'

'Then we will have to find a solution!' We both look round to see Scott standing in the doorway. He has his hands in his pockets, thumbs extended outside them, looking every inch the debonair businessman that he is. With Scott, it's not for show. He lives it. 'You need somewhere more affordable to live, right?'

Deanna nods. 'Yes, that's about the crux of it. I have to pack, but I don't have much, to be honest.' She glances at me.

Scott comes closer, laying a hand across my shoulder. 'We have space in the basement conversion,' he says, gently squeezing my shoulder. 'It's not much, but it's a private part of the house with your own bathroom, a separate lounge area and you even have access to the basement courtyard garden.'

'Hang on,' I say, but Scott is in full flow.

'We never go down there, do we, Sophie? So it would be your own space. You even have access by your own door down the steps from the street above. There's an alleyway access on the far end of the garden courtyard to the rear as well.'

'I couldn't possibly—'

'Of course you could,' Scott says, glancing between us. He nods at me, as if seeking approval without giving me any opportunity to give it. 'We can even charge you a nominal rent, if that would make you feel better? You'd be available full-time for Katie's studies that way, as well. Problem solved.'

'I...' Deanna looks at me and she's trying to mask her excitement. 'I guess, if it's all right with you both?'

'Of course it is,' Scott says, arching his eyebrows at me. I nod, but I have reservations. Strong reservations. It's all very... convenient, somehow. 'There you go,' Scott says. 'It's done!'

Deanna's face splits into a broad grin. 'It's done!' she repeats.

'Done,' I whisper.

Is this what is best for my daughter, for everyone? Am I being selfish; should I put my feelings aside? Why do I have a gnawing sensation in the pit of my stomach that this is a very bad idea?

TWENTY-ONE

The garden flat, the basement level, of our Georgian terrace is larger than many apartments in central London. At the front, there is a small courtyard garden with a stairwell up to street level, and there are vaulted storage rooms that stretch out beneath the road above. We seldom use them. There are two windows that allow light in, and you would only know you were below ground on the darkest of days. To the rear there is a small garden area, rare in this part of the capital, and beyond that a gated access to a rear passage linking us to the next street.

I flick on the light switch and the forward-facing room, the lounge area, is illuminated. An occasional sofa is butted up against the wall to the right. There is a small fireplace, likely once used by staff to either heat the room or to cook with, perhaps both seeing as this was once the scullery. It's far more modern now, carpeted and decorated in keeping with the rest of the house. The fireplace is a period detail, if not original to the house, with open shelving to either side of a marble mantel-piece. To the front is a small courtyard; a door opens out onto it, and there are steps up to street level. From here, the natural light comes into the basement, unless it's a gloomy day.

I never got to meet the previous owners of our house, but whoever they were had this room kitted out as a study and it was far too small for Scott's liking. He transformed two of the upstairs bedrooms for his use, knocking them into one room to suit his purpose. We didn't need an extra room on that floor anyway and Scott likes the space and to be able to see across to the park opposite the terrace.

I know the neighbouring properties use the basement level for staff. Scott has never entertained live-in assistance before, believing it adds an artificial element to the family. I can see what he means, and Scott has always been very focused on the family as a unit. Introducing people from outside the home into our family dynamic has never been part of our plans. So, it is a bit surprising how quickly that position shifted but, then again, Scott is also something of a pragmatist.

'This would be your personal space,' I say, glancing sideways at Deanna. 'We never come down here, so you could use it as you wish. I know there's not a lot of furniture now, but we could get you some more if you let us know what you might want.'

'I share this same space with three people at the hostel,' Deanna says, referring to her dorm presumably, 'and it doesn't smell badly here.'

I back out of the room. 'And to the rear is the bedroom.' I push the door off the basement hallway open to reveal another room similar in size to the one we just left. Only this one does have a double bed in it; the mattress is still wrapped in plastic. It was a standard double rather than a king size, my mistake, although I was certain at the time that was what I was supposed to order. It was part of a clearance sale, and I was unable to return it, so it ended up stored down here.

This was originally planned to be a playroom, but by the time we'd completed the renovation having lived elsewhere, Katie was at an age where she either wanted to be around us or be in her own bedroom. The need for a playroom had passed and this space became a storage room. There would be no more babies coming into the Morton household. Statistically, I should still be able, but something about me just means it isn't going to happen. Mother Nature is not particularly kind to everyone and despite our desire to extend the family, Scott and I had to face the reality that more children weren't going to be in our future. That saddens me deeply, and I believe it hurt Scott too. It kills me that I can't give him what he wants.

The room is a bit dusty, but it's only because of a lack of use rather than from the build-up of dirt or grime. I look over at Deanna. It's not much, a little pokey and gloomy, perhaps, but she's almost jubilant as she takes in the space.

'Just through that door is an en suite,' I tell her, pointing to the door at the end of the room to the left. 'It's arguably the smallest en suite in the world, but it—'

'Is perfect!' Deanna says, her smile broadening. 'I can't believe it, this is amazing.'

'At the end of the hall there's a utility room, where you'll find the door into the courtyard at the front. There is plenty of space, a sink, cupboards. We could probably get you a few bits and pieces down there, too, set you up as a self-contained unit.'

Deanna turns to face me, reaching out and taking my hands in hers. 'Thank you. This is...' I can see her welling up. 'I can't believe it,' she says again. I was about to say it's not much, but I suppose to Deanna, it's more than just her own space, and more like her own home. 'I could never afford anything like this. It would cost thousands a month on the rental market—'

'Well, it's not on the rental market and Scott is pretty generous with things. You'll be able to afford it, I'm sure.'

'I just can't believe my luck.'

'Say that when Chas wakes you up stumbling in in the middle of the night from one of his student parties!'

Deanna looks at me, smiling. 'I'll manage Chas, don't

worry.' She moves around the room, inspecting the en suite facilities and then checking the view out of the small window facing onto the back of the property.

'You access the garden from the door at the end of the hall.'

I let her explore for a while, and my focus drifts back to work, scenarios I might face in the coming days with Michael, Sam and even with Magda. I'd be much happier if my co-host would move on to other projects and then I could share the sofa with someone I really connect with, but he'll not be going anywhere. I fear he's such a part of the furniture, much like the sofas themselves, that he'll be carried from the studio in a pine box, and even then I suspect he'll make a fight of it.

As for my producer, Sam, he's fixated on my wardrobe while I'd just like to focus on what I'm good at, taking people to task. Those who need it anyway, and there are plenty of them kicking around these days. There are some big announcements coming up in the next week or so regarding policy decisions in the run-up to the general election this summer. The big hitters will be touring the studios and I want to be ready, not stressing about a contract extension and how much that depends on what dress I'm going to wear.

'Is that okay?'

I look up at Deanna. She's right in front of me. The last I saw her, she was disappearing back into the shower room. I blink at her. 'Sorry, what did you say?'

'Can I go and get my things today and move in right away?'

'Erm, yes, of course. Are you okay getting everything over here?'

Deanna laughs. 'It is only two bags, and one of those is in your kitchen with my laptop inside it.'

'Is that all you have?'

She shrugs. 'I had to leave most of my things behind when I came back to the UK. At my last place, I had several wardrobes chock-full of clothes. I had an allowance to spend on my appearance, a different outfit almost every day.'

I sigh. 'I could use some of that.' She looks at me hesitantly. 'It's work. They don't approve of my styling. It's become something of a running battle between me and, well, everyone else. I never had a problem with things like this before but...' Suddenly I'm feeling self-conscious. Why am I telling her all of this?

'Would you like some help?' she asks, and my expression must have shifted because she immediately back-pedals. 'Sorry, it's none of my business—'

'No, no. Actually, I would like some advice, if only to bounce ideas off someone. Between my co-presenter, my producer and my agent, I'd end up looking like a streetwalker if I did what they wanted.'

Deanna giggles. It must be her default laughter. 'Men are really something when it comes to what they expect us to look like, aren't they?'

'One of them is a woman!'

'Is she not on the side of the sisterhood?'

'I'm beginning to wonder,' I say, thinking of Magda. When it comes down to it, I'm confident Magda will always be on the winning side. Whichever that side happens to be.

'Seriously though, I'd be happy to help. In my last position, I worked for an executive who was high up in an Italian fashion chain. I wasn't allowed to dress normally, just in case the paparazzi snapped us out together. She was *very* particular about my appearance—'

'Hence the clothing allowance?'

'That's right. I'm sure I can help, although I don't think there's anything wrong with your style. You look amazing.' I can feel myself flushing. I've never been good at accepting compliments. It's lovely of her to say so, but I assume she's only flattering me. 'I mean it, I'd be happy to help.'

'Thanks, that would be great.'

'Okay, I'll run out and collect my things. Then, maybe we could have a look through your clothes later? Oh, and I'll need to go shopping. I've been eating out most nights. Nothing fancy but there isn't much in the way of facilities at the—'

'You could join us for dinner, save you the trouble today, and then you can get yourself sorted tomorrow.' I regret the offer as soon as I say it.

'Great,' Deanna says, almost bouncing on the spot with excitement. 'And we could have a look at your wardrobe after we eat.'

The thought of allowing Deanna to style me, the *intimacy* of it, makes me feel vulnerable somehow. But I know I'm just being insecure. She's being perfectly lovely; I have no reason to doubt her intentions.

At least, I think so.

TWENTY-TWO

Dinner was nothing fancy. Fortunately, we are pretty well served by way of mini supermarkets, both chain and independent shops, dotted around the perimeter of Regent's Park. Usually, Martha would only shop in the latter seeing as they cater well with artisan foodstuffs, fresh local produce and organics.

However, these places will provide exceptional quality but not necessarily convenience. This morning, on my way home from work, I went with the convenient option. Therefore, dinner consists of a tray of ready-made lasagne along with garlic bread and a couple of bags of mixed Italian baby leaf salad.

'What did you put in the salad?' Scott asks as he finishes up, lifting his glass to his lips and sipping his wine – from a bottle of red I hurriedly chose from the cellar storage, I have to admit without first checking it would go with the food.

'Nothing much,' I tell him. The truth is, I threw the bags away without looking. 'Spinach, rocket, cos, I think and, um...'

'Green Batavia, isn't it?' Deanna says. That's one I could never have named even if I was given the rest of the night to come up with it. I figure that's what comes from working closely with, and beside, an Italian family.

'Yes, I think so,' I say masterfully. 'Was it okay?'

'Yes, of course,' Scott says, sipping more of his wine. 'I was just curious.' We usually end up pouring at least half a bottle of wine away when we've opened it. Scott will only ever have one glass with dinner, and he rarely finishes it anyway. I tend not to drink at all these days. In recent years, I've been known to become irritating to everyone including myself once I've had a drink and so it's better for me to abstain.

Scott poured Deanna a glass as well, but she's hardly touched it. I wonder if she doesn't drink and was too polite to decline, or maybe she doesn't want to drink in front of us, seeing as we are now her employers as well as her landlords. Chas raised his hand for a glass, but Scott won't let him drink on a school night. Eighteen years old or not, he'll get no encouragement from his father. For her part, Katie is absently toying with her food, shuffling it around her plate with her fork.

I catch Deanna watching Scott. *Watching* is possibly an exaggeration. She's definitely looking at him though. I catch her eye and she shifts in her seat. 'Is something wrong, Deanna?' I ask.

'No, I... it's nothing really.'

'Something on your mind?' Scott asks, curious.

'It's a bit awkward really, and, with everything you've done for me, I feel bad for even thinking it.'

'Thinking what?' Scott asks, resting his elbows on the table, interlocking his fingers before his face. Deanna wrinkles her nose and furtively glances at me then back to Scott.

'It's just, I've sort of used all of my budget to get home and find accommodation, and eating out has sort of stretched me.' My eyes narrow. 'And I know I've got no right to ask but—'

'You need an advance?' Scott asks.

'I... I need to settle up with the hostel. They've been great, but I can't take the rest of my stuff, as little as it is, unless I pay them what I owe.'

Scott's brow furrows. 'They won't let you take your things?'

'No,' she says, shaking her head. 'They're withholding the last of my things. I can't blame them, not really.'

'I didn't think you came back with much,' I say.

'Well, I don't have a lot anyway. There's only one more bag over there, but it's clothing I really need.'

'They can't do that,' Scott says, incredulous. 'That's tantamount to theft.'

Deanna shrugs. 'I guess, but from their point of view I could leave and they'll never see me again.'

'I'll get you some cash, not a problem.'

'Thank you, that's so kind of you, again.' She smiles at him and then looks across at me. I return her smile, although mine is artificial. She's good, I'll give her that. I get up and start collecting the plates. 'I'll help you clear away,' Deanna says, rising from her seat with me.

'No, not tonight you won't,' Scott says, holding up his hand to stop her. 'We'll clear the table. Tonight, you're our guest.'

Deanna looks awkward at this suggestion, but sits back down. Scott looks at me and nods with an easy smile and I accept the plate Deanna passes to me.

'Thank you,' she says. I meet her smile with one of my own.

'No problem,' I say, but the words stick in my throat. Katie is very quick to pass me hers, and there is still a fair bit of food on it. 'Are you not hungry, love?'

'Not my type of thing.'

'What's wrong with it?'

She shrugs. 'It's very processed. Martha makes it from scratch.'

'Good for Martha,' I say, taking her plate. 'I'm sorry it didn't meet with your approval.'

'That's okay,' she says, completely missing the sarcasm in my voice.

'Shall we go upstairs soon?' Deanna asks and all eyes turn to me.

'What's this then?' Scott asks, and I note he hasn't got up to help. 'All girls together?'

'Deanna has offered to help with my styling conundrum, that's all.'

Scott hesitates and then is finally spurred into action, taking Chas's plate from him. 'You have a conundrum?'

'Sort of, yes. It's a woman thing.' Hopefully that will be enough to make him seek the solace of ignorance. I'd rather not get Scott involved in the question of *how much is enough* when it comes to revealing my body to the world.

'Ah, in that case I'll steer well clear.' He looks at our children in turn. 'Perhaps then, the two of you would like to help clear the table and give your mum a break.'

Both Chas and Katie react as one might expect, Chas groaning and Katie rolling her eyes. Scott launches a napkin at our eldest, who catches it deftly.

'Thank you for dinner,' Deanna says as we leave the dining room.

'You're welcome, but I warn you, that is almost the limit of my culinary talents. I can manage to throw together a half-decent breakfast and simple lunches are my forte, but evening meals are usually a disappointment.'

Deanna laughs. 'Well, it beats the options nearby I've been existing on this past week. Don't get me wrong, I like fried chicken and burgers as much as the next person but living off them, no thanks. I swear I've piled on the pounds in the last couple of weeks.'

I appraise her as she leads the way upstairs. If she's gained weight, you wouldn't know it. She's incredibly lean. I hate that.

Fifteen minutes later, we have a number of outfits laid out on my bed in the guest suite.

'I think these are great,' Deanna says but she's reticent, I can tell. Maybe she doesn't like my style as much as she said. 'But...'

'But?' I ask, biting a ragged fingernail.

'I can see what they mean, I think we can do better! Can we have a look at the rest of your clothes?'

Downstairs in the principal bedroom, Deanna flies through my wardrobes plucking out one thing after another and with frightening speed comes up with several outfits that appear different but maintain consistency and continuity of style. There are several that are more daring than I feel comfortable with, but Deanna is insistent.

'That's the one you should wear tomorrow.'

'Really?' I'm not so sure, looking at it laid out on the bed. 'I used to love it but...'

'But what?'

'It's so bold.'

'It's heritage chic.'

'It's short.'

'Classic.'

'I'm not sure,' I tell her, fearing the hem riding up. Deanna must have read my mind.

'No, look, when worn with these tights,' she says, holding a pair of black checked, 100 denier tights. 'And these boots.' Having tossed the tights onto the bed alongside the red dress, she's now fished out a pair of knee-high boots. I have to admit, it is a great look. 'Simple, stylish, and not too revealing.'

'It is above the shoulder—'

'Trust me, people will die for you in this dress. The red and black combination of the figure-hugging knitwear dress, the boots, you will knock them dead.' Deanna looks around.

'It's the figure-hugging bit that I'm worried about.'

'Nonsense, you look great. Everyone will think so.' I'm still not sure, but if I'm going to ask for advice then I probably should take it. 'Where do you keep your accessories? We need something extra.' The dress is tight, with long sleeves and a Bardot neckline, so there is nothing across my upper chest and back. It isn't necessarily revealing in a daring way but does show a fair amount of skin.

'Jewellery?' I ask and Deanna nods. I open a drawer of my vanity unit and produce my box. It's not a large box. I keep the items I tend not to wear very often in this, usually rotating between the same three earring sets. I'm not a huge fan of jewellery anymore; I'd hate to be accused of being too showy.

Going through the various items, none of which are expensive or sentimental to me – I never ask for jewellery as presents anymore – Deanna pauses. 'This is it,' she says, holding aloft a small blue velvet-lined case. Staring at it for a moment, she turns to me, holding the box open.

Inside the box is a delicate gold necklace with an accompanying pendant. It is understated but decorated with an intricate pattern. 'This is it,' she repeats, passing it to me. I take it from her and carefully lift the necklace out, the pendant nestling in the palm of my hand. 'Where did you get that from? It's beautiful.'

'I don't recall. I imagine it was a gift from Scott, but not recent.' In the early days of our relationship, Scott still bought me jewellery but now I tend to prefer other, more practical, gifts. I don't remember this one though and it's not what I would choose for myself.

'He has great taste. You should put your hair up and wear this tomorrow. It suits you. You have such a lovely skin tone and' – she lowers her voice – 'you'll look sexy as hell too.'

I take a breath and look at the clothing laid out on the bed, imagining myself in it on the set. It's more the look I would have gone for years ago, before I was married, and I'd have had the confidence to carry it off then, too. It is in tune with what the studio wants though, I'm sure of that. 'What do you reckon? Are you up for it?' Deanna is smiling at me.

'Yes,' I say, nodding. 'I'm up for it.'

Deanna claps her hands excitedly. 'You are going to be the talk of the town.' I'm not so sure I like the sound of that. Being the talk of the town is one thing, but when the town is London, then it is on an entirely different level.

TWENTY-THREE

Once again, I'm lying in my bed wide awake, trying very hard not to calculate just how few hours of sleep I will manage to get if I was to fall asleep right now... which I won't, obviously. The room is partially illuminated by the digital clock, casting a dull-green glow across the room. Despite my best efforts, I glance at the display and it is after ten.

Less than five hours. Provided I fall asleep immediately, and that is not going to happen. The rain is still coming down, driving against the windows in gusts but I've always found rain strangely comforting as long as I'm not walking around in it. Despite Deanna's assistance in helping me with my outfit, I'm still feeling a sense of dread about presenting tomorrow morning. I never used to feel this nervous, going to work. The comments made about my appearance, and the anxiety they've caused me, are distracting me from what I love about my job, speaking to interesting people from all walks of life.

They don't have to be celebrities or people of power and influence, though. There are everyday people who lead extraordinary lives, be it in their communities or in the field of work. I interviewed a man whose hobby was being a detectorist, once. Arguably the dullest person I'd ever met, but he uncovered one of the greatest Anglo-Saxon burial grounds in history, completely changing how archaeologists view that period as a result. An unassuming man who changed the view of an entire profession.

A sound caught my attention a few minutes ago but I ignored it, imagining it was a trick of my overactive mind. But there it is again. Usually, I can't hear anything from the guest suite and, believe me, I've been awake often enough over the last few weeks and months to have heard odd sounds should they arise, as they do in any home at night. This is different though.

Slipping out from under the duvet, the air feels cold against my skin. My pyjamas are silk, beautifully soft and spacious, but they offer little warmth. Scott bought them for my birthday this year. I would rather sleep in warmer clothing, especially when it's dank and dismal as it is at the moment, but Scott smiles when he sees me wearing them.

Cracking the bedroom door, I listen intently. The landing is in darkness with only a modicum of light penetrating the interior through the small window at the rear of the building on the half landing above me. All I can hear is the rain... but there it is again, that sound. Scott will be in bed by now, Chas in his room, probably gaming, certainly not studying, and Katie will be asleep.

Perhaps it is Deanna moving around, but she is in the basement and these houses are solidly built. The sound doesn't carry all the way up here. There it is again. It's not distinct voices or music, but there is an element of that. Edging out onto the landing, I peer down into the stairwell and I can see a bit of artificial light two floors below. Only Katie's bedroom and Scott's study are on that floor. Scott could be up late working, but he doesn't make sounds like this in his study.

I slowly walk down the stairs, peering into the gloom and looking to see where the light is coming from. It's creeping out from under Katie's door. She should be sound asleep by now. I feel a flash of anger stab at my chest, but I quell it. How many times has she stayed up like this without either me or Scott noticing? She knows full well her bedtime routine begins at eight and the rule is *lights out* by nine o'clock, nine thirty at the latest.

I'm tempted to listen at the door but even though I want to read her the riot act, I still wish to protect her privacy. I remember having none in my home when I was growing up, never knowing when either a sibling or my father was going to walk in on me. They didn't mean any harm, but all the same, I never felt like I had my own space and as a result, I've been adamant that I won't allow the same for my children. When they flagrantly breach the rules, though, it is very hard to keep to that promise.

I knock lightly on the door and when I hear nothing, I turn the handle and enter. Katie has her back to me, headphones on. Looking past her, I can see the screen of her tablet, propped up on a stand on her desk next to her laptop screen. She's on a video call with someone.

'Katie!'

She leaps in fright, turning to face me and pulling her tablet off the stand and knocking it face down with such a thud I think she must have cracked the screen. 'What are you doing?' she shouts. It's worse than I thought. She's wearing make-up and has spent time styling her hair since we ate this evening.

'What *are you* doing?' I counter as she tears off her head-phones, and gets up from her chair, moving to intercept me. 'Who are you talking to at this hour?'

'None of your business.'

'I'll have you know it's all of my business. What are you playing at? You know full well you're still grounded, banned from speaking to friends and using the internet, and you should be asleep. Now who was that?'

'No one!' she says, turning on me.

'It didn't look like no one.' I try to pass her and she steps across, blocking my path. I sidestep her and despite her best efforts, I reach for her tablet and pick it up.

'Hey! That's mine!'

The screen locks but I caught a glimpse of a woman from the call just before the call ended. 'Who was that woman?'

'What woman?'

Her petulance is irritating. I point at the screen. 'The woman you were talking to. Who was she?'

'No one.'

'Katie!'

'A friend—'

'At this hour? Which friend?'

'None of your business!'

I tap the home button and the password prompt comes up. I enter it. Denied. 'You changed your password code?'

'Yes, it's my tablet and—'

'We are supposed to have access to your tech, you know that. It's one of the rules.'

'Your rules, not mine!'

'House rules, and it may have escaped your notice, but this is my house.'

'It's Dad's house.'

I'm stunned by her attitude. 'How dare you. This is our family home. Now, Katie, I demand to know who you were talking to.' I'm defiant. I can be just as stubborn as she is, and besides that, I'm concerned about how she's altered her looks to make an impression on whoever it was.

I'm trying to remember what the woman looked like. For a second, I thought there was something familiar about her, but she didn't seem to be a teenager, and now I'm struggling to recall any details at all. I'm not even sure if it was a man or a woman. I think it was a woman but is that wishful thinking, my mind filling in the blanks? What if it's an older man? Could she be that stupid? She's still a child, even if she doesn't realise it. 'Katie, the world can be a dangerous place, and bringing someone into your bedroom, even via the internet, is a dangerous thing to do.'

'Oh, please! What do you take me for, an idiot?'

'Who was it?' I ask in my sternest voice. She folds her arms across her chest, but I can see she's not quite as steadfast as she'd like me to believe. She's nervous and that makes me nervous. 'Tell me, right now!'

She rolls her eyes which is usually enough to send me to the moon, but properly losing it will only make this situation worse. If that is at all possible. 'Argh, why can't you just respect my privacy? I have a life, you know.'

'You, young lady, are twelve years old. You're not supposed to be online at this time of the night talking to heaven knows who!'

'Oh, this is so typical of you!' She's yelling at me, and my voice has gone up a few notches, but hell, if I can't be angry about this then what hope is there for decent parenting in this world?

'Katie, you can't—'

'What, I can't have a life unless I run it past you first? Why do you have to control everything?'

'Because I'm your mum, and—' I feel someone next to me, brushing against my arm. If I wasn't so riled, I would have heard them approach. It's Chas, dressed in his ever-present pyjamas, and he looks at me before casting a somewhat bemused glance at his sister.

'What on earth is going on here then? Trying to wake the dead, are we?'

I turn to look at Chas. 'Not a time to be flippant, Charles.'

The smile disappears from his expression, and he looks away. 'If you're proper naming me, I think I'll go back to my room.' He makes to leave, and I try and stop him by grasping his sleeve but he's too quick, beating a hasty retreat.

'And you can get out, too!' Katie yells at me. Now Scott appears on the landing outside, cutting off Chas's escape, and he hurries to my side. He looks perplexed and tired, with heavy bags beneath his eyes. We must have woken him.

'What's going on?'

'That's what I would like to know,' I tell him, looking at Katie. 'But this little madam is playing up.'

'Get out!' she screams at me. There it is. This is the moment I'd been trying to avoid, and that ripple of anger, frustration and resentment is now tearing through me. How dare she behave like this.

'Just who do you think you are, talking to me like that?'

'Get out!'

'Katie, I will not have you speaking to me like this. You will show me proper respect. I am your mum—'

'No, you're not! You're not my mother, and you can get the hell out!'

Her words hit like a hammer blow to my chest.

I almost stumble as I take a step away from her.

She knows.

TWENTY-FOUR

I can see Scott looking behind me, but I'm transfixed on my daughter. Katie is staring at me, her eyes gleaming, burning with hatred and outright disgust, and she is aiming everything at me.

Scott moves past me but Katie takes a step away from both of us. 'Katie, why would you say such a nasty thing to your mum?' Scott asks steadily.

'She's not though, is she? She's not my mum, she just sleeps in my mum's bed.'

'Katie!' Scott's voice raises, but I can see him pause and take a breath. When he speaks again, his tone is back to being measured. 'That's no way to speak to your mum.'

'Stop saying that, Dad. She's not my mum and we all know it, so why carry on with the lies?'

I can feel the tears welling up now. My hands are trembling at my sides and I cup them together in front of me to try and stop it, but it doesn't work. I feel sick. The anger I had only moments ago has left me; everything has left me. Now I just feel hollow, as if my entire core has drained out of me, emptying onto the floor at my feet.

'W-Why... why are you saying this, Katie?' The words

tumble from my mouth, but we all know the indignation is nothing but a sham. Scott glances at me. How did it come to this? Who told her? Katie defiantly takes a step closer, catching both of us off guard.

'*Because it's true!*' she says with a sneer, the words dripping with venom.

'Katie,' Scott says coming between us just as I can feel myself shrinking away. 'Why ever would you think such a thing?'

'*She* said so!' Katie says, jabbing a finger in the air towards me. Scott stares at her, as do I, but she is unfazed, immovable, resolute. 'She told me. Are you telling me I shouldn't believe her?' Scott's gaze drifts around to me, disbelief written in his expression.

'I... No, I didn't—'

'Liar!' Katie screams, attempting to push past her father but she can't force her way through and Scott blocks her. 'You're a liar! My whole life is a lie!'

'No, no, that's not true, darling,' I say but I'm whispering, wilting in the face of her aggression. 'I am—'

'You told me! Say it! Say the truth, I dare you!' Katie screams and I can't. I can't stand here and argue with her. She knows. I don't know how she knows, but she is speaking the truth. Scott has both his arms spread wide. He's not seeking to restrain her, but he's keeping her from getting into my face and confronting me. 'Say it!' she demands, leaning around him, her face flushed, tears in her eyes.

'Katie, I love you. I love you so much.'

'Get out!'

Scott looks at me, and something passes unsaid between us. I retreat slowly, my legs feeling numb, then I turn and run from the bedroom out onto the landing, bouncing painfully off the door frame as I pass through. My chest has constricted, and I cannot breathe. I sink to the floor, burying myself into the corner of the landing where two walls meet at the top of the stairs. Collapsing into myself, I hug my knees and I'm crying. Great wracking sobs that I couldn't control even if I sought to.

Katie knows the secret we've kept from her all her life.

Did I really tell her, somehow? And if so, what else did I say?

What else does she know?

TWENTY-FIVE

DEANNA

So, here it is, the chaos I knew would come. The moment I've been waiting for.

It is delicious.

Clearly, no one knows quite how to react. Chas wants the ground to open up and swallow him whole, that's obvious. I've never known a teenager, so outwardly confident and self-assured, to be so timid in the face of an emotional reaction.

They haven't seen me yet, so I could just slink away back to my basement apartment and pretend I hadn't seen or heard anything. That would be the prudent thing to do, but I'm rather enjoying this.

Sophie turns to say something to Scott and I step back so she can't see me. She's shell-shocked. I guess she didn't see that coming, did she.

Then Scott looks past Sophie and does see me, followed soon after by Chas, who looks almost apologetic. Not that he has anything to be sorry about.

Is Scott displeased that I've witnessed this little family exchange or is he dumbstruck, much like his wife?

Sophie is acting like I'm not here, which is probably for the best. For my part, it's like watching a car crash happen in slow motion. One I saw coming. In fact, it's all unfolding exactly how I planned.

'Sorry,' I mouth silently as Scott momentarily holds my gaze. He tilts his head, acknowledging my apology. He's a picture of smouldering anger, but I'm sure that's not aimed at me.

I can see Katie has tears in her eyes, the poor thing. But it can't be helped. Chas turns and beats a hasty retreat, and I do the same.

Picking up the pace, I try to put a bit of distance between Chas and I, but his strides are a lot longer than mine.

Back on the ground floor, I round the newel post and head for the stairs to the basement. That's probably the safest place for me right now.

'Deanna?'

I stop and slowly turn to see Chas at the foot of the stairs, and I act like I didn't know he was behind me. 'Yes?' He looks awkward, avoiding making eye contact. 'Are you all right?' He shrugs. He's not all right and you don't need to be particularly adept at reading people to see it.

'Do you want a cup of tea?' he asks.

I don't really drink tea, at least not tea in the traditional British way. It's all those years living abroad. Coffee is more my thing.

'Do you have any chamomile?'

It's like I've asked him for something illicit. 'I can look.'

I smile. 'Okay.'

Chas returns my polite smile with a weak one of his own and walks past me into the kitchen. I follow, waiting as Chas goes into the pantry returning moments later with a small box containing a number of coloured boxes and foil packets. 'One of these will be chamomile, I'm sure,' he says as he begins rifling through. 'I know Martha always liked herbal teas.'

'Martha? She's the housekeeper, isn't she?'

Chas pauses his search momentarily, glancing up at me thoughtfully. 'She was, yes.'

'Not anymore?' I heard Sophie mention her by name earlier, but I've never met the woman.

'No, she had to go away. Something to do with her mother, or sister, or someone. I don't remember. Dad told me.'

'That's a shame. Will she be gone long?' Chas shrugs.

'Is this chamomile?' Chas asks, holding an open packet aloft triumphantly having removed the clip. There is nothing on the exterior of the foil and he hands it to me.

'That's peppermint.'

'Oh, is it? Are you sure?'

'Well, it smells of mint, which is a giveaway.'

'Ah, right. It does.'

I think Chas either smokes a bit of pot on the side, like many university first-year students or he's just naturally a bit spacey. 'Peppermint will be just fine.' His mood lightens and he smiles, moving to switch the kettle on. I point at it.

'What?' he asks.

'You need to put more water in there.'

Lifting the kettle, he examines the water gauge. 'Ah, right.'

I pull out one of the stools beneath the breakfast bar, the legs screeching a bit on the tiled surface, and climb onto it. 'Does this happen often?' I ask, lowering my voice.

'Katie's meltdowns?' Chas asks, taking two mugs from a high cupboard and setting them down in front of me. 'No, well, yes, but tonight was something else. I've never seen her that bad before.'

'She is young,' I say.

'Yes.' Chas makes a show of making tea, but his mind is elsewhere. 'I think we need to...'

I look over my shoulder. 'Need to what?'

He shakes his head. 'I don't know. Katie is going through a

lot, and they're giving her a really hard time. I don't think it's fair on her.'

'Sometimes life isn't fair though, is it?'

He nods slowly. Then he's holding my eye and he's as serious as I've ever known him to be. 'You might get more than you bargained for in coming here, Deanna.' I stare back at him, trying to gauge his meaning. Is that why he ushered me into the kitchen, to give me a warning?

If so, he has no idea what I am capable of.

TWENTY-SIX

SOPHIE

I don't know how long I've been here, slumped against the wall. I'm cold, so cold. Is that caused by shock? Perhaps. I don't want anyone to see me like this, but I don't want to move. I can't move.

'Sophie?'

My head snaps up. It's Scott. Where did he come from?

'Sophie? Can you hear me?'

I can hear him, but I can't speak, so I nod almost imperceptibly. Looking past him, I can see Katie's bedroom door is closed. Scott is crouching beside me, concern etched into his expression.

'It's not true,' I say quietly. 'It's not true. She is my daughter, in any way that matters.'

Scott looks down, breaking eye contact with me, pursing his lips and frowning. 'Why, Sophie? Why did you tell her?'

I shake my head firmly. 'I didn't. I swear I didn't.'

'She says you told her, that it came out when you were angry...'

'When? I couldn't have—'

Scott clamps his eyes firmly shut, shaking his head slightly. 'Back when she was suspended from school, last month.'

'I don't know, I don't know...'

'I don't understand how you could say that to her. We talked about this. The timing had to be right otherwise the damage it might do to her—'

'I know, I'm sorry,' I tell him, reaching out but he doesn't accept my hand, and instead he pulls away from me. 'I'm so sorry, Scott. I don't remember. Honestly. I'm so, so sorry.' He pinches the bridge of his nose, his forehead creased as he starts to get to his feet.

'How could you be so stupid? I mean, there's thoughtless and then—'

'I know, I'm sorry!' I'm blubbing now, properly wailing and I can't stop. 'Please, please don't leave me,' I say, clawing at Scott, desperate for him to tell me everything will be all right. He gets back down, allows me to put my arms around his neck. All I want is for him to kiss me, tell me we can make this right. But I can tell he's reluctant to feel my touch; his body is tense. At least he's not rejecting me, not yet anyway. 'I can make this right. I know I can.'

'How, Sophie?' he asks, and I can hear the regret, the sadness in his voice. 'How are you going to make this right?'

'I... I don't know but I will. Please forgive me. I'll do anything.'

He exhales heavily, his lips pursed. 'Okay. We'll find a way to fix this, somehow.'

I feel the tension in his shoulders soften fractionally and I lean forward, angling my face so I fall into his sight-line. 'I'm so sorry. Please believe me, I'm really, really sorry.'

He relents, sitting down on the floor beside me and, taking my hand in one of his, he draws me to him, putting his other arm around me and hugging me close. 'We'll find a way,' he repeats, making soothing sounds to me. I cling to him like a terrified child after a bad dream. Of all the things I could do to harm my family, this one is right up there.

And I don't even remember doing it.

TWENTY-SEVEN

DEANNA

Scott clears his throat as he walks into the kitchen, glancing around. Seeing Chas and I, he hesitates before coming over. Most of the lights are off, with only the three pendants hanging above the breakfast bar switched on. They are dimmed, ensuring we are softly lit.

'Are Katie and Sophie all right?' I ask, innocently.

Scott doesn't meet my eye. 'Chas, do you think I could have a moment alone with Deanna, please?'

'Sure,' Chas says, his eyes flicking across to mine, where they linger for a moment, and then he looks away again. 'It's late. I should head up to bed anyway.'

'Good idea. You have lectures tomorrow,' his father says without looking at him. Chas nods, although he's more sullen than I've ever seen him. I suspect he had more to say but his father coming down has quieted him.

'I've a long day tomorrow.'

'Chas,' I say as he makes to leave. 'You forgot your tea.'

'That's okay,' he says, turning and backing out of the room. 'I don't really want it anymore.' I smile and glance down at his untouched mug, steam rising gently. It's full of hot water and nothing else.

Scott slowly approaches me now, one hand gently rubbing his cheek and his chin. Although I can't read his expression, it's patently obvious he's lost, struggling to know what to say. I smile inwardly, feeling the power I hold, of being the only person in this household who has any control over the situation. 'I'm sorry for coming upstairs—'

'No, no, don't be,' he says, holding up a hand. 'I think that little episode caught all of us off guard. This is your home now, too, so—'

'I never wanted to intrude.'

He shakes his head. 'Don't worry. It's happened now, and' – he hesitates, his brow furrowing deeply – 'and it is what it is. A bit of a surprise, I don't mind telling you.'

'Yes, I can see that. Is Katie all right, do you think?' I repeat.

Scott sighs, folding his arms across his chest but not in a defensive pose, more like he's trying very hard to appear able to take this in his stride. To me, though, it has the opposite effect. He's cracking, weakening, I can see that. 'She's taken to barricading herself inside her room.'

'That sounds rough.'

Scott smiles but without humour; he looks pained. At last, an expression I can read. 'Barricaded is probably an exaggeration. She's wedged her chair beneath the handle. I could probably force my way in...'

'If you had to.'

He lifts his eyes to meet mine and nods, an unreadable expression crossing his face. 'Yes, if I had to.'

'And Sophie... is she—' Scott winces. 'Sorry, it's none of my business.'

'Well' – he draws breath – 'it is – while you're living under our roof – very much your business.'

'I don't wish to pry.'

'No, of course you don't,' he says. 'But I think you are owed an explanation—'

'You don't owe me anything...'

'Well, perhaps not, but I doubt you thought you'd be letting yourself into all of this' – he waves a hand in a circular motion in the air beside his head – 'when you agreed to work for us and certainly not when you agreed to move in.'

'All families have their...' His gaze narrows. 'Well, you know?'

'Their secrets?'

'Um, well, yes.' I'm making a great show of feeling very self-conscious, like I've overstepped. Quite frankly, I deserve an Academy Award.

'That's probably true. I think you should be aware of a few things, seeing as you witnessed tonight's' – he glances behind him and up, as if he can see through the floor up into Katie's bedroom – 'episode of the classic drama *The Mortons*.' I can't help a smile, and Scott cracks a wry smile of his own.

'Is it true then, what Katie said?' His smile fades and I think I've certainly crossed the line this time. I need to be careful, slow down. The last thing I need is to get myself fired, not when I've only just begun. 'Sorry, again.'

Scott pulls out a stool from beneath the breakfast bar and sits down beside me, resting his elbows on the counter. He frowns, carefully choosing his words and speaking in a very controlled and measured way. 'Katie's mum – her biological mother – passed away shortly after she was born.'

'Oh, that's so awful.'

Scott nods. 'Yes, it was a very traumatic time for all of us, not least Katie, although she'll have no memory of her mother now. As I say, she was very small at the time.'

'How did it happen?'

'She, er, it was very sudden. She...'

'Sorry, none of my business again.'

Scott exhales, drawing his hands down across his cheeks, ignoring my apology and taking a deep breath. 'The truth is, she took her own life. She went out to run a few errands, pick up a couple of things. Things I was supposed to be coming home with, and sometimes I wonder...' He shakes his head. 'Anyway, she never came home.'

'That's so sad.' I meet his eye, trying to show him that I empathise. That I'm on his side. 'Was she having a tough time, struggling with things?'

'Yes, you could say so.' Scott's taken on a faraway expression now, haunted even. 'My wife was a fragile creature, and she found day-to-day life challenging. Add to that the demands of a baby and it just got too much for her.'

'The poor thing, and for you and the children too.'

'Yes. It was a tough time.' Scott arches his eyebrows, looks at me and then away again. 'I don't like to think about it too often. It's too upsetting.'

'I'll bet. And Katie, she doesn't remember any of this?' Scott shakes his head. 'Then how does she know? About Sophie, I mean?'

Scott arches his eyebrows, seemingly genuinely confused. 'I really had no idea she knew.' He draws a deep breath, his lips pursed. 'Apparently, Sophie blurted it out to her in a... a... fit of rage!'

'No!' I exclaim, widening my eyes.

Scott inclines his head and nods. 'Yes, I'm afraid so.' I can hear the change in tone. He's not impressed with his wife at all. Understandable. Good. 'I can't believe she did it, I really can't.'

I pause. 'So, you met Sophie soon after your wife's passing?'

Scott snaps out of his reverie and exhales heavily. 'Yes, it was a bit like that, sort of. Sophie and I fell in love. I guess I was on the rebound,' he says, glumly. 'That sounds awful, I know, but I mean I was dealing with the emotions of it all and Sophie was there for me. We sort of found each other.' He looks at me.

'I know it all happened very quickly, but you don't get to choose when you meet people you fall for, do you?'

'No, that's true.'

'And we realised we were a good fit.'

'That's nice.'

He smiles. 'And she wasn't put off by my being a single parent with two children. I think a lot of people would have been, you know?' He fixes me with a look of consternation. 'We always planned to tell Katie someday, but when is the right time to deliver that kind of news?' He sighs. 'She knows now anyway, so it's all academic I suppose, and Sophie *is* Katie's mum in every other way. She's raised her, loved and cared for her as best she can, as any mother would. She is, by any measure, her mum. Even if she' – he looks away – 'struggles sometimes.'

The way Scott is able to articulate his thoughts so indirectly is rather telling. I can see how he came to be such a successful businessman. He would make a half decent politician if he ever chose to be one. 'I understand.'

'Do you?'

I'm taken aback by his tone suddenly. There's an edge to it, matched only by his piercing gaze. He's attempting to read me. I nod. 'Yes, I think so.'

His expression softens again. He looks tired now. Scott strikes me as the kind of guy who takes what is thrown at him, methodically working through the problems, and never gets flustered. Not yet anyway. 'Sorry, I didn't mean that to sound so harsh. It's just that Katie's outburst has thrown me off a little tonight and... all of us, to be honest. I'm sure you can appreciate just how traumatic it is.'

'Of course. It's a lot to take in. And children can be a challenge.'

'Yes, they can.' I reach across and place a hand gently on top of his, offering him a gentle, supportive squeeze.

He looks up and smiles, but he doesn't withdraw his hand,

and I leave mine where it is. I'm making progress, tonight. 'Thank you.'

'You're welcome. What do you think you'll do?' I ask him as I slowly withdraw my hand.

'Tonight, with Katie?'

I nod. He frowns and then shakes his head. 'I think I'll just leave her be for the night. I know she was out of order, but she is hurting. And I don't want to start making demands on her. I think she'll dig her heels in if I do that. She's a lot like her mum in that respect.'

'Sophie, you mean?'

He nods. 'Anyway, I think it's time I got some sleep. It'll be a long day tomorrow otherwise.' He slides off the stool and then frowns deeply. 'Damn.'

'What is it?'

'I forgot. I have a meeting at the office tomorrow morning. One of my producers is flying back from Ecuador and I promised to meet him straight after he lands. It'll be early. Sophie won't be home before I have to leave. Usually, Martha would watch Katie and—'

'I can take care of Katie before we start our lessons, if you like?'

He looks at me and I think he's about to cry; he's certainly emotional at least. 'Would you? If it's not too much of an imposition? It'd be a great help to me.'

'It's the least I can do after what you've done for me. I can take care of everything, breakfast, get her ready for studying, I mean, I'm here anyway, so why shouldn't I help?'

'It's above and beyond what we're paying you for though.'

'Nonsense. I'd be happy to help.'

'Thank you,' Scott says, visibly relaxing as if a weight has just been removed from his shoulders. 'You're very kind.'

'I'm happy to help and it might ease things in the morning for her to see a neutral face after, well, you know?'

'After what's happened tonight, yes, certainly. That wouldn't hurt at all. As long as you don't mind? I wouldn't want you to feel we were imposing on you. And Sophie will be home by ten o'clock, I should think.'

'Honestly, it's not a problem,' I tell him, holding both hands up before me. 'No problem at all. I'm pleased to be able to help.'

More than he can possibly know.

'Thank you, Deanna. I'm so glad you've come into our lives, and not just because you're going to get me out of a hole tomorrow!'

I beam at him. 'I'm pleased to be here too.'

Scott smiles and leaves the kitchen. It's all quiet and peaceful now. I am in my element, sitting in this gorgeous home, in a place where I have quickly become necessary. They need me; there's no going back now. And I am exactly where I want to be.

Who would have thought that a sprinkling of seeds can be sown and then, in a matter of a few short weeks, they can come to life in such dramatic fashion? I lift my mug and sip at the tea Chas made, savouring the taste.

Scott and Sophie have absolutely no idea who they've let into their home.

But before I'm through, they're going to know just how it feels to see everything they love destroyed before their eyes.

TWENTY-EIGHT

SOPHIE

Tuesday

The alarm vibrates, and eventually I'm roused from my sleep. It seems like only a moment ago that I was staring at the ceiling unable to sleep no matter what I tried to do. Scott insisted I go to bed when all I wanted to do was to be with Katie.

I feel empty inside. It feels similar to the day after suffering a migraine where the pain has eased, replaced by an emptiness of both mind and body. You feel detached and yet still present somehow. It's a really strange sensation.

I've never seen such hatred in my daughter's eyes, such utter disdain. We've fallen out before, indeed often in recent months, but this was entirely different.

At least with anger, frustration, screaming or shouting, you know it's coming from an emotional place and she is reacting to *me*. The argument matters. I matter. This time, though, it was different. All of those emotions were present but there was more; I was nothing to her. My place as her mum was of no value. *How did she find out? How could I have allowed myself to say such a thing out of anger? And then how did I forget?*

Throwing off the duvet, I stumble into the shower room on wobbly legs, taking off my watch and laying it down beside the basin. I dare not look at my reflection until I've woken up a little. I feel dreadful, so I must look even worse.

I set the water temperature a few degrees lower than normal. A cold hit will wake me up faster, get my blood pumping and the senses going. I just can't get the image out of my mind: Katie glaring at me as if I'm some kind of a threat. She *is my daughter*, and I don't need a DNA match for that to be true. I feel it in my heart. I guess that's why it hurts so much.

I don't feel much like wearing the outfit Deanna helped me put together yesterday, but that's probably exactly why I should. If it was left to me, I'd wear my baggiest hoodie, a pair of joggers and I'd hide for the rest of the day beneath a blanket on the sofa.

I can't remember the last time I wore this dress, but it certainly turned heads and Scott couldn't wait to get me out of it when we arrived home that night. The boots are heavier than I'm used to wearing. I wore them often in the past, but Scott doesn't like them because it makes me so much taller than him. It will be good to get some wear out of them again. They still look brand new.

Presenting myself in front of the mirror, I have to admit, I look fantastic. If you don't pay attention to the telltale signs around my eyes of a fraught night's sleep anyway. Despite feeling tighter, I actually think the dress looks better on me now than it did before. I'll certainly catch the eye, which is what Sam and those above him want.

Admiring myself in the mirror, I think there's something missing, but I can't remember what. Never mind, Saif isn't here yet and with a bit of luck, I'll remember in time.

'You'll do, Sophie Beckett. You'll do,' I tell myself as I turn side on to the mirror, checking myself out. I haven't felt good about how I look in so long that this is a welcome, very pleasant change. Then Katie comes to mind again, and the hint of positivity I had evaporates. 'Come on, Sophie, pull yourself together. One thing at a time.'

Making my way downstairs, I half expect to find Katie on the landing, waiting for me. But she isn't. I try her door and I'm pleased to find the chair beneath the handle has been set aside allowing the door to open. Peering through it into the darkness, I can see she's sound asleep in her bed, an arm across Tiggy, the cuddly tiger she still sleeps with every night. A sense of guilt hits me. 'I'm so sorry, darling,' I whisper.

Retreating from the room, I head downstairs, taking care because the heels on these boots are high and I'm out of practice. Usually I'm in flats.

At the foot of the stairs, I think I hear something coming from the kitchen, but the lights are off and the ground floor is in darkness. It must be my imagination, hearing things that aren't there. I'm certainly on edge. As I'm focusing my attention on the open door into the kitchen, I feel a pain in my chest and I realise I'm holding my breath. Releasing it, I edge towards the kitchen but yes, it is my imagination. There's no one in there.

Everything has been cleared away. I know I didn't do it. Scott must have cleared everything up. My eyes are used to the dark now and despite the cold shower, my head is still in a bit of a fug so I don't switch the lights on. Walking through to the front of the house, I crack open the shutters and look out onto the street. Saif still isn't here and I check my watch. He's running late. He's never late.

Turning, I gasp and my heart skips. A figure is standing there. Deanna steps into what little light the open shutters offer, looking at me without speaking.

'Deanna...'

'Sorry, I didn't mean to startle you.'

'Startle me? You scared the hell out of me!'

'Sorry,' she repeats.

'What are you doing here?'

'I live here now, Sophie.'

'I meant at this hour?'

'I couldn't sleep. Would you like something to eat or drink? I could make it for you, if you like?'

'N-No, thank you.'

She smiles briefly, looking around the kitchen. 'I cleaned up for you last night.'

'Oh, so it was you. Thank you.' I walk forward, slowly, but Deanna's blocking my route. There's something very odd about her expression and I'm wondering if she's sleepwalking. 'Sorry, do you mind if I get past you?'

'No, you go ahead, please.' Deanna steps aside.

'Do you often have trouble sleeping?'

'No, not usually. I've not been able to get myself straight since I got back.' She shrugs. 'Staying in a hostel doesn't help. No one keeps regular hours in that place. It's chaos.'

That makes sense, I suppose. 'Yes, of course.'

She narrows her gaze, studying me. 'You're not wearing the pendant.'

'What?' I ask, reaching to my neckline. That was it. Saif isn't here. I have time, although negotiating the stairs in these boots again? I could take the lift but I'm not a fan of confined spaces, never have been. I was trapped in that lift for almost eight hours once and I've refused to use it ever since. 'It'll have to wait until next time.'

'No, don't say that. It really caps off the outfit!'

'I know, you're right,' I say, wincing as I look at the stairs.

'Is it the boots?'

I laugh. She doesn't suggest I take the lift, thankfully. I'm embarrassed to tell people I'm scared to stand in a lift for thirty seconds. 'Yes, that's it exactly.'

'I'll go, if you want? I know where it is, still on your dresser in the guest room?'

I'm ready to say no, and Saif's car has just pulled up outside.

I can see the headlights illuminating the park opposite. 'I'm not sure I have time—'

'I'll go! I'll be super quick.'

'Yes, okay, if you can, but please hurry.'

As I wait for her, I put my coat on, open the door and wave to Saif, just to let him know I've seen him and he waves back before getting out of the car, standing beside it.

Deanna returns, smiling warmly with the pendant in her hand. I lift my hair aside and she puts the delicate chain around my neck.

'There,' she says, standing back. 'Gorgeous.'

I can't help but smile. Instinctively, I reach out and grasp her hands in mine. 'Thank you.'

'You're welcome. And don't worry, they're going to love the new you.'

I smile again and nod. I needed that little confidence booster. 'Thank you.'

'And,' Deanna says as I make to leave, 'don't worry about last night. All families have their moments. Don't think too much about it today.' My little flame of confidence is extinguished in that moment and that must be obvious in my face as Deanna looks surprised and then concerned.

'Last night?' I don't know if I should be embarrassed or angry. I didn't know she heard or saw us. Did Scott speak to her afterwards? Deanna is standing before me, confident, unfazed by my awkwardness. What business is it of hers anyway?

'Sorry, maybe I shouldn't have brought it up. I'm sure once everyone's slept on it, everything will be fine.'

I feel my face flushing. 'Yes, you're right. I have to go.'

'Of course,' Deanna says, stone-faced.

She hands me my bag and I step out into the night air. Saif is still waiting beside the car for me but he's looking past me and towards the house.

I look over my shoulder, Deanna is there watching me leave,

framed by the painted woodwork of the doorway architrave and the soft glow from the interior light behind her.

I wave and she slowly lifts a hand in return, then she closes the door. I turn back to the car. Saif, his arms folded defiantly across his chest, is staring up at the house. He hasn't offered to open the door for me as he usually does.

'Saif?' He doesn't flinch; he doesn't even blink as he stares straight ahead. 'Are you okay?'

He snaps out of it and looks at me, a strange expression on his face, and then he smiles broadly. 'I'm fine, Miss Sophie.' Lowering his arms, he opens the door for me, closing it once I'm sitting inside and walking around to the driver's side.

'You have a new friend?'

I meet Saif's gaze in the mirror. He's never asked me a question about my home life before, ever. 'You mean Deanna?' He doesn't reply but maintains the eye contact for a few seconds longer until he has to negotiate a set of upcoming traffic lights where the road narrows. 'She's my daughter's new tutor.'

'You know her?'

'No, not really. For a few days.' I look into the mirror and he's still looking at me.

'And she is in your house now?'

'Yes,' I say, remembering Scott's insistence on letting Deanna stay. Something about his concern has elevated mine. 'Why do you ask?'

'In my country we are very hospitable,' Saif says, concentrating on the road now. 'But we are wary about strangers we welcome in the house. People... can be frightening. We can't always trust them.'

'I'm sure she's fine, Saif.'

His eyes flicker up to the mirror again. I'm not fooling him, or myself. Saif doesn't say another word until we reach the studio.

'Have a good day, Miss Sophie,' he says, holding the door open for me as I get out.

'Thank you, Saif. You too.'

TWENTY-NINE

DEANNA

It feels special to be in a family home, once again. I've wanted this for so long. I was up and dressed before dawn, enjoying a cup of coffee on the terrace as the sun rose. There is something about that time of the day, where I am at peace. I know what I will be doing; I have it all planned. It's like lining up for the start of a race, only not everyone knows it's about to begin. I'm already out of the blocks before they know the race is on.

For many people, the morning seems to stress them out, running from room to room in search of everything they need: the misplaced wallet, car keys, or that list you scribbled out late the previous night.

For me, though, it is emblematic of a life worth living. Everyone has somewhere to be, a purpose to be fulfilled. Just like me. I've prepared everything, left nothing to chance. All I need to do is follow the steps. The finishing line is in sight.

Scott enters the kitchen looking just as I expected. He's sporting a navy three-piece suit with a crisp white shirt beneath, all immaculately pressed. It is a tailored slim fit and he's chosen to forsake the tie, his collar open to the first button, revealing a glimpse of a tanned chest. His features are supremely groomed, as is his shock of wavy hair. It's like he's just stepped out of a magazine shoot for a high-end fashion house. He must be the envy of almost every man he meets and an object of desire for most women.

His eyes light up as he spies the breakfast table. I've laid it out as we found it every day when we lived in Buenos Aires. There was an expectation placed on all the staff who lived and worked in the Puerto Madero neighbourhood, and if you failed to meet it then you wouldn't work there for very long.

The table was covered with a pristine white cloth, folded at the corners and pinned beneath, out of sight. Breakfast plates, bowls and side plates were set out for every member of the family, along with glasses for water and freshly squeezed fruit juices, available from a chilled jug. A wicker breadbasket that I found in the pantry was placed in the centre of the table as well, with a variety of sliced offerings.

Now, not everything was readily available in the Morton house, but I made do and compromised where I could.

'Good morning, Dad,' Katie says from her place at the table. She is already eating her bowl of Cheerios, and I have toasted a slice of bread for her with strawberry jam. Not the healthiest of breakfasts, but sometimes children just need to be eating first thing in the morning. We can always look to improve the nutritional offering at a later stage.

'Um, good morning, darling,' Scott says, smiling at me. Katie looks back to her food and Scott shoots an unspoken query towards me. I shake my head almost imperceptibly. He crosses to where she is sitting and leans down to kiss the top of her head in greeting. 'What is all this?' he asks, looking at me.

I shrug. 'It's always good to start the day well, wouldn't you say?'

'Yes, absolutely.'

'Good,' I tell him, hurrying over and pulling out the chair opposite Katie and ushering him into it.

'Now, sit here and relax, chat with your daughter while I get your breakfast.'

'There's no need for you to go to all this—'

'It's fine, Scott. I know you have a busy morning, and so I've taken care of everything.'

'Okay,' Scott says, cracking a smile. 'Then, I'll leave it to you.'

He turns to face Katie while I bring a pan of hot water back to the boil. I've already oiled the cling film, draped it across two ramekins and broken the eggs into them. Wrapping them, I reduce the heat and lower the eggs into the simmering water.

'She's making you your favourite,' Katie tells her father in a hushed tone.

'And who told her what my favourite is?'

'That'd be telling,' Katie says, spooning another mouthful of Cheerios into her mouth.

'How are you feeling this morning, Katie?'

She lifts her head and shrugs as she meets his eye. 'I'm okay.'

He nods slowly. I try to make myself look busier than I am. There's an elephant in the room, and it is the incident last night. 'Did you sleep okay?'

Katie angles her head but doesn't answer. She's avoiding her father's gaze now.

'You know, about last night...' I see Katie hesitating over her food, twirling the spoon in her hand. 'I think it's important that we clear the air, and don't let things fester.' He glances at me and I pretend not to be listening, but I am, obviously. How is he going to handle this? 'I'm sorry, Katie.'

Katie's head snaps up to look at him. 'Sorry? What for?'

Scott frowns, lips pursed. 'Sorry that Sophie said such a thing to you. Your mother is not quite herself at the moment and she can say things that she doesn't mean.' He holds her gaze. 'Things that aren't necessarily true.' I have to admit, I'm rather surprised at this approach. 'Your mum is having a tough time—'

'Are you actually telling me it isn't true?' Katie asks, sitting forward and staring hard at her father, gauging his sincerity perhaps. He tilts his head in reply. 'Really, you're telling me she was lying?'

'She is your mother, I promise you. I don't know why she said what she did. Like I said, she's having a tough time and when adults – anyone – are struggling they can say, and do, things that seem at odds to good judgement, or even common sense.' He holds her eye, looking earnest. 'Do you understand what I'm saying? Nobody is perfect.'

'Yes, sort of.'

Scott nods approvingly. 'Just cut your mum a bit of slack, could you?' He holds his hands up in a gesture of supplication. 'I know what she said is unforgivable, and it wasn't true. But it wasn't calculated or said with malicious intent. She—'

'Is having a tough time.'

'That's right. And I am sorry. I know your mum will be too.'

Katie pauses, staring at the table in front of her. 'Okay.' She nods and Scott's demeanour relaxes, if only a little.

'Thank you for understanding, darling. I appreciate it.' Turning his attention to breakfast, he picks up a napkin and lays it across his lap. 'You know, you didn't have to go to this amount of trouble.' He is speaking to me now and I look over as if unsure he's addressing me. 'All of this,' he says with a sweeping gesture of his hand.

'It's no trouble, honestly. This is how I lived growing up.'

'Oh, where was that?'

'All over, my father worked abroad a lot, so we travelled.'

'Mine too. Your father, he always took you with him?'

I shrug. 'Mostly, but not always.' The toaster pops up.

Chas walks in, sweeping his floppy hair away from his eyes as he looks around. His dishevelled appearance has been meticulously cultivated, I am quite certain. It's the fashion among teenagers now. His eyes light up. 'What's all this?'

I look at him blankly. 'Breakfast. Take a seat.'

'Damn right, I will,' he says, hurrying to join his sister and father at the table.

'You're up early,' Scott says to him. Chas smiles. He doesn't share his father's physical stature and their smile is very different too.

'I smelled food and came to investigate. It's an evolutionary throwback.' Chas throws a comforting arm around his sister as he sits down. She leans into him. The bond between the siblings is clear despite the age difference. That simple gesture tells Katie that her brother both loves her and is there for her. They're good kids. They deserve the right mother.

'Come to think of it, you're all up early. I rarely see either of you if I'm heading out for an early meeting,' Scott says.

'Yeah,' Chas says through a mouthful of toast, 'but now Martha isn't here, you have to go out later.'

'Not anymore,' I say, coming to stand behind Chas and placing a gentle hand on his shoulder.

'Sounds good to me. You can stay as long as you like,' Chas says much to his father's embarrassment, judging from the withering look he offers his son.

'Please pay no attention to my waste of space of a teenage son, Deanna.'

'Hey!' Chas says with mock indignation. 'Waste of space, future lifesaver and specialist surgeon.'

'Hmm, yet to be proven, but I certainly hope so.' Scott looks to me. 'You are, of course, welcome to stay with us as long as you like, Deanna, but you don't need to do all of this every day.'

'Noted,' I say, smiling and touching him gently on the shoulder before hurrying back to the hob to rescue the eggs.

'Well.' Scott frowns as I'm walking towards him. Coming to stand beside him, I slide the plate before him, poached eggs on toast and smoked salmon. He glances down at it and then up at me, smiling. 'Thank you, Deanna. This looks great!'

'You're welcome.' I hurry back to the counter, returning with a small jug of Hollandaise sauce. 'I hope you'll enjoy it. I'm sorry, I didn't have time to make the sauce from scratch.'

Scott laughs. 'There's no need to apologise, this is all incredible.'

'I can make you something too, Chas. What would you like?'

He fixes me with an optimistic look. 'A little scrambled egg wouldn't go amiss.'

'Coming right up!'

Chas sits back, grinning, looking between his sister and father. 'I like her. I like her a lot.'

'Well, Deanna is not here to wait on you, or the rest of us, for that matter.' Scott looks over at me as he says that and I wink at him. He wipes his mouth with the napkin and places it neatly alongside his plate before rising. 'I'm afraid I won't be able to finish it, delicious as it is, Deanna. I really must get into the office for that meeting but thank you for making such an effort.'

'That's no trouble, Scott.' I look over my shoulder toward the pantry. 'I can see you're missing some things. There's a list on the fridge door. Would you like me to pop out and take care of it later?'

Scott frowns. 'I thought Sophie went out for that lot yesterday.'

'I checked, and there isn't much from the list in the fridge or in the pantry.'

'You don't need to do our shopping. Sophie will take care of it—'

'Okay, but I think she has a lot on her plate right now. She seems very burdened.'

Scott sighs. 'That's true, I can't lie.'

That's a bit rich bearing in mind the conversation he's just had with his daughter.

'Then let me help. I can duck out to the shops later while Katie prepares for her spot exam.'

'I have an exam?' Katie asks, dejected.

'Yes, but don't worry. I'm just trying to assess where you are at. It will help me plan our lesson schedules.'

'You are very organised,' Scott says, coming to stand beside me and placing his plate down on the counter. The knife and fork are aligned perfectly at six o'clock.

I shrug. 'I like to be organised. It makes life so much more efficient.'

'I agree completely. You're a woman after my own heart.'

'Thank you,' I say, blushing. I see Chas raise a solitary eyebrow in our direction.

'And thank you for breakfast, I mean it.'

'So, do you want me to go to the shops for you?'

'Only if you don't mind.'

'It's no imposition, honestly.'

Scott smiles and takes his wallet from his back pocket. He produces a number of credit cards and selects one. Passing it to me, he says, 'I tend not to carry cash. The PIN code is 4031. If you have any trouble using it, just give me a call at the office.' He also hands me a business card bearing his mobile number. 'I'll call in on a cashpoint on the way home and get that advance you asked for.'

'Thanks,' I say, holding the card aloft before tucking it into my back pocket. Another point to me. 'Any problems, I'll call.'

Scott smiles, returning to the table to kiss Katie goodbye on the top of her head. 'Thanks for being so grown up about last night,' he says to Katie and she smiles slightly. Scott then nods at Chas, who returns it with a similar gesture. Public displays of male affection are clearly not the done thing in this house.

As Scott walks past me, he brushes my forearm with his fingertips. 'Have a good day.'

'I will,' I say, smiling warmly, 'you too.' That touch of his speaks volumes. To the unsuspecting it looks casual, friendly, but I know better. He wants to present himself that way, fearing perhaps that his family will see inside his head. And make no mistake, I am in his head. Scott wants me to know he appreciates me. He is approaching the line, and now I just have to lure him across it.

THIRTY

DEANNA

It doesn't take long for Chas to finish off the plate of scrambled eggs I made for him, along with the last of the smoked salmon I found in the fridge.

How easy it is to integrate yourself into someone's life always surprises me. People who struggle to make friends or join established friendship groups amaze me. Some say to be yourself, but I'd argue there's a much easier way. Just be what they want you to be. Be what they expect you to be.

I can see Katie keeping half an eye on the clock. She's nervous, and I'm sure that has nothing to do with the little exam I have prepared for her. She's already thinking ahead to when Sophie walks through the door at her usual time. Chas gets up and brings his empty plate over to the dishwasher, loading it into the machine rather than leaving it on the side. For a teenager who is supposed to be feckless and absent-minded, he's actually not too bad. He seems to have a lot of his father in him, conditioned to clean up after himself. Either that or he's trying hard to impress me.

'Is everything all right, Katie?' She glances over at me and at the same time she can't help herself and looks past me to the wall-mounted clock.

'Sure.'

'Really?'

Katie shrugs but it's a forced gesture, bravado in the face of the coming storm. Chas returns to the table and puts an arm around his sister. She leans into him and they hug. He is saying something to her, but he's lowered his voice so only she can hear it. Then he pulls back and Katie smiles at him, nodding slightly. What a good brother he is.

'Right!' Chas says, drawing himself upright. 'Time to crack on. We all good here?'

Katie nods again.

'Thanks for breakfast,' Chas says to me, striding from the kitchen.

'You're welcome. Have a great day.'

I finish rinsing the pan and add the remaining debris from my food preparation to the waste bin and the dishwasher, drying my hands on a tea towel. Folding it neatly before laying it down on the counter I walk over to where Katie is absently toying with her fountain pen, staring at the revision notes I gave her earlier. She's not actually reading them though. I perch myself on the edge of the table, hands resting on my thighs, smiling down at her.

'It's going to be okay, you know?' She lifts her head with a look that demonstrates she couldn't believe me less if she tried. 'It will, trust me.'

'I said some awful things last night.'

I nod. 'Yes, I heard.'

'Did Dad tell you?'

'I was there.'

'You were?'

'On the stairs just below the landing. I came to see what the fuss was all about.'

Katie shakes her head. 'Dad won't have liked that. He doesn't like us airing our dirty laundry.'

'Don't worry, I can manage your father. And it is quite normal for someone not to like their private family matters being openly discussed in front of strangers.'

'You're not a stranger.'

This brings a smile to my face. I've made a connection with Katie. I've won her trust. 'Thanks.'

'I mean it. I can count on you, I know it.'

'What about your mum? Can't you count on her too?'

'I've always been able to, in the past. But things are different now; they've changed.'

'But your dad said—'

'I don't care what he said,' Katie tells me. 'Everything's changed, and I don't trust her anymore.'

'Can you...'

'Can I what?' she asks.

'Make an effort for a little bit longer? Maybe try not to make too many waves? I promise you, it's going to work out. You just need to hold on for a bit. You can trust me.'

She shrugs.

'It will be okay,' I tell her, placing a supportive hand over hers. 'You'll see. I'll be right here the whole time, and we'll get through it together.' Her expression softens then and she smiles weakly.

'I shouldn't have said the things I said last night.'

'It wasn't wise, no.'

Katie is glum. 'She must hate me.'

'I doubt that. From what I've seen, Sophie loves you very much.'

'If you say so.'

. . .

We both hear the front door open, and Katie shoots a nervous glance my way as I smile reassuringly back.

'Morning!' I say, trying to be upbeat but not overly so as Sophie comes into the kitchen, walking stiffly, eyes scanning the room. Katie keeps her head down, focusing on her revision. Sophie looks over at her, her gaze lingering, but Katie doesn't react. 'How was the show? Did they like your new style?'

Sophie's expression softens then. She's nervous too, I can tell. 'Yes, they loved the style. I think Sam was over the moon.'

'Sam?'

'The producer. He's been the mouthpiece for channelling the thoughts of the higher-ups who want change.'

'Oh, and he was pleased?'

Sophie nods and shoots me a genuine smile now. 'Loved it, yes.'

I clap my hands gleefully, grinning. 'I'm so pleased for you!'

Sophie reaches out and takes my hands in hers. 'Thank you. It was your idea, after all. At some point, you're going to have to help me with some more selections.' She looks down, appraising herself. 'I can't wear this every day.' Her eyes dart across the room back toward Katie, who still has her head down, attempting to look like she's studying. I think we both know she isn't. 'How is...'

'We've had a great morning so far, haven't we, Katie?' She nods but doesn't look up. 'Do you want to show your mum what we have lined up for today?' Katie shrugs.

'Maybe later then,' Sophie says, and I can hear the disappointment in her voice. Katie, stoic and silent at the table, quickly gets up, gathering her study materials together and shoves them into the little backpack she uses for her schoolwork. 'Katie, darling...'

Katie swings the backpack over her shoulder and crosses the kitchen, keeping her head down and avoiding eye contact with Sophie. 'I'm going to revise in my room.' As she approaches us,

Sophie thinks about intercepting her, and I see her inching to her left into Katie's path. This will be interesting.

'Katie,' Sophie says, reaching out to touch her daughter's arm. Katie flinches, snatching the arm away and avoiding the contact. 'Katie, please,' Sophie says, her arm still extended.

'Leave me alone!'

'But' – I hear the exasperation in Sophie's voice, threatening to crack with the emotional strain – 'what about your studies?' It's a lame response but I guess she has nothing else if Katie won't engage.

'Don't care.'

'Don't walk away from me, Katie!' There's the flash of that anger, that fierce rage I always knew was somewhere in her. Buried, waiting to come out again.

Katie responds by turning to face her, petulance darkening her expression.

'What?' she asks defiantly. Sophie flounders.

'I... I...'

'Is that it?' Katie asks. 'Really. You've got nothing to say?'

'I'm sorry.'

'Sorry for what? Dad spoke to me earlier.'

'Oh, he did? What did he...? What did he say?'

'He said you were lying to me.'

Sophie seems startled. 'No, I wouldn't lie to you. You have to believe me when I say I've only ever acted in what I thought was your best interest.'

'Oh, is that right? So either you were lying to me then or Dad's lying to me now. Which is it?'

'I...'

'Because it can't be both, *Mum*. Did you send Dad to lie to me, to cover for you? To clean up a lie with another lie?'

Sophie's mouth opens and she looks to me. I could excuse myself and give them their much-needed space. Most people probably would, but I'm not going anywhere.

I must admit, I didn't expect Scott's attempt to pacify Katie to unravel this quickly. Katie is vehement in her stance and I admire her courage. Sophie takes a step closer, reaching out to Katie.

'Your father, what exactly has he said?' Sophie asks, shaking her head.

Katie stares hard at her and then tilts her head to one side. 'I can't believe you pretended to be my mum. You disgust me.'

With that said, Katie turns and leaves without waiting for a reply.

'But I am your mum,' Sophie says and I can see her welling up as we watch Katie leave. Katie stops at the foot of the stairs and looks back, only at me though. 'Give me a call when you're home from the shops and I'll come down.' The change in her tone, from visceral to matter-of-fact, ice cold in its delivery, is quite something.

Sophie is taking rapid, sharp intakes of breath. I think she's bordering on hyperventilating. She stumbles to her left and luckily I am there to catch her and prop her up against the breakfast bar.

'Sophie, are you okay?' She doesn't reply, still staring at the hallway and where Katie had been standing. 'I'll get you some water.' I guide her to the table. I don't think I should sit her down on one of the stools, fearing she'll topple off.

I fetch her a glass of water and bring it back to her. She's looking pale, fatigued, sitting with her hands in her lap. Vacant. Lost. A familiar expression. 'Here you go,' I say, putting the glass in her hand but she doesn't acknowledge it, let alone take a sip. 'Sophie?' I ask, crouching before her, and she looks at me, eyes wide.

'She hates me.'

To be fair, it's hard to argue. 'She'll come around.'

Sophie shakes her head. 'No, she won't. I've ruined it.'

'Ruined what?'

'Everything.'

I pull out the seat next to her and sit down. Sophie doesn't seem to notice me. 'Listen, children can say the most horrible things, but they rarely ever mean them.'

'Oh, she means them. Did you not see it in her eyes?'

'Yes, but she's hurting, and she'll try to hurt you just as much, if not more, to try and make herself feel better. It's a bad strategy, but it's what people do.'

'What was she saying about Scott? Do you know?'

I do, obviously. Not that I'm going to say. That's something she needs to take up with her husband. I'd like to be a fly on the wall when that happens.

This couldn't have played out better for me, if I'm honest. Katie is pushing all the right buttons and I couldn't have set it up any better myself.

'How was Scott this morning?'

'Scott? Fine, absolutely fine,' I say. 'Why do you ask?'

'Oh, it's nothing really.'

I can see that it is something, really. 'He was on good form. We had a lovely breakfast, the four of us.'

'You did? All of you?'

That's upset her; I can hear it in her voice and see it in her face. 'Yes, it was very pleasant. I made Scott breakfast and then Chas joined us too.'

'And Katie?'

'Of course. She was a little subdued but lightened up after a while. As I say, it was lovely.'

'Oh, I see.' Her expression clouds. 'Scott never normally joins them for breakfast. Martha usually sorts out the children.'

'Is Martha coming back anytime soon?'

Sophie's brow creases and she thinks hard. 'I'm not sure. I can't recall her saying what to expect.'

'Scott will know.'

She looks at me with a faraway expression. 'Yes, probably.'

'Are you sure you're feeling all right, Sophie?' I ask her, looking into her eyes. Her pupils don't look right to me.

'I just have another headache. I've not been sleeping well lately.'

'It's the odd hours, I suspect, plus a bit of family drama doesn't help. Shall I make you a coffee?'

'Um, I don't know. I might go for a lie-down.'

'Oh, okay. I was hoping you would watch Katie for me while I pop out.'

'Where do you need to go?' Sophie asks before laughing at her own question. 'I'm sorry, I can't believe I just put an obstacle in the way of watching my own daughter. Of course I'll stay with her if you have somewhere you need to be.'

'I'm just going out to the shops to get a few things for the house.'

'There's no need,' Sophie says, looking past me into the pantry. 'I went yesterday and got what we need.'

'Oh, really? Only...'

'What?'

'I read down the list pinned to the fridge and well, I couldn't see a lot of it.'

'That's impossible,' Sophie says, brushing past me and hauling the fridge door open. She scans the interior, shaking her head. Closing the door, she strides into the pantry and then reappears moments later, a mixture of bemusement and anger in her expression. 'I don't understand.'

'What is it?'

'I went to the shop yesterday and I got everything on my list, well, almost everything, but it's not there. I don't understand.'

'Maybe you missed a few things,' I say, trying to be kind.

'I didn't *miss* anything!'

'Sorry, I don't mean to offend you.'

She looks at me and her expression changes. She's not angry

now, more confused. She goes to her handbag, rifling through its contents. 'It's okay. I thought... maybe I didn't get everything.'

'What are you looking for?' She pauses her fruitless search, looking at me, confused.

'The receipt. It should be in my bag.'

'And it's not?'

She shakes her head. 'I could have sworn I...'

'The weather was bad and you'd been working,' I tell her, doing my best to reassure her. 'We can all get confused and forgetful, caught up in our busy lives.'

'Y-Yes, that's true.'

'Or maybe you left a bag at the shop. That happens! They'll keep a note of things left behind. You should ask next time you're in there.'

'Yes,' she says, looking ready to cry. 'I should.'

'Anyway, if you can keep an eye on Katie, I'll be back as soon as I can.'

'Okay, yes. Of course.'

'She's just doing some last-minute study for an exam I'm giving her. Tell you what, I'll make you a cup of coffee. It might perk you up.'

'I... I... okay, yes. Thank you,' Sophie says, staring straight ahead.

She's already falling apart.

And it's only just started.

THIRTY-ONE
SOPHIE

My mind is reeling over Katie's words. The pain in her face, the hurt I've caused her. I watch Deanna, who is making me a cup of coffee. She's proved something of a godsend, even if I'm perturbed by how comfortable she is in my home, or is it more how comfortable everyone else is around her? She makes it all seem so effortless. Martha could do that too, but she didn't have the emotional connections that the family, and Katie especially, have forged with Deanna.

I remember how it was when I came into this family all those years ago. Scott was already a very successful man working in the media, a young wife and a new baby to cope with on top of his work. Chas was a precocious prospective tearaway even back then. He hasn't changed much over the years, as it happens. When you get to know him, you see how sweet and lovely a young man he is, but there has always been that hint that if he ever decided to forego his studies, then he could go off the rails in one way or another. Thankfully, I still think he'll make it. And if Chas wanted to go wild then I'm certain he'd do it in style.

Her present issues aside, Katie has grown into such an intelligent, beautiful young lady, and she really didn't have the best start in life. Her mum, Cecilia, was struggling from the moment they brought Katie home and Scott desperately wanted to alleviate the burden the newborn baby was putting upon his wife. That is where I came in.

What did I know about looking after a baby? Nothing, as it turned out. I had no nieces or nephews, no experience of being around children, but I threw myself into it. The job was my last-ditch chance of staying in the country. The ski season was over and the demand for staff cleaning the chalets and serving drinks was coming to an end for another year. I'd have no option other than to fly home, and that meant home, home. Not just the UK, but back up north. I'd left with a few hundred pounds in my pockets and I wasn't relishing the prospect of heading back.

Don't get me wrong, I have a deep affinity to where I'm from, a lovely place and great people, but I couldn't see myself finding work in the town or travelling into Manchester or elsewhere every day. I wanted more, something different to what all my friends, and my siblings, were already doing.

So, when I was introduced to Scott one evening by a mutual acquaintance, and we made small talk and conversation shifted to home life, I saw an opening. I didn't pursue it, but Scott made the suggestion and I bit his arm off. I didn't know where it would lead though, and never would I have thought it would bring me to where we are today.

'Sophie?'

Deanna is standing before me. I must have drifted away for a moment. 'Sorry, what did you say?'

'Here's your coffee,' she says, handing me a cup. 'I wasn't sure how you take it, so I didn't add milk or sugar.'

'Thanks, it's fine just as it is.' I move to take the cup and we both flinch, bumping hands and the cup tilts, splashing hot coffee down my front. The heat is a shock, and I yelp. Deanna is horrified, quickly putting the cup with what remains inside it down and grabbing a tea towel from the counter, then frantically dabbing at my chest and lap to absorb the liquid.

Fortunately, the dress material is thick and I'm not scalded. '*I am so, so sorry!*' Deanna says, wiping down my front, dabbing at the material to try to limit the potential for staining.

'It's okay, don't worry...'

'But your dress, it might be ruined!'

'It's fine. It'll be okay. It was just the shock.'

'I'm such a clumsy oaf,' Deanna says.

'It'll wash out.'

'Look what I've done. That'll have to be spot cleaned immediately, or taken to the dry-cleaner's.'

'We can sort it, don't worry,' I tell her.

'Don't worry about what?' We both look round to see Scott standing at the entrance to the kitchen, his jacket across his forearm and briefcase in the other hand. Neither of us heard him come in. 'What's all this?' he asks, looking at us both with a half-smile.

'I'm a clumsy idiot,' Deanna says and Scott frowns. He looks at me and I shake my head.

'Just a minor spillage of coffee. It was an accident, no one's fault.'

His eyes drift to my dress and he looks me up and down, his eyes lingering on the stain. Then, after a few seconds, he nods, wincing.

'That's quite a mess. Did you burn yourself?'

'No, it's just the dress.'

'I'm going to run it to the dry-cleaner's,' Deanna says.

'There's no need—'

Deanna appraises the dress. 'You know, looking at it, I think I can take care of that.'

'I can't make you do that—'

'One more task in my day won't hurt.'

Having one less thing to do would help, I have to say. Scott comes between us, slipping an arm around my waist and edging me aside. He takes out his wallet and produces a wad of notes which he hands to Deanna. 'As promised.'

Deanna's eyes light up. 'Oh, thank you so much. You're a lifesaver.'

Scott smiles. 'Funny thing,' he says and both Deanna and I look at him. 'On my way back here, I thought I'd save you the trip, and so I called in at the hostel.'

'You did?' I ask him. Scott nods, glancing at Deanna.

'Yeah, I thought seeing as I was passing, I'd call in, settle your bill and collect your bag for you. I figured it would save you having to make the trip.'

'Oh, that's kind,' Deanna says, but she doesn't seem particularly enamoured by the gesture.

'The thing is,' Scott says, frowning, 'the person at reception had no idea who you were.'

'Really?' Deanna says, surprised.

'Really.'

'Who was it, on the desk, I mean?' Deanna asks, uncertain.

'I didn't get his name. A tall chap, blond hair, a nose stud, just here,' Scott says, pointing to his left nostril.

'Oh, that'll explain it. He's quite new. I think I only met him once. Besides, I'm registered with them on my birth name from my passport, Deianira. That guy could never pronounce it right.'

'Ah, yes, that's probably it,' Scott says. 'Pity though, because you'll have to make a special trip yourself now.'

'Thanks for thinking of me though,' Deanna says. 'I appreciate it.'

'Right,' I say. 'I'm going to change.'

Scott smiles at Deanna, and then hurries to catch up with me as I climb the stairs. 'I'll come up with you.'

'Your meeting finished early,' I say to him.

'Yes, it was brief. It was more of a meet and greet. We'll go into more detail once he's settled in.'

'Where did he fly from again?' I ask as we reach the landing of our bedroom suite.

'South America, landed this morning.'

'I'm surprised you came home.' I'm struggling to undo the clasp on my pendant, and I'm worried I'll catch it in the dress. 'Could you help me with this, please?'

'Yes, of course,' Scott says. I lift my hair and turn around to give him access. He rests his hands gently on my shoulders, thumbs at the base of my neck and the thought occurs that this is the most intimate contact we've had in weeks. 'Where did you get this?' he says, unhooking the clasp and lifting the pendant away from me.

'You gave it to me, didn't you?'

He studies it, holding it in the palm of his hand. 'Did I?'

'I think so.'

'I don't remember you ever wearing it,' he says, arching his eyebrows. 'It's pretty though.'

'It is, isn't it? Deanna found it in my jewellery box. It pairs well with the outfit, don't you think?' Speaking of my outfit, I've now removed the dress and I'm standing in the bedroom in only my control pants; I feel a bit daft. Scott is my husband, and we are married, warts and all, but even so, two minutes ago I looked pretty good even with coffee down my front, and now I feel a bit vulnerable. Scott hasn't noticed. He's still examining the pendant, stroking it gently with the forefinger of his other hand.

'It looks good on you, yes,' he says. Then he notices my lack of clothing and inclines his head towards the dress on the floor. 'And that red dress, you wore that to one of my company events a while back?'

I think hard whilst rummaging through my wardrobe for something else to wear. 'Yes, I think you're right.'

'It was an awards celebration, best independent picture, the second time I won that.'

'You've got a good memory,' I tell him, wishing I had the same skills. I don't. At least, not anymore.

'You certainly turned heads that night!'

I laugh, pulling on some yoga pants and a woollen jumper. 'That was a long time ago.'

'I'm sure you still turned heads today, too!'

'That's very sweet of you to say. But the fit is definitely a bit snug this time around.'

'Well, you look lovely.'

'And you, husband dear, are a silver-tongued little devil,' I say, holding out my hand. He looks at it, then lifts his head. 'Can I have the necklace? So I can put it away. I wouldn't want to lose it.'

He smiles, looking at it in the palm of his hand. 'No, of course not.' He passes it to me, and I put it back in the top drawer of my jewellery box, pushing it closed.

I take a deep breath. 'Did you speak to Katie this morning?'

'I did. She seems okay. I think I smoothed things over a bit.'

'Really? I think you made them worse.'

'How's that?' he asks.

'Did you... um... tell her that I made it up, about me not being her mum?'

Scott pauses, his brow furrowing. 'Yes, I thought it best if she thinks—'

'That I lied to her and told her the most spiteful, hurtful thing possible?'

Scott's face darkens. 'I think that Katie having faith in the family unit is more important than her having to face what happened to her mother right now, and that everything she thought was true all her life is a lie.'

'So, she gets to think I'm a nasty, cruel bitch instead?'

Scott exhales deeply. 'Look. Maybe I should have run it by you first—'

'Maybe?'

'Sophie!' Scott says, his mood descending lower. 'I had to make a decision. You'd left me to it—'

'*Left you to it?* Scott, I went to work, for crying out loud.'

'Please don't use that tone with me, Cecilia.'

'Sophie!'

'What?' Scott snaps his head up, meeting my eye.

'My name's—'

'Yes, yes, yes, sorry,' he says, flapping his hands in the air to placate me. 'It's just Cecilia was on my mind, after yesterday. I'm tired. Look, I... made a call on it, and I thought it for the best. Nip it in the bud, so to speak.'

'Well, she doesn't believe you.'

'Really?'

'Yes, really. And what's more, she thinks I might have put you up to it.'

Scott closes his eyes and turns his face heavenward. 'I didn't mean for that to happen.'

'How could you put me in this position?'

'Me?' Scott points at his chest. 'This is your fault, Sophie. You told her!'

My anger dissipates. He's right. I rub my face with both hands. 'Okay, I know. I'm sorry. I don't remember saying it, and I would never have planned to. Not like that.' Scott comes to me and pulls me into him. I rest my head on his shoulders.

'I have to tell you something else.' I pull back from him, worried at his tone. 'I spoke with Deanna this morning, before...' – he hesitates as our eyes meet – 'before I spoke to Katie. I felt I had to say something to her.'

'About what?'

'Last night, about what she saw.'

'What does she know?'

Scott shakes his head. 'She knows everything.'

THIRTY-TWO

We talk for a while, planning our next steps. Scott withdraws from our embrace finally, stooping to pick up my dress. 'This is quite a departure from what you usually wear.'

'Yes, it's the studio. They want me to... I don't know, change up my style a bit.' His eyes narrow as he searches my face. He works in media, is a savvy guy, and I'm sure he's clocked what's going on.

'They want you to be more revealing with your clothes?'

'Daring, they would prefer to call it.'

'Would they now,' he says, flatly, looking at the red dress in his hands.

'Yes, that's a well-sanitised adjective, isn't it?'

'I see.' He nods, and I know he's unhappy, but it is his world, his industry. He knows how it works, especially for a woman who is on the cusp of reaching *a certain age*, I think the saying goes. Not that I believe I'm past it by any stretch, but in broadcast television the rules of the game are different. 'You'll be careful?'

'I won't go too far, if that's what you're asking?'

'Just be yourself,' Scott says, forcing a smile. 'Otherwise, you'll lose everyone... the execs, your floor team, and the viewers too.'

'I know.'

'I could make some calls?'

That would be such an easy option for me to take, to have Scott wade in with the clout he carries, but this is my problem to deal with. 'Thank you, but I can handle it.'

'Are you sure? Because recently...'

I don't like the look on his face. 'What?'

He cocks his head, apologetic. 'You've not exactly been yourself lately, have you?'

'What's that supposed to mean?' I know I'm sounding defensive, but I think I know where this is going. 'Well, it's *not exactly* been an easy time lately.'

'I appreciate that but—'

'You *appreciate* it? Really?'

'Yes, of course.'

'That's odd because it sounds like you're attacking me.'

Scott sighs, looking heavenward. 'I'm not attacking you, Soph, but you have to admit that you've been a bit out of sorts lately.'

'I'm trying to keep this family together whilst holding down a high-pressure job and—'

He holds up his hand in placation. 'I know, and you're doing wonderfully, but things at home... the kids... it's all slipping.'

'And all of that is my responsibility?'

'Well, no, it's our responsibility.'

'And yet you seem to be laying the blame for the current state of things at my feet and not yours.' I can feel my anger rising along with my voice.

'Calm down, Sophie.'

That's an instruction likely to lead to the exact opposite reaction. 'Calm down? What is it you think I'm letting slip, exactly?'

Scott frowns. 'Well, it's not so much slipping but you're clearly struggling. Look at how much you rely on Martha, for a start. More than we pay her for.'

'Heaven forbid, we have a housekeeper and I rely on her. Why is it that I rely on her and not *we rely on her*? Is it because I'm a woman? The grocery shopping, the cleaning, looking after the family, it should all be my responsibility, is that it?'

'That's not what I'm saying at all.'

'That's odd, because it sounds like that's exactly what I just heard, Scott.'

He shakes his head. I don't know if that's the frustration of not managing to articulate his point properly or he's bothered by my response. He's surprised, certainly. This time last year, anytime in the last decade, I'd be apologising to him. But not now. Now, I'm making something of myself, I'm finally carving out my own path, as a result of my hard work. And it's changed something in me.

'I'm worried about you.' He meets my eye, and I can see pain in his expression which tugs on my heart.

'Then help me, don't attack me and blame me for everything that's wrong in our home, our family.'

'I'm *not* blaming you,' he says earnestly. 'I just don't want what happened before to happen again.'

'It won't—'

'You can't say that, not in light of recent events, Soph. Things are getting a bit much, aren't they? The signs are there and you can't bury your head in the sand.'

He does have a point. 'I know, and I appreciate your concern. I have it too.'

'Then, perhaps, we should give Doctor Sheldon a call. What do you think?'

That name brings a stab of fear – and a sense of shame – to my mind. I don't want to go down that road again, although I never had much of a choice last time out. 'No, I don't want to.'

Scott takes a step closer and tentatively reaches out, and I allow him close enough to touch me. We sit down on the end of the bed.

'I understand, but it will be different this time.'

'Will it?'

'Yes, very different. This time we will be initiating treatment—'

'So, you think I need treatment?' I say curtly, more pointed than I'd intended.

'Bad choice of words, but this time it would be on our terms and maybe that's what you need? We can get ahead of it.'

I shake my head firmly. 'No, Scott. He'll just pump me full of even more pills, and I don't want that.'

'I think it's a bit more tailored than that.'

'Do you remember the last time? I wandered around like a zombie for months!'

'Which is why we should do something now, so things don't get that bad again.'

That feeling of shame is hard to shake off. It was bad enough for anyone to see me in that state, especially my children, but if the studio or the press had got wind of it? If I was found naked, sitting in the street in the middle of the night now, then the press would have a field day. As it was, only Scott saw me that night at my worst, and Chas I suppose, but Katie was too young to remember. Scott found me, gathered me up in his arms and brought me back inside and no one was any the wiser, thankfully.

I was a hot mess that particular night having been trapped in the lift of our house for eight hours straight during the day. Scott had taken the children out on an adventure day, and I was there alone, sitting in that stainless steel, mirrored coffin. It is what I imagined being buried alive would feel like, knowing that no one will come to rescue you, dying a slow and lonely death.

'No. I can't go there, not again. I don't want to stop feeling again.'

'Sophie.'

'No! Things are different now. It'll be fine.'

My words sound hollow, even to me, but Scott nods silently. I can see the disappointment in his face, tinged with an element of fear too. I still feel intense shame about having put him through what happened before. He didn't sign up for any of this when we got together. He thought he'd found someone to replace the love of his life – no, not replace, that's unfair, to follow on from maybe – along with a mother for his children, and what he has is a basket case who can barely hold it together long enough to do the shopping.

'I'll... think about it, okay?'

He smiles and nods. 'Thank you.' He pulls me into him, and I rest my head on his shoulder. 'I just want what's best for you, Sophie.'

'I know you do.'

I believe him. The problem is neither of us has any clue as to what *the best for me* looks like.

Despite my assurances to Scott that I'm in a better place, deep down I know he's right. The signs are there, but I am choosing to ignore them. Last time, I didn't see it coming. This time I see the signs, and Scott sees them too, and I've no idea how I will cope if it happens again.

I've no idea what I will do, how far I will go.

THIRTY-THREE

I don't see Scott for the rest of the day. He barely leaves his study, and I don't want to interrupt him or get in his way. Deanna has been to the shops and returned with several bags and, whilst Katie has been working through the exam paper Deanna has set for her, we both set about packing the shopping away.

I'm getting serious déjà vu as I'm stacking items in the pantry. I could have sworn I did much of this yesterday but I'm obviously mixing up my memories. It could well have been last week.

Scott's suggestion of involving Dr Sheldon has triggered me. I know it comes from a good place but to up my medication again just feels like such a massive step backward. Mind you, if Scott knew what course of action I took when I landed this new job, then he'd lose it, I'm sure. If I speak to Dr Sheldon, then it'll all come out. The pills were dulling my senses, making me numb to the world. I couldn't be a statue on the breakfast show, so I stopped, there and then. I've been flushing my prescription down the toilet every couple of days. Scott would lose it if he knew. His experience is greater than mine, bearing in mind what happened with Cecilia.

I haven't thought about her for a while. I try not to, seeing as I'm something of an interloper, living the life she should have lived and indeed was living until I appeared. What happened to her wasn't my fault though. I know this, everyone knows this, but I still feel guilty about it. She should be here unpacking the bags and putting the shopping away, not me.

I look out through the open door and across the kitchen at Katie, head down, furiously writing as the clock ticks. She looks so much like a mini version of Cecilia. Katie could be her double and probably will be when she grows up. Not that that would raise a red flag with anyone because she also looks a lot like me. Several people have commented that she has my eyes.

Well, without a surgical procedure, that won't be possible.

She could be my daughter, though. She is my daughter, and I don't need the DNA or my name on a birth certificate to prove that. I love this girl with all my heart, no matter how trying she can be.

Deanna comes into the pantry and her appearance snaps me out of my ruminating. I catch her eye and something in her expression piques my interest. Is it her eyes? They're beautiful but it's not that. The way she's standing, perhaps? Her poise. I don't know, but it dislodges something in my memory that I can't quite grasp. The thought, irritatingly, fades just as quickly as it came to mind.

'What is it?' I ask her.

She shakes her head. 'Nothing. You were lost in thought for a moment there.'

I smile. 'Yes, I was just recalling something and then I saw you...'

'Oh, intriguing. What is it?'

'I don't know. I was just thinking about Katie, and someone saying she looks just like me.' Deanna's eyebrows arch ever so slightly, and I remember, she knows. 'She *is* *my* daughter,' I say defensively, more so than I intended.

'Yes, I can see how much you love her,' Deanna says, lowering her voice and glancing over to where Katie is working, with her back to us. 'And I think she knows it too.'

'I don't want you to think badly of me—'

'Why would I?' Deanna says, studying my face.

'Because it is quite a secret to keep but, well, we have our reasons.'

Deanna maintains the eye contact and then nods. 'I'm sure.'

'And we didn't make these decisions lightly, just so you know.' I don't know why I'm feeling the need to justify our actions to her.

'It's really none of my business,' Deanna says quietly. Is that disapproval I hear in her voice, or is it just my imagination seeking out the most negative response it can? Deanna forces a smile. 'Look, I'm sure you have your reasons. I grew up in an environment where... No, I shouldn't say. As I said, it's none of my business.'

'No, please. Say what you were going to say.'

'Well, my childhood was very stable, or so I thought. My parents were together a long time and we travelled with my father's job – a lot – and for the most part that was fantastic.'

'I sense a but coming.'

Deanna smiles ruefully. 'Isn't there always? My parents split, and I stayed with my father, unusual at the time I suppose, but particularly so bearing in mind how much he moved around the globe with his work.' Her expression clouds. 'Anyway, my life changed then, forever. And it was all because of secrets no one thought would ever come out.'

'But they did.'

She nods. 'That's just it. They always do, and the longer they are kept, the more damaging they are when they do see the light of day. I've seen, first-hand, how secrets and lies can destroy lives.'

I feel sad for her and then I look beyond her to the twelve-year-old daughter I have, and I will always call her my daughter, no matter what. What a choice to have. What a predicament to be in, although I'm well aware it is purely one of our own making. Do we shatter the illusion of her life now, or at some random, or pre-planned, point in her future? Whenever it is, it will turn her life upside down, that's true. She might suspect that I'm not her mother, despite Scott's cack-handed attempt to reassure her otherwise. But she doesn't know everything. Not yet.

'What about your mother?' I ask, shifting my focus back to Deanna. It's far easier to discuss other people's lives than your own.

'I didn't see much of her after that. The odd phone call around Christmas or my birthday, cards and presents in the post if I was lucky.'

'You didn't get to see her?'

'Oh, I did. My father would arrange to put me on a plane from time to time, and my mother always seemed keen to see me when I arrived. But...'

'But?'

Deanna shrugged. 'I often felt like I was in the way, hampering her life just by being there.'

'That's so sad.'

Deanna rocks her head from side to side. 'It was the way it was. I've made my peace with it.'

'Do you still see her?'

'No, she passed away some years ago.'

'You said you have no family close here.'

'No, I don't. My father passed away last year, and so I'm sort of on my own.'

I reach out and take her hand. 'And then you come into this mess. I'm sure this isn't the stability you were expecting.'

Deanna smiles then, and it reaches her eyes, lifting the mood. 'It's fine. I'm pleased to be here with all of you, and Katie is awesome.'

'Yes,' I say, observing her in the background. 'She is.'

'Change of subject,' Deanna says. 'I didn't know what you had planned for your dinner this evening, but looking at the shopping list I figured it might be a curry. Is that right?'

'That's right. One of my favourite recipes. It used to be something Katie wouldn't touch, but she has finally begun branching out and being a bit more adventurous and as long as I don't make it too hot, she likes it. Would you like to join us?'

'Oh no, not tonight. I have plans of my own.'

'Heading out?'

She laughs. 'No, nothing like that but I have bought some things to eat, and they'll go out of date if I don't have them tonight. Anyway, I have a great book to read, so I was going to hunker down and have a bit of quiet time.'

'Sounds lovely. If you're sure? You don't have to hide from us, although I can see the temptation after last night and today. Cooking for you will be the least I can do seeing as you've done the shopping I was supposed to do yesterday.'

'No, it's fine, honest. Thanks for the offer though. I can help prep the vegetables if you like?'

'Thanks, Deanna.'

'No problem. I enjoy cooking.'

'No, not just for that. I mean, thanks for being here.'

She smiles at me, and I can see something in her expression that shifts something inside me, again. It's not quite satisfaction, is it? I can't quite put my finger on what it is, but it is certainly momentarily unsettling.

THIRTY-FOUR

DEANNA

I set the table whilst Sophie finishes up the meal preparation.

'All done,' I say, coming back to find Sophie perspiring and looking a little flustered. 'Everything all right?'

'I think so,' she says but without confidence.

'Is there anything else I can do for you?'

Sophie looks around. 'No, I have everything under control.' I hope so, but to be honest, the kitchen has been devastated. I almost feel sorry for her but that's because I'm very finicky about cleaning as I go, and Sophie doesn't appear to have the same mindset when she's cooking. Each to their own but the scene is one of culinary devastation as I look around. 'I just need to get the naans out of the oven and we're good. Oh, do you think you could call the children down for me?'

'I can do that.'

Walking out into the hall, I peer up the stairwell and call Katie, whose head soon pops over the balustrade and meets my eye.

'Your dinner is ready. Could you let your brother know as well, please?' Katie smiles and disappears. There is no need to call Scott as he descends moments later having remained inside his study for the whole afternoon.

'Something smells wonderful,' he says, as he passes me and I follow him back into the kitchen. Sophie is busy putting rice onto plates and I think she's slightly behind. The curry is still bubbling away on the hob, and I can smell burning but I don't want to suggest she attends to it for fear I'll annoy her. When I'm cooking, the last thing I want is a back-seat driver telling me what I should or shouldn't be doing.

Scott moves past Sophie, placing a hand on her waist and peering over her shoulder and then over to the hob. 'Should I...'

'Yes, please. I think it's caught on the bottom of the pan.'

Scott picks up a wooden spoon and stirs the contents having first lifted the saucepan off the heat. Footsteps sound behind us as Chas and Katie come down for dinner.

'Right, I'll leave you to it,' I say, turning to leave.

'You're not joining us for dinner?' Scott says, sounding disappointed.

'No, I have plans.'

'Are you eating out?' he asks, and I shake my head.

'Deanna has already made arrangements for a quiet night in,' Sophie says, cursing under her breath. All eyes turn to her, and she hurries to the oven, opening the door as steam billows out. Apparently, the naan bread is a little overdone. 'I forgot,' Sophie says, waving the cloud of steam away and looking up at the smoke detector. I think we all hope it's not going to sound off. 'And I set the temperature too high on the oven.'

'But have you eaten?' Scott asks, looking at me.

'No, not yet, but I have a salad bowl to eat and—'

'Well, that won't do. You can join us for dinner,' he says.

'No, really, I—'

'I insist,' he says sternly, fixing his eyes on me. 'Come on, there's plenty to go around.' He glances at the table. 'Chas, set Deanna a place.'

'Of course,' Chas says.

'She can sit next to me!' Katie announces eagerly. I see Sophie's eyes dart towards her daughter and then at me. I don't think she liked that one bit.

'I'll sit wherever,' I say, smiling through my awkwardness. 'Besides, Katie, I thought you'd be sick of me by now.'

'Oh yes,' Scott says, 'the exam. How did you get on with it, Katie?'

She shrugs and it's left to me to elaborate. 'She smashed it. You have a very bright child on your hands.' I can see the pride reflected in Scott's smile as he hugs his daughter. Katie breaks off from him, beaming triumphantly, before coming to me and throwing her arms around my waist, taking me off guard. Sophie is looking at me with a strange expression.

I think I've got under her skin.

'Is there anything I can do to help, Sophie?' I ask sweetly.

'Yes,' Scott says, turning to face his wife. 'What can we do?'

'Nothing. It's all done,' she says flatly. 'If someone could put the salad bowl on the table, that'd be great.'

'I can,' I say, picking up the bowl and taking it to the table. The family appear to eat in the extended kitchen rather than the formal dining room. Presumably, they only use that for when they have guests.

Sophie points out which plates belong to whom and the family move as one to the table. I am sitting next to Katie, in between her and Chas. Sophie comes over last with a plate bearing the naan breads. They do look a bit stiff.

'So, Chas, how was your day?' Scott asks. Chas shrugs. 'As good as that, eh? I'm curious to hear what you say on a bad day.' Chas shrugs again, only to a different depth of his shoulders. Scott frowns with an exaggerated sigh.

'Oh no!' Sophie says, and I look at her. She's desperately trying to remove the food from her mouth without spitting it out. Has she eaten something too hot?

Katie yelps, her breathing increasing as she looks around, frantically flapping her hands in the air. I reach out and place a comforting hand on her forearm and she looks at me, pleading. 'What's wrong, sweetheart?'

'H-Hot!' she says, just before spitting a mouthful of food onto her plate.

'Damn hot!' Chas says, swallowing hard before shovelling another forkful of food into his mouth. He's already red-faced and sweating. 'It's good!' he adds, whilst chewing. Scott tastes his food and manages to put the contents of his mouth back on the plate but with more dignity than his daughter. He glances apologetically at his wife, who looks on the verge of tears.

'But I followed the recipe... I don't understand.'

Scott arches his eyebrows then winces in sympathy. 'How much chilli powder did you add?'

Sophie, shaking her head, thinks hard. 'I cut it back so it wouldn't be too hot for Katie—'

'It's all good,' Chas says, still eating although his cheeks are now flushing crimson, the perspiration increasing.

'I don't understand,' Sophie whispers.

'Did you mix up teaspoons and tablespoons?' Scott asks softly, folding his napkin and laying it down on the table neatly beside his plate.

'No! Of course I didn't,' she says, but without a great deal of conviction. 'At least, I don't think so.'

Katie has gulped down a glass of water and is pouring herself another one but she looks ready to cry as well.

'I'll get you some natural yoghurt from the fridge. I bought some today,' I tell her. 'Anyone else?' I ask but Chas appears quite happy with setting his mouth alight, while Scott is sitting in silence, hands cupped before his face, elbows on the table. I know family mealtimes are important to Scott, and he clearly isn't pleased, but probably doesn't want to be too critical either. He doesn't respond to my question and neither does

Sophie. 'I'll get some bowls and I'll just put the tub out,' I say quickly.

Moments later, Katie seems more comfortable as she is spooning mouthfuls of natural yoghurt from the bowl I've given her into her mouth. Chas is already eyeing the untouched plates in front of everyone else, through a sheen of perspiration I should say, and using his napkin to wipe the sweat from his face. I'm impressed with his fortitude. There's enough spice in the sauce to fell a rhino.

'Well,' Scott says calmly, 'I think we'll have to order something in.'

'Don't worry,' I say. 'There's plenty of ingredients in the fridge. I can throw a quick pasta sauce together. It'll take fifteen to twenty minutes, if everyone is all right with that?' Scott inclines his head, answering me but remains looking at Sophie, who's averting her eyes from his gaze. It's as if he's waiting for something to happen.

'Thank you, Deanna. I don't know what we would do without you.'

Sophie slams her palms down on the table, startling everyone. Getting up from the table she practically runs from the room with her head down. I think she is in tears or likely will be soon. Scott takes a deep breath and places a hand over one of Katie's, patting it gently and smiling at her. Katie nods and returns to eating the yoghurt, only this time she doesn't bother spooning it into her bowl and eats straight from the tub.

'I'll, er, get on with making the pasta,' I say quietly.

Scott nods. 'Thank you, Deanna.' He slowly rises from the table and follows his wife. I notice Chas watching me carefully, as I start clearing the table. I avoid his gaze.

THIRTY-FIVE

SOPHIE

The door creaks slightly as it closes, and I hear the latch thud as Scott releases the handle. I'm alone again, thankfully. I can't bear to face him right now. This evening had to be the most humiliating thing I've endured recently. Although it's not like I don't make an idiot of myself with alarming regularity.

If I'm not embarrassing myself at work by missing my cues or hiding in the toilets, I'm losing my keys or leaving the shopping behind at the supermarket. Throwing a tantrum and running out on my family in front of Deanna comes pretty close to the worst of the lot though. I've made that meal a hundred times, if not more, and I still managed to make a mess of it.

Scott came after me, of course, as he always does. I resorted to my professional diversionary tactic: that of hiding in the bathroom, locking the door and refusing to respond to his appeals. It worked and soon he left me alone, no doubt going back downstairs to smooth things over. As always, he has to clean up after me.

Once I thought I could leave the sanctuary of my bolthole, I crept down to the lower landing. The right thing to do, the adult thing, would have been to rejoin the family and thank Deanna for bailing me out of my mistake.

I almost did it as well, but hearing the laughter and friendly conversation coming from everyone only made me feel worse. Not that I was worried about anyone being angry, well, perhaps Scott, but my appearance would have changed the dynamic. Walking in there would only increase the humiliation as all eyes turned to face me.

And so here I am, lying in the dark hoping for this day to end. I will be up early in the morning and I can slip out to the studio before anyone else rises. By the time I get back tomorrow all of this will be forgotten. Probably not, but it will be yesterday's news and we can all move on. I can save face, what little of it I have left anyway.

This is why when Scott crept into my bedroom just now, I kept my eyes closed and even exaggerated my breathing to make it seem like I was sound asleep. He wouldn't disturb me whilst I'm sleeping. I was right. He came over to the bed, whispered a greeting – one I didn't respond to – and then he leant over me and kissed my forehead, before wishing me goodnight.

I don't deserve him. I really don't.

I'm in the garden and I can feel the warmth of the morning sunshine on my skin. It's pleasant right now, that time of the day when the sun is rising but there is still a little shade on offer at the rear of the house. By mid-morning I won't be able to bear the heat as the sun rises higher in the sky, and Katie certainly won't be able to cope.

I put my coffee cup down on the table. They have high quality coffee in these parts. It is part of the natural diet, not these fad diets that are so popular, but an unwritten, national diet of coffee and cigarettes. I'll take the coffee each and every day, but they can keep the latter. I've never cared for smoking, and I know Scott would hate it anyway.

I can just make him out through the trees, taking a morning stroll. He's got that shock of dark wavy hair, naturally unkempt but always looking styled. He is just a handsome guy. As much as I'm saddened for his loss, it is my gain which is a bit mind-bending for me. Right place at the right time, or right person at the right time? One of those sliding door moments that you hear people speak of.

Why, then, do I feel lucky and guilty at the same time? It's not like I chose for any of this to happen. Life has a way of coming at you pretty quickly sometimes.

Katie stirs, but it's not time for her to be awake yet and I hope she'll let me enjoy this moment. I can hear Scott's voice carrying on the gentle breeze. He's talking to someone but, glancing over my shoulder into the house, I can see his mobile on the table.

He moves into view, and I can see he has someone alongside him, a woman. She has her arm looped through his and they are laughing. The familiar pang of jealousy stabs at my chest.

I remember this day, but it was ten years ago. Why are we back here? It's like our wedding never happened. The last decade or more of my life has been wiped away. This isn't possible.

The two of them move out from the shadow of the trees and I want to yell at them, at her, to leave my husband alone. To my surprise, it's not Cecilia walking alongside Scott, but Deanna.

That's not fair. I am with Scott now! *This can't be happening.* I try to stand but my legs feel strange, and I struggle to rise. Scott is walking away from me now and Deanna isn't there anymore. Cecilia is laughing at whatever Scott just said.

No!

Cecilia has had her chance, and she chose to leave him, and her family, and now it's mine. Why does she think she can walk in and disrupt everything after all the damage and devastation she wrought upon it? And Scott, how dare he do this to me? I'm here, watching over their child, the child *she* chose to abandon.

She leans into him, and he stops, turning her to face him and pulling her into his body. His arms curl around her waist, Deanna's waist, and their faces close. They kiss. I want to scream but no sound comes out of my mouth. I'm just watching them, fascinated, angry, so incredibly angry. I'm trying to run to them, tell them to stop and that I am here but I'm paralysed.

I can hear Katie crying from her crib. I must go to her. But I can't move.

THIRTY-SIX

It's dark now, and I can hear the repetitive drumming of rain falling steadily against the window. My eyes are slowly adjusting to the meagre light filtering in from outside, the soft glow from the streetlights interspersed with movement as tree branches sway back and forth, casting dancing shadows across my bedroom.

Something catches my eye, deep in the shadows between my bed and the closed door. Movement. Something, or someone, is there just out of sight and they are watching me. I need to move but I can't. I'm still paralysed, just as I was in my dream a moment ago.

The shadow edges a little closer and I can make out their figure now, not threatening, just standing there watching me. There's a pain in my chest, almost as if someone is sitting on it, stopping me from breathing. And I'm not breathing. I want to but I can't inhale. A new sensation, *rising panic*. The figure takes another step, and they are at the foot of the bed, almost within touching distance and still, I can't move.

I open my mouth to scream but nothing comes out. My route to the door is clear, if only I could get out of this damn bed. My eyes are locked on this thing, this apparition which must be what it is because that's all I can make out. No face. No discernible features at all. It reaches out, slowly, purposefully. I want to move my feet away, but I can't. I am completely helpless. I clamp my eyes shut, shifting my head to one side, as if not seeing it will end this nightmare and send this thing back to where it came from.

It's not real. *You're not real.*

I open my eyes, and the rain is still falling outside, but at the foot of the bed I can see nothing. It was a dream, a nightmare within a nightmare, and I gasp as I draw breath, savouring the sensation of air passing into my body.

Looking at the clock on my bedside table, my gaze lingers. I've seen this before. The picture beside the clock, mounted in a simple silver frame, is of Scott standing with his arm around a woman who looks just like me. But it's not me. It's her. It's Cecilia.

Throwing off the duvet, I run for the door, but the handle is stuck, and I can feel the flush of panic rising once more as I wrestle with the handle.

'No, please!' I say as I tug at it, but the voice doesn't sound like mine. The door flies open and I half run, half stumble from the bedroom onto the landing. My legs don't seem to work properly, and I pitch forward, landing on the floor at the top of the stairs. My left knee feels like it is on fire, and I grasp the balustrade, hauling myself upright and stumble down the stairs. 'Scott!' I scream through tears. I didn't realise I was crying. My legs almost give out and I slide the last few steps before finding my feet on the lower landing and stumble towards our bedroom.

Scott has heard me. I think the entire street has heard me, and I collapse into his arms just inside the bedroom. 'Sophie!' he says, holding me tightly and we both sink down to the floor. 'What is it?' I can hear his fear. 'What's going on?'

'In my... my bedroom...'

'What?' Scott says, and I look up to see him staring out of the bedroom at the landing towards the stairwell. 'What is it?'

'Someone...'

'Someone's in your room?' Scott asks. I try to speak but I can't. He eases me aside, but I grapple with him. I don't want to be alone in the dark. I need him to be with me, to hold me. 'Sophie, let go. I need—'

'No, don't leave me, please!'

He relents, tightening the grip he was loosening only moments before, but his eyes are still flitting toward the stairs. 'I won't leave you,' he says. I'm sobbing, completely and utterly broken, my face pressed into Scott's chest.

'Please don't leave me,' I all but whisper. He leans down and kisses the top of my head.

'I won't.'

I hear movement from behind us but my eyes are closed to the world. I am safe and I don't care about anything else in this moment.

'What's wrong with her?' It's Katie. She's frightened.

'Your mum is just having a nightmare—'

'No!' I scream at him, opening my eyes and pushing away from Scott. I see Katie flinch in my peripheral vision, taking a step back. 'I'm not dreaming! There was someone in my room.'

Scott holds up his hands in placation as I back away from him on my hands and knees, putting my back to the wall, lifting my knees to my chest and hugging them.

'Katie,' Scott says calmly, 'please can you go back to your bedroom and get back into bed.' Katie is about to protest but something in her father's expression makes her think better of it. She nods, backing out of the room, her eyes darting to me before she turns and disappears from my sight. Scott fixes his eyes on me, squatting down. 'Sophie—'

'I'm *not* imagining it!' I hiss at him.

'Okay, okay,' he says softly. 'Stay here.'

I have no intention of moving and I stare at him, following him with my eyes as he leaves the room and I hear him make his way upstairs.

'I'm not imagining it. I'm not imagining it,' I tell myself, rocking gently back and forth which, perhaps strangely, feels comforting. I can't hear anything aside from the rain, nothing but the rain. My heart is racing; is it from rushing downstairs, or from adrenalin and fear?

Time is passing so slowly. Where's Scott? What's taking him so long? I'm staring at the doorway, waiting for any flicker of movement but there is nothing. Nothing but the darkness and the rain. My breathing, which was laboured, is coming easier now. My chest still hurts, but the panic is subsiding at least. Where is Scott?

I yelp as a figure steps through the door. Startled, I would expect to scream, to run or to fight but I do nothing of the sort. Instead, I sit on the floor with my back to the wall, paralysed by fear.

'There's no one there,' Scott says, standing over me for a moment before coming down to my level again, his elbows resting on his knees. 'There's no one there, Sophie.'

'There *was* someone there.' He looks at me with nothing but sympathy in his eyes, but he doesn't believe me. I can see it. 'I'm telling you: *someone* was in my bedroom.'

He slowly shakes his head. In the past, he would humour me. Not now. He is despairing of me. He's had enough. 'Soph, there's no one in your room.'

I stare at him, narrowing my eyes defiantly. 'There was someone in my room.'

'Sophie.'

I haul myself upright, pushing off the wall behind me and Scott reaches for me, but I bat away his hand. 'There damn well was!' I scream at him as I push past him. I stride from the room, and I can sense he is following me back up the stairs.

'Sophie,' he repeats. He must be a few steps behind judging from the sound of his voice. He's irritated, I can tell.

I break into a run, and my legs feel fine now, taking the stairs two at a time, Scott hurrying after me. I charge into my bedroom and flick the light on, stopping at the foot of the bed. Soon he appears beside me, breathing heavily but not as heavily as I am, whilst my eyes survey the room.

'See? There's no one here,' he says, 'and there wasn't anyone here before.'

I scan the room, searching every corner, every hiding place, but he's right. There is no one here and no sign that they were. My duvet is cast aside; I'd flung it off when I ran for the door. The windows are closed; the shadows cast by the trees in the streetlight are still there, dancing on the far wall of the bedroom. On the bedside table, my digital clock reads 1.30 a.m., and the glass of water I always take with me to bed is standing alongside it.

There is no picture frame, no photograph.

'But I... I saw...'

'What?'

'There, it was right there.'

'Sophie,' Scott says, placing his hands gently on my upper arms from behind and giving them a supportive squeeze. 'It's okay.'

'No! It's not okay,' I say, shrugging off the contact and turning to face him, welling up. 'I know what I saw!'

'Sophie—'

'*I know what I saw!*' He smiles gently, but I can see in his eyes, those beautiful brown eyes of his, that he is at his wits' end. He doesn't know what to say and neither do I. I glance at the bedside table again. 'I know what I saw,' I say again, but now I'm whispering, doubting myself. 'I think...'

Scott reaches for me again and this time I don't push back or dismiss him. His arms encircle me, and I allow him to pull me to him. I try to speak but I'm choked up. What the hell is wrong with me?

'I'll call Doctor Sheldon in the morning,' Scott says, holding me firmly, but lovingly. 'See if he can make a house call.'

I feel safe again, in his arms. I'm not going to argue. I can't. Not anymore.

THIRTY-SEVEN

Wednesday

My alarm still goes off at the usual time and Scott stirs beside me. I was already awake anyway. After catching fragments of sleep disturbed by nightmares, my mind has been throwing up memories, bombarding me with an onslaught of snapshot images. I can't settle. It's like I'm uncomfortable in my own skin.

Sliding out from beneath the duvet, Scott murmurs, shifting onto his side, facing away. I gather my dressing gown about me and leave the bedroom. I've no idea what I'm going to do. I'm not hungry, despite missing dinner, and I am absolutely shattered but I know I'm not going to sleep.

Cracking the door into Katie's bedroom open, I can see she's sound asleep, none the worse for having a basket case for a mum. Her little chest is rising and falling beneath the duvet.

Monkey say, monkey do, is one of those parental phrases my dad used to repeat whenever he talked about people's behaviour. As a parent you set the tone, you set the example. Now, as an adult, you can no longer point the finger of blame at those who did their best by you. As long as they did their best anyway. Some parents are awful by intention, but most are doing the best they can with the only set of skills they have.

I can see Katie's stuffed tiger has fallen from the bed. If she wakes during the night and can't find it, she'll be upset, regardless of how often she claims she doesn't care about such things anymore. She does. And that's okay.

I creep over, my knee is aching, and slowly crouch down to retrieve Tiggy from the floor beside the bed before tucking her under the duvet beside Katie. 'She'll be there if you need her,' I whisper, gently moving the hair away from her brow. Katie stirs and for a moment I fear I've woken her, but she soon settles again. I touch my fingers to my lips and then gently place the kiss on her cheek, fearful of waking her but chancing my luck anyway, and back out of the room.

Making my way downstairs in the dark, my eyes have adjusted and I'm grateful for Scott's decision to go with light, pastel colours on the walls and a satin white finish for the woodwork. They reflect what little light penetrates from the exterior, a light that is very welcome given my current state of mind.

Even so, I hear something which makes me stop still partway down the last flight of stairs before reaching the ground floor. On the half landing, I peer down into the gloom. Chas could be up, but at this hour on a weekday it would be unusual even for him. Perhaps it is Deanna again. Images of Deanna and Scott together come fleetingly to mind, and I push them aside only for the same images to reappear a moment later.

I listen but I hear nothing else. If Deanna is there, then I'd probably turn and take flight back to my refuge in the guest suite. I'm embarrassed to walk into my own kitchen just in case she is there. That's ridiculous. This is my home.

I'm having this internal debate and considering going back to bed when it dawns on me that I'm supposed to be heading to the studio in about half an hour. I haven't told a soul that I'm not going in. My mobile phone is in the pocket of my dressing gown, but I can't face making the call. I know I won't sound ill and I'm too old to put on a fake voice like my children are wont to do.

I'll make a cup of tea, and then do the adult thing: send them a text message. In the kitchen, I put the lights on above the breakfast bar, dimming them to the lowest setting. The bright lights hurt my eyes so much lately, not just in the early hours, but all of the time. I can't be in a room with spotlights for very long; the intensity brings on a headache. The studio lights are becoming almost unbearable.

The text message I send to Sam is succinct:

I am ill. I won't be able to present today. S.

I don't want to go into details. What would I say anyway? That I've lost the plot and can't face – let alone risk – being on air just in case I have a very public meltdown?

I hear a car outside and, crossing to the window, I peer through the shutters to see Saif pull up in his hybrid Toyota. He will sit there all night unless I let him know. Ensuring my dressing gown is tightly wrapped around me, I slip into a pair of Scott's shoes that are in the cupboard next to the front door.

The cool night air takes my breath away and I hunch my shoulders, shrinking away from the light rain that's still falling, and dash out to where Saif is sitting in the car. If he is surprised by my appearance, he doesn't show it, calmly opening his door and getting out. 'I'm sorry, Saif,' I say, raising my voice, 'but I won't need you today. I'm not working.' He looks at me, puzzled, and it's as if the rain isn't falling upon him or he's just not paying any attention to it.

'Is everything all right, Miss Sophie?'

'Yes, yes. I'm just not feeling well, that's all.' He looks at me and I see his eyes move, almost as if he's appraising me. 'I'm sorry. I should have let you know earlier.'

He shrugs. 'It is okay, Miss Sophie.' His gaze shifts beyond me and towards the house, and the move is so clear that I look back myself. The door is open, but what he's looking at I don't know. 'Are you sure everything is okay, Miss Sophie?'

There's something in his tone, something I can't quite pinpoint, and I look back at the house again. My hair is getting wet and I can feel water on my neck trickling down past the collar. 'I'm fine, Saif. Honestly.' He takes a step toward me but he's still looking at the house, only this time up at one of the upper floor windows. I follow his gaze and see a figure looking down upon us. There is someone in the guest suite.

Someone is in my bedroom.

I look back at Saif, but his expression remains unchanged. 'If you're sure nothing is wrong, Miss Sophie?' I want to say no, I'm not sure at all. He can see something in my expression, and he takes another step toward me. 'Miss Sophie?' I look over my shoulder, up at the window again. Saif does too, coming to stand beside me. 'What is it?' he asks.

'At the window.' I look at him and he frowns.

'What?'

'The pers—' I look again and there is nothing there. No figure, no silhouette, no person. The curtains are open and the streetlight has illuminated what I can see of the interior. Nothing. 'You saw them, right?'

'Saw what, Miss Sophie?' Saif has a peculiar look on his face and he's eyeing me strangely.

'I thought...'

Saif places a hand on my forearm, and I look at him. He seems concerned in a way I have never seen from him before. 'Miss Sophie?'

'No,' I say, looking at him apologetically, smiling awkwardly and shaking my head. 'Saif, everything is fine.' He still has his hand on me, and I place my other hand over his. The touch is momentary, and he smiles.

'If you are sure?' he says.

'I am, thank you.'

The rain is increasing in intensity now, and I withdraw my arm from Saif to move the wet hair that's hanging across my eye and clinging to my cheek. 'Wait for one moment, please,' he says, turning and hurrying back to the driver's side of the car, reaching inside and fumbling for something. I can't see what he's doing and I'm blinking rainwater away from where it has caught in my lashes.

Saif returns with something in his hand, and he extends it to me. I take it without thinking, looking down at a thin leather, beaded necklace. The beads are wooden, all of a similar size but varying in colour. Different types of wood, I guess. I look up at him, perplexed with a half-smile on my face. 'What is this?'

'In my homeland this is a...' – his face wrinkles as he searches for the correct term – 'it is used for the blessing of a troubled soul. It will protect you from evil spirits.' I think he's joking but his expression is as serious as I've ever seen from him.

'I don't need...' I protest, but he holds my eye and I smile gratefully. 'Evil spirits, you say?'

He glances up at the bedroom window once more, and I follow his gaze, and then his eyes lower back to me. 'You must keep it with you at all times. May God bless you this day, Miss Sophie.'

I don't know what to say, and Saif doesn't wait for a reply. He walks back to the driver's door and gets in. I hurry back into the house, hoping to get clear of the rain and wave as I reach the front door, open it and step into the hall. My dressing gown has parted slightly, and I draw it around me again, tightening the cord around my waist. Saif waits in the car, watching, and I only see him move off once I close the door to him.

'Hello, Sophie.'

Startled, I turn, step backwards and bang my head against the door. It's not possible. *It can't be.*

'C-Cecilia?'

THIRTY-EIGHT

She steps out from the shadows as my breath comes in short, ragged gasps. I swallow hard. 'Sophie, it's me, Deanna,' she says, peering at me out of the gloom with a curious expression. 'Are you feeling okay?'

'No, I mean, yes. I'm fine. You just... you gave me a fright is all.'

'I'm sorry. I seem to be making a habit of that, don't I?'

'You can say that again.' I have a trembling hand placed flat against my chest, clutching the beaded necklace against my heart which is beating like the clappers.

'You're not going into the studio today?'

'No, I'm not feeling right.'

'Is there anything I can do for you—'

'No, thank you,' I say as I stare at her briefly; the image of Cecilia comes unbidden to my mind again. I need to be alone. I brush past her, picking up the pace as she calls after me.

'Are you sure? You seem upset.'

'I'm fine,' I say, pressing the call button for the lift. Right now she scares me even more than it does, and that's saying a lot. It'll be the fastest way out. The doors don't open, and I can hear Deanna coming toward me, so I take off up the stairs having first kicked off Scott's shoes, leaving them where they land.

'Sophie?' I hear Deanna say but I don't stop, rounding the turn of the half landing and continuing up the stairs without looking down. I don't stop until I'm into the guest bedroom, my sleeping quarters in exile, and close the door, leaning my back against it and sinking to the floor.

Only now do I recall the figure I saw, or thought I saw, whilst I was outside talking to Saif. Pushing off the ground, I rise with my back against the door, listening intently and making ready to turn and run if the need arises. I can hear nothing besides the sound of my own breathing.

My eyes, once they have adjusted to the darkness, search the room for signs of someone else being present. *There is nothing to fear but fear itself.* That's what my therapist used to tell me, making me recite it again and again. I wish it was true.

Looking at the bedside table, the picture frame isn't there and now I doubt it ever was. But it all seemed so real.

Mind you, I just mistook my daughter's tutor for a woman who's been dead for the better part of the last twelve years, so maybe I can't trust my own eyes. And if I can't trust what I can see, what on earth can I believe?

A few hours ago, I wasn't sure about seeing Dr Sheldon, although I accepted the need, but now the morning can't come soon enough. 'It'll be okay,' I whisper, closing my eyes and trying to regulate my breathing.

I used to regularly practise these exercises to calm my mind. Following the advice of my therapist, I started attending classes in mindfulness and meditation, offered free by the local Buddhist group, until it became too difficult with Scott's work schedule and looking after the children. I'm trying hard to recall the techniques now, and wondering why I ever ceased the practice, when I open my eyes, and something catches my attention. Is there something on the bed?

I stiffen and edge towards it. There, lying on the edge of the bed is a soft toy. Katie's tiger. 'But I—'

The door starts to open behind me then and I yelp, throwing myself against it with all my weight to stop it from opening. I lean onto it, wondering what I should do just as someone bangs their fist against the door. 'Sophie?'

It's Scott and I turn, yanking the door open and throw myself into his arms, collapsing into him. He holds me up, his arms encircling me.

'What is it?' he asks, surprised, as we both sink to the floor, me crumpled in his arms. 'You're all wet. What have you been doing? Have you been outside?'

'Cecilia.'

'Cece? What about her?'

'She's back,' I say, looking up at him.

'Sophie,' he says, looking at me sternly. 'Cecilia is gone and she's never coming back. You know this. Whatever has got into you?'

'I saw her.'

His eyes narrow. 'What do you mean, you... that's not possible.'

'I know, I know it's not possible, but I saw her. And she was here. Right here in this room.'

'Sophie,' Scott says, and I recognise the tone, and he's shaking his head, 'you were having a dream again or something—'

'But someone was in here, *in this room*, looking down on me when I was outside.'

'When?' he asks, glancing at the window.

'Just now, before.'

'What were you doing outside?'

'I... I had to... it doesn't matter, but I saw someone up here and—'

'Sophie,' he says, squeezing me tightly, 'it couldn't have been Cecilia. Come on, you know this is nonsense.'

'But the picture and—'

'I thought we'd covered all of this? Look, there is no picture and Cecilia hasn't come back from beyond the grave to... I *don't know what* you think she would be doing. It's all...' He hesitates, and I can see the words catching in his throat. 'It's all in your head, Sophie.'

'No, it can't be,' I say, lifting my head from his chest but my fingers are still clutching the folds of the T-shirt he's been sleeping in. I dare not let go. 'If it is, then...'

'Then what?'

I respond in a whisper. 'Then I'm losing my mind. Scott, I'm scared.'

He says nothing, but he holds me more tightly still. The safety of the embrace is reassuring, but I know it's only temporary and sooner or later, he is going to have to let go and I'll start falling again, and I'm terrified that I'm never going to stop.

'It's going to be okay,' he tells me, but I know from his tone that he's speaking without conviction. 'What is that?'

'What?'

'That, in your hand?'

I look at my right hand and I'm still clutching tightly to the necklace Saif gave me whilst I was outside with him. I let go of Scott and open my palm. 'It's a charm of some kind, I think.'

'Where did you get it?' Scott asks, carefully taking it from my palm and holding it in the air, examining it in what little light there is available to him.

'My driver, the one the studio sends, gave it to me.'

'You're accepting gifts from strange men now?' There's no accusatory tone in the question; he is teasing me to lighten the situation.

'Saif isn't a strange man. He's been my driver since I started on the national programme.'

'And what is this charm supposed to do?' he asks, curiosity getting the better of him as he angles it in the air.

'It will ward off evil spirits.'

'It does? He really thinks that.'

'That's what he said.'

'I'll bet you can get these ten-a-penny from beach hawkers all across the Med,' Scott says, placing the necklace back into my palm. My fingers encompass it. 'Besides, you don't need any tat like that or religious artefacts to protect you from evil.'

'I don't?' I ask, feeling my lips forming a half-smile, reflecting Scott's.

'No, you have me to do that for you.' He draws me back to him and I rest my head on his chest. His heartbeat is measured, as always, my rock in a sea of turmoil. 'And I'll never let anyone hurt you, Sophie. Never.'

We sit there on the floor in silence, Scott kissing the top of my head, making reassuring sounds, but I'm looking across at the bed where I can see the head of Tiggy peeking over the edge of the bed, looking straight at me. The same Tiggy I tucked under the duvet in Katie's bedroom not half an hour ago.

At least, I think I did.

THIRTY-NINE

Dr Sheldon has a curious way about him. In his sixties and approaching retirement, he has a shock of white hair seemingly sprouting from above the ear line and a bald pate, wisps of thin hair sticking up as monuments to what once stood there, much like the pyramids do for a past empire. He peers over the rim of his spectacles, searching my expression with an unreadable one of his own. He has an air of authority, a knowledge deeper than anything I can fathom. He should be a reassuring figure, but I find him somewhat unsettling.

'And how have you been finding things with the medication?' he asks, and I shrug slightly, the second time I've made the same reaction to his questions. The last time is the reason he was peering over his glasses at me in the first place.

'Fine.'

'No side effects?'

I shake my head. 'No, none at all.' He nods solemnly, releasing the finger grip on my wrist as he finishes measuring my pulse. He purses his lips and I feel the need to elaborate. 'I mean, I felt a bit woozy from time to time.'

'Hmm. From time to time,' he repeats quietly, arching his

eyebrows momentarily before glancing at the bedroom door. It is still closed. We are alone. 'And when did you stop taking them, Sophie?'

I pinch my lips together. He knows his stuff, but then you would having had a career in medicine spanning forty-plus years, I guess. 'Stopped?' He fixes me with an uncompromising look.

'Yes. I haven't issued you with a repeat prescription for' – he looks at his notes – 'three months. Now, I am a physician and not a mathematician, but I can count,' he says gently.

'A while ago.'

'Didn't you think it would be a good idea to discuss this with me first?'

I shake my head, feeling my face reddening like I've gone back in time to being eight years old and my dad's caught me raiding the kitchen for biscuits just before dinner. 'I don't want to live my life through the prism of medication. I want to be normal.'

'And how is that working out for you at the moment?' he asks drily. There's no accusation in his tone, but it is a rhetorical question. After all, he wouldn't be here before eight o'clock in the morning if I was flying straight and level.

'Not great.'

'Not great,' he repeats softly, setting his palms down in his lap. It feels odd having him here, perched on the side of my bed in his tweed suit. The bedroom, either the marital bedroom or the guest suite, is my safe space where I can close the door on the world. The plush carpet, my accessories scattered across my vanity unit, the easy chair to the right of the bed, are all mine to do with as I please. This man is invading that space and bringing with him my vulnerability, holding it aloft before me like a mirror so I can see it in glorious technicolour.

He takes a breath, fixing me with a serious look before adjusting his waistcoat. I'm sure it cost a fortune, his suit, but it has seen better days. I don't think Dr Sheldon is too bothered about making a statement with his wardrobe. It's alright for some. 'I think we need to discuss a plan for the future,' he says.

'That sounds ominous.'

'It doesn't have to be, Sophie. I prescribed you the medication to help, not hinder, your recovery.'

'I didn't feel like I was getting better.'

'How did you feel?'

'Like I was drifting through my days, my life, like a zombie. Unfeeling, like a ghost of myself. If that makes any sense?'

'Yes, it does.' He nods slowly, thoughtfully. 'But, in that period, you have made a successful step ahead in your career advancement, become a national celebrity no less.'

'A celebrity, no. My face is fairly well known, it's true, but celebrities are people who are famous for being who they are and not just for what they do. No one really knows me, and if they did, then I wouldn't be a celebrity for very long.'

'I'm sure that isn't true, but my point is that perhaps the medication helped you to focus, to put you in a better place to move forward in your life. Have you considered that?'

I shrug again. He's not a fan of me shrugging, I can tell. His bedside manner is a bit old school: *do as I say because I know best*. He probably does, to be fair. At least from a medical, if not psychological, point of view. But it's my body and my life. 'I suppose it might have, but I still don't like how it made me feel.'

'Did you sleep better when you were taking them?'

'Yes.'

'And your work life improved?'

'Yes.' I can see where this is going.

'What about your relationships at home?'

'In what way?'

'Were they more harmonious?'

'Everyone else was very happy, yes.' He picked up on that comment; I saw a flicker in his eyes.

'But not you?' I look down. I really don't want to be pumped full of sedatives and beta blockers. 'Scott tells me you've been having some domestic trouble of late, with your daughter.'

'Yes, she... well, it has been difficult.'

'Is her behaviour related to your state of mind, do you think?' That's a loaded question if ever there was one.

'Who said that?' Offence is the best defence, after all. Dr Sheldon doesn't answer. He begins packing away his equipment into his little leather case.

'It is my opinion that you should go back on your medication, Sophie.' I'm about to protest but he hasn't finished. 'And I would also recommend something to help you sleep. The two combined should help to stabilise your condition—'

'It will turn me into a—'

'A zombie, yes, I feared you would say that. I wouldn't put it quite that way, but you are right that you will feel different; your emotions will be somewhat muted. However, I think it is the best course of action for the time being, and perhaps we could look at some cognitive talking therapy, which may also help alleviate some of your anxiety.'

I sigh. Someone knocks on the bedroom door, and I'm terrified it's Scott. Grasping the doctor's forearm, I whisper urgently, 'Please don't tell Scott.'

'Tell him what?'

'That I've stopped my medication—' He doesn't get a chance to reply as the door opens and Scott walks in with a mug in his hands. Steam is drifting up from the contents and he smiles as he sets the mug down on the bedside table next to me.

'So, what's the verdict, Joseph?' It concerns me that Scott is so close to his family doctor to be on first name terms. I would prefer a degree of separation for the family, to maintain an independent medical opinion, but Joseph Sheldon has been Scott's family practitioner for the entire time I've known him. Even when we got together whilst living in Switzerland, Dr Sheldon was always the first port of call for a diagnosis. Scott takes the man's word as if it was the word of God. Okay, that's not literally true, but his opinion carries more weight than anyone else's. Certainly more than mine.

'I think we have someone who is overwrought,' Dr Sheldon says, glancing between me and my husband. That's a relief, I have to say.

'Do you think we should up her medication?' Scott asks.

'No, I wouldn't say so.' Scott is visibly surprised by that. 'I think that I can prescribe something to help her through the night' – it's like I'm not here now, and the two men are discussing me like I'm a defective engine part or something – 'and, if she sticks to her original treatment plan too, then I think we will see an improvement.' He casts his eyes sideways at me and something unsaid passes between us. 'I'll issue a repeat prescription alongside the sleeping aids.' That is such a nice way to describe sedatives.

'Thank you, Joseph. And many thanks for coming out at such short notice,' Scott says warmly.

'It's no trouble, Scott. I'm always at your service, you know that. I know how these situations can impact upon you.'

Upon him, *upon Scott*. It's true, with the history of mental illness Scott's had to cope with in his life, especially with what happened with Cecilia, he is very dialled in to mental health awareness. This kind of drama must bring back so many bad memories. That thought brings on a wave of guilt and shame, but at least I recognise that now. In the past, I was so detached, so delusional that my reality trumped everything and everyone else. I was so selfish.

Dr Sheldon produces a small brown bottle, shaking it performatively and passing it to Scott. 'These should tide you over until you are able to reach a chemist.'

'I'll go today,' Scott says.

'I can go myself,' I say but neither man is encouraging me to do so with their looks. 'I'm not dying.'

'I'll go,' Scott says, smiling weakly. 'You should rest.' He holds the bottle in his hand aloft. 'If you're going to sleep then you probably shouldn't drink that cup of tea. I'll get you a glass of water.' He's right. I'm bone weary and the day has only just begun.

'Listen to him, Sophie, he's right. Get some rest and consider what we talked about. Can you do that?' I nod and I can see Scott searching me with his eyes in my peripheral vision. He's picked up on something and I hope he won't press either me or Joseph on what the doctor meant. 'You'll be back to your old self in no time.'

'Thank you, Doctor Sheldon.'

The GP smiles and stands up, picking up his case and nodding to Scott. 'I love what you've done with the place, Scott. You've really brought the house on.'

'Thank you, Joseph. I'll see you out.' Scott smiles at me, leans over and kisses my forehead. 'I'll be back in a minute with that water.'

I watch the two men leave, Scott striking up a conversation as they exit the room, closing the door behind him, leaving me alone once more. I don't want to go back on the medication but I know that's selfish on my part. I'm struggling to see the line between reality and fantasy already, and my experience tells me that it will only get worse from here on in. I can't put Scott and the children through all of this again. It's time to act.

FORTY

I'm sitting up in bed, a bank of pillows and cushions supporting me, watching the branches of the nearby trees lining the edge of the park across the street gently swaying in the breeze. In my mind, I can hear the breeze rustling through the leaves, but the windows are closed. I'm half tempted to open them and let the fresh air in, but Scott always says that will upset the balance of the air conditioning. I'd rather go with the natural over the artificial, personally. Maybe that's another reason I prefer not taking medication.

My phone vibrates and I search for it, finding it wrapped up under the duvet. I've no idea how it got in the bed. It's a message from Magda, straight to the point.

You're not in the studio.

I reply that I'm not feeling well. It's a short message, too. I'm not in the mood to explain myself, not to Magda and not to anyone. The bedroom door opens, startling me. Scott pokes his head around the door and then enters with a glass of water in hand. 'Everything all right?'

'Yes, why?' I say, glancing at the next message that comes through.

Turn on your television NOW!

'You look, I don't know, pained.'

'I have a headache, that's all. Lack of sleep, I suppose.' Scott comes over to the stand beside the bed, putting the glass down and sits on the edge. I angle my mobile away from him and then bury it beneath the duvet, so he can't see the messages. I don't know why. Scott holds out his hand; there are a couple of pills in his palm. Joseph Sheldon's pick-me-ups, I figure.

'Looking at your phone screen isn't likely to help with a headache, is it?'

'No, probably not.' I take the pills from him and smile appreciatively.

'I'm just going out to the pharmacy to get your prescription. Deanna is downstairs with Katie.' At the mention of her name, an image of Scott walking arm in arm with her flashes into my mind and I force it aside.

'Okay, thanks.'

Scott looks at me and I avoid his gaze, fearing he wants to ask me something I'd rather not talk about. There are a number of things that come under the category of *don't tell Scott*: my dreams, visions of the dead and the quiet dispensing of taking my medication are the most pressing. I'm sitting here, propped up on my pillows hoping he won't press it, at least not for now. I can't articulate the thoughts in my own head, let alone explain them to someone else, even my husband.

Thankfully, he takes the hint and simply places a gentle hand on my leg, patting it gently with a look of resignation. 'I'll not be long. Will you be okay?'

'Yes, of course.' I smile at him as he leans into me and kisses my cheek. I can see he's hurting, and it's all my fault.

Scott has been so wonderful to me ever since we first met. With everything he's been through with his family, after Cecilia, he deserves some happiness and yet he ends up with someone like me. He's so caring and he always wants to help others, and I guess that means he tends to be attracted to fragile women. Maybe that's unfair, on him and me. Cecilia too.

Scott gets up and drags his hand lightly over mine as he walks away. 'I won't be long. You can call me on my mobile—'

'I'll be fine! I'm not on my deathbed.'

He laughs awkwardly. 'I know, sorry. I just—'

'Worry. I know. And I love you for it.'

'See you in a little while.'

Scott leaves and I lift my phone. It is on silent, as I set it each night, and there are two missed calls and another text message.

Seriously. TURN IT ON.

Throwing off the duvet, I cross the room to where I left the remote and switch on the wall-mounted TV. I'm in time to catch the morning news round-up and my breath catches in my throat as I see a picture of myself up on the screen beneath the headline *BREAKDOWN*.

My phone starts vibrating on the bedside table, the monotonous buzzing amplified by the solid surface. I don't react, my eyes fixed on an image of a bedraggled me, no make-up, wet hair clinging to my face as I stand in the street in my dressing gown with odd-looking shoes on. The sound is muted on the television, but I don't need to hear it. A picture paints a thousand words, so they say, and this picture is mortifying.

Snapping out of it, I hurry over and pick up the phone. 'Magda. What's going on?'

'You're asking me?'

'I... I... this was last night,' I say, barely able to string a coherent sentence together. 'How did they—'

'If you are having problems, Sophie darling, then you really needed to speak to me. This really isn't the way to make it public—'

'I'm not, I mean, okay, I am.' My head is an absolute skip fire right now. 'I can't believe this.'

'Who is the man in the video?'

'There's video?' I ask just as the VT starts rolling on the screen. The images of me outside in the middle of the night start moving, the camera pans out to encompass part of a car and I see a man approach me, passing me something and then we hold hands.

'Who's the guy? Is he your dealer or something?'

'No!'

'Do you always meet dodgy-looking men in the street in the early hours of the—'

'For heaven's sake, Magda, he's my driver. He takes me to the studio every morning!'

'Ah, well that's not what they are saying in the media outlets.'

I can't believe this. My breath is coming in ragged inhalations, and I can feel my face burning, a hot flush like nothing I've ever experienced previously.

'What did he give you?' Magda asks. 'The gossip columnists are dying to know.'

'Tell them it's none of their damn business.'

'I have to tell them something, Sophie darling.'

'Why?'

'Because we have to get out in front of this thing, to own it otherwise someone else will provide the narrative, and, well, because they are speculating you're having a breakdown—'

'Yes, I can see that!' I shout, pointing at the television as if Magda isn't watching the same feed. 'It's all over the television.'

'What's going on with that man?'

'Nothing is going on. This is all a fuss over nothing. He came to collect me as usual, but I was ill, and no one had asked him not to.'

'It's a shame you're not in the studio today. Why is that?'

'I told you, I'm ill!'

Magda pauses, and I can imagine her thinking hard. 'They'll say there's no smoke without fire.'

'I told the studio, just like I'm telling you now, I'm not well.'

'Well, in the pictures I'm looking at, you certainly don't look great, it's true. Are you on something?'

'No, I'm not! And I'm not having a breakdown either. I'm just not feeling myself just now.'

'That's good. I'm as new-age as the next agent, you know me, and I can work with general illness but it's difficult to keep things clean if I don't know whether I'm going to find you in the street scoring a bag off some random—'

'Magda, please!'

She goes quiet and I sink to the floor, my back against the foot of the bed, eyes transfixed on the screen. It's a rolling cycle of footage, me in my dressing gown, standing in the rain. It's like watching a car crash unfold in slow motion, only I'm driving the car and being hit by it at the same time. 'This isn't happening.'

'Oh, it is definitely happening,' Magda says and her words tail away as I lower the phone from my ear and my hand settles into my lap.

'This can't be happening,' I whisper again to myself, and then I put my head in my hands, and I can hear screaming. And it's my voice.

I can't look at this anymore. I just can't watch my life self-destruct on live television. The pictures of me talking to Saif come back onto the screen and it's clear this is the main news story of the day. I can hear Magda's voice, detached and far off.

My mobile is still in my hand and an overwhelming need to silence everything courses through me.

It feels like what I imagine an out of body experience is as I get up, hurling my phone at the television. The strike sends multiple cracks shooting out from the impact point, almost dead centre. The screen flickers with a rainbow of colours, then flashes black and white for a second or two before going dark. The sound, though, keeps playing through the speakers and I run over, grasping the bevelled edge and twisting and pulling with an enraged strength I didn't know I possessed.

The fixings give way, and the television topples toward me. I leap back and it pivots momentarily, desperately holding onto the final connection with the bracket but then it too gives, bends and snaps and the screen hits the carpeted floor.

I have the silence I craved, but the noise in my head is only just getting going. And I know what comes next. *What am I going to do?* I can't breathe; I want to run but there is nowhere to run to. I can hear noise outside, unusual for Chester Terrace at this time of the day, or any day in truth. Backing away from the smashed television screen, I retreat across the room to the window, feeling a sharp pain in the ball of my foot, but I ignore it. Cracking open the slats in the shutters, I peer down to the street below.

On the far side, on the edge of the parkland, people are gathering. But they're not ordinary people. These are not members of the public; they have cameras, cables trailing the floor around their feet. They're professionals. The vultures have arrived.

What am I going to do?

My eyes drift to the bedside table and the glass of water Scott brought me. Beside it is the bottle of tablets Dr Sheldon left. I can't remember how many he said I should take.

I tip the bottle upside down and three fall out into my palm, and I put all three into my mouth and wash them down with half of the water.

I know that's wrong, one should be enough, two at the most, but I need to get away from all of this. I need it all to stop.

FORTY-ONE

My eyes open and for a moment I'm unsure of where I am. It's dark. The wind is blowing a gale outside, but I feel strangely comforted by the sound. I slowly adjust to the room. A shaft of artificial light has crept in through the crack of the open door from the landing beyond. I can hear muffled voices, but I don't think they're nearby.

Was it all a dream?

My eyes close on the space on the wall where the television used to be. The bracket is still fixed to the wall, although it is twisted and bent in an unusual way. Where did I find the strength to do that? Because it was me. It was all me.

I'm not dressed. I don't remember getting undressed. My body feels relaxed, but I'm lethargic.

I've no idea what time of the day it is, and my digital clock is blank. Has there been a power cut? If so, why are the lights still on, on the landing? Propping myself up on my elbows, I crane my neck to see the floor at the foot of the bed. Someone has cleared away the mess I made. How they did so without waking me, I'll never know. Rolling onto my side, images come to mind. Cecilia. Dr Sheldon. Magda. The paparazzi.

The bottle of tablets is still on the bedside table beside the half-empty glass of water. How long have I been asleep? A figure passes outside on the landing, a shadow breaking the shaft of light, all that is illuminating the bedroom.

'Scott?' My voice sounds lighter in my head than normal, disembodied somehow. The figure returns, hovering on the other side of the door but I can't make out who it is. 'Scott, is that you?'

Staring at the door, I'm half expecting it to open but nothing is moving. I can see a flickering light coming from the en-suite bathroom but it's unlike anything I would expect. Slipping out from beneath the duvet, a familiar smell reaches my nose, toxic and unpleasant. I tentatively approach the door to the en suite; it is cracked open, and the flickering is reflected in the mirror mounted on the wall behind the twin basins.

Easing the door open, I see the last recognisable piece of the photograph as the corner curls in upon itself, blistering and crackling as it is consumed by the flames. Scott and me, entwined on the beach on our wedding day. I leap forward and turn on the cold tap, the last flicker of flame immediately extinguished by the water. Stepping back, I waft away the acrid smoke and wonder if it will set off the smoke detector in the bedroom.

I catch movement on the landing in the corner of my eye. Whoever it is steps aside, but I'm sure they are still there. I can't see or hear them though. The landing light goes off momentarily before whoever it is passes by the bedroom, scurrying away. Hurrying across the bedroom to try and catch a glimpse of them, a sharp pain stabs at the sole of my foot and I pull up, quickly sitting down on the bed. I lift my foot and it's wrapped in a bandage; a dark liquid has permeated through the dressing. A gentle probing sends more pain shooting through my foot and I hiss at the sensation. Why didn't I feel this when I just got up?

Tentatively, I get up and hobble across the room to the door, pulling it open further just in time to see Deanna making her way downstairs. Moving as fast as I can to the balustrade, I peer down at her. 'Deanna?' She doesn't answer, increasing her pace and then I see it.

How dare she. She's wearing it. That's my dress, the one she was supposed to be cleaning. 'Deanna!'

She's gone and part of me wants to chase after her, catch up with her and tear my dress from her youthful body. But I'm calm. I'm not angry. I can't feel the pain in my foot anymore. I'm not sure exactly what I'm going to do, but I'm determined to fix this.

I sit up in bed. Rain is drumming against the window, much as it was last night. I have no idea what time it is. The clock beside my bed says it is nine forty-five p.m. I've been out of it all day! The room is in darkness, and I am alone. The glass of water is half-empty, beside it, the bottle of tablets left for me by Dr Sheldon. *Was I dreaming all or any of it?* My eyes shift to the television and it isn't mounted on the wall anymore. I definitely didn't dream that.

Reaching beneath the duvet, I feel for the injury to my foot, finding the bandages still in place. It was real. Throwing back the duvet, I swing my legs out and tentatively put my feet down. I'm wearing my underwear this time, at least. Looking at the window, at the intensity of the rain, I wonder if the press are still outside. Creeping across the bedroom, I hug the wall to the right of the sash window, peering around the shutters and down into the street. I can't see anyone but there are several vans parked up, partly across the pavement. Maybe they've left for the night. Either that or they've hunkered down inside.

Hurrying to my wardrobe, ignoring the pain in my foot, I open the first door and scan the rail. The red dress isn't there, but I know Deanna took it. She was going to clean it or take it to the dry-cleaner's. I can't remember which. If she kept it, then she would have it. Did I stain it, or am I imagining that too? I open the second door, and it's not here either. I push aside the dresses one by one, but it isn't here. I open the next wardrobe, increasing the speed of my search but I already know I'm not going to find it in here. I know where it is.

Running from the guest suite, I almost lose my footing as I go down to the next floor, cursing my throbbing foot, using the wall to steady myself and run into our bedroom. My day-to-day clothing is still in here. I only keep what I wear to the studio in the guest suite. I don't even think to turn on the bedroom lights; the wardrobes have their own motion sensors anyway. I'm not methodically looking now, like I was upstairs; it's as if I'm set on autopilot pulling out hanger after hanger and casting everything aside to the bed, the chairs, or the floor, I don't care.

I'm aware enough to know I'm having some kind of an episode but not enough to cease acting upon the impulse.

I have to know. I have to be sure.

Someone appears in the bedroom; I see them in my peripheral vision but I'm too focused on ransacking the wardrobes. I've emptied mine and now I'm tearing through Scott's clothing, discarding anything and everything that isn't my red dress.

'Sophie?'

I ignore him. He wouldn't understand. He can't possibly understand.

'Sophie!'

I turn on him. 'No!'

He looks at me with a mixed expression, confusion, irritation and something else. Amusement? No. He couldn't find this funny.

'No what?' Scott asks.

'No, I will not stop.'

Scott stays where he is, casting his eye over everything I have removed from the wardrobes. A burglar would have made less of an impact.

'What... what on earth are you doing?'

'You'll see!' I announce triumphantly, wagging a pointed finger at him. '*You will see.*'

'Sophie, can you—'

'Can I what?' I ask, glaring at him and I can see he's taken aback. 'What *can I do*, Scott?'

'Can you take a moment, take a breath, and try to think straight. Perhaps you could tell me what this is about?'

'Oh, I am thinking straight, Scott. Believe me, for the first time in months, I am thinking straight.' He must see the determination in my face, just as I can feel it empowering me. I stride past him and I see him roll his eyes before turning and following after me.

'Sophie, what is all of this about?'

'You'll see,' I state confidently, heading down the stairs towards the voices I heard earlier. Was it earlier or was it yesterday? The day before? I don't know what day it is. No matter. Happy voices, pleasant communal conversation. All without a care in the world. Well, I'll give them something to think about, that's for damn sure.

The kitchen is full. At least, it is full when you consider what the norm is in our house. Conversation ceases. Everyone turns to look at me and I don't care. Chas is open-mouthed; the three people chatting with him over snacks and bottles of beer – university friends I guess – are staring at me with equally shocked expressions. I wonder what could *possibly* have brought Chas's friends here tonight of all nights. No doubt I'm some sort of peculiarity for them to examine. A case study for their next psychology assignment, perhaps? After all, I'm across the papers, the talk of the entertainment media with their vampires camped outside looking for the next image to prove I've lost the plot. I'm inclined to go outside right now and give them exactly what they want!

Katie is observing me from her place at the breakfast bar, playing some board game with Deanna. *Deanna.* I ignore everyone else and stare at her.

'Where is it?'

She coughs awkwardly. 'Where is what?' she asks, playing dumb, slipping off the stool.

'Where is—'

'Sophie!' Scott barks from behind me, but I ignore him as well, just as I'm ignoring the teenagers staring at me, half-dressed, standing in my own kitchen. It's my house and I'll do what I want.

'The dress. Where is it?' I ask, steeling myself. Deanna looks past me at my husband but I'm not letting her off the hook. 'I want it back.'

'The... the one I cleaned?'

'Yes! The red one you took to the dry-cleaner's!'

Deanna's eyes flit to Scott and back to me again. 'The coffee stain came out. I had no need to take it to the dry-cleaner's.' I take a step toward her, and she mirrors the action but steps backwards.

'I know you want it. I know you want to be me. You want my life.'

'I... don't understand,' she says, nervously. 'I hung it in your wardrobe. I thought that's what—'

'You're lying.'

'I-I'm not lying,' she says, in a whisper.

'Well, we'll see about that, won't we?' I turn around and walk purposefully out of the kitchen, knowing they are all exchanging confused looks with one another. I don't care. Scott reaches for me, gently grasping my forearm but I shrug him off, walking into the hall.

'Where are you going, Soph?' he asks, falling into step. I pick up the pace. If I let him get in front of me then he'll stop me, bar my way. He matches my pace, and I can hear other footfalls behind us on the stairs as I descend to the basement level. 'You can't go into Deanna's personal—'

'I think you'll find that's exactly what I'm doing. You'll see why.'

Scott grabs my arm from behind, more forcefully this time, and it takes a concerted effort to shake him off, but I manage. He tries to pull me back but I make it down to the basement level and I make a beeline for Deanna's bedroom, barging in before Scott can stop me. Hauling open the wardrobe, I don't have much time to prove my case. Scott is shouting at me now, his words lost in a mental fog. I'm so focused. Deanna really doesn't have many clothes, so it won't be hard to find what she's stolen from me.

'Sophie!' Scott shouts and I turn on him just as I'm throwing Deanna's clothes onto the floor. 'You can't behave like this! It's not on.'

I'm out of clothes. There's nothing left in the wardrobe. I don't understand.

'Sophie,' Scott says, coming to stand behind me. His tone has changed. The situation has changed. It's not here. She doesn't have it. I turn to face him, and he places both his hands on my arms. I'm tense, fists balled at my sides. He slides his hands down and takes mine into his. I relent and he squeezes them gently. 'It's all right,' he says. 'It's going to be all right.'

I look past him. Deanna is standing in the doorway. Chas is behind her with his hands on Katie's shoulders. I can see something in her expression I've never seen before.

Fear.

My eyes dart between them and Scott. 'I'm so sorry,' I say quietly. Three simple words that catch in my throat as I say them. My confidence, my assuredness, it's all gone. Did it ever exist? I feel my eyes tearing up, my face and neck warming. The embarrassment. The shame. I'm six years old again. My father is standing before me, with that look. It's always that look.

'Sophie?' Scott says and my father isn't in the room anymore. My husband is here. He looks scared too. Everyone is frightened. I've done that. It's my fault.

'This is all my fault,' I say, pushing past Scott and running for the door. The others part to the side, averting their eyes from mine, and I hustle my way through them, back upstairs, ignoring the pain I feel with every step, ignoring the blood I can feel seeping through my dressing.

FORTY-TWO

I don't know what is happening with me. I'm feeling everything and nothing but all at the same time. I'm out of breath as I stumble onto the landing outside the guest suite; my lungs feel like they're ready to explode, my legs have so much lactic acid in them that they won't move properly.

Scott appears at my side, and I relinquish my hold on the newel post and fall into his arms. How did he get here so quickly? I see the lift doors close behind him. His embrace is comforting, and I feel myself go limp and I'm crying. He hasn't said anything at all. I'm such an embarrassment. I don't want anyone to see me like this, not even Scott, but I won't push him away.

'I'm so sorry,' I say, forcing the words out between racking sobs. I must look a state. 'I don't know what's happening to me, Scott.' I sink down to the floor, Scott coming down with me. I can see smears on the carpet, blood from my foot, on the carpet. My skin is crawling. It's as if it's alive and I'm probing my forearms with my fingertips but it's not helping. If anything, the itching, the unpleasant sensations are only getting worse.

'It's going to be all right, Sophie.'

'It's not,' I say, scratching at my arms with my fingernails. My legs are prickling as well now. 'How can you say that? Everything is falling apart. I'm falling apart.'

'We can fix it, we... Sophie? Please, can you stop doing that?' Scott asks and I pull away from him, looking up into his worried, handsomely chiselled face.

'What is it?' He is looking at me curiously, his eyes not meeting mine. I follow his gaze down to my arms. I'm not gently scratching them now, as before, but I'm raking my fingernails over the skin, leaving great tracks, bright red and angry. 'I can't stop.'

'Maybe you're allergic to something?' he says, firmly grasping my hands to stop me from clawing myself. 'Come on, let's get you into the shower.' He scoops me up effortlessly and carries me into the guest suite. My skin is alive. It feels like it's burning and I don't know if that is self-inflicted or something else entirely.

Scott sets me down in the bathroom; the tiles feel so cold against my skin, and I'm scraping at myself again within moments. I hear the squeaking of the taps and then I hear the water starting to flow. I don't even wait to take off my underwear and crawl into the shower cubicle. The water is freezing cold, but I couldn't care less. I want to wash this feeling, the sensations off me. I want to wash everything away.

'Sophie?' Scott asks, staring at this fragile wretch of a person who used to be his wife. I can't bear to look at him, to see the disappointment in his eyes at what I've become. I crawl further into the cubicle, the water cascading over my head now, and I want to find the corner and curl up into a ball, hide from the world.

Moments later, strong arms encircle me. It's Scott. He is alongside me, drawing me to him, and I bury my head into his chest, the water falling onto the two of us. I can feel the water soaking through his shirt.

'I'm so sorry.'

'You have nothing to be sorry about,' he says above both the roar of the water striking us and the roar of voices screaming at me in my head.

'I was so sure, my red dress, I was so sure she had it.'

'Don't worry about that now.'

'Why? Why do I do this to myself?'

'We just need to get you better, that's all.'

'I was so sure,' I whisper, and I don't know if he can even hear me.

'We can fix this, I promise.'

I don't believe him. He says this often, but he couldn't fix what happened to Cecilia. Not really. And now he won't be able to cope with what's happening to me. I'm too much, and not enough, all at the same time.

My father is a lot like Scott in many ways. He was always in control, always able to deal with whatever life threw at him. Scott has tried, but he's not built from the same stuff. My father knew that. He tried to tell me, but I love this man with all my being. It was always Scott, for me. Without Scott, I'm nothing. He is my everything. But I wish my father was here for me now. Maybe things would be different.

Scott couldn't save Cecilia and he won't be able to save me either. No one can.

I am broken.

Everything is much quieter now. Whatever it was that Dr Sheldon prescribed for me, it has certainly done the trick. I'm sitting before the vanity mirror in the guest bedroom, staring at the reflection of the woman I hardly recognise, but at least she's calm. The pain, all of it, has relinquished its hold on me.

Scott is passing a brush through my hair, ensuring it's not tangled. He's sporting some clean and, more importantly, dry clothing. He finishes and steps back, meeting my eye in the reflection.

'There, much better.' He's tentative. I know he's in shock and putting a brave face on it. I'm in shock too. Where do we go from here? I know the studio have called. I also heard Scott talking to Magda on the phone a little while ago as well. Everyone wants to know what is going on with me. If they ever figure it out, then I'd like it if they could share it with me too. 'What do you think?'

I smile. It's not much, but it is the best I can do for now. I can see it doesn't reach my eyes though. My eyes are sunken and hollow, and I look sad. There is no amount of make-up that will bring this vacant expression back to life. It's like I'm looking at a fragile copy of myself. A smile is the response I think Scott's looking for. *Progress.* Nothing more, nothing less. He has managed to improve the situation, somewhat.

Right now, I'm numb. Numb to my shame, my humiliation and, most importantly, numb to my emotions.

'It's much better,' I hear myself say without thinking. It doesn't sound like my voice, but I saw my lips moving in my reflection.

'Let's get you into bed. A good night's sleep will change everything. Things will look brighter in the morning.'

My father used to say something similar. *The day is always darkest just before the dawn.* And he was right. He knew a lot about this particular subject. I stand up, with Scott's help, and he guides me to the bed. My legs, although they are no longer itching, feel like jelly. Scott supports me again as I sit down, then he passes me a glass of water before reaching for the bottle of tablets on the bedside table and unscrewing the cap.

I don't really want to be taking drugs but stopping them and not telling anyone was arguably not the greatest decision of my life recently. Scott holds out his palm and I take the two pills he has in his hand from him. They look different to when I saw them earlier, when Dr Sheldon gave them to me, but I wasn't really paying attention. Putting them in my mouth without argument, I swallow them with a mouthful of water. I struggle as they are quite large. I'm so tired now I can hardly keep my eyes open.

Heaving my legs up into bed, I roll onto my side and Scott pulls the duvet up over me and I snuggle into it. 'You'll have more peace up here, away from my snoring.' He leans over and kisses my forehead as I close my eyes. 'I'll come and check in on you later.'

'I love you,' I whisper as he withdraws, seemingly hesitating for a moment.

'I love you too, Sophie. So very much.'

I slip into a fitful sleep, dreams of Deanna and Scott flashing through my mind. They are so real. Deanna is with Scott, and I am forced to watch as they embrace. She is wearing my red dress, and Scott is approving of how it clings to her figure. I want to yell at them to stop. I want to turn away, but I can't. I'm locked in place, watching as my life disintegrates before my eyes.

Deanna turns to face me, mouthing the words *I love you*. She isn't saying it to my husband. She is saying it to me, just as she brandishes a kitchen knife, holding it aloft at the foot of the bed.

I want to scream, but I can't. I'm lying in my bed. I'm paralysed with fear.

FORTY-THREE

DEANNA

Thursday

I'm doing my best to appear busy in the kitchen, clearing up behind Chas and his friends. They beat a hasty retreat from the house after Sophie lost the plot, and who could blame them? Scott had the doctor visit Sophie yesterday, and since then I've not seen her. Scott told us all she was sleeping, that she was overwrought. I can see he wasn't exaggerating, based on her appearance this evening.

Pouring away the half-empty bottles of beer and gathering up the empty crisp packets, I'm wondering how things are going upstairs. As soon as Sophie took off, I knew Scott would follow. What else could he do? Chas, for all his bravado about taking on the world, was like a rabbit caught in the headlights and as for Katie, well, the poor thing shouldn't have to see an adult, her supposed mother at that, going through something like this. Sophie would never have acted like that if she was in her right mind, but of course she isn't right. She never has been.

So, it fell to me to take the lead. Chas didn't know what to say to his student friends who were enjoying a relaxing evening one minute and then had their friend's half-dressed mother screaming in the kitchen.

They were okay. I ushered them out the back way, down the alley toward the adjoining street. With a bit of luck, I knew the paparazzi camped on the front doorstep wouldn't have colleagues around the back and if they did, they might not realise where the young party emerged from. Hopefully, Chas has chosen his friends well and none of them will speak to the press. It's one thing to orchestrate a headline – which went far better than I could ever have imagined – but I don't want to push it too far.

After all, it would not be helpful if the media coverage becomes so intense that I will never be able to get away with what I have spent months planning. No, we need things outside the home dialled down just a notch or two. Behind closed doors is another matter entirely.

I set a glass of warm milk down in front of Katie, who is looking lost amongst all this adult stuff. She's probably too old for this to work, but it always helped me to settle of an evening when we were kids. She may have seen things like this before, Sophie certainly has a chequered background with her mental health, but it doesn't get any easier and she's only twelve. Should I feel guilty? Possibly. But there is more at play here than one woman's mental health. One day she'll realise. She'll understand why all of this had to happen.

'What's this?' Katie asks, observing the glass suspiciously.

'Warm milk. My mother used to make it for me when I was troubled.'

Katie glances at the liquid and nods appreciatively, wrapping her fingers around the glass but she doesn't drink any of it. 'Was your mum ever... ever, you know?'

'Emotional? Like Sophie?'

'Yes.'

'No, she wasn't. My mother and father were always very calm, very measured in their responses to everything in life.'

'Sounds like my dad,' Katie says, and I smile.

'Yes, it does, doesn't it?'

'What sounds like who?' Scott asks, entering the kitchen. Chas looks up glumly from where he's sitting at the table beside the front window overlooking the street. He's cracked open one of the shutters so he can see outside, watching the comings and goings.

'You,' Katie says. 'Deanna's dad sounds just like you.' Scott raises one eyebrow towards me in query and I nod.

'Calm under pressure.'

'Ah, yes, that's me alright,' he says, putting an arm around Katie and she leans into him. He gives her shoulder a squeeze and smiles at her.

'How's Mum?'

Again, Scott glances at me and his expression says a lot. 'Your mum's tired, and so she's gone for a lie-down. You'll see her in the morning. Okay?'

Katie nods but she's visibly bothered by all of this. Fair enough. I have been trying not to think too much about how it would be affecting her, but it is impossible not to after Sophie's episode this evening. Scott runs a hand through his daughter's hair, trying his best to sound upbeat.

'Now, I think you also need to get some sleep, young lady. Chas?' He turns to his son, who continues to peer through the shutters at the small group of photographers outside on the pavement, braving the elements for the chance of a shot for the morning papers.

'They're still out there, you know? I reckon they're staying for the night.'

'Chas?' Scott asks again and his son turns his head to face him. 'Can you take your sister up to bed for me?' Katie doesn't protest. She takes a sip from the glass of milk before leaving the rest of it and hopping off the chair. Scott gives her a hug but she doesn't reciprocate. 'I'll come up and tuck you in soon.'

Chas walks past and shoots me a glum smile, passing his father and leading Katie up to her bedroom with a supportive arm around her shoulder. Free from the prying eyes of his children, Scott sinks into the nearest chair and puts his head in his hands.

'What am I going to do?' he asks me, sounding incredibly dejected. It is what I figured all along. The air of calm and assuredness he conveys is a front he hides behind. Everyone has insecurities. Everyone has weaknesses. You just need to push the right buttons to determine what they are. We appear to have stumbled across Scott's. Losing control. Control is an illusion, but men like Scott don't understand that.

This is playing out just as I figured it would. Men are simple creatures, and this one is no different. He makes out he is, but I know better.

'What do you mean?'

'I mean, Sophie is having a full-on breakdown...'

'Is it really that bad?' I ask, seeing Scott lower his head further, his shoulders sagging. I place a supportive hand on his shoulder and take the seat next to his. 'I mean, she's having a tough time but—'

'It's more than that, Deanna.' He shakes his head and instinctively I gently rub his shoulder. He reaches his hand across his body and places it onto my hand. 'I've seen all this before. I just can't believe it's happening again.'

'Cecilia, you mean?' I withdraw my hand and he turns to face me in his seat, nodding.

'Yes, the woman I was married to before Sophie.' He seems reticent and I don't push him to open up, but I sense he wants to speak, so I give him the space to do so, doing my best to hide the tension in my body. 'She struggled for a long time. We thought that having a baby – Katie – would fill that emotional void, that need she had to be, well, needed.'

'What happened, if you don't mind me asking?'

He sits up and leans back in his seat, shaking his head. 'She couldn't cope with the baby. I mean, she tried, certainly. But the stress around that and the pressure she felt to be a perfect mother just seemed to eat away at her. I did my best to help her, but eventually...'

Scott's expression takes on a faraway look. 'She walked onto a train track... and just kept walking.'

'That's terrible. What a horrible way to die. Poor you, and poor little Katie!'

'Yes. The police weren't sure if it was an accident or whether she chose to do it but, knowing how much she was struggling, I think I know.' He sits forward, his elbows on the table's surface and resting his chin on his hands. 'So, you see, I've seen how this ends and I can't let it happen again.'

'What will you do?'

He sighs, a sound like he's letting out years of frustration in that second. 'There are places that Sophie could go to.'

'You mean hospitals?'

'Of sorts, yes. There are residential clinics, specialist places, to get her head straight.' He shakes his head. 'They work for some. Then maybe later, she can be more like the Sophie we know and love again.'

'It works for some, but not for others.'

'That's right,' he says, glumly. 'Some people just struggle all their lives with this sort of thing. I...'

'What is it?' I ask him, sensing he stopped short for fear of how I'd react.

'I shouldn't say.'

'No, go on, please. I'm here for you.'

He smiles weakly. 'I wouldn't want you to think less of me. That's all.'

'I won't. I promise,' I say, taking one of his hands in mine.

'I'm not sure I can go through all of this again. And I don't think it's fair on the children. Not only because Katie has enough on her plate as it is, but Chas was older and although he was away at boarding school when Cecilia got sick, I know he still felt the pain as much as I did.'

'I know you'll do the right thing, Scott.'

He smiles at me. 'Thank you. I hope so. If I don't do something, I fear what happened earlier this evening is just the start.' He offers me a wry smile. 'I think, if I'm honest, you should probably consider your decision to remain with us.'

I'm taken aback. 'You want me to leave?'

'No, no, heaven no, that's the last thing I want,' he says, and I believe him. 'It's just, I want you to feel safe here and I can't guarantee that things won't get worse before they get better.'

I place my hand in his again, squeezing it tightly. 'I'm here for the long haul with you, Chas and Katie,' I tell him, and he smiles. 'You can trust me to be here for all of you. I won't leave you. I won't let you down.'

Scott leans in toward me, his tired eyes full of gratitude, and I can feel the warmth of his breath on my face. 'Thank you, Deanna. I don't know what I'd do without you.'

FORTY-FOUR

'I'll make us some tea,' I say, rising from my seat beside Scott.

He smiles appreciatively. 'I meant what I said, you know?'

'What's that?' I ask, over my shoulder, filling the kettle.

'Before.' He turns in his seat, resting one arm across the back of the chair. 'When I said I don't know what I would do without you.'

'It's nothing.'

'No, it's far more than nothing! Since Martha left and Katie was expelled, it was only a matter of time before the wheels came off, so to speak. That's why I decided to make some changes around my work.'

'What changes?'

'Working from home a bit more, for a start, but there's more.'

Scott looks out towards the hall, checking we're alone I suppose. 'What else?'

'Well, I'm at a stage in my career where I can do almost whatever I want to do.'

'What do you mean?' I ask, perching on the edge of the table.

'I've made something of a habit of moving around, between companies and geographically.'

'Ah, right. You don't like to stay anywhere too long, is that it? I can relate to that. Why do you think you like to move around so much?'

Scott shifts in his seat. 'It's just how I'm built.' As if that answers my question. 'Anyway, I've made a decision.'

'That sounds ominous,' I tell him, playfully batting his upper arm. He smiles.

'It is, from a certain point of view.'

'So, are you going to tell me or do I have to guess?' The kettle boils and I return to it, pouring the water but maintaining eye contact and encouraging him to continue. Scott looks nervous, eyes flitting beyond the kitchen, fearing we'll be interrupted, I suppose. It's not a state I remember seeing him in.

'I've given notice.'

I hesitate, staring at him. 'On your—'

'Job, yes. I leave next month.'

I must admit, I hadn't expected that. 'I... when did you decide this?' I'm trying very hard not to react to the fact he's holed my plans beneath the waterline with this one.

'If I'm honest, I've been mulling it over for a while. Recent events have convinced me it is time for a change.'

'Where will you go? I mean, what will you do?'

Scott inclines his head, lips pursed. 'I think the whole family needs a fresh start, away from' – he waves his hands in a circular motion in the air – 'from all of this. London, the number of people, the pressure, all of it.'

'W-What does Sophie think about all of this?' Sophie has been very key to my plans, and being in London is rather necessary as it happens.

'She doesn't know,' he says quietly, fixing me with a stern look. 'And she mustn't either. She's far too emotional and vulnerable right now.'

'Right. That's definitely big news.'

Scott rises and comes over to me. 'I hope you don't mind me confiding in you?' I shake my head. 'It's just that I've felt something of a bond between us since you joined the family. I feel like you understand, like I can talk to you. I haven't felt anything like it for, well,' he sighs, 'not for a long time. It's been lonely, walking on eggshells around Sophie, unable to talk to anyone about what my home life has been like.'

'Thanks,' I say, touching his hand. He doesn't pull away and instead his fingers massage my hand with a delicate touch as he holds my gaze.

'I'm so glad I met you, Deanna. I don't know what I'd do without you.'

'I'm glad I met you, too,' I say, allowing myself to form a half smile. 'But you are leaving,' I say, withdrawing my hand and busying myself making us both that cup of tea.

'Yes, but you are well travelled. I can tell.'

'I am, yes.'

'And you have no ties here, no family, right?' I incline my head, but I have my back to him now so he can't see my face. This is a very unexpected move on his part, but I'm sure I can turn it to my advantage. 'What about friends? You haven't mentioned any.'

'No, it's pretty much just me. I'm on my own.'

'Well, you're not alone now you're with us, Deanna. And if you haven't got any ties here there's no reason you couldn't consider, well...' He smiles sheepishly. 'How about we all keep an open mind, shall we?'

'Yes,' I say, brightly, as I turn and pass him a cup of hastily made tea. 'Keep an open mind.'

Scott walks over to stand before the front window overlooking the street. I watch him, one hand in the pocket of his chinos, the sleeves of his shirt folded up toward his elbows. He really does cut quite a dashing figure of a man. I'll bet everyone wants to speak to him, spend time with him, and generally looks forward to being in his company. He catches me looking and I avert my eyes but not before allowing something unsaid to pass between us. I pretend there was nothing in it, but we both know that isn't the case. He shoots me a knowing smile and I return it with a coy one of my own.

'What happened to Martha?' I ask, casually.

'Martha? Oh, she had a family thing. She left suddenly, and I have no idea if she'll be coming back. If she does, it won't be anytime soon.' Scott goes quiet, ruminating. I would love to know what is going through his head.

'Penny for them?'

'Sorry?' he asks.

'Your thoughts. What's on your mind besides the obvious?'

Scott sighs, pulling out a chair for me and we both sit down. 'Sophie, earlier, she thought she saw Cecilia.'

'What, here?'

He nods. 'It's a bit scary, to be honest. Bouts of depression are one thing but this hallucinating she's been doing, it is a whole new level of weird.'

'The medication will help, won't it?'

He shrugs. 'I hope so, but they're sedatives and beta blockers, I think.' He glances at me. 'I'm not really up on the whole medication thing. She'll need a professional diagnosis I reckon. What Joseph gave her – he's our family doctor – is just to get us through this latest episode. It's all such a mess.'

'You have had a lot to deal with, Scott. Is there anyone who can help take the weight off you a bit?'

'You mean, besides you?' he asks, laughing a little.

'Besides me. Family, perhaps?'

'I don't have any family,' Scott says. 'I was an only child. My father said my parents tried for another baby, but it didn't happen.' He leans into me, lowering his voice conspiratorially. 'I don't really believe him.'

'Why not?'

'I'm not sure, but it's just a feeling. I never had the impression he was all that bothered about having children. I think he was content with just my mother for company and tolerated me when I came along.'

'I'm sure that's not true. What about your mother?'

'What about her?'

'Did she want more children?'

'She never said so. I suppose she might have, but she was obsessively tidy. It sounds silly, but it was a huge deal to her, and children aren't conducive to achieving that. I think one was all she could handle.'

'Are they still around, your parents?'

He shakes his head. 'No, they both passed away many years ago. What about you, do you have any siblings?'

'Me?' I hesitate, unsure of how open I should be, but Scott is sharing and it's an opportunity to get closer to him. 'No, none. I'm also an only child.'

'Ah, something else we have in common. So, what's your story?' Scott asks, sipping at his tea.

'No story to tell, not really.'

'Oh, come on, everyone has a story. Even if it's uneventful, there is still something to say. You've lived and worked abroad. You must have met people.'

'Bad people, mostly. Nobody I wanted to keep in my life.'

Scott laughs. 'You must have had good times?'

'Bad times, and plenty of them.'

'I'm sorry to hear that.'

'Well, I'm hoping that I've turned a corner now.'

Scott smiles. 'You've found a place with us, and you are welcome to stay as long as you like.' I tilt my head and nod appreciatively. 'You said you lived abroad, in Argentina. Was that with your parents?'

'I did, yes. My parents divorced when I was very young. I

don't really remember my mother. I don't even have a photograph of her.'

'So you went with your father?'

'That's right. He worked abroad a lot, and so we moved around from place to place. It's hard to settle that way.'

'Something else we have in common. I made a lot of new friends. I loved it.'

'I find making friends difficult.' I smile and Scott returns it. 'People often say that kids who move around struggle to make friends, don't they?'

'Not my experience.' Scott shrugs. 'I made friends everywhere I went because I had no other choice but to relate to new people. I'd argue it's become a skill, to walk into a cold room and make conversation with complete strangers.'

'You're a natural.'

He laughs. 'Thanks.'

'Do you find that the relationships you do make are fairly superficial though?'

'How do you mean?' Scott asks, his brow furrowing.

'Well, they are friendships on the surface, but you never get too close to them because you know you'll be on the move again soon enough. You sort of hold back a little, to keep yourself safe rather than give them everything you have.'

He tilts his head to one side. 'I suppose that's true, yes, up to a point. But... think of everyone you know, and be honest, do you ever know what's going on inside their head? I mean, how could you? You never really know people anyway and sometimes they can surprise you.'

'Yes, sometimes even when you're looking right at them,' I say before looking away when Scott catches my eye. 'We never really know what someone is thinking, do we?'

'No,' he says. 'I guess we don't.' He's offering me a coy smile as well now. This could be my moment. I'm not entirely sure the timing is right, but I have the sense things have been building to this point since I first arrived.

'Do you know what I'm thinking?' I ask softly. Scott's eyes narrow. 'Do you have any idea?'

'I...' He laughs awkwardly, holding my eye for a moment before breaking the contact and looking down at the mug he's slowly turning in his hands. 'I should probably go and tuck Katie in, and check on my wife.'

'Yes, you probably should.'

Scott stands up, putting his mug down on the table and moves past me. As he does so, he hesitates, stopping beside me for a moment and I can see in his expression he is thinking about something, biting his bottom lip. I reach out and gently touch the back of his hand, stroking it with the lightest touch of my fingertips. 'Thank you.'

'What for?' he asks, looking sideways at me. I cock my head.

'For being you.'

He looks down at where I touched his hand, flexing his fingers slightly but he doesn't meet my eye. Instead, he slowly leaves the room. I think it is fair to say, I have ignited that flame.

Now I just need to fan it.

FORTY-FIVE

SOPHIE

This is the strangest sensation. To feel apart from your body, watching yourself tossing and turning in bed while being completely detached from the experience. It is as if this is all happening to someone else.

I should feel calm as a result, but I don't. I can't stop thinking about them. Cecilia. Scott. Deanna.

What is that noise?

Deanna is recurring in my thoughts, over and over. It's like my subconscious is trying to tell me something, trying to make me understand. I feel almost like I can reach out and touch it, a message made whole in physical form. If I did then all of this would make sense, I'm sure of it. Every time I think I have it, though, the thought recoils from me and I'm tumbling back into darkness.

I'm feeling cold now. I shouldn't be. The duvet is a heavy tog, and I'm fast asleep. Drifting in and out of fitful dream states, that's true, but whatever Dr Sheldon has left for me it's having an effect. I'm numb. I cannot feel my body at all.

I do wish that noise would stop.

I can see so much of Deanna in me. Maybe that's why she

makes me so nervous. It was over twelve years ago that I was in a similar position to her. I came into this family, a family who from the outset appeared to have it all. They had money, a dream marriage, two wonderful children. They were the epitome of what success looks like to someone like me. They were everything that I craved out of life.

That's it, isn't it? Deanna is me... only a younger me. I'm so cold.

I can see Cecilia now, walking through the garden – Switzerland, I think – arm in arm with Scott. It's that same memory repeating again and again. Only, Cecilia isn't there anymore. Now it's Deanna. Although, I think at one time it was myself and Scott who were walking among those same trees. Or am I remembering a fantasy of my own crafting, something that never really happened?

I'm behind a window now, outside in the cold, looking in on Scott and Deanna having dinner. They seem so happy. We were happy like that once, Scott and I, weren't we? No, he looks much happier than I ever remember him being with me. *It's so cold now.* The wind is chilling my bare skin. The windowpane is so cold to the touch of my palms.

There's that banging again...

FORTY-SIX

DEANNA

I'm worried I have overstepped the mark with Scott. That's always been part of my problem, I'm far too impulsive. Patience has never been my greatest strength, but I have learned to develop it over the years. In the past, when I had a sense of what I wanted to achieve, I threw myself into it without consideration for the outcome. I got into a lot of trouble living like that.

I promised that this time things would be different, and I hope I haven't messed everything up. Scott hasn't come back down. Maybe he's staying with Katie for a while. I wouldn't be surprised. She was very upset at seeing her mother – Sophie – coming undone like that. I feel badly about that, but there isn't anything I could have done to stop it. Not once things were put in motion anyway.

I can hear footsteps coming at speed down the stairs, but they sound lighter than an adult's. Katie bursts into the kitchen, eyes wide, struggling to catch her breath. Instinctively, I run over to her and clutch her upper arms. 'What is it, Katie? What's the matter?' I can see terror in her eyes. She glances back towards the stairs, but she hasn't yet been able to catch her breath and she's panicking. 'It's okay, deep breaths, don't try to speak, just focus on breathing.' She's holding tightly to her favourite cuddly toy, tucked beneath her arms and I can smell the toothpaste on her breath.

Katie doesn't have time to steady herself before I hear shouting coming from upstairs. It sounds distant, probably coming from the top floor. 'Wait here, darling.' I give her arms a supportive squeeze and she nods. 'Sit yourself down and I'll come back in a minute.' I leave her in the kitchen.

Heading upstairs, the shouting has stopped but I can hear someone laying into something. It could only be Scott, or Chas I suppose, but he seems so placid that I doubt it's him. I'm reticent to go further but the intensity of the banging is increasing. I find Chas on the second-floor landing, peering up the stairwell as I come to stand beside him. 'What's going on?' I ask.

'I don't really know. It's Dad and Sophie.'

'Wait here,' I tell him with an air of confidence and authority. Continuing up, I look through the balustrade and across the landing into the guest bedroom. Scott is hurling himself against the door to the en-suite bathroom. I can't see Sophie.

Hurrying up the last few steps, I run to the bedroom door and hesitate before entering. 'Scott! What's going on?'

He looks at me, his cheeks are bright red from the exertion and he's sweating and breathing heavily. 'It's Sophie. She's locked herself in the bathroom and I can't get her to open the door.' I step inside and come to stand alongside him. The door is showing signs of damage – Scott's a strong guy – but it's made from solid oak and the fittings don't want to give way without a fight.

Turning my face to the side and pressing my ear to the door, I listen. I can hear water running. I glance down and water is seeping out from beneath the door and soaking the carpet. I meet Scott's eye and then look at the bed beyond him. Sophie was in bed; the sheets and duvet have been disturbed.

'Sophie?' I ask, gently knocking on the door in case Scott's hammering at it has frightened her. 'It's Deanna. Are you okay?'

'I've tried to speak to her and she's not answering me,' Scott says, breathing hard and doing his best to steady himself, but I can hear the panic edging into his tone. 'She won't open the door.'

'Does it have the child lock?' I look down at the handle. Usually, you can unlock a bathroom door from the outside, just in case a child locks themselves in by accident.

'Yes, but it won't budge. It's stuck firm, I tried.' I try the handle myself, but it won't move.

'Do you have anything we can use to pry it open?'

'Like what?' Scott sounds exasperated.

'It's okay. We'll figure something out. How about the loft hatch?'

'What about it?'

'You open it with a metal hook. It might fit in the crack here between the door and the jamb; we might be able to jimmy it open.'

Scott shakes his head. 'That door's solid. There's no give in it at all.' He comes over and I step aside as he leaps forward and slams a foot against the door again. 'Sophie!' The door remains in place but, undeterred, he moves back and takes another run at it, grunting as he makes contact, but it's no use.

'If the door is too solid, we should focus on the latch or the hinges. That's where the door will be at its weakest. Force that...'

'How?'

'Wait here.' I run out onto the landing, and I can hear Scott inside the room, pleading with Sophie to let him in. On the floor below, I open the airing cupboard and inside is what I'm looking for, a two-foot-tall fire extinguisher.

Chas is at my shoulder, peering into the cupboard. 'What are you going to do with that?'

The extinguisher is bulky and I'm struggling with manhandling it upstairs. 'Feel free to step in and help me anytime, Chas. Don't stand on ceremony or anything.' He ambles forward and takes much of the weight. With his help, we get it up to the bedroom and Scott immediately realises the plan and takes it off me, hefting it effortlessly into the air.

Using the extinguisher as a battering ram it takes three attempts, each taking a little longer as Scott's strength flags, but on the third blow the angle is right and the latch gives way. The door swings open and we see Sophie lying in the bath, water overflowing the rim and cascading down onto the tiled floor, spreading out to the bedroom. Her right arm is hanging over the rim; her left is submerged along with most of her body, her hair dancing beneath the surface with the ebb and flow.

'Sophie!' Scott screams and runs in before I can react, his feet splashing through the surface water. What have I done?

That moment of indecision lasts a mere second or two but then I follow Scott into the bathroom, raising a hand to stop Chas from entering behind me.

The thought that I'm sure passed through everyone's mind dissipates quickly as we all see the clear water Sophie is lying in. There's a knife lying on the floor beside the bath, but the water is clear and transparent. Sophie is unconscious but otherwise unharmed, her face floating just above the waterline. Scott slips his hands beneath her shoulders and elevates her head away from the water. She mumbles, but it's almost inaudible and certainly incoherent.

'Is she okay?' I ask. That's probably the dumbest question I could have come up with, but it fills the silence.

'She's cold,' Scott says and he tries to lift her from the water, struggling to do so. Sophie is almost a dead weight. Reaching past him, I help support her and between the two of us we get her out of the bath and onto the floor. The water is absolutely freezing. She must be well out of it not to have woken from her sleep. 'The sedatives. I think she may have taken too many by mistake.'

My eyes shift to the knife, and I quickly move it aside. This doesn't look like an accident. I grab a couple of bath towels and we wrap her in them. Scott, resting on his heels, has Sophie lying in his arms. I turn off the taps that were still running and I'm soaking wet now anyway, so I reach into the water and release the plug. Water begins swirling out of the bath.

Meeting Scott's eye, I get up to leave the bathroom. He doesn't speak, looking utterly shell-shocked. Chas is standing beside the bed. He holds up the bottle of pills that were on the bedside table, giving them a shake as my eyes settle on them. He tosses the bottle to me, and I catch it deftly. 'How many were in the bottle before?' I call through to Scott.

'I'm not sure, maybe it was just over half full.' I look at Chas and he has his hands on his head, pushing his hair up and away from his forehead, stunned. I examine the bottle.

'She hasn't taken many. There's still almost half a bottle left.' Opening her wardrobe, I find her clothes have been stuffed inside without hanging them up or organising them. They must have been hurriedly put away after Sophie's outburst around the red dress. I root through the clothing and find her dressing gown. It's a plush, thick material, and I take it through to where Sophie is still lying in Scott's arms, laying it over her. He looks at me, water running from him now too.

'Enough is enough. She can't be here anymore. She's a danger to herself' – he looks at the knife I've set aside – 'and to everyone else.'

Sophie stirs in his arms. 'I don't need help. I just need you.' Scott leans down and kisses her forehead, moving the wet hair aside from her face. He looks at me, again, shaking his head.

'No, wait!' I hear Chas exclaim and I turn to see Katie standing at the doorway, looking in on us, her mouth open, Tiggy on the floor at her side with only the end of the tail still in the girl's grasp. She shouldn't be here. I should never have allowed it to come to this.

'Katie, she's going to be all right,' I tell her, but I don't think she believes me. She glances at me before turning and running from the en suite as fast as she can, bouncing off the door frame as she passes through it. Scott and I exchange a brief look and I hurry after her.

FORTY-SEVEN

Friday

It must be night-time. The bedroom feels cold outside the confines of my duvet and the heating switches off overnight, coming on again shortly before dawn. My eyelids feel so heavy and it hurts to open them. I'm vaguely aware of someone else in the room. It must be Scott, but he's not beside me in bed.

'Scott?' I say but I'm mumbling. It's like it's someone else entirely. 'Is that you?'

'No.'

The voice is stark, matter of fact. Managing to force my eyes open, it takes a moment for them to adjust to the darkness. The figure is standing at the foot of the bed. For a second, I think it's Katie, but she's taller than my daughter. I should turn on the lamp beside my bed but, weirdly, I can't move. 'Katie?'

'No.'

My eyesight is improving although it's not just the lack of light, but my vision is blurry at the periphery. My head is pounding. 'Deanna?' I say, hearing the surprise and a hint of fear in my voice. 'What are you doing here?'

'I have something to ask you.'

'What?'

'What happened to Katie's mum?'

This has to be a dream. I am Katie's mum. 'What are you talking about?' I want to sit up but it's like I'm bound to the bed. I can't see or feel the restraints, but I can hardly move. 'I'm Katie's mum.'

'No, you're not.' Deanna moves to the side of the bed and the light from the streetlamp outside the bedroom window reflects via the mirror on my vanity unit, partially illuminating her features. They are set, her eyes narrow, her lips pursed as she stares hard at me. 'You're not her mother.'

'I am! Cecilia left her. It was her choice, and I *am* Katie's mum.' Panic flares in my chest but Deanna remains where she is, looking down on me, her arms by her side.

'You took her daughter from her. You and Scott.'

'I didn't!' I whisper, shutting my eyes tightly, willing Deanna to leave me alone. 'That's not how it was, not at all.'

'Then tell me how it was.'

I shake my head. 'You're *not* real. This is a nightmare; this is not real.'

'You took her daughter, her life, away from her. Everything. Her husband, all that she was... taken from her in an instant.'

'It wasn't my fault,' I say, opening my eyes and seeing Deanna still standing over me, watching, her expression set in stone. 'Cecilia was ill. I was there for her at her worst. I saw how she was—'

'And the best way to help her was to take her life, her family? You could have helped her through it but instead you helped to destroy her.'

'I did help her. I was there. I took care of her baby. I took care of Katie.'

'And you took care of her husband!' Deanna speaks to me in

a measured, and yet menacing tone. I shake my head. 'You stripped everything from her and left her with nothing.'

'I didn't. I swear I didn't. Scott and I, we fell in love later, much later. Cecilia was gone. She left them.'

'You think you can absolve yourself for what you did by providing Katie with the mother you took away?'

The feeling in my body is slowly returning. I can move my arms a little. 'Why should I feel guilty? I did nothing wrong.'

'You stole Cecilia's motherhood from her. Why?'

'I love those children like they are my own.'

'Why?'

'Because I can't have children of my own, and I so desperately wanted to—'

'So you took Cecilia's.'

'No, it wasn't like that. I love them. I love them so much.'

'I think you are lying to me, Sophie—'

'No, I'm not, I swear.'

'And you are deluding yourself.' She leans away from me, the pale skin of her face, the red lipstick disappearing into shadow. 'Scott is right.'

'Right? About what?'

'You cannot be here anymore.'

The panic returns in an instant and I can't swallow. I'm holding my breath. 'But where will I go?'

'Somewhere else, Sophie. Somewhere else.'

'But I have nowhere to go.'

'You can go and be with Cecilia, if you like?'

'No!' I whisper, feeling my eyes tearing. 'I don't want to die. I can't die. I have to be here for Katie.'

'I can't allow that for you, Sophie.'

'No.' I'm thrashing my head from side to side, desperate to get out of bed but I still can't manage to get up. 'That's not fair—'

'Life isn't fair, Sophie. If it was then Cecilia would be here with her daughter instead of you.'

'No. Please, I'm all that she has.'

'No. You're not. She has her mother.'

'But Cecilia is dead.'

'No, she isn't,' Deanna says, hovering above my face again, her eyes drifting over me from head to toe.

'Yes, she is, she died. She killed herself.'

'Just as you tried to do earlier tonight? You tried to abandon your daughter.'

'I didn't. I'd never put them through that, not again. Not Katie, or Scott.'

'But that's exactly what you did, Sophie.'

'Why are you doing this to me; why are you saying all of this?' I can feel tears tickling my skin as they roll down my cheeks. 'I'm a good person.'

'What comes around, goes around, Sophie.'

'Why do you want to hurt me? I've done nothing to you. Why are you taking my life away from me?'

'What have I taken from you, Sophie?'

'You stole my red dress from me ...'

Deanna is still leaning over me, staring into my eyes now. Her pupils are dilated. She doesn't blink. 'Cecilia is coming home. This is her home, Sophie.'

I'm full on crying now, the tears blurring my vision further. I blink to clear them. 'No, she can't, she's dead.'

'Cecilia has been in Switzerland for the last twelve years, Sophie, but she's found her way home, and she will take back what is hers.'

'No, that can't be true, it's not possible.'

'She blames you, Sophie. You helped to put her away. Helped to keep her in the asylum, locked away from the world, away from her family.'

'What? No, I didn't.'

'And Scott thinks you are to blame, too.'

'Why, what have I done?'

'You've let the family down, Sophie. You've betrayed them all.'

'No, please...'

'Rest now,' Deanna says, brushing her hand over my face. My eyes involuntarily close to the sound of her soothing tone. Her voice is drifting away from me. 'You need your rest, Sophie. Sleep well.'

FORTY-EIGHT

I wake with a start, wide awake like you do on those nights when you just know something is wrong. Very wrong. *Deanna!* I sit up, my eyes sweeping the room for her. Every corner, every dark recess, my mind seeing movement in the shadows. I'm sweating profusely.

But I'm alone, or at least I think I am. My clothes are scattered all over the floor and I'm naked. I don't remember getting undressed. The display on the clock on my bedside table tells me it's one thirty in the morning.

Am I dreaming? I was dreaming before, I think, but I don't know what is real and what isn't anymore. My foot is throbbing. That's real at least.

How long have I been asleep? My head is dulled, but it's not the lethargy that comes with waking abruptly from a deep sleep. This is something else, something new.

The tablets.

I reach for my bedside lamp and switch it on, blinking at the brightness. The bottle that I remember being beside it, the one left for me by Dr Sheldon, isn't there. I think Scott gave me the sleeping pills he prescribed.

Memories that were previously so vivid are fading as I try to recollect them. I remember Scott... and I remember emptying my clothes from the wardrobes, all of our wardrobes. That was an odd thing to do. Why on earth did I do that? Katie's face pops into my head, distraught, running away from me and the feeling of paralysis where I couldn't go after her. Did that happen as well?

Deanna!

Deanna was here, just now. I can remember what she said.

All of it. And everything makes sense now. Throwing back the duvet, I get out of bed and stumble to the wardrobe, rooting through the contents and coming up with a pair of joggers and a jumper which I quickly throw on.

The sudden burst of movement has made me feel light-headed and a wave of dizziness passes over me when I try for the door. I reach out to steady myself, my hand finding nothing but air, and I stumble, grateful when I bump into the wall. I feel sick.

Taking a moment to steady myself, I use the wall to work my way along to the bedroom door, reaching for the handle. It won't open. It's locked. *I'm locked in!* Why would someone lock me into the bedroom? I shake the handle, tugging on it and then it turns and the door swings open. It was only stuck.

The landing outside is in darkness and I listen intently, seeing figures in every shadow. I can't hear anything but a gentle wind buffeting the skylight in the pitched roof above me. Edging out onto the landing, I peer into the gloom. I know what I have to do.

I make my way downstairs, avoiding every squeak that will give me away. I know this house. This is my home and I know which tread will let her know I'm coming.

I see it all now. She planned all of this. She came into our home, my home, with one intention and that is to destroy it. To take away everything I've worked for. To take my husband and my children. I need to make Scott see sense. He'll know what to do. On the next landing, I see Scott's bedroom door is closed.

For a moment the thought comes to mind that I'll find them together, Deanna in bed with my husband, much like Cecilia would have done if she had come to Chester Terrace a week or so after we returned to the UK. But she couldn't come home, then or now, because she died after what happened that day on those train tracks. Didn't she?

The memorial service, held on a cold and wet day in March. Cecilia wasn't close with many people during their time living in Lower Valais, a French-speaking canton of Switzerland, where Scott and Cecilia had made their family home. Very few would travel to London for the memorial and, with no family members to invite, it was with barely a handful of friends and acquaintances in attendance that we said farewell to Cecilia. I stood there beside Scott, holding Katie, a baby at that time, in my arms as we bade farewell to a woman I only knew by reputation and from photographs.

I hadn't planned to fall in love with Scott nor he with me. It happens sometimes; such is the way of life. You don't choose when you meet the love of your life, you just find one another. And if it's under difficult or strange circumstances, then you have a choice to make: to be happy or to stay as you are. The timing wasn't great, but there was no one there to judge us. I was there for Scott when he needed someone, and in turn, he was there for me. We just... sort of fitted neatly together.

Scott couldn't live in the past and I couldn't run away from a ghost.

This particular ghost has unleashed an avenging angel upon us in the form of Deanna. I can't allow her to destroy what we have worked so hard for, what I have sacrificed so much to build. What we have here is special, Scott and me. I see it all now. I must make him understand before it's too late.

Taking a deep breath, I steady myself as I grasp the handle

of our bedroom door. What if I am too late? I put my ear to the door and listen. If I find Deanna in our bedroom, in *my bedroom*, with my husband, I really don't know what I'll do. Brushing aside another wave of nausea threatening to upset me, I know this is something I have to face, and I open the door.

The bed is empty, made up, and not slept in. My heart sinks. Where is he? Where is my husband? I can see into the en-suite bathroom and the light is off; Scott isn't in there. Backing out of the bedroom, I walk along the landing and looking over the bannister see the door to Scott's study is slightly ajar, a thin shaft of light escaping from within.

I carefully tread down the next flight of stairs. Gently pushing the door open, I peer inside, blinking at the brightness of the artificial light. Despite the overhead spots being dimmed, it still hurts my eyes and amplifies the pain in my head. 'Scott?' But he's not there. The lamp upon his desk is on, illuminating some paperwork he has on the surface, and his laptop is also open.

I enter and peer through to the far end of the room, wondering if Scott is in the corner out of sight. 'Scott?' I ask again, but he definitely isn't here. I wonder what he could be working on at this hour.

I cross to his desk, resting my hands on the back of his chair, the paperwork having caught my attention. They are not official documents or letters but brochures, all written in Spanish by the look of them. I don't speak it but I can recognise it when I see it written down.

Is he planning a holiday? It certainly seems like it as I casually flick through the glossy images of new build apartments, beach front townhouses and the associated facilities nearby. Closing this brochure, I flip it over and on the rear page there is a map of where these properties are located, close to La Dehesa, an area to the north-east of Santiago, the capital city of Chile.

Only, it's not a luxury holiday complex but a development

of new residential homes. Scott had a meeting with a colleague who'd flown in from South America; that must be why he's interested. The bottom drawer of the pedestal to the left is cracked open; something red is protruding from the side, stopping the drawer from closing properly.

I slowly bend over and pull the drawer out. I recognise the material. My red dress.

I don't understand.

In the drawer, lying beneath where the dress had been, is a small velvet box. I lay the dress out across Scott's chair and reach for it. I realise I'm holding my breath as I open the lid. Inside is the pendant Deanna selected for me.

Scott's laptop is open, and my eyes are drawn to his list of unopened emails, one in particular, titled, *Sorry to miss your leaving party.*

'What leaving party?' I whisper quietly. I switch the screen to the internet browser, finding it open in the background. The open tab is, again, written in Spanish. I refresh the page and allow it to translate the contents into English. The *Nido de Aguilas International...* why is he looking at schools? Sitting down in his chair, I turn my attention back to the drawer, looking for anything that might explain this. I find two more brochures for property developments in South America. I think Scott had a meeting with someone flying in. Were they coming from there? I can't remember.

Rooting around, I hear a familiar rattle and I stop. Pushing back the chair, I reach to the back of the drawer and find a small brown plastic medicine bottle. The writing is all in Spanish and it doesn't look remotely official. It's more like it's home-made. Turning the bottle round, I can't find anything that looks like a proper name I can understand. There's something written in German, I think it's German anyway, *Lysergsäure-diethylamid*, but that's all.

Using Scott's laptop, I open a new incognito tab in the

browser. I don't want him to see I've been using his computer. I type in the name and hit return. I can barely read it, let alone say it.

'It's LSD,' I say quietly. 'What the hell?'

Looking down the list of search results, the first two take my breath away. *Side effects.* The main effect of LSD is psychological, with intense visual and auditory hallucinations, euphoria, and an altered sense of space, body, and time. Scrolling past the scientific paper and medical website references, I come to others focused on the use of psychedelic drugs by shamans, ayahuasca, for instance. My eyes drift to the bottle of pills on the desk and I pick it up, closing my hand around it.

Why would Scott have this? Was it some kind of gift from his South American contact? I know he took some drugs during his ballerino days, but surely that's long behind him?

'Sophie?' I jump, startled by the voice behind me and slam down the lid of the laptop. 'What do you think you're doing?'

FORTY-NINE

Scott is standing at the entrance to his study, watching me. 'Scott, I was just looking for you.'

'Were you?' Scott asks, slowly closing the door behind him, but he stays where he is, observing me with a watchful eye. He nods towards his desk. 'Did you think you would find me in the drawer, or were you looking for me inside my laptop?'

'No, I was just...' I look down at the desk and then the laptop, then back at Scott. 'Why are you looking at schools in Santiago?' I ask, cocking my head, secreting the bottle in my hand into my pocket. 'Are we going somewhere?'

'Why are you snooping through my things?'

'I wasn't, n-not really.'

'Because you know how I feel about you going through my things, Sophie.'

'I was waiting for you and...' – I cast my hand in the air over the desk – 'it was all just here and—' Scott takes a step forward and then stops, holding up his hand to silence me.

'I think we need to talk.'

'Yes! We do. That's why I came looking for you. I think I know what's going on, what's been happening—'

'I think I should speak first, Sophie, if you don't mind? It's been quite a day, and one hell of a week, to be honest.'

'I know, it seems like things have been going wrong for—'

'Ages, yes.' He sighs, lifting his right hand and rubbing the back of his neck, grimacing. 'Listen, I know you've been struggling lately. It's obvious that things have been getting a little overwhelming for you.'

'No,' I say, coming out from behind his desk. 'Scott, I can explain.'

He shakes his head slowly. 'No, Sophie. I think we're past that stage now, don't you?'

'What do you mean?'

'I mean we're past talking. You need help, and it's more than I am able to give you. No matter how much I wish I could.'

'No, you don't understand, I can explain—'

'I do, Sophie. I really do understand. I knew something like this was going to happen when you moved from regional to national. I saw it coming and I should have acted then.' He sighs, staring straight ahead and shaking his head. 'Damn, I should never have got you into the studio as a weather girl—'

'*You got me into it?*' I can't believe he would be so dismissive. Is that what he thinks, that without him I'd never have got the opportunity? 'Is that what you think, that without you I would be nothing?' I can hear the hurt in my voice, let alone feel it in my body. It's pain, real pain.

'No, no... I don't mean it the way it sounded.'

'Then why did you say it?'

He raises his gaze to the ceiling, dragging a palm across his mouth. 'It wasn't meant the way you took it, that's all. I just meant...'

'What?' I ask, coming to stand before him.

He looks resigned, and then shakes his head. 'I don't know what I meant.'

'I worked hard to get that job. I know you got me in on the

ground floor with your connections but after that I had to earn my place on the national programme. I work damned hard—'

'Do you hear yourself? You sit on a sofa every day talking about who knows who, who was wearing what dress at some awards ceremony the night before. I mean, come on, does anyone really care?'

'Thanks, Scott. That's possibly the most hurtful thing you've said to me, in the last five minutes.'

'Oh, Sophie.' He draws breath, then purses his lips. 'To think we have to have this conversation in the middle of the night?'

My hands are clenched into balled fists, held at my sides. 'My husband belittles me and my achievements, but let's not speak about that, or about the little tramp in the basement who's trying to get his clothes off—'

'Sophie! You're out of line!'

'Am I?'

Exhaling heavily, Scott's expression tenses, his right cheek involuntarily twitching. It does that when he's angry, and right now, I can see how angry he is. 'Deanna has been a breath of fresh air to this family, and if you're feeling threatened by her presence, then I am truly sorry, but you have to be able to see that you're at the root of our troubles.'

'No,' I say, stepping up to him. 'This is what I'm trying to tell you. *I'm not the root cause.* It's her, it's Deanna.'

'Sophie, please don't—'

'No, don't you see, it's all happened since she arrived—'

'It hasn't though—'

'Scott, hear me out, please!' He meets my eye, and his gaze lingers on me for a moment. I can't figure out what's going through his mind, but I only need a couple of minutes to explain. Surely he will give me that. He nods curtly.

'Okay, go on then. Say what you have to.'

'Don't you see, since Deanna came into our lives everything

has been going wrong. The things going missing, objects randomly appearing and disappearing.'

'Sophie—'

'The evening meal I prepared being ruined, after she helped me with it, and she miraculously swoops in to save the day. And then she's cosying up to Katie—'

'Which is what we wanted, Sophie!' Scott flings his hands into the air. 'We needed a tutor for Katie to get her back on track after she was expelled, get her some stability in her life. Deanna is offering us exactly that, something that you can't. Or are we blaming Deanna for something that began months before she was even back in the country?'

'And what about you?'

'Me?' he asks, looking at me curiously. 'What about me?'

'Tell me you haven't seen how she's been making moves on you since she arrived. I mean, we didn't even have a chance to check her references before you invited her to come and live with us. Now she's made sure she's slotted right in—'

'Okay, I think I've heard enough of this, Sophie. Seriously, Deanna has bent over backwards to help us through this period, to *help you* through this. And this is how you repay her, by making up some weird conspiracy against her?'

'It was her in my room, Scott!'

'What?'

'She's been in my room. She's been going through my things.'

'She didn't take your things, Sophie.' Scott points at my dress on the other side of the study. 'I did that, and it was for your own good.'

'You took my dress? Why?'

'To save you from flaunting yourself to the entire country, just because you felt pressure from your bosses. It's embarrassing, and it's beneath you.'

'I... That's not what I'm talking about, Scott,' I say, feeling thrown. I'm not sure how to handle what he's just said, but it's not the most pressing thing I have to deal with right now.

'Then what?'

'She was speaking to me in my room, saying things… *such awful things!*'

Scott is shaking his head in disbelief. 'What things?'

'About you. About me and Cecilia. She says Cecilia is coming to take her revenge on me for what I've done—'

'Sophie,' Scott says, closing his eyes and pinching the bridge of his nose between thumb and forefinger, 'this is utterly *insane*. You've gone too far—'

'But it's the truth,' I say, pleading with him. 'You're intoxicated with Deanna, aren't you? But you can't see her for who and what she is. It's not real, *she's not real*—'

'Sophie, stop! Please!'

'You don't understand, Scott.' He moves to turn his back on me, to walk away but I haul him around to face me. 'You have to believe me, Scott! Deanna is poisoning you against me. She's poisoning this family—'

'*She* has been nothing but supportive. And all you can do is slag her off. If anyone is poisoning this family, it's you.'

'No! She knows so much more than she is letting on. She knows about Cecilia.'

'What does she know, Sophie? Tell me, what can she possibly know about Cece? Cecilia is dead!'

'No, that's what we all think but maybe she's not.'

Scott puts his hands on my upper arms, gripping them firmly – so firmly that it hurts – and staring into my eyes, but I don't care. He's listening to me now. He has to understand. 'Cecilia is gone, Sophie. And right now we have to focus on making you better, take you someplace where it is safe for you. Somewhere you can mend and get well.'

'No! I think Cecilia is coming back. *Deanna told me.*'

Scott shakes his head, clamping his eyes shut in frustration and tightening his grip on my arms.

'You're hurting me,' I whisper. He doesn't want to believe. He is fighting it, but I must make him understand. Our lives depend upon it. I've never been so sure of that as I am now. But Scott wants to walk away from me, dismissing what I know to be true. Why won't he listen? 'Scott, please.'

Turning, Scott releases me and shrugs off my fresh attempt to stop him walking away, taking hold of the door handle. He speaks without looking back. He can't say this to my face. He must really hate me. 'Enough, Sophie. That's enough!' he snaps. His shoulders sag and he hesitates. 'You have to leave. I'll... call Joseph in the morning and make the arrangements.'

'No! Scott, please!' I grab his arm and pull on it.

'I said, that's enough!' Scott barks at me, turning on his heel and glaring at me, throwing my hand off his arm. 'I can't do this anymore—'

'But what if Cecilia didn't die on that train track,' I say, tears streaming down my face. I can taste the saltiness as they reach my lips.

'Sophie, stop!'

'We have to face up to this' – I glance back at Scott's desk, gesticulating with my arms – 'and we can't run away from it, hiding someplace like... like... Santiago!'

'Sophie!'

'Don't you understand, Deanna said Cecilia's been in an institution all this time—'

'What did you say?'

'Cecilia is in a mental institution, in Switzerland, a-and she's coming back. She wants what's hers. She wants her revenge, for what we did.'

Scott stares at me for a moment, an unreadable expression on his face. 'This was her home once,' he says quietly, his eyes moving around the room. 'And I took it away from her.'

'What? You bought this house when we were leaving France and coming back to the UK. I don't understand.'

'No. This was our home, mine and Cecilia's, and when I brought you here it was after I'd changed everything, erased her presence from our lives, from the very fabric of this building. It was a fresh start, for all of us.'

'You didn't erase her completely, though. What about the picture?'

He fixes his gaze on me. 'What picture?'

'The one of you and Cecilia that Deanna left beside my bed to...'

'Yes, to do what exactly? Why would she do that, let alone dare we ask the question *where would she get such a picture from?*'

'And the photograph, *our photograph*, that she set light to in the bathroom?'

'Set light to? What are you talking about?'

'Oh...' That's right, I didn't tell him about that. I should have. 'I didn't tell you. I'm sorry, I should have.'

'What photograph?'

'The one taken on our wedding day! You've always kept it there...' I spin on my heel and point at where the photograph of us taken in the Seychelles is usually displayed. And it's there, on the mantelpiece, exactly where it should be. How is that possible?

'You mean, this one?' Scott asks, picking it up and holding it aloft.

'It-It was burned,' I stammer. 'I... it's all designed to unsettle me, to make me look...'

'Psychotic?' Scott asks, putting the frame back and immediately I see he regrets saying it. 'I'm sorry, I shouldn't have said that.'

'You don't believe me.'

Scott winces. 'It's not that. I think you need help, that's all.'

'You don't believe me,' I repeat. I don't think I could ever be prepared for this feeling; the person I trust most in the world has no faith in me.

He looks at me flatly. 'How can I? Honestly, if you were me? Put yourself in my shoes and ask yourself, would you believe what you've just told me? It's... it's...'

'Madness,' I whisper.

And there it is; finally, I see the truth. I don't want to believe it, but it's staring me right in the face.

'Maybe it's not Deanna, or even Cecilia, after all,' I say, taking the bottle from my pocket. Scott has the door open, one hand curled so tightly around the handle that I can see the whites of his knuckles. But he's looking at me, rapt. I have his attention. 'Maybe it's all been to do with these.'

'What are they?' he asks slowly. There's a distinct change in his tone, but I don't know what it means.

'They look like my prescription tablets. They are the ones I've been taking,' I say to him, drawing a deep breath and mustering as much courage as I can, 'and *you've been giving them to me.*'

Scott's head twitches ever so slightly.

'I found them in your desk, Scott. Have you been giving me a psychedelic drug? Why would you do that?'

Scott slowly turns away from me, glancing out onto the landing before gently closing the door. With one hand placed flat against the architrave, he presses his forehead against the panel door, gently tapping his head repeatedly against it, with his back to me. When he speaks, he does so in a whisper, and everything's different. I don't recognise his voice.

'I wish you hadn't found that bottle, Sophie. I really wish you hadn't.'

FIFTY

'Scott?' I say but he doesn't hear me or, if he does, then he doesn't react. His right hand slowly reaches up to the handle and I hear the lock click as he turns it. 'Scott?'

Turning to face me, a shroud of darkness descends over his expression. He's never looked at me like this before. His eyes are cold; his lips are pressed together, the corners of his mouth upturned, forming a half smile.

I can see his chest steadily rising and falling as he watches me, his expression set. 'Oh, Sophie,' he says quietly, shaking his head, his lips parting as the smile broadens.

The tone. The look. I take a step toward him, lifting my hand to touch him but I hesitate. His manner. It's all off. I take a step back. 'Scott? It was you, wasn't it? This whole time. Why?'

'You had to do it, didn't you?' he says, moving purposefully toward me. I back away again, glancing over my shoulder.

'I–I... had to do what?'

'All we needed around here was a little bit of control, some order to everything.' His advance continues and I'm backing away. 'Then everything would have been all right, but you had to have it, didn't you?'

'Have what?' My legs bump into Scott's desk. 'I don't understand.'

'All you had to do was manage the house, take care of the children, and you couldn't even do that, could you? You had to be famous, a celebrity. You needed Martha to help you be the mother you are supposed to be—'

'Martha, what? I don't—'

'You relied on her too much, so I had to get rid of her. We weren't enough for you, were we?'

'That's not true. You're enough for me, all of you...'

'No, having a family just wasn't enough, was it? You're just like all the others. *Selfish.*'

'Scott? What are you talking about?' I ask as he moves within arm's reach. 'What do you—' I yelp as he lashes out with his right hand, striking me across the face. I'm stunned into silence. Then both his arms fly up and before I can react, he plants his hands on my chest and forcefully shoves me backwards across his desk. Then he's upon me and I can feel the fingers of his powerful hands curling around my throat.

'Scott,' I garble, his weight upon me, pinning me down, his fingers curling around my throat, compressing my windpipe. I want to protest, no, to plead for him to let go but the pressure is increasing and I'm looking into his face, into the eyes of the man I love, my husband, my rock. I don't recognise him. It's like a veil has been drawn over those kind eyes and replaced with a darkness, a malevolence seeking nothing other than destruction.

'Please,' I whisper, struggling to free myself, clawing at his hands, scraping with my fingernails but he is unflinching, his grip tightening.

'You're the same... the same as Linda, as Cecilia.' Linda? I'm panicking now, I can't breathe, and I can feel the energy draining out of me, panic flaring, as I rake my hands across Scott's face but he's snarling, teeth clenched, eyes bulging as he squeezes the life out of me.

'Scott,' I whisper.

'This would go much easier,' he says, spit dripping from his mouth as he leans closer to my face, 'if you would just... stop... fighting.'

I let go of his hands. His grip is too strong for me, but I won't give up. I didn't get this far in life by giving in, by accepting my fate. I've survived through sheer strength of will, and up until this very moment, I think I'd forgotten that.

My hands are scrabbling on the desk to either side of me, thrashing around for anything that will offer me salvation. I can see shadows growing in my peripheral vision, feel Scott's warm breath on my face. Sound is muffled and if not for the terror I'm feeling right now, I'd believe this was yet another nightmare.

But I don't. This is real. Scott has every intention of killing me. My vision fades to black and then returns before flashing dark once again. I must act, or I will die here in my husband's study, prostrate across his desk. My fingers touch something solid, slender and cold on the desk and I grasp the thick handle. It threatens to slip from my fingers, and I know my strength is rapidly filtering out of me, but panic pulls me back into the moment and I swing my right hand up, driving the point of the makeshift weapon into his side.

Scott screams and suddenly I'm free to breathe. I gasp, drawing air into my lungs then I cough, my lungs burning as I inhale raggedly. Scott recovers from the shock attack, refocusing on me. I pull back my hand and I stab at him again, not once but twice, and a third time only he manages to deflect the blow aside with a flailing arm. I lose my grip on the letter-opener and it clatters to the wooden floor. And now it is Scott who rolls off me, trying to put some distance between us, staggering to his right, clutching his side.

The bitter taste of fresh blood is in my mouth. *But I'm not dying tonight.*

'You evil, utter...' Scott curses, staggering back, inspecting the left side of his abdomen. Blood is seeping through the fingers he has pressed against the wound, and I can see a crimson stain expanding as the blood seeps into the material of his shirt.

I'm off the desk now, back on my feet and still drawing in huge gulps of air, light-headed as I make a break for the door. Scott sees me move and hurries to intercept me, throwing a punch which glances off the side of my head, but it still sends me sprawling to my right and against the mantelpiece. I slump down onto my knees, my head ringing, using the ornate period surround of the fireplace to keep me from pitching forward.

I feel a stabbing pain in my forehead, just above my right eye and liquid flows into and over it. Blinking furiously to clear my vision, I don't need to check what it is. I know the impact has cut me. Scott is between me and the door now, my only escape route. If I thought he was angry before, now he's a mass of seething rage. He's glaring at me, wincing with one arm pressed to his side. At least he's hurt too. I might still get out of this. Without looking, I reach out to my right. I know it's there and my fingers feel the cold of the metal. Taking a firm grip, eyes fixed on my husband, I ready myself to get up, one hand braced against the mantelpiece.

'I should have taught you a lesson years ago. You never knew how to handle yourself, Sophie!' His tone is measured and yet every word is spoken with an ice-cold fury. He takes a step forward and I watch him approach, unflinching. I have one shot at this. As soon as he is almost within arm's reach, I launch myself to my feet and swing the poker I picked up from beside the fireplace, aiming at Scott's head. I miss, the swing is too wild, uncontrolled, and he sways aside and away from it but, off balance, I'm able to push my way past him and run for the door. Scott stumbles to the side, growling.

The door is secured with a simple thumb-turn lock and no key, thankfully, and I'm out onto the landing with Scott's curses behind me. He'll be following, I'm certain. He'll be upon me in seconds. In my haste, I lose my footing on the first tread at the top of the stairs, slip, and find myself tumbling downwards, head over heels. I lose my grip on the poker, and I hear it clattering against the tiles as I fall. Sharp, painful sensations punctuate my body as I bounce off the wall and the balusters, finally coming to a stop on the half landing, colliding with the wall.

I'm in a crumpled heap on the floor, staring back up to the landing above waiting for the monster – my husband – to descend. Then my eyes drift down to the next floor where wide, watchful eyes are staring up at me.

Katie. She's there at the foot of the stairs in her pyjamas, looking at me. My girl, my daughter.

'Katie,' I say, forcing myself up and bracing my back against the wall. Pain tears through my side and I wince. I've broken something, I'm certain. Reaching down with my left hand to inspect the damage sends sharp pains through my side and I gasp. Gently probing the area, slipping my fingertips through a tear in my top, they disappear into a wet opening in my side. The poker is beside me; the pointed end is bloodied.

Surprisingly, the wound itself doesn't feel painful with my fingers inside it.

'What's going on?' Katie asks me, her voice trembling as I retrieve the poker and force myself up, clutching my side and putting my back against the wall for support before sliding along it, descending the stairs towards Katie on the lower landing. Her eyes are fearful. 'You're bleeding.'

I can taste the blood on my lips and I swallow what's in my mouth, the bitter, metallic taste making me feel sick. 'Come with me,' I say, steering her alongside me with my left hand; the right is still holding the bloodied poker. Reaching down, I take her hand, almost having to drag her as I feel resistance. It's not enough to slow us down and I haul her along the landing, into the stairwell, and we begin the descent.

All the while I'm shooting nervous looks back up the way we've come, knowing I'll see Scott at any moment.

'What's going on?' Katie asks, pulling on my hand. There is sound from above and movement just beyond my view. He's coming.

'Sophie!' Scott's voice bellows from above, his voice reverberating through the stairwell.

'What's wrong with Daddy?' Katie asks and I can hear the fear in her voice which only makes me take the stairs faster, so fast that we stumble and almost fall. 'You're hurting me!' she says, but I won't let go. I can't let her go.

'Daddy's not very well, love. He's angry.' I stop, she's digging her heels in now, and I pull her around to face me, bending down to meet her eye. 'Don't worry, it'll be fine, but you have to come with me, now! You understand?' But I don't wait for an answer; I'm dragging her downstairs again, but she's still resisting.

'Why? What's happening?' she says, pulling on my arm to slow our descent. 'Why is Daddy so angry?'

'Not now, Katie! Just do as I say.' She wrenches her hand free of mine as we reach the hall. I reach for her again, but she repeatedly bats my hand away, shrugging me off. I know Scott's coming, and we must get out. I'm scrabbling with her arms trying to get control of her with my free hand, shooting furtive glances back at the stairwell, holding the poker aloft like a sword in my other hand.

'No!' she screams.

'Katie, please listen to me.' I'm wrestling with her, trying to pull her towards the front door and our escape route.

'No!' she screams again, throwing me off. 'Let me go!' She breaks the hold I have on her pyjamas, dragging herself beyond my reach, and before I can get a hold of her again, she's off and running along the hall back into the house.

'Katie, wait!' She pauses at the top of the stairs and then she flees down into the basement.

'Katie, no!'

'Deanna!' Katie screams, and then she's gone from view, down into the basement.

'Katie! Not Deanna, you can't trust her—' I don't hesitate, moving to follow her. I'm not leaving this house without my daughter.

A shadow crosses my sight-line as I reach the stairs and I stop, staring up into the darkness. It's Scott. He's coming. I have a decision to make, run after Katie and face Deanna, running the risk of Scott coming upon me from behind or... I can make my stand here, in the hallway.

I can't take on two opponents. I'm not sure I can face one, to be honest. I must protect Katie. Taking a deep breath, I fight to suppress my urge to run, to quell the almost overwhelming fear. I'm staring up into the darkness of the stairwell, my eyes flicking across to the light switch. Should I turn it on, put a stop to his element of surprise?

But the darkness is my ally too.

I curl both hands around the handle of the poker now, setting myself at the foot of the stairs, adjusting my grip, holding it like a baseball bat. And I wait. All I can hear is the sound of my own breathing, short and laboured. I stare into the shadows. And I wait.

'Where are you, Scott? I'm here, and I'm through running,' I whisper, more to bolster my confidence than for any other reason.

To my right, a tiny amber light flickers in the darkness drawing my eye, and I turn just as the lift doors silently slide open, and I'm rooted to the spot. Scott is leaning against the mirrored wall, his head tilted forward, eyes focused on me, sweat beading on his forehead, and he smiles.

Before I can move, Scott pushes off the wall and drives at me. I swing the poker but I'm too late and he's upon me, the poker missing its target as he easily brushes my arm aside. He lands a blow to the side of my head which sends me sprawling across the marble surface. My lungs explode as I hit the floor and I lose my grip on the poker. I watch helplessly as it slides away from me, tantalisingly close but still out of reach. And then Scott is standing over me, hauling me up by my hair with his powerful hands, my feet trying to gain purchase on the slippery surface beneath me but to no avail.

He drags me forward, grunting and cursing, pain shooting through me as he practically lifts me into the air and launches me face first into the mirror. The glass smashes, I hear it rather than see it, and I slump down in a heap on the floor, broken glass cascading to the floor around me. Turning my back to the wall, I press myself against it.

Scott is advancing on me, great clumps of my hair still in his balled fists which he casts aside, yelling as he approaches. 'Did you really think I would let you take *my daughter, my family, away from me?*'

FIFTY-ONE

Scott closes the gap between us, and I try to stand only for him to accelerate his advance, kicking a leg at me and striking me in the stomach. I scream as pain shoots through my abdomen, and I sink back down to the floor. Scott towers above me, grabbing my hair with his left hand and pulling my head to one side.

I strike out with my right fist, thumb extended, and drive it into the dark patch of crimson soaking his shirt. He screams and I know I've found the right spot. I push further, driving my thumb deeper and twisting my hand with all my strength. The sensation of my hand inside his body should disgust me but all I can think of is my survival, my daughter's survival, at any cost.

The pain stems his assault, and he falters, arching his back and turning his head to the heavens, howling like a beast out of control. Releasing my hand from his wound, he recoils from me and staggers back. I'm able to slide out from beneath him, roll over and scramble clear on my hands and knees through the shards of glass littering the floor. My hands, elbows and knees are cut, I'm bleeding but desperately trying to stand and run at the same time.

A figure steps out from the shadows of the kitchen and I slide to a stop, off balance.

'Chas?' I ask, but he says nothing. I can see the illuminated screen of his mobile phone in his hand by his side. He doesn't move towards me or back away. He stands silently like a solitary sentinel bearing an impassive expression as he looks from me to his father. 'You have to run, Chas.' But he doesn't seem to hear me. He's still looking past me at his father. I grab his arm and shake him, but he doesn't respond. 'Chas!' I try to drag him away and now his eyes slowly move to meet mine.

'No, you have to run, Sophie,' he says, taking a step back into the kitchen.

'What?'

'Run!'

I blink the sweat and tears from my eyes. *I have to protect Katie.* I don't want to, but I must leave him. Scott is upright now and lumbering towards me, Chas slinking back further into the shadows of the kitchen. Scott has one hand clamped against his side. He's not moving as well as he was. I've hurt him, badly. I catch a last, fleeting glimpse of Chas raising his mobile to his ear before he disappears from view and I leave, praying my son will be okay, setting off down the stairs with only a quick backward glance to see Scott following me.

Descending to the basement level, everything is in darkness, and I hit the first bank of light switches at the foot of the stairs, illuminating the corridor, the living room and the exterior garden lights to the rear of the house.

'Katie!' I shout, scanning the living room and seeing no sign of her. Running to the bedroom door, I throw it open but find the room empty and in darkness. The bed hasn't been slept in. Crossing the room, I open the door to the en suite and it, too, is empty. 'Katie, where are you!'

Back in the corridor, I try the door to the rear garden, but it's locked and the key is missing. The lights go out and I'm plunged into darkness. Spinning around, I put my back against the door and peer back into the gloom. My eyes will need time to adjust again. I should never have put the lights on. Seeing the switch on the wall beside me, I try it but flicking it on and off does nothing.

He's cut the power.

Whatever I do, I can't stay here. Inching back along the corridor, I listen intently, not knowing what I'll do when he shows himself. My breathing is heavy, coming in ragged bursts as I creep through the darkness. I have to find Katie and we must leave this house. Reaching the bedroom door, I peer into it again just in case, but the room still appears to be empty.

I see a flicker of movement through the window from the courtyard garden, or is it my imagination playing tricks on me? Either way, it's the only way out and Katie must have gone that way. With luck, she's up in the street looking for help. I move in that direction, taking care as I approach the foot of the stairs. I chance a look around the corner. There's no sign of Scott or Chas. And no sound either.

Where is he, where's Scott? I fear for Chas. Surely Scott wouldn't hurt his son.

I don't know why but I stand there, staring up into the darkness, and I'm half expecting to see Scott descending. Whether I manifested it or not, he does appear, leaning against the wall and breathing heavily. The dark patch soaking his shirt has spread now, across his lower body and I can see his blood smearing the wall as he uses it for support, taking each step down towards me with care.

'Sophie!' he yells, and I'm stuck. I can't run. It's like my legs won't respond to instruction anymore. Scott has one hand against the wound in his side; the other is wielding a kitchen knife.

'Stop this, Scott!' I scream at him, but he takes the next step, his legs moving with exaggerated actions, more lurching than walking, awkwardly bracing himself against the wall with the hand bearing the blade. 'Why are you doing this?' I scream. His hand on the wall slips and he stumbles, pitching forward and his arms flail around in the air for a moment before his feet come out from beneath him and he tumbles down the stairs.

Be it self-preservation or abject terror, I don't know, but I'm spurred into action. I turn, running for the courtyard as Scott clatters to the foot of the stairs, narrowly missing me but he still manages to slash at me with the blade in his hand. The door to the outside is unlocked but it is stiff, made from wood and possibly warped by the inherent damp and humidity of the basement level and I'm struggling to free it. The door is caught on the jamb, and I'm still wrestling with the handle as Scott makes it back onto his feet, lumbering towards me. He's sweating profusely now. Wiping his face with his forearm only smears blood across it. What little light on offer is reflecting off the smooth, polished steel finish of the kitchen knife he's brandishing at me. He must have taken that from the kitchen. *Chas.*

The hinges shriek their protest as I finally manage to haul the door open and a draught of cool breeze, along with the faint hint of moisture, crosses me as I pass out into the darkness. The cobbled floor is slippery, damp from the night air, and I stumble over to the steps leading up to the street above. Mounting them, I almost lose my footing, so slippery are they underfoot and at the top I find the gate onto the street is locked. The railings are slippery too, and the spikes atop them are designed to stop anyone from climbing over. I'm sure they were never designed to keep people in.

Even if I wasn't bleeding from my side, I don't think I'd manage to get over them. I'm trapped. I shake the gate as if the lock will give way, but I know it's futile.

Headlights turn onto Chester Terrace, and I stare at the approaching vehicle. 'Help!' I scream. 'Please help me!' The car pulls into a space between two cars, a couple of doors down from ours and the lights go out. I frantically wave my hands in the air. 'Help! Please—'

I feel something grab my ankle and before I know it, I'm unbalanced and I'm falling through the air, arms flailing, desperate to gain purchase on something, anything... and I hit the cobbles, face first. One thought comes to mind before everything goes dark: no one is coming to rescue me.

FIFTY-TWO

I'm not sure where I am. I'm lying on something cold and wet to the touch, hard and unforgiving. Opening my eyes, the shapes and images I can see are dark, blurry and no matter how hard I try, I can't quite bring them into focus. I can hear muted words; at least, I think they're words. I want to get up but my body aches, protesting at the slightest movement. Lifting my head brings a wave of nausea and I vomit. That's enough to give me a boost and I roll away from the contents of my stomach, the odour permeating the air around me. I'm on my back now and I push away with my feet. I'm moving, painfully slowly, but at least I'm moving.

A face hovers above me and I stop. I sort of recognise them, but they don't stay still long enough for me to focus. One eye feels like it's closing; my sight from it is almost useless. The other isn't much better. I still can't focus, seeing only shapes and colours in shades of grey or black. I push again with my legs but only one foot seems to be working. When I put pressure on my left foot, the ankle buckles and stabbing pains shoot up my shin and into my knee.

Working my way up into a seated position, my back against the wall, my vision improves and there he is.

Scott is in front of me, squatting with his elbows resting on his thighs, head cocked, watching me. The orange glow from the streetlights above casts macabre shadows across his face. He is bleeding from several wounds to his face, as am I. I can feel blood trickling down my face, taste the iron and salt combo in my mouth. He's toying with a blade in his hands, turning the handle over in his palm, staring at me.

His lips are moving but I can't hear him. Is he speaking? All I can hear is a loud buzzing in my ears, along with a sensation that feels similar to being underwater, but at the same time able to hear the sound of the surf breaking on the shoreline. Something is tickling my neck just below my left ear and I tentatively reach up to scratch at it. Withdrawing my hand, I can see a dark liquid on my fingertips. Blood is leaking from my ear. My head is thumping now as well, but my focus is returning, my hearing improving. I'm able to distinguish between different sounds on offer.

'You could have had everything,' Scott says in that low, controlled voice he has. Looking at him, I don't recognise who he is. He must be possessed by something; there's no other explanation. Where is the man I fell in love with? He shakes his head, looking at me with utter disdain, jabbing the pointed tip of the blade in my direction. 'You know, I didn't ask you for much, but you couldn't even show me the respect I deserved, the care our family needed.'

'I... I-I tried, Scott. I really did.' I can feel the blood trickling down the side of my face now as well. The pain in my head is increasing too.

'Not hard enough.'

'I know. I can do better, I promise.'

He slowly shakes his head. 'No. It's too late. We're past that now, Sophie.' He winces, clutching his side.

'You're hurt,' I say, trying to put compassion in my tone. 'I can help you.'

'Yes, you can,' he whispers, leaning forward, raising the blade in his hand. 'You can make way for a new start, for me, for my family.' There is nothing I can do. I've failed and this is where it ends. I want to close my eyes, to look away. If I don't see the end coming, will I feel it?

'Scott...'

He hesitates, the knife raised above me.

The voice came from behind but it's not one I recognise. The speech is slurred, not drunk, sounding more like an impediment of some kind.

Looking past my husband, I see a figure step out from the door into the basement area, the same door I fled through barely moments ago. I half expect to see Katie, but it's not her. Nor is it Deanna, although at first, I thought it might be.

She's of a similar height and build as Deanna, slim and dark haired, but she's putting her weight on her right side as she walks forward with slow, deliberate movements, compensating for the odd gait by leaning heavily on a cane.

Scott's head turns and I see a flicker of recognition. His eyes narrow and he slowly rises to face her. I am forgotten. All I want to do is close my eyes, to go to sleep, and perhaps wake from this nightmare because surely that is what this is, a nightmare.

Scott turns his back on me, and I try to rise, to attack him while he's distracted but the first movement sends another wave of nausea through me, and I struggle not to throw up again. I'm done. Whatever happens from here is beyond me.

Scott advances cautiously on the newcomer but falters as another figure steps out from the shadows, from the vaults beneath the street, the storage rooms we barely use. It's Deanna, and I can see Katie hiding behind her in the folds of her long coat, hands before her face, peering around Deanna at her father, then at me. They've been hiding in the vaults.

I see Scott look between the two women, and I hear him laugh, a deep booming sound and I don't understand. It is lost on me. His focus is split, with Deanna and the other woman either side of him. Beyond Scott, someone else steps out of the basement, and I'm relieved to see Chas a half step behind her. I don't know her, but she's tall, pale skinned but the detail of her features are masked by a large hood. Scott pauses, looking between all three women. The hooded woman raises her palm, indicating to Chas to remain inside.

My gaze turns to Katie, who is looking at me, eyes wide. I can see the terror in her expression. I lift my hand and extend it towards her, opening and closing my fingers much as we did to one another when she was a toddler, summoning her to me. She breaks free of Deanna, who doesn't try to stop her, and runs to my side, throwing her arms around me. I draw her into my embrace, ignoring the pain of her weight upon me, and I kiss her head as she buries her face into my chest. 'I've got you, baby,' I whisper to her.

She's trembling. I can feel her fear in my arms, and I wish I could take it all from her, draw it into myself. Scott hesitates, blinking perspiration from his eyes as he surveys the scene. Then he inches forward, first to his left and then to his right, uncertain as the three women cautiously spread out around him. The blade in his hand is by his side. He's caught in two minds as to what to do. I wrap my arms around Katie, making soothing noises and doing my best to shield her. I don't know what comes next.

Deanna takes a step forward and I see her raise her arm; something is in her hand and Scott reacts, moving to intercept her. From his left the woman lifts her cane and with a surprising burst of speed and dexterity, she sweeps it in an arc through the air, bringing it down and connecting with the side of Scott's head before he's able to adjust and react.

He grunts under the impact and stumbles but doesn't fall,

only for Deanna to continue her assault. She swings her hand in a downward motion and a gut-wrenching thud sounds as something wooden makes contact with flesh and bone. Scott takes another step, staggers and drops to one knee, head bowed. Then the third woman, the one with the hood, steps forward, towering above him, eyes focused on Scott and nothing more. He raises a defensive arm above his head, and I'm sure he makes eye contact with her for I see her eyes widen at the moment she strikes out with something metallic, flashing through the air in a downward motion, buckling Scott's arm and landing a crunching blow against his skull.

Scott's head wobbles under the force of the impact and he sways but doesn't fall. Another strike from the woman with the cane and I wince at the sound, encircling Katie with my arms and hugging her even tighter, desperate for her not to see or hear this. Deanna strikes a second blow and Scott teeters, pitifully attempting to lift a hand in defence. He reaches out, grasping Deanna's coat and pulling her towards him. Another strike from the cane, this time to the arm brandishing the blade, but Scott doesn't relinquish his grip, but neither can he wield the weapon effectively. Instead, he slashes at Deanna, narrowly missing her as she moves aside.

Undeterred Scott hauls Deanna towards him and I hear her scream. The hooded woman, looking every inch the part of the Grim Reaper, leaps forward and her weapon, a hammer, knocks into Scott's arm. He immediately drops the knife and releases his hold on Deanna. She stumbles away from him, off balance, and trips and falls to the cobbled floor.

Scott, exuding some strange gurgling sound, lunges towards the fallen Deanna, the hooded woman moving to intercept him, but he's found some reserves of untapped, hidden strength, and he's upon Deanna, hands encircling her throat.

'Stop!' I scream, but the words are barely audible, even to me. A flurry of blows follow from the other two, Scott seemingly taking each one without feeling the impact as he slowly chokes the life out of Deanna. Blow after blow, stabbing and slashing, a frenzy of attacks without end... and finally Scott falters, his grip loosening. Deanna manages to free herself from his clutches and scrambles out from underneath him, eyes wide, terrified.

The other women stand back as Scott crumples, swaying from left to right. His eyes glaze over, his pupils dilate, and he slowly sweeps them around the courtyard until they come to settle on me. It's as if all of them are frozen in time, unable to process what has happened, just waiting for the final moment. Including Scott. I meet his gaze, still clutching Katie in my arms and I see his lips curl into the trace of a sad smile.

'I do love you, Sophie. I loved all of you...'

Scott's eyelids flicker and close, never to reopen. I see his chest heaving for a few moments more and then it settles too. He doesn't move anymore.

So, this is where it ends.

FIFTY-THREE

I can hear voices, muffled and distant, but coming closer. Opening my eyes, my vision is blurred, the lights overhead are too bright and I blink furiously, my eyes watering. 'She's awake.' I don't recognise the voice.

I'm aware of someone beside me along with others in the background, moving around. 'Where am I?' I ask no one in particular. A face appears above me, the features blurred and indistinct, and I realise I'm lying on my back but I'm not outside. The surface supporting me is soft and I'm warm, but I'm not in bed.

'It's okay, Sophie. Everything is going to be all right.'

'Deanna?'

'Yes, I'm here.' Her features sharpen and I can see her smiling softly, gently moving the hair away from my face. She glances to someone nearby. 'Is she going to understand all of this?'

'We'll soon see,' the other woman, the hooded Grim Reaper, says. I definitely don't know her. I look to my right and see her as she removes her hood. She's blonde, pale skinned. I recognise her face, but I can't pinpoint how I know her. I'm sure we haven't met. A knot of fear manifests inside me. Images of this woman repeatedly striking Scott with a hammer and then slashing at him with his own blade leap to mind, and I recoil from the thoughts, trying to move away from her now.

Deanna places a gentle restraining hand on my chest as I try to rise, perhaps recognising my agitation for what it is. 'Relax, Sophie. Everything is all right. You're safe now.' She looks away from me again. 'Perhaps we should dim the lights a little.' The other woman rises from beside me and goes over to the panel, lowering the lights.

I don't care what Deanna says. I don't feel safe, but I look at her, the softness of her expression, the reassuring smile. Was it real? Did all of that happen? My ankle throbs, almost as if it has woken along with me. I wince and look down at it. I'm not imagining the pain; it's acute. My foot is heavily strapped, up to and including my ankle.

'You'll need to keep the weight off it for a couple of days, as best you can,' the blonde woman says, returning to my side having dimmed the lights. I can see better now. The light is no longer hurting my eyes. My head is clearing, at least a little. 'And I suspect you have a concussion, so you should take it easy for the next couple of days, and' – she glances at Deanna, reticent to continue; however Deanna inclines her head slightly, encouraging her – 'if your headache gets any worse or if you're still vomiting when you move around you should go to the hospital. Get yourself checked out.'

I look at her and then at Deanna, who nods. 'Linda is a doctor.'

'I was,' Linda says from my right, peering at my face and tentatively inspecting the wound above my eye. 'But that was a long time ago, before Scott.'

'Before Scott what?' I repeat, confused.

'Before I married Scott, and before he broke me.'

Deanna touches my arm gently. 'He broke all of you.'

I don't understand, and my thoughts are scrambled as another figure comes into the room. A dark-haired woman, leaning on her cane. From her side profile, she looks so much like Deanna. The angle of her cheekbones, the same eyes, and she probably once had the same hair colour, too, although now hers is heavily shot through with grey. She only differs from Deanna in age and with the pronounced limp.

She comes into the room, evidently struggling with her restricted movement and as she turns to me I study her face. I can see the left eye, cheek and mouth droop somewhat and the left side of her body, from shoulder to fingertips, follows in the same fashion, hanging lower than the opposite side. She carries a haunted expression, pained. Despite this, she seems familiar. Has she had a stroke? No, it's more than that. Putting her weight entirely on her right side, it's like only half of her body functions, supporting the burden of her left.

When she talks, her speech is slurred. 'You must believe me, this was not how we planned this to end.' I stare at her. It can't be. It just... it can't. 'We knew how enthralled you were with him. We needed you to see him for who and what he is. Only then could we free you from him.'

'Cecilia?' I ask, as I spy the pendant around her neck. That is my pendant, the one Deanna picked out, the one that caught Scott's eye.

'Yes, it's me.' She follows my gaze, reaching up and gently holding the pendant between thumb and forefinger. 'This belonged to our mother,' she says, glancing at Deanna.

'So, it's true? You didn't die?'

'Scott told you what you needed to hear,' Cecilia says, her speech restricted by the lack of facial movement. Deanna takes my hand in hers and squeezes it.

'We wanted to show you who Scott really is, but we knew you were so infatuated with him that you wouldn't listen.'

Linda looks at me, apologetically. 'We knew you had to see

him yourself, for what he is.' She nods towards Cecilia. 'We were in exactly the same position as you are once. We know how it happens...'

'How what happens?' I whisper.

Cecilia continues. 'How he makes you feel special, like you are *the one*. You are the person he has been looking for. The one who can save him and be the focal point of his existence. Only you can complete his family and bring fulfilment to his life.'

'And you believe it,' Linda says. 'Not because he told you, but because you can feel it for yourself.'

'And once you are enraptured with him, secure within the relationship,' Cecilia says, lowering herself onto a chair Deanna has placed beside me, 'he sets about removing you from every connection you hold dear. Stripping you of friends, family and colleagues. Every relationship must be sacrificed for the benefit of *the family*. His *precious* family unit.'

My thoughts drift to my father, my brother and sister.

I haven't seen them in such a long time.

'You are not allowed anything of your own, Sophie,' Cecilia says. 'Where you work, where you go, what you wear, all the way down to what you eat and where you sleep, is all controlled by one man.'

'Scott,' I whisper.

'Scott,' Cecilia says. 'And should you not measure up to the impossible standards he sets for you,' – she looks at Linda – 'you will be replaced.'

I look at Linda, her expression softening now. 'You.'

'I married Scott after my boyfriend ran out on me. I was a naive twenty-something, pregnant, and just beginning a career as a general practitioner. I met Scott,' – her expression takes on a distant look – 'and he comforted me, helped me visualise a bright future for me, and for—'

I stare at her, studying her features. The eyes, the slim nose and the angular line of her jaw. 'Your son.' She looks at me then, nodding solemnly.

'For Chas.'

'Scott isn't his father?' I ask, stunned. Linda shakes her head.

'Nor is he Katie's,' Cecilia says flatly.

'But that can't be true.'

Cecilia fixes me with a solemn look. 'Scott is unable to have children of his own.'

My mind is reeling. 'He told me it was my fault we couldn't have children—' We had gone for tests with Dr Sheldon, who called Scott and gave him the results. I'll never forget the devastation in his face when he told me the news, and it felt like my world had fallen apart. He was so believable, so convincing, that the problem was all mine and there was nothing we could do. And all along it was a lie.

'The only way Scott could have a family was to take someone else's,' Linda says, and, looking into her eyes, I know what she says is the truth, and it's like something has struck me, deep inside, and I'll never heal from it.

I could have children. I could have children, and he told me I couldn't.

I look at Linda. I can't believe she would leave her child with such a monster. She averts her eyes, and I think she can read my mind. 'I tried to leave Scott once,' Linda says quietly. 'I had a plan, money, and a place to go. He found out and he locked me away for three months.' I see her eyes tearing. 'Three months of darkness, alone and separated from my son in a damp cellar. Little food, only water, and scant measures of that too. He said he needed to *teach me a lesson.*'

'Much like the one he taught you that day,' Cecilia says to me, and I'm puzzled, 'when Scott trapped you in the lift, in this house, for eight hours.'

'The lift broke,' I whisper.

'No, it was recently installed, Sophie,' Cecilia says. 'He needed to crush you, for you to experience the powerless nature of your life, and that only he was here to be your saviour.'

The memory of the panic, the abject terror I felt that day rears its head in my mind. 'What lesson did you learn?' I ask Linda, fearing the answer.

'The only way I leave the family is through death,' she says softly. 'He taught me well, and so that's what I did. I arranged it. One day, I drove out to a known viewpoint on cliffs far above the ocean, some way from our home, and I vanished.'

'He thought you were dead?'

Linda nods. 'And then I watched, and I waited for the chance to get my son back.' Chas appears in the doorway behind her, his hands resting on Katie's shoulders, standing before him. He smiles at me and Linda at him. 'I never thought I would have to wait this long but, over time, I managed to bridge that gap with my son.' She extends her hand to him, and he takes it in his. 'We met, in secret over the years, I earned his trust again, and we worked together to end all of this.'

'And I couldn't leave,' Chas says to me. 'I couldn't leave without Katie. I couldn't just leave you at his mercy either, so I stayed. I'm sorry you had to go through all of this,' he says to me, apologetic. 'We had to pull the veil from your eyes.'

'You were never supposed to get hurt,' Deanna tells me. 'We underestimated how far, and how fast, things would escalate. You were supposed to see him for who he really is and then—'

'And then?' I ask.

'The plan was that you would use your position on national television to expose him for the man he is.'

'I could never have done—'

Cecilia places her right hand over mine, laying in my lap. Her left hand is hanging useless by her side. 'You will never know just how far you can go, or what you are capable of until you are truly tested, Sophie.' She looks at Linda, the two children and then Deanna. 'My sister taught me that. And I am grateful to her for finding me after all these years apart.'

My eyes drift over Cecilia. She looks unrecognisable from the woman married to Scott. My predecessor, the woman who I replaced. The woman I thought was dead. Katie's birth mother. I've seen her in photographs mainly, for she was already in the hospital when I moved into the house in Switzerland to care for Katie while her mother received treatment for her injuries. Injuries that I thought eventually led to her death soon after. Injuries sustained in her suicide attempt.

Cecilia has me under a watchful eye, examining her, and she nods. 'Yes, I also tried to find my own way to escape the nightmare. I married Scott, I loved him, but when I realised who and what he was, I sought comfort and support in another man. For a time, I managed to keep my new relationship secret as I tried to find a way to escape the monster I'd married. But I underestimated him. When I fell pregnant' – her eyes close on Katie and she smiles her lopsided smile – 'Scott realised I was having an affair, and then everything changed. I...' – she glances at Linda – 'was also taught my lesson.'

'You couldn't leave with your child?' I ask, struggling to understand how they could both leave their children with such a man, Cecilia choosing to walk onto a train line rather than live that life anymore. 'Why did you try to kill yourself?'

'Scott dismantled me,' Cecilia explained, 'and then put me back together in the image he wanted.' Cecilia closes her eyes, and Katie leaves Chas, coming to her mother's side. Cecilia loops her right arm around her daughter's waist. 'I could no longer live a life where I was a mere shadow of myself, an empty shell, drifting mindlessly through each day. But I didn't try to end it in the way you think. I tried again to leave, only for Scott to pursue me. I wasn't very good at running, even then.' She glances down at her left leg. 'Less good now, obviously,' she says with dark humour. 'It ended when Scott had my daughter in his arms,' she says, hugging Katie tightly; God only knows what she's making of all this, 'and he gave me an ultimatum.'

'What?' I ask, seeing her fingers curl even tighter around Katie's waist.

'I stand on the tracks, or...' – she looks at Katie, tears welling and pulling her closer – 'he does... along with my baby daughter.' A solitary tear escapes her right eye; the left eye is emotionless, and I realise it is fashioned from glass. 'I survived. I don't know how, but I survived, and in carrying out that one act to save my daughter, I handed Scott the perfect reason to have me locked away for the rest of my life. Afterwards, he got to bring my daughter back to the UK, to our old house in London, pretending to be making a fresh start with you by his side. He replaced me with you.'

'But the house was a new project—'

'That is what he told you; he wanted to pretend it was a fresh start,' Cecilia says, her eyes lifting from me and scanning the room. 'This was my home, where we lived before we moved to Switzerland. It was where we were going to return, to raise our family. Before I disappointed him.'

'I... I'm sorry,' I say to her. I see all the faces around me; every one of them is looking at me. 'I'm so sorry.' Deanna takes my hands in hers, squeezing them.

'None of this is any more your fault than it is Linda or Cecilia's, Sophie. What happens from here, though, is up to you,' she says firmly.

'I don't understand.'

'We have a new plan, and we think it will work. We will take care of everything, but it all hinges on you.'

'Me?' I feel the familiar knot of anxiety forming in my stomach.

'Scott was leaving you. He resigned from his job and he was planning to take his family to South America.'

'I know, I saw the paperwork in his study...'

'We suspect he was going to have you committed. We still think Scott should leave the UK for South America, Sophie,' Deanna says, holding my gaze. 'You will be heartbroken, of course, but you can restart your life. Your children,' she says, smiling at Katie and glancing at Chas, 'will go to live with their biological family but,' – she inclines her head – 'of course you will maintain a strong relationship with them. They love you as much as you do them, and they always will.' Katie breaks away from Cecilia and throws her arms around me again, hugging me tightly. I hold her closer.

'I'm so sorry about how I treated you,' Katie says, drawing back from me. She's crying. I don't remember the last time I saw her cry because of anything but anger. 'When Aunty Deanna came to me—'

'When did she come to you?' I ask. I need to know how long this has been going on.

'A year ago, or more,' Katie says, nervously. 'I found out about my mum, and I was so angry with you for the part you played in everything that happened to her.'

'But I didn't know, darling—'

'I know that now. It was Dad and not you.' I'm crying now too. 'I had to help them. Do you see? I had to!'

'You helped?' I ask Katie. 'All of this? The fire at the school, getting yourself expelled? It was all on purpose?'

Deanna nods. 'We had to break the family, wreck every-thing about it, in order for him to want to rebuild it. We had to sow doubt in his mind, play to his obsession about the perfect family... it was the only way to escalate things and show you his true colours.'

'What did you do to me?'

'We knew Scott was trying to break you but despite his best efforts you are a success. Don't you see? That's why he had to step it up, drugging you with hallucinogenic drugs, and removing the support you had from Martha.'

'Her mother is ill.'

'No,' Deanna says quietly, shaking her head. 'Scott sacked her. He wanted you to fail, but you didn't. I had to add something to the mix.'

'Like what?' I ask, feeling the resentment festering within me.

Deanna shrugs. 'Dressing you in Cecilia's jewellery in an attempt to trigger Scott. Moving your things around, ruining your cooking and hiding the shopping—'

'I knew I wasn't going mad!'

'I'm so sorry, Sophie,' Deanna says. 'But without you falling apart, Scott would never have revealed himself for what he is. It wasn't all me; he was drugging you, trying to make you and everyone else believe you were losing your mind.'

'As it happens,' Cecilia says, 'things were escalating far faster and much farther than we'd anticipated. We thought Scott would try to remove you from your career, and maybe keep you at home. It was only when Chas called us, Linda and me tonight, that we realised just how far he was prepared to take things. We knew he would try to drive you to suicide, like he has before, and after what happened in the bathroom we were going to step in soon before it was too late.'

'But we never thought he would try to murder you first. We put you at great risk, and for that, we are sorry,' Deanna says, and the others nod.

I can't handle all of this. It's too much.

'I'm so sorry,' Katie says again, burying her head in my chest. I tighten my hold on her, relishing what I know could be the last touch I have from her for some time to come.

Deanna looks at me apologetically. 'I did try to tell you, the other night, but you were so far gone that I didn't know if you were understanding anything I was saying.'

So my fevered dreams were real, at least in part. Deanna is also right.

'What about... what about Scott?' I ask. 'He can't really go to South America, can he?'

Cecilia draws a sharp intake of breath. 'We will take care of him; we have a plan. No one will look for Scott. He has contacts, but nobody outside of the family is really close enough to him for them to miss his presence. It is unlikely he will be missed. All you need to know is, Scott has left you.'

'Give us some time, Sophie,' Deanna says, placing her hand on my forearm as Katie detaches from me and returns to her mother. 'We'll come back later tonight and take care of Scott. You don't need to see him again, and by the time the sun comes up, he will be gone.'

'I'll be alone,' I whisper.

'No,' Deanna says, squeezing my arm and looking into my eyes. 'You'll never need to be alone again. I promise you.'

I think about the letter I've been keeping secret from Scott. The letter from my father. Some people say everything happens for a reason, be it God's plan, Allah or fate and destiny. A higher power in one form or another. I've never held to that so far in my life, but maybe there is something in it after all. My father. He is still here for me, despite everything.

Perhaps now is the time.

EPILOGUE

One year on...

The red light blinks and I smile to camera. It's not the usual artificial greeting I manufacture for the viewers. Tonight, this is different. Everything is different. This time, I'm not the presenter. Tonight, I am the star name on the sofa for the studio's most popular entertainment programme, predicted to be watched by the second largest network television audience of the year. Yesterday was the largest on record, and I was centre stage then, too.

'Joining us this evening is the recently crowned dance hall champion, as well as the newly announced host of the channel's flagship news and current affairs programme. So, how did it feel to win last night, Sophie Beckett?'

The presenters, the audience, fellow guests and the crew offer me rapturous applause as I sit there, clutching the trophy in my lap, a glitter ball the size of a football mounted on a delicate crystal stem. My smile broadens. 'I can't quite believe it. It hasn't sunk in yet,' I tell them, and it's not a rehearsed line, it's the truth.

'Which part?' the co-host says, smiling. He's a former winner of the same dance competition.

'All of it,' I say, smiling coyly as I feel my face flush beneath the make-up. 'It's been a heck of a year for me!'

'Hasn't it just? Well...' Both hosts turn to camera, smiling warmly. 'Before we chat to Sophie about all things dancing – and we'll definitely ask her about the prospect of a reported romance with her Italian dance partner, don't worry – but first, here's a recap of the journey she's undertaken.'

The montage of the last three months starts to run, the studio audience cheering as footage of my journey from ball-room dancing novice to being crowned winner in December is displayed on giant screens above their heads. The two hosts look at me, smiling and Darren gives me a quick wink. After all, he sat on this side of the sofa only a year ago, so he knows how big a deal this is for me and my career.

Watching the VT, the video recap of my experience from the original announcement of me taking part in the competition, through to the training and the televised performances, my mind wanders. It's been a hell of a year. I've not only been through a very public break-up, where my husband ran off with someone younger and disappeared as I faced the intense pres-sure of the subsequent media scrutiny – beautifully managed by my agent, Magda, I have to say – but I've made great strides in my career.

Being able to take control of my life for the first time in over a decade, I've fostered a renewed sense of my own achieve-ment. Following a brief sabbatical, where I was reunited with my father and siblings, I returned to work with them at my back. I feared they would reject me, that too much water had passed under the bridge... the same bridge that I burned years ago, at Scott's request. They didn't though. They welcomed me back with open arms. My father told me how he watched me on television every morning, seeing the pain in my eyes that I hid from the world, but couldn't from him. He waited as long as he could before reaching out. As for the timing, was it an intervention by God? Destiny? I don't know, and I don't care enough to contemplate the way the universe works. That's beyond my pay grade.

However, with my family's support, they gave me the strength to come forward and own my truth. I would no longer accept only what was on offer to me. Sam, his bosses, and even my co-host would no longer control me. I have taken back control of my life. Little did I know how many others felt as powerless as I had. When I spoke out about my treatment in this industry, rather than be attacked, as I expected, I found a vocal majority standing with me.

The paparazzi who'd been camped outside my home months before, looking for salacious shots, were suddenly replaced by serious broadcasters seeking knowledge of events, knowledge that only an insider could have. My days of being tagged as a sex object were soon replaced by an acceptance of my strength as a broadcaster, a courageous advocate for equality and as a hero to many.

Of course, the real heroes are the best among us, often going under the radar and never receiving the praise they deserve. I was inspired by those who I can never name in public, my secret sisterhood who saved my life.

But I've taken my hits, earned what I have through my determination, and I have my scars to prove it. My life has begun anew.

My eyes catch my father's, sitting as he is in the front row of the audience, just as he was last night when my name, along with Paulo's, was announced as the winner at the grand final show.

What a year.

'Sophie, how was it, seeing all of that compressed into a two-minute reel?'

'Wonderful, although my knees and ankles can still feel the agony,' I say, drawing a laugh from the audience.

'Now, we definitely want to speak to you about the dancing, and your new role which was confirmed yesterday, but first we really must ask you about the recent scandal involving high-profile figures within the media. One of those convicted is known to you, isn't he? You worked with him for a while.'

'Michael, yes. I worked with him on the breakfast show,' I say, nodding, pursing my lips. 'And I think we should be so grateful for those brave women who put their head above the parapet and called out his behaviour.'

'Yes,' Darren says, checking the Autocue. 'A total of five women, seeing him convicted on thirteen counts. He attended sentencing only this morning and was sent to prison for seven years. What's your reaction to that?'

'I think it sends a message to men everywhere, that they may well try to abuse their position of power, and might get away with it for a time, but there is justice in this world and' – I look at the camera – 'eventually, it will be served, one way or another.'

'Beautifully put, Sophie.'

They continue talking about the cases that are steadily working their way through the system, but I'm barely listening. Looking into the camera lens, I have other thoughts in mind.

I don't know exactly where Katie and Chas are, or when I will get to see them again, but I'm given great comfort in the knowledge that if they ever want to see me, all they need to do is switch on their television. My children, for that is who they always will be, are never far from my thoughts. I think about them every day, and I miss them terribly.

But in a curious way, I feel like they are my guardian angels now, alongside Deanna, Cecilia and Linda.

They are always watching and if I ever need to, I know how to reach them. And I believe they would come.

A LETTER FROM JASON

I would like to say a huge thank you for choosing to read *Homewrecker*. This is my first foray into penning a psychological thriller, and I had so much fun creating a set of believable characters and fleshing out the twists and turns of the storyline. I hope you enjoyed reading it as much as I have enjoyed writing it for you.

If you would like to keep up to date with all my latest releases, please do follow the link below. I know how much we all value our privacy and rest assured, your email address will never be shared, and you can unsubscribe at any time.

www.bookouture.com/j-m-dalgliesh

One of my pleasures around writing, of which there are many, is that I am given the licence to build a world for my characters, their likes, dislikes, wants, needs and desires, but also their idiosyncrasies, flaws, and downright distasteful behaviours. With a bit of luck, you were able to see a little of Sophie, Katie and Deanna in those around you – hopefully less of Scott – and could relate to them as much as I could whilst writing. Perhaps they made you laugh, cry, or you found one of them inspirational? Maybe you were touched by the vulnerability in Sophie, the pain Katie carried, or took pride in the triumph of good over evil, the perceived weak overcoming the strong?

I would absolutely love it if you were willing and able to leave a short review of *Homewrecker*. When readers leave feedback on a book it makes such a difference in persuading others to give an author a chance for the first time, and it would mean the world to me if you could take a moment to do so.

Thank you for supporting my writing, I really appreciate it.

All my best,

Jason x

www.jmdalgliesh.com

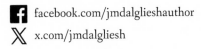 facebook.com/jmdalglieshauthor
x.com/jmdalgliesh

PUBLISHING TEAM

Turning a manuscript into a book requires the efforts of many people. The publishing team at Bookouture would like to acknowledge everyone who contributed to this publication.

Audio
Alba Proko
Sinead O'Connor
Melissa Tran

Commercial
Lauren Morrissette
Hannah Richmond
Imogen Allport

Cover design
Henry Steadman

Data and analysis
Mark Alder
Mohamed Bussuri

Editorial
Rhianna Louise
Lizzie Brien

Made in the USA
Middletown, DE
07 September 2024

60571185R00205